BEING THERE

Frank Price

UPFRONT PUBLISHING
LEICESTERSHIRE

BEING THERE
Copyright © Frank Price 2002

All Rights Reserved

ISBN 1 84426 017 8

First Published 2002 by
UPFRONT PUBLISHING
Leicestershire

BEING THERE

FOREWORD

When I hear so-called self-made men, who from humble beginnings have risen to the top of the pile, say that their success was due only to hard work, I know that they are kidding. If wealth be the judge, I never did get to the top of the pile. I made a lot of progress up the greasy pole and I did work hard, but I suspect like most of them, it took a combination of dedication, being in the right place at the right time and a hell of a lot of good luck, and in my case it was also due to always getting up whenever I was knocked down.

I still can't quite believe my good fortune. For years I had a recurring dream that I was back where I began, waking up in a cold sweat thinking that those around me had found that I wasn't as clever as they had thought!

At school, the teachers constantly reminded me that I wasn't as bright as my older brothers. They need not have bothered; I was only too well aware of the fact. I can only conclude that I 'made it' because lady luck smiled kindly on me, thinking it odd that I kept getting up instead of staying down where I belonged.

For the children of the poor, a good education was hard to come by in the 1920s and 30s. It wasn't until I was thirteen years old that I began to comprehend the difficulties with which my parents had to struggle just to keep our collective heads above water. When it sank in, I began my search for knowledge and this led me to become adversarial; it's a habit I have since found hard to break.

Today, having lived a very varied life, I find when a place, event or name is mentioned in conversation it invariably strikes a chord and I tend to 'rabbit on' a bit. A number of my kinder listeners have urged me to 'get it down on paper'. Having hesitated for the past fifteen years I have now actually done it and hope that the effort has been worth it.

Throughout my life I made notes of the interesting people I've met, the conversations I have had, and the things that happened around me. My personal secretaries – Muriel Cope, Gwen Hill and June Pell – all kept scrapbooks and diaries which have been of immense help. Mu was with me for over twenty-five years. She was immensely patient, loyal and blessed with a faultless memory. Without her support I would have been lost. During my days with the British Waterways Board, Gwen Hill and June Pell were equally loyal, efficient and again, very patient.

There are others I should mention: Tommy Thomas, who I first met when I was appointed to help save Dawley New Town from 'going down the tube'. He was a tower of strength during the early years as we turned Dawley into Telford. It would never have reached the measure of success it has had he not been there; Trevor Luckcuck, who as Secretary of the British Waterways Board shared the slings and arrows which a number of ministers in both Tory and Labour Governments rained upon us during our long battle to save the canals, a fact still not fully appreciated or even recognised.

Contents

Chapter I
ROOTS

Trying to adequately describe the conditions which my family and thousands of others were forced to endure in the backstreets of Birmingham is not easy. Conditions were not to dissimilar to those which existed in the nineteenth century. Looking at old photographs, I find they fail even to scratch the surface.

My life had changed dramatically by the time I was put to the test of trying to explain this when asked by someone very far removed from these conditions. When asked the question, 'What was it really like?' I hardly knew where to begin.

What follows will appear to some to be name-dropping, and I guess it is. But it seems to me to be the best way to underline how difficult it is to tell someone far removed from the scene just how it was 'being there', at a time and in conditions that were a world away from those in which they and people like them lived.

On 20 May 1980, I was standing by a window in an enormous, splendidly furnished upper floor room, looking down at the people peering through the railings in the hope of catching a glimpse of the family who lived on the other side. I had done the same at the age of twenty-seven when paying my first visit to London. Never in my wildest dreams did I think that one day I would be on the inside looking out.

My invitation card said 12.45 for 1 p.m., but I'd been delayed by heavy traffic and was late. It was fortunate that the tall, elegant and friendly Lady Dugdale was there to receive me. We had met before. Looking down at me – I'm 5'6" in my shoes – she quietly admonished me but added, 'Not to worry, his nibs thought he had to wear a uniform and has gone back to change.'

She was referring to Prince Philip. She surprised me further by telling me, 'As guest of honour, you will be escorting Her Majesty in to lunch.'

Reacting to my thin smile, she gave me a reassuring wink and guided me to the broad stairway leading to the reception room in which the nine other guests were already assembled. I recognised Sebastian Coe and Jimmy Hill.

The Queen appeared in a simple knee-length dress with a minimum of jewellery, closely followed by the Prince, now suitably attired, along with the two corgis. Whilst sherry was served, they and the dogs mingled with the guests. The Queen moved towards me when it was time to go in for lunch. With a smile and a nod of the head we led the party into the dining room. As we entered, she signalled to the dogs and they scurried off each to a separate corner of the room leaving no doubt as to who was in command.

I had visited Buckingham Palace on a number of occasions, but never to join the royal couple for a meal, and I was feeling uncomfortable. I had heard that the Queen had a way of putting people at their ease but didn't expect her opening remark.

'Sir Frank, I understand that you were raised in the centre of Birmingham.'

Realising that she had been fully briefed I guessed that she meant in the backstreets, but just in case I asked, 'Do you mean the slums, ma'am?'

Looking straight at me with twinkling eyes she replied, 'Yes indeed,' and with a captivating smile added, 'please tell me, what was it really like?'

So I did.

I doubted that she had ever been near a slum dwelling or had held a conversation with anyone who had lived in one. Considering who I was speaking to, describing the district of Hockley, its people and the kind of houses in which we lived during my early years was difficult. I tried but she pressed me to describe in more detail what I had called a 'backyard'. Although the memories came flooding back I found it hard to paint an adequate word picture of the ill designed, overcrowded and appalling property in which I was raised. I picked up the menu card which lay in front of me, turned it over and drew a plan of Court 13, Great Russell Street.

So intrigued was she that our conversation went on through

the lunch to the exclusion of the other guests until the last course was served. She then turned to Dr Kilcade, who was seated on her left, leaving me wondering how the hell I had got there from Court 13, Great Russell Street.

I escorted the Queen back into the reception room where coffee was being served. Feeling that I had hogged her attention long enough I moved back to the window to stare once more at the crowd, unable to clear my mind of the memories she had stirred up.

It can't be true, but it seemed that it rarely rained when I was young. My earliest memories were of squatting on the floor near the open door during a heavy thunderstorm. Our house was one of eleven similar small linked dwellings crammed into a backyard, connected to other backyards with houses of the same design, near the heart of the city. I remembered that day, sitting there, blowing through a comb with a piece of tissue paper placed over it, playing, 'Rain, rain go away, come again another day'.

Looking up the yard I could see other open doors and kids looking back at me. The doors were left open during thunderstorms because it was generally believed that if a thunderbolt struck the house it would come down the chimney and roll out of the open door. With the door closed, it would burn the house down. Crazy, I know, but the residents of the slums believed it. The thought that the missile might decide to crash through the roof instead didn't occur to them.

Now, standing in Buckingham Palace, these memories went flashing through my mind, and I thought of my mother and how hard she had struggled to rear us and how she would have felt if she could see me now. This reverie was interrupted by a member of the staff who told me that Prince Philip would like to have a word.

He was standing at the far side of the room chatting to Sebastian Coe, the Olympic athlete who was yet to enter politics. As I got near, I saw Coe, who like me is rather small, looking up at the Prince in deep conversation. Seeing my approach, he interrupted Coe, saying, 'Look out, here comes trouble.'

Coe turned to me with a startled look.

11

'Don't fret, I have grown accustomed...' I began, but before I could finish the sentence, the Prince said, 'See what I mean!'

I had met him a few times by then and felt I understood what made him tick. I felt sure that he tired of those he met who fail to speak their minds when faced with members of the Family. It seemed to me that in despair he sought to stir up a different response from that of 'Yes sir, no sir, three bags full, sir'. Having said that, he did come on a bit strong on our first encounter (see the chapter entitled 'First Citizen'). I had risen to his bait on a number of occasions but all this was a far cry from the days when I lived in the place I had earlier tried to described to the Queen.

Great Russell Street was part of a densely populated area made worse by the concentration of factories and workshops spewing out dust and fumes polluting the air we breathed. One of the huge multi-storey factories owned by Joseph Lucas threw a continuing shadow over nearby houses. It also overlooked St Matthias Church School, where my brothers and I were educated, and Burbury Park, where we played.

To call this small island of railed-in concrete a park was a cynical exaggeration. The barren area was relieved by a few dust-covered laurel bushes in one corner which we called 'the jungle' and a row of swings, a roundabout and a slide. It was the only local public open space available to hundreds of kids in this treeless, grassless and overpopulated area. The park was opened up at seven in the morning and closed in the summer at dusk.

In those days Birmingham was known as 'the city of a thousand and one trades'. There was a plethora of small workshops in the slums, some sharing backyards with the houses. They brought extra income to the landlord, and noise and pollution to the tenants. These workshops were usually run by one or two self-employed men polishing metal components. They pumped clouds of dust into the yard and the houses; the Public Health Department did nothing to stop it.

This scene was commonplace in an area crowded with back-to-back slum dwellings and shops. Pawnbrokers and pubs seemed to occupy every street corner. I was born and raised in this jungle of 30,000 appalling tiny two-up and one-down terraced houses joined at the back as well as on two sides. They were crammed into over 3,000 grim backyards, hanging around the neck of the city centre like a rotting body.

Living in these conditions the future was less than rosy. It must have been even harder for my father, Frederick, who had been raised in better circumstances. His parents lived in an area referred to by the less fortunate as 'respectable'. It meant that the houses were not joined back-to-back, that they had a separate dining room, living room and kitchen, a private garden and – more important – they didn't have to share their lavatory with others.

His father had played for Aston Villa Football Club as a semi-professional when William MacGregor, one of the founder members of the Football League, was a leading figure at the club. He owned a factory in Newtown Row, a few blocks from where we lived. He manufactured case balls, now called footballs, and football boots. The balls were made up of a series of thick leather panels stitched together. The top panel had an opening with holes on both sides for a leather lace. A rubber inner tube was placed inside and inflated and the ball was then laced up. When it rained, the water soaked into the leather making the ball so heavy that heading it was strictly for heroes. The goalkeeper had a pretty tough time too.

Football boots were also made of thick leather with a very hard toecap; they needed to be softened by rubbing tallow fat into them so that they would be easy on the ankles and feet. The studs, also made of leather, were nailed onto the bottom of the boots. It doesn't take much imagination to realise that in those days football could be a crippling game in the true sense of the term.

MacGregor had a sports shop fronting on to 'the Row'. In the 1920s, when Aston Villa won the FA Cup, he made the mistake of displaying this large piece of solid silver in the shop window. A few days later, it was stolen, never to be seen again. It was rumoured that it had been melted down within the hour.

Just after the start of the 1914–18 wars, our future dad enlisted in the Royal Engineers without his parents' knowledge; he was just seventeen. He also kept from them the fact that he was courting one Lucy Bayley. His parents were Protestants, Lucy's Catholics. In those days mixing the faiths was frowned upon far more than it is today. The Catholic priests were fearful of losing control of any issue from such a marriage and threatened damnation and excommunication on the offender. The Protestant clergy were not too happy either. The fact that the Bayley family lived in the slums and that Lucy was 'on the stage' didn't help. Fredrick knew that his family would not accept her.

Her family consisted of four girls and two boys, brought up as serious Catholics. Their father, Joseph, was a small, quiet, gentle man who worked as a blacksmith in a local foundry. I was about six years old when he died but had got to know and love him. However poor people were, pride made it obligatory to leave something when they died. Granddad Bayley left each of his grandchildren a silver threepenny piece we called a 'Joey'.

Whilst my father's family resided in a moderately prosperous neighbourhood on the top of the hill in Gerrard Street, Lozells, my mother's lived in the valley in Great Hampton Row. It was a grand name for a street made up of a variety of shops at the front, hiding grim yards full of slum houses and workshops at the back. Great Hampton Row was categorised by the locals as having a 'Queen Anne front and a Mary Anne back'.

During the Depression, the two oldest Bayleys, daughter Gertrude and son Jack, left to join those who were seeking a new life in America. Gertrude was single; but Jack, who had a family, took his wife and young son and daughter to settle in New York. Gertrude went on to the west coast and subsequently became a Barrister and married a Barrister named George who became a well-known Judge in San Francisco.

Jack's daughter, Polly, followed my mother, Lucy, by going onto the stage. Both beautiful and talented, she was to become a member of the famous *Ziegfeld Follies* playing on Broadway. She was in the musical *Making Whoopee* with Eddie Cantor and Ruby Keeler, who were great stars at the time. As understudy, she took over the lead when Keeler left the show to go to Hollywood to marry Al Jolson, then the most famous singer in America.

The studios decided to make a film of this successful Broadway musical and Polly went to Hollywood with the cast; but Ruby Keeler, who had by this time become a movie star, returned to take up the leading role.

Polly's mother, a devout Catholic, had insisted on chaperoning her daughter whilst she was in Hollywood. Harry Lisle Crosby, who was at the time one of a trio singing with the band run by Paul Whiteman – known as the King of Jazz – began to court Polly. He had a reputation for wild drinking and chasing women, which according to his biography he never lost. He didn't fit Polly's mother's idea of a suitable swain, so he was given his notice.

We heard these glamorous stories from our mother but none of us really believed that Bing Crosby had chased after one of our family. Years later, when I met Polly in New York I had the opportunity to look through her scrapbooks I apologised to her – mentally – for ever doubting the stories.

Far removed from the glamour, my mother lived in Great Hampton Row, which was a bustling thoroughfare. Double-decker tramcars travelled from the Great Western Railway Station at Snow Hill in the city centre, to Villa Cross Lozells via Great Hampton Row. They were narrow, about thirty feet long and more than eighteen feet high. When travelling at speed on a narrow gauge rail system they tended to sway alarmingly. It was nothing short of miraculous that they didn't jump the inverted rails, which were sunk into the ground.

The district had its share of colourful and enterprising characters, ranging from gunsmiths to tailors. Living in our yard was an old man named Onions who had his own small workshop. He was said to be the best gun barrel rifler in the business and much sought after. His glasses were always covered with graphite spots from his work; I never saw him without them on, but the spots didn't seem to bother him.

In Great Hampton Row, a Jewish tailor by the name of Loo Bloom had a large shop trading under the title 'My Tailor'. His brother was well known in the theatrical profession. When clients were working and too busy to visit the shop, he called on them wherever they were appearing. They would choose the cloth, he would measure them and return to whatever theatre they were playing for fittings. I doubt if there was another tailor in the country providing such a service. There were times when these famous thespians or vaudeville stars would visit the shop, having no idea of the conditions that existed behind it.

Birmingham had a number of theatres. My mother, who was an auburn-haired green-eyed beauty and a capable dancer with a pleasant singing voice, was appearing at the Prince of Wales Theatre in Broad Street, Birmingham, playing the part of Goody in the musical *Goody Two Shoes* when my father fell in love with her. Lucy became known to her extended family and the neighbours as 'Goody' Bayley. Today, stage and film folk are lionised, but in those days, being a poor Catholic girl *and* on the stage was considered by some to be beyond the pale.

The Great War was in its second year when the Army decided that Dad's outfit was to be posted. On his week's leave he and Lucy married. They were both under age and knew that their parents would never have agreed. They gave their age to the Registry Office as twenty-one and their home addresses those of friends. Fred returned to his unit with his secret and Lucy wore her wedding ring on a ribbon around her neck so her parents wouldn't know. During his embarkation leave, Lucy conceived and was soon forced to confess to her parents. Neither of the families was too happy, but it took many years for Dad's parents to forgive him. They couldn't possibly have known that the girl he chose to marry was as courageous and dedicated as she was beautiful, and that she was to keep him and their family's heads above water during the long years of Depression that were to follow. Neither did they suspect that he would remain in love with her until the day he died.

Their firstborn, my eldest brother, Freddie, arrived on Christmas Day whilst Dad was serving in Salonika. Released from the Army in 1919 suffering from malaria with no disablement pay, he had difficulty finding work. With no help from his parents, he, Lucy and their baby had to set up home in a low-rent, small back-to-back house in Hockley. There they raised their family – my three brothers and me.

Our house had a living room measuring twelve feet by fourteen feet. With no hallway, the front door led straight from the backyard into the room. In this tiny area, illuminated by a central gas mantle, was squeezed a table with a pine top scrubbed white, six chairs, a sofa and a sideboard. The floor was laid with quarry tiles and our only carpet was made of jute. It lay in front of a small cast-iron fireplace which had a space at the side to keep food warm. The grate was rubbed with a black lead paste and polished so that it shone. A gas cooker stood in the narrow pantry, which had a stone sink. Not until 1932 did the landlord install a tap and cold running water. Until then all the neighbouring families got their water from a tap in the yard.

There was a narrow pantry with steps leading down to a coal cellar. In one corner of the living room, a door opened on to a steep staircase leading to a bedroom and then further up to a tiny attic with a sloping slate-covered roof. The bedroom had a gaslight; the small attic where my brothers and I slept was lit by candles.

There was a gas meter in a corner of the living room which accepted pennies. There were times when we would sit in the dark and Mom would tell us, 'Sitting in the dark is good for your eyes.' But we knew then that pennies were in short supply. When times got too hard to deal with and there was no money for food, some neighbours broke into their gas meter and faced up to the consequences later.

Living in overcrowded small dwellings built back-to-back and linked on each side at as high a density as possible, the tenants had a constant battle with vermin. On the first day of spring, the families would spray every nook and cranny with a paraffin-based mixture designed to kill off anything that crawled. It stank the place out for days. In spite of the hardship, most of the women fought to keep their homes clean and wholesome both inside and out.

Dad suffered severe recurring bouts of malaria. As he lay in bed covered with a single sheet, the sweat poured out of him. Then he would begin to shiver and Mom would cover him with blankets, coats, and anything else she could lay her hands on to keep him warm. The only medication available was large doses of quinine.

Looking back, I can understand that having to live in the slums and struggle to find work just broke my father's spirit. Had it not been for the grit my mother was to demonstrate for the more than twenty years that followed, I dread to think what would have happened to him, and to us.

In the Thirties, married women also found it difficult obtaining employment. My mother bought a second-hand bicycle; a type called 'sit up and beg', took off her wedding ring and rode out of the area to find work. She got a job at Joseph Lucas in their Foremans Road Factory in Tysley. It was well away from Great Russell Street and no one knew her there.

It took a good hour's hard ride from our home to get to work; so she would rise at six o'clock to prepared our breakfast, usually toast spread with lard or dripping, and in the winter gave us hot porridge. She would cut sandwiches for our lunch and then get us out of bed, making sure that we were washed and tidy before she left the house. Returning just after 6.30 p.m., my brother Eric having prepared vegetables, she would mix them with canned meat or the remains of the Sunday joint, the only day we had fresh meat. If the joint was big enough and there were leftovers, she would mince the meat in an old cast-iron mincer which she screwed onto the table, and make a meat and potato pie or some other concoction to fill her brood's stomachs.

The fact that she went out to work resulted in Dad becoming even more depressed. In order to earn a few shillings he helped a local decorator to paper the walls of large houses in the Handsworth Wood district. Watching this man work, he thought that if he could learn the tricks of the trade he could start decorating on his own account. He was able to obtain enough wallpaper left over from one of the jobs to cover our meagre ceiling. So, one evening he set about putting into practice his newfound skills.

We helped him clear the pine-top table and sat to watch him dip a brush into the bucket of paste he had prepared and paste the first sheet. Leaving the bucket on the floor he went around to the other side of the table, climbed on to it, and began to instruct us on the art of paperhanging.

Lifting the pasted paper on to the end of a broom and holding it against the ceiling, he began to show us how the professionals did the job. With the broom handle in one hand and a brush in the other, he began to walk along the table, swishing the paper up as he went.

Moving one foot in front of the other, concentrating on the job, he forgot just how small the table was. He stepped off the end straight into the bucket of paste! We couldn't contain ourselves. Not so Dad; his dignity offended, he walked out of the house. By the time he returned, Mom, not wishing to see the paste grow hard, had finished the job. He never tried paperhanging again.

His self-esteem took another knock when brother, Freddie, left school at the age of fourteen and went to work for Boots the chemist at their city centre shop in Colmore Row. His wage was eight shillings a week, less deductions for unemployment stamps.

A few weeks later we had a visit from an official known to the locals as the 'Means test man'. I can still remember him standing in his raincoat with his bowler hat still on his head, a notebook in hand, listing our possessions. This was in the only room where we were able to spend time whilst we were in the house, other than when we were in bed.

Having checked our belongings to ensure that we were not living above our means he dropped his bombshell. Addressing my father, he said, 'Now that you have a breadwinner—' he was referring to Freddie, '—your unemployment allowance will be accordingly reduced.'

His 'breadwinner' comment cut my father to the quick, filling him with despair. It kept the family below the poverty line.

Dad was 5'9", thin, almost bald with sunken cheeks, a pale complexion and sad, dark brown eyes. Due to the effects of the war and the circumstances in which he found himself, he never mixed with the neighbours other than giving a passing nod. He kept very much to himself; they never got to know him and considered him to be something of a mystery.

His father was always well dressed, slim, standing tall and straight as a ramrod. His heavy grey eyebrows and moustache added to the overall effect of a man of quality. I can only recall him visiting our house once. Although I was very young I can remember it as if it was yesterday.

He was wearing a plum-coloured overcoat with a velvet collar, a starched white shirt, wing collar and cravat, and on his head was a grey trilby. Carrying a rolled umbrella, he walked down Great

Russell Street causing quite a stir among our neighbours. When they discovered his identity, it added to the mystery surrounding my father's background.

Although it was more than seventy years ago, his face and general appearance is still etched in my memory. He must have asked for a slice of toast because I remember sitting near his feet while holding the bread on the end of the wire toasting fork against the fire.

He sat on a chair next to the table, still in his overcoat, resting his hands on the handle of his umbrella. Sitting on the floor, I couldn't take my eyes off him. He poked me with his umbrella saying, 'Careful, boy, you are burning my toast.' There was no grandfatherly softness in his tone; in fact these were the only words I can remember him ever saying to me.

Unlike most of the men in the slums, my father didn't drink; so he couldn't find friendship or solace as most of the men did in one of the numerous pubs in the neighbourhood. He enjoyed listening to opera and classical music, his favourite tenors were Beniamino Gigli and the American, Richard Crooks; he considered Richard Tauber a crooner.

He played records on an old wind-up gramophone, carefully wiping them with a duster kept for the purpose. Inserting a rare fibre needle in what was called a soundbox, he would gingerly lower the arm on to the record, then sit with eyes closed for moments of escape from his miserable surroundings and personal desperation.

Every Sunday morning, come rain or shine, a Mr Saunders, who worked in the offices of the Birmingham Corporation's Electricity Supply Department, called to collect our penny subscription to the Ward Labour Party. He too was a classical music fan. Every so often he would bring his well-protected records to our house so that he and Dad could enjoy a musical evening.

Although we were a close-knit family, I never really understood my father. Even now I ponder about what was going on in his head during what were, for him, the dark days of the 1920s and 30s. I would dearly love to be able to communicate with him now and try to grasp what it was that destroyed his will to fight the system.

Although he was a mild, kindly man, I can't ever remember him giving me any praise or word of encouragement. He was like that all the time I knew him. Whatever I achieved in my life, he left me with the impression that he could not quite make out why, or how, it had been possible.

He liked to watch boxing and would walk miles to the Smethwick Baths or Walford Road Rink to stand at the back of the hall and watch regional and national professional champions. He took my elder brother, Freddie, to the Aston Amateur Boxing Club which was based at the Holte Hotel – really a large pub – situated at one end of Villa Park, the home of Aston Villa Football Club. Freddie possessed a sense of survival, so he didn't stick at it. Much later, I joined the club without my father knowing. He only became aware of the fact once I was established.

The street in which we lived was called Great Russell Street, a name that conjures up an image of grandeur. In reality, it was four mean streets in one: straight, long, narrow, and very depressing.

The top end had a T-junction called Tower Street, where stood the church known as St George's in the Fields. Needless to say, the fields had disappeared long ago under a dense forest of slum houses. This first section ended at Brearley Street.

The second section had a slow gradient; it was here where my family resided. It ended at New John Street West. The third section was on a very steep gradient ending at Bridge Street West, best known for its local police station – the finest-looking property in the immediate area. The fourth flattened out and came to an end – in name only – at Farm Street.

It was on the steep section in Great Russell Street that, like most kids in the neighbourhood, I discovered the art of balancing on two wheels. It was a simple, highly dangerous riding course, but very effective. To be successful, the novice had to follow a strict pattern.

First came a visit to Mr Scrivens, a stern but understanding shopkeeper who supplemented his income by hiring out bikes by the half-hour. They ranged from small three-wheelers to the large 'sit up and beg' variety, common in those days. They had all seen better days and most could fairly be described as 'boneshakers' with brakes which belied the name and were usually found only on the front wheel.

The intrepid learner would sit astride the machine and, with teeth gritted and a nod of the head, be pushed to the brow of the hill. There, watched by a circle of friends, he or she would be given a hard push to career at a gathering speed down the steep incline. The rider then had to remain upright, miss people, dogs, cats and the greengrocer's shop on the corner of Bridge Street West – along which vehicular traffic passed regularly and, exhilarated but scared, resist the urge to apply the brake, which would have resulted in being catapulted over the handlebars. Then, just sticking with it, he or she would slow down on the level part at the bottom of the street by scraping both feet along the ground, having successfully overcome the hazards and discovered that he or she had learned how to ride a bike. Not the best way, to be sure, but most certainly the fastest.

Those who failed the test were faced with a long lonely trek up the hill, so-called friends having fast disappeared, carrying a busted bike and planning on how to leave the battered machine outside the Scrivens' shop and to beat an undetected retreat.

At the Farm Street crossing, Great Russell Street became Clifford Street. After continuing on a level for a short distant it began to rise sharply to a T-junction at the top. This street was where Denis, later to become Lord Howell of Aston Manor, was born, and lived until his family went upmarket. They moved to a larger house in Guildford Street, which ran parallel.

Entrance to the backyards was gained via a narrow tunnel. The houses in one yard were physically joined to houses in the next. Our backyard had a cast-iron number plate nailed over the entrance with the legend COURT 13. In it there were eleven dwellings, with three fronting the street.

All the houses had small rooms on the ground floor, a bed-room on the first floor and an even smaller attic over that. There were four called 'cottages' which had one bedroom but were all welded together on three sides. Density was considered by the owners to be all-important.

The houses in each yard, along with those fronting it, formed a community. In our case it consisted fourteen families, or forty-nine human beings. We shared six outside lavatories – eight persons plus per lavatory – and two garbage pens called miskins, each containing three dustbins. It meant at times queuing for the 'lav' and overflowing dustbins most of the time.

Every yard had either one or two washhouses called – goodness knows why – the brew house; in the local tongue, 'bruhus'. They were single storey, with a slate roof and a glassless window and a doorless entrance. In other words, they were, save for the roof, open to the elements.

The 'bruhus' was where the women took turns to wash the family laundry. With fourteen families in our 'community' it meant that washdays had to be allocated, and for most of the week the yard was full of washing hanging out to dry. In each 'bruhus' there was one, sometimes two, large basin-shaped copper receptacles called boilers, which were set in a brick housing, under which there was a place for a fire. There was a cold water tap and a ceramic sink about two feet long by one and a half, and three inches deep.

Buckets of water were poured into the boiler, the fire was lit and when the water was bubbling a handful of a black tar-like substance called 'soft soap' was dropped in along with a Reckitt's blue bag. The water was constantly stirred with a wooden boiling stick. This was a must. It made sure that the soft soap had properly melted, otherwise it would adhere itself to whatever was being washed.

Once the water was considered ready, in would go the washing. This would also be stirred with the stick which was used to lift the contents out from time to time to be rubbed on a scrubbing board, which in the sixties were used by skiffle bands. When considered adequately clean, the washing was dumped into a tub full of cold water and pounded with a maid or dolly, a castellated chunk of wood on the end of a pole with a handle.

The washing was then hauled out and the water squeezed out by a mangle. This had two long wooden rollers operated with gears at one end and a large wheel with a handle at the other. The washing was placed between the rollers and the wheel turned, which required two strong arms. The wooden rollers squeezed out as much of the water as possible. This helped the washing to dry more quickly when hung on the lines which were stretched across the yard. Not a pretty sight.

I have tried to describe this in order to show just how hard wash days were. They were hard enough in the summer; in the winter they were sheer hell, which underlined the fact that the women in the slums were a very special breed.

When they were pregnant, there were no pre or post-natal classes to guide the women of the slums. They couldn't afford a maternity ward, hospital balanced meals or professional nursing to reduce the risk and the pain of childbirth. They were lucky if the local midwife was at hand. If not, they were on their own or left to a local lady who could be counted on to bring babies into the world or to 'lay out' the dead ready for the next.

My mother went into Labour on 26 July 1922 whilst engaged in doing the family wash. I was told that she was helped by the local midwife to bring me into the daylight, but having learned of the family's financial situation at the time, I doubt it.

In the mid-1930s, the weekly rent charged for slum houses crowded into backyards where the sun hardly penetrated was about seven shillings. It was collected on the same day at the same time each week by the owner's agent. Other than seeing this rent collector, none of the tenants had any contact with the owner, let alone knowledge of who the owner was.

Later on in my life, I found out that most were owned by well-known, well-to-do families who were pillars of their local church. They named some of our mean streets after their sons or daughters: Ann, Charles, Henrietta, Henry and Mary Street was commonplace. It made me wonder what went on in the minds of these people.

Their estates of slum properties were slung around the neck of the city so close to the centre that we could hear the chimes of Big Brum. This was a clock designed like, but as a much smaller edition of, London's Big Ben. It stood over the council house, the name given to the administrative centre where the city council hold its meetings. I was destined to spend a good part of twenty-five years of my life in its committee rooms.

I don't know whether it was due to the fact that the families lived so close to each other, the shared poverty or the kinship that prevailed, but in our street, which was described as mean, I can recall being very happy at times. The area had a warmth and seemed to breed 'characters'. It's difficult to find either on modern housing estates nowadays.

The house in front of ours faced the street and was occupied by the Judd family. Mrs Judd was enormous, 5'8", and she weighed in at twenty-two stone. You could tell when she was waddling up the entry into the yard, because other than a little light coming from over her shoulders the rest of it was blocked out by her immense body.

Her husband, Billy, was a complete opposite. He was three inches shorter than his wife and as thin as a rake. They had two daughters; one died very young of diphtheria, a common enough occurrence in the slums at the time. My youngest brother, Norman, caught the disease but thankfully survived. The other daughter grew up to be a talented and beautiful young woman. A competent dancer, she tried the theatre but gave up because she didn't want to travel. Why, I couldn't understand. Although her mother doted on her, living there couldn't have been pleasant.

The Judds were hawkers selling fruit and vegetables from a cart in the Bull Ring. They saved enough to open a fruit shop in Great Hampton Row and, according to our standards, were relatively well off.

Billy Judd had a pretty bad time of it. With a wife almost three times his weight, he was no match for her. He became what the neighbours described as a quiet drinker – meaning that he could drink anyone under the table and often did without any outward effect. He was a decent man who never caused the neighbours or the police any trouble.

The streets were illuminated by freestanding gas lamp posts, about four to each section. With no automatic switches, the Corporation had an army of lamplighters who had the job of cleaning the glass, replacing gas mantles, and turning the lights on at night and off at daybreak.

The week the country celebrated King George V's Silver Jubilee, the neighbours decorated the yards, the streets and the lamp posts. My mind boggles at the thought that we were living in a relatively small country which was one of the richest in the world, yet the gap between the haves and the have-nots was almost as wide as it had ever been. Yet, these poor sods saved up their pennies so that they could celebrate *their* King's Silver Jubilee.

They hung streamers zigzagging across the street from bedrooms to bedrooms. The women, who had collected money for a whole year, laid on a street party for the kids in the afternoon and the adults on the night. The King's picture was displayed in windows, hung on every lamp post and on the commemorative jugs and plates they bought. I still find that astounding.

There was a band playing, and at about eleven in the evening a cry went up: Billy Judd had entered the bottom of the street, having abandoned his seat in the pub. With music going strong, bowler hat in hand held high, he danced up the length of the street doing high kicks like a member of the *Ziegfeld Follies*. How he kept this up in a state of complete inebriation was nothing short of miraculous. As I mentioned, our street was full of characters, Billy being just one. This was definitely one of our good days.

Most families had two or more children, so in almost every street in the slums there was an army of kids who had to make their own amusement. In the late 1920s and 30s, motorcars were a rare sight in the area, so there was little danger when we played our games in the street.

Tipcat, hide-and-seek, kick the can, or jump the camel. Tipcat was a game played with a piece of wood about two inches long whittled at both ends like a pencil; it was called the cat. The other piece of equipment was a chunk of wood, usually salvaged from a discarded orange box, which we shaped into a bat.

The cat would be placed in a circle marked with chalk in the middle of what we called 'the horse road'. The player would strike the whittled end causing it to rise sharply and then whacked it as far as possible. It was like a game of rounders. Unfortunately, the fast flying missile could prove dangerous to passers-by or to the windows of the houses fronting the street. Being warned not to play this game only made it that much more exciting.

Complaints were made to the local bobby, who was a fellow we knew as 'Ginger the Cop'. He was, as most of the policemen were in those days, big. He had sandy hair – hence his nickname – and, unfortunately for us, a turn of speed which should have earned him a place in the Olympic sprint team.

Although clad in a uniform which included heavy boots, when he turned the corner at the top of the street he came at us so fast that there were few who escaped. On a day when I was in to bat with my back to the oncoming Ginger, he had collared me before the cat was high enough to strike.

He seemed to know all our names, where we lived and who were our parents. He whisked me home giving me a clip on the ear and a warning in front of my mother. Unlike today, there was a mutual respect regarding the police. I cannot remember anyone verbally or otherwise abusing them, or they in turn being too heavy-handed.

The only trouble my father got into was when he tried to help an old drunk who fell whilst being marched off to the nick. The Desk Sergeant, who was new to the area, put dad in a cell for 'interfering with the course of justice'. Ginger was on night duty, and when he called in to report at Bridge Street police station he spotted Dad behind bars. He knew he didn't drink so asked what he was in for. On being told, he spoke to his Superintendent and Dad was on his way home. That was the way it was in those days.

The Great Western Railway Company had their stables not too far from us, and our street was en route to and from their main station at Snow Hill. We had great fun riding on the back of the carts and there was an income to be derived from the by-product. Horse manure was the only fertiliser to be had, so we would rush out with a bucket to collect the steaming droppings in order to sell it to those houses that had small gardens and the others that had window boxes.

During the summer months, when the sun seemed to shine every day, we played our games. Our backyard was paved all over with blue bricks; it was not pretty but ideal for games. With a piece of chalk we drew goalposts on the wall, tied old newspapers rolled into a ball with string, and the game of football was on. When the ball wore out we just made another.

A French Canadian came to live in Court 13 with a lady whose husband had left her. Her name was Elsie Waldren; his was

Thérioux – pronounced *te–ree–oo*. He was a barber. To 'make time' with the neighbours, he cut the kids' hair free of charge. To make time with the kids he would make a toffee he called 'stick jaw'. A piece would take hours to chew and almost extract our teeth in the process.

He organised games during those summer evenings and so with us he was very popular. However, some of the more conventional neighbours just ignored him. To them he was Elsie Waldren's fancy man and as such was considered unacceptable in a respectable neighbourhood.

Our simple pleasures were few during the dreary winter months, made tolerable on Sunday mornings by the call of the Periwinkle man. For a penny he would use a half-pint beer mug to measure the winkles and he always provided a straight pin to extract the tasty morsels.

In the afternoon sitting by the fire we would hear the ringing bell and the cry 'fresh pikelets' – called muffins in the south – which we could buy when we had money. Toasted and spread with Echo margarine, they tasted like food for the gods.

Unlike the housing estates today, the slum areas were full of shops. There were seven in our small section of Great Russell Street. A fish and chip shop, newsagent, greengrocer and a number of grocers who sold everything from bootlaces to bacon.

There were also two pubs, and two pawnshops proudly displaying their statutory three brass balls. On Monday morning, women queued to pledge their families' Sunday clothes, which they reclaimed on Friday night when their husband came home.

Around the corner in Great Hampton Row was Knight's, the pork butcher. He didn't just sell pork, he killed the pigs in his slaughterhouse alongside his shop. We would ask Mr Knight if he had any pigs' bladders. Cleaned, we blew them up and tied the end with strong cotton and they lasted a lot longer than balloons, and cost us nothing.

We were also lucky to have a number of what we called picture houses in close proximity. On Saturday afternoon, a visit took us into a different world. There was Newtown Picture Palace in Newtown Row, the Metropole in Snow Hill; the Great Hampton Picture House was named after the street, not its structure. It was small and facing heavy competition. The manager tried his best by handing out free comics at the Saturday matinee but try as he might to fill his cinema, the enterprising man was fighting a losing battle. The cinema was built over a railway tunnel, and when the trains came thundering through, the floor would shake and the noise would drown out the sound coming from the screen.

The Metropole was where we saw our first talking picture. Sitting on planks in the gallery behind a large lady with straight hair dyed jet black, sobbing her heart out, we watched Al Jolson in *The Jazz Singer*, billed in Britain as *The Singing Fool*. The whole cinema broke into tears when he sang 'Sonny Boy'.

I remember sitting there with my brother Norman one Friday night just before the last war; we were watching *Things to Come* based on an H G Wells novel. The last scene was of a very young Raymond Massey pointing up at the night sky and saying excitingly, 'There, there they are – do you see that faint twinkling light?'

He was pointing to a manned rocket that had been launched in search of another planet. It sent a shiver down my spine. We walked back to our little house in Great Russell Street in silence.

When Mom could spare the money, as a young boy l would go on Saturday afternoon to the Newtown Picture Palace to watch Tom Mix, Hoot Gibson or Tom Tyler, all famous silent screen cowboys. I would come out after the film, leap on to my imaginary black and white pinto and gallop up New John Street West shooting everybody in sight.

Reaching Court 13, I would tie my horse to the lamp post at the bottom of the entry and saunter into the house. My mother would bring me down to earth by giving me a piece of bread and jam and I was back in the real world. Unlike many pundits, I'm convinced that films and television have an effect on people's behaviour.

Living on the third part of our street – the steep section – was the Kirby family. Their name means nothing today, but then Bert Kirby was the uncrowned lightweight boxing champion of Great Britain. Uncrowned, because everybody who watched the fight for the championship knew that Bert had beaten Jackie Brown, the reigning British champion, but the referee thought otherwise.

Bert's brother, Jack, was the middleweight champion of the Midlands. He was the bad lad of the family. Being caught just after midnight carrying a safe on his back in the centre of the city of Worcester, when asked, he told the police that he was moving it for a friend and was surprised when they didn't believe him. Not too bright, he was in and out of trouble for most of his life.

Their nephew, Freddie, an amateur with me in the Aston ABC, was a nice lad. He was a classic boxer loaded with talent who, had he not been killed during the Italian campaign during the war, would have made it to the very top.

We had another great professional lightweight champion who lived in Ormond Street just off Summer Lane. His name was Owen Moran. He fought for the World Title in the United States and lived there for a time. His sister, Katie Moran, was a drinker, her favourite pub being the Salutation on the corner of Snow Hill and Summer Lane.

I remember seeing the police carrying her back to Bridge Street Station fighting all the way. Those who had the job of handling her were in no doubt that had Katie been a man she *would* have been a world champion.

From time to time there would be a fracas outside one of the pubs at closing time on Sunday afternoon. I can recall vividly the one-legged hawker who hobbled around on a crutch, having lost a leg during the war.

He lived round the corner from us in New John Street West and wasn't very old. Owning a flat cart and a pony, rain or shine he would sell fruit and vegetables around the local streets. This particular Sunday he had been caught up in an argument which spilled out into the street at closing time.

He threw his crutch down and hopped about on his one leg, throwing punches at his opponent like a champion. How he remained upright on his one leg having imbibed a quality of the local brew was astonishing. He kept going until the police arrived. Physically you could say the area was miserable, but there was never a dull moment.

There was a young fellow of indeterminate age who, whatever the weather, could always to be found standing on the corner at the top of the steep hill in Great Russell Street. Hunched up, wearing an old pair of long trousers and boots that had seen better days, cold or wet he never wore a coat, just a threadbare pullover.

His parents scratched a living by visiting the market, gathering boxes that had been thrown out and chopping them up to make and sell bundles of firewood. How they earned money during the summer months I never knew.

Their son was severely mentally retarded and, as far as I am aware, never went to any kind of school. We called him Cary Custard because those were the words he would sing repeatedly. With his hands stuffed deep into his trouser pockets and his shoulders hunched up, he would do a shuffling jig, singing, 'Cary Cary Custard, Cary Cary Custard!' He did this every time we stopped to talk with him.

It really wasn't a case of being with him because he never said anything that we could understand. It appeared that he looked at you with eyes that couldn't see; he was in a world of his own. John Lennon wrote a song about a man on the hill who watched the world going round. It could have been based on someone like our Cary Custard.

In later years, President Kennedy's sister, Eunice Shriver, was to talk me into helping young people like him... but that's another story.

Chapter II
THE WAY IT WAS

Despite the trials and tribulations there was always a feeling of kinship between neighbours, sharing both the happy and the not so happy times. There were dramas now and then but these were soon forgotten.

In the homes where the father was unemployed the children dressed in hand-me-downs; in some cases the clothes were handed on to families even worse off than they were. I can't remember wearing socks or pullovers that were free of darns until I was fourteen.

A son of the Brutons, one of a large family living in the next yard, knocked our door on a Sunday morning to say, 'Me mom asked if you have any old clothes to spare.'

If it hadn't been so pathetic it would have been funny. This wasn't unusual and the Brutons weren't looked down upon, because we were all in the same boat. We shared an understanding born out of the adversity we experienced in common.

Poor people didn't stray too far from the family. When a son or daughter got married they couldn't afford to buy a house so they usually moved in with the family or rented a room from a neighbour, if they were lucky enough to find one, but it would not be too far from their family.

When the area in which they lived was redeveloped, and that didn't happen until the 1950s, the so-called Housing Managers and the elected members – not just in Birmingham but in all the big cities – simply failed to comprehend what would happen when they broke up the extended family unit when the time came for them to be rehoused.

A study was carried out in the East End of London on the effect of splitting up of families, friends and neighbours after the bombing flattened the area in which they had lived. It was called

Family and Kinship in the East End of London. The study was illuminating and should have been noted by those in whose power the movement of people lay. Unfortunately it wasn't. But I'm getting ahead of myself.

After the First World War, the government's declared intention to build 'Homes fit for Heroes to live in' was an empty promise. Coupled with the Depression that followed it caused too many decent men to lose their dignity, and with it their confidence.

Disillusioned, some tried to find solace in the company of those sharing the same kind of fate in one of the numerous pubs amply provided by the local brewers. They found warmth, cheap beer and a camaraderie which helped them to forget their miserable existence, if only temporarily. Nearing the time that the towels were placed over the beer pumps and the publican was shouting, 'Time, gentlemen please!' They would be singing away as if they hadn't a care in the world. My brothers and I were lucky – our parents didn't drink.

When our neighbours found an excuse, any excuse, and the money to spend, they would pool their resources and break the monotony by inviting a few friends home on a Saturday night to have what we called 'a knees-up'.

They would buy jugs of draft beer and bottles of cheap port to mix with lemonade. Some would bring sandwiches, others meat pies, cheese, onions and pickles, and they would spend a few hours putting their problems behind them. In the summer, the party would spill out into the yard and everybody would join in.

More often than not they asked my mother, whom they knew as 'Goody Bayley who was once on the stage', to sing for them. As I've already mentioned, she was attractive, so she always took one of her sons with her as a chaperon. We would stand in front, and with her hands on our shoulders she would sing all the popular songs. Before we left, the host would wrap up some sandwiches and pies and back home we would have our own party, minus the booze.

At the time, the centre of Birmingham had four variety theatres and there was another closer to us in Newtown Row called the Aston Hippodrome. One of the first music halls to open in the city, the price for admission here was much less than the others.

The cheapest seats – really wooden planks – were in the gallery at the top of the building right under the roof, which we called the gods. My parents loved the music hall and when they could afford the shilling for the whole family to sit in the gods, we got there early to catch the first of the two evening performances on either Friday or Saturday.

We reached the seats by climbing hundreds of stone steps which spiralled up a narrow staircase. Reaching the summit, we were faced with frighteningly steep gangways. Leaning slightly backwards, we would carefully make our way to a vacant row of planks as near to the front as we could get. From such an elevated position the stage appeared to be quite small but at least we had an unimpeded view. Although it was a second-string theatre we saw many great stars who were on their way down… and some yet to be on their way up.

On winter nights we would buy baked potatoes from the mobile oven with a fire underneath. The cart had a wooden box on its side filled with salt; a few pinches helped to improve the taste.

Newtown Row was a thriving market place full of character with kerbside hawkers who had acetylene lamps so at night you could see what they were selling. There were one or two large stores and rows of small shops which were far more interesting that their counterparts today.

If you had the money you could buy Indian or China tea served from large black canisters; the grocer would weigh and bag the tea of your choice. The smell of freshly ground coffee wafted in the air. The grocers had a large lump of fresh dairy butter on a marble slab which they would slice and pat into a quarter-pound oblong shape with wooden paddles, and there were various cheeses on similar slabs which the shop assistant would cut with a piece of piano wire coupled to the counter.

There were greengrocers', butchers' and bakers' shops, some having open fronts with large acetylene gaslights to brighten up the night scene. There was nothing mundane about any of the traders, they all played a part in adding to the atmosphere and gaiety of the place.

The butchers didn't have refrigerators, only cold rooms with blocks of ice delivered daily to keep the meat relatively fresh for short periods. On Saturday night at about 8 p.m. they would hold Dutch auctions in order to get rid of their stock. Whether you wanted to buy or not, the auctions were entertaining.

We would get as near to the front to watch the butcher standing outside his shop on a box so he couldn't be missed. When his audience was large enough he would entertain us with his patter. Holding up a piece of meat he would describe it in the most glowing terms, then announce its weight and the price he wanted. With no takers he gradually brought the price down until he had a bid. This was the way we got our Sunday joint and he got rid of his stock.

At the end of the Row there was a small market hall. I remember it because a gypsy had a stall there. He would tell the women their fortune, which would have been easy had he told the truth. But he knew only too well the life they had to live so he told them what they wanted to hear.

In 1949, 'the Row' became part of what was called of the Summer Lane slum clearance area. Its shops and market hall, along with the surrounding decrepit dwellings, were torn down. In the 1950s, a modern shopping precinct was built to replace the old shopping area. It was without either charm or character. Whilst writing, I was happy to hear that this too had been torn down and a far better shopping precinct built in its place. However good it looks, it will never be able to attain the magical atmosphere of the original 'Row'.

Like most of our neighbours, my mother had to shop around for bargains.

On Friday night one of us would accompany her to Barrow's store just before it closed. It was in the centre, Birmingham's equivalent of London's Fortnum and Mason. The Barrow family were Quakers and a number of their family had served on the city council.

We would stand with our backs to the wall near to the bacon counter waiting for the last customer to leave. The assistant, who knew our family, would gather up the leftover bacon ends, put them in a bag and hand it to my mother in exchange for a few coppers. In May 1965, more than thirty years later, my mother reminded me of this (see the chapter entitled 'First Citizen').

The time I'm referring to had been tough on her but she worked hard to protect us, always pretending that everything was fine. Home entertainment was the wireless or the wind-up gramophone and the games we played together. There was a once-a-week visit to the cinema and rare visits to the theatre. The libraries and the parks were free, and to be able to watch a Aston Villa or Birmingham City football game we would wait until they opened their gates at half-time so that those that couldn't afford to pay could get in to see almost half of the match for nothing.

The streets were our stage. Every Sunday there would be one parade or another. The Boy Scouts, Boys' Brigade, the Salvation Army or the British Legion. Organ-grinders would appear, at times with a dancer, and street singers were commonplace – and sing they could.

We had traders who pushed their carts through the area, all adding colour to the scene and to our lives. There was the diminutive moustached Italian salt seller who carried oblong blocks of salt on his open cart. He would serve his customer by sawing a piece off with a wood saw. He had a fine tenor voice and to let people know that he had arrived in the street he would sing some aria or other. His voice would reverberate, bouncing off the walls in the narrow streets.

There were rag-and-bone men, who collected old clothes and worn-out pots and pans in exchange for a few pennies or a balloon. There was a young happy-go-lucky fellow who pedalled a tricycle with a gaily-painted box on the front with the words *El Dorado*. He sold flavoured coloured ice on a stick for a ha'penny and attracted attention by yodelling. We kids loved him.

In those days there were lots of horses hauling railway carts, milk floats, bread vans, or fruit and vegetable carts. On May Day, every horse would be decorated with coloured ribbons plaited around their manes and tails. Their brasses and leathers would be highly polished and some of the carts would also be decorated.

On Easter Sunday, the Catholic community held their colourful Easter Parade. These were huge and attracted hundreds of people who would line the city centre streets three and four deep to watch the floats and the children dressed in white, parading through the city centre before going to St Chad's Cathedral to celebrate their annual Easter Mass.

A walk to the city centre from our house in Great Russell Street would take about thirty minutes. Some Saturday afternoons we would go to mix with the crowds looking round the street market in the Bull Ring where there would always be someone performing. Escapologists, conjurers and the like. Indoors there was the rag market and the Market Hall.

We returned home via Snow Hill, where halfway down the hill was an eating house. In the window, the faggots, peas, sausages and mashed potatoes kept hot over deep trays containing piping hot water, made our mouths water. If times were good we would stop and have our Saturday supper sitting in a booth enjoying the atmosphere and the food.

In the slums we lived close to a great variety of people; it was an education. Studying human nature began early for me and paid dividends over the years. There were a lot of children in Hockley and we had six schools to cater for us. The school in Summer Lane – another name conjuring up a picture which was far from the real thing – was the largest. It and Burbury Street were state schools which were administered by the city's Education Department; St George's and St Matthias, by the Church of England; St Mary's and St Chad's by the Catholic Church.

Education at all of them ended when their pupils reached the age of fourteen. Although my mother was a Catholic she had been isolated when she married out of the faith so we were sent to St Matthias. It was the smallest, with just two hundred pupils, ages ranging from five to fourteen. It was small enough to make an indelible impression on me.

I can still remember all the teachers and most of my contemporaries. A Protestant church school, it had limited financial support from the Education Department and consequently was always short of facilities. It was old and badly designed and yet it attracted dedicated teachers. Being small had its advantages, but I was to discover that being attached to a church had its downside.

I sang in the choir, and when I was twelve a new vicar arrived. He had returned to England from Singapore. His name was Bishop and he acted as if he actually represented this position in the church hierarchy. He was tall and rotund, with a large flabby pink whisker-free face and small inset eyes – at least, that's how I remember him.

He made no bones about letting everyone know that he was not happy to have been directed to minister in a church in the slums of Birmingham, even though his church house was in leafy Handsworth. Unlike the teachers in the school to which the church was attached, he was totally insensitive to the conditions being suffered by the people he was there to serve.

Prior to the day in autumn when the church celebrated what was known as Harvest Festival, the vicar visited the school to tell – not ask – that we bring a gift of food to the church to be placed on the altar steps during the service.

Inside, the church was beautifully decorated for the occasion and the pews were full. At a given time, the pupils from the school walked down the aisle to place our Harvest Festival gift on the altar steps. The majority of us came from families which were in dire straits. Not too well fed and mostly poorly dressed, with outstretched arms and upturned hands, as instructed, we bore our gifts, some of us carrying a solitary Oxo cube. It caused us and our parents to suffer agonies of embarrassment but it went straight over the vicar's head.

I wondered then, and still do, why it hadn't occurred to this representative of the Christian faith, that he had press-ganged his *poor* parishioners into giving gifts of food they couldn't afford, to be distributed to the *poor*. The thought angers me still.

For a short time I was a member of the church choir overseen by the verger who doubled as choirmaster and organist. He was old, small, very short-sighted and immensely kind. At this time I was also a member of the Old Edwardians Boys' Club which was housed in an abandoned pub in Barr Street, otherwise occupied by small factories. The funds to provide this had been given by the governors of King Edward's School Foundation.

It was a nice, relatively small club, its objective being to keep the boys in the slums off the streets and from slipping into a life of crime. The teachers from King Edward's Grammar Schools gave up some of their spare time to help out at the club which they had affiliated to the Federation of the Boys' and Girls' Union which enable us to entered into many of the Federation's inter-club competitions.

I had the honour of being chosen to play for our team in the table tennis tournament. Unfortunately, one of the matches fell on the night of the choir practice. Caught in a dilemma, I decided that this was just one night and the honour of representing the club took precedence over choir practice. I was soon to find out that the vicar took a different view.

On the following Sunday morning, along with the other choirboys I was standing outside the vestry waiting for the verger. The vicar arrived just as the door was being opened and we stood aside so that he could enter. He looked down at me to ask why I had missed choir practice. I tried to explain that I had been chosen to play table tennis for my club.

'Table tennis – you stayed away to play table tennis.' It was more of a statement than a question. He then slapped me hard across the face.

'If you want to play table tennis you can play with me!' he shouted, and stomped into the vestry.

The embarrassed verger guided me and the rest of the choir indoors. I donned my cassock and surplice, picked up my hymn book and stood in line ready to march with the other boys behind the vicar into the church. As the organ struck up, I stopped, took off my choirboy's outfit, placed it with my hymn book on a chair, and left.

My mother, seeing me back home so early, asked if there was anything wrong. I told her what had happened, and she put her arms around me and gave me one of her pieces of homely advice.

'Whenever you feel sure that you are not in the wrong, never make excuses and never explain.'

I didn't fully understand it then but have remembered it with gratitude many times since.

On another occasion, when she realised that something was burning up inside, she counselled, 'If you have a bee in your bonnet, better let it out before it grows so big it will burst your brain.'

It was a piece of unnecessary advice in my case, because I have always been *too* open. It's got me into many scrapes which could have been avoided had I kept the 'bee' in a little longer than I did.

My choirboy days were, along with my reverence for things ecclesiastical, at an end but I remained a member of the Old Edwardians Boys' Club. Why it went by that name was a mystery; its membership was made up solely of elementary school kids.

In August, the club took us to The Wrekin Public School where we camped on their playing fields and was allowed to use their sports facilities. It was where I was taught to play tennis by one of the masters, a man named Bell-Scott who played as an amateur for the Warwickshire County Cricket Club.

At St Matthias school, the classes were mixed until we were old enough – nine years – to enter the seniors. Then, for reasons which escaped me, the boys and girls were educated separately. Looking back, I think because it was a church school the governors felt that as we were older it would be in our best interest not to be placed in a position were we might suffer temptations of the flesh. They really had nothing to worry about; there was no television, films we were allowed to see were limited to the cowboys and Indians variety, and pornography was not then generally available, although we *had* seen some 'rude' paintings when we were taken to the City Art Gallery.

Our teachers came from a totally different background from us, but were nevertheless both caring and sympathetic. They were aware of the poverty being endured by the families in the area and marvelled at our pride. They arranged to provide free dinner tickets which they handed out unobtrusively to the children whose parents applied. The recipients left the school at twelve o'clock and made their way to a church hall in Farm Street where they were served a hot meal. Although my father was out of work and there were four boys to feed, my parents were too proud to apply.

During winter months, a Salvation Army mobile soup kitchen travelled the streets in the central areas. On a day it pulled up in Great Russell Street and I got into deep trouble when my mother was told that I had queued for a bowl of carrot soup. I had shamed the family. Fact was, that it tasted more like water; the carrots had been boiled in rather than soup, but I guess it was the thought that counted.

Poverty was so rife that the *Birmingham Post* and *Mail* newspaper group formed what they called the 'Mail Christmas Tree Fund'. The Trust raised money to supply the children of the poor, with what we called 'Daily Mail boots'. Of heavy thick leather and with hobnails in the soles, they were made to last. It didn't matter how highly you polished them, you couldn't disguise them from what they were. Thinking that he was helping, the Headmaster put forward my brother Eric's name, and he was duly issued with a pair but was never allowed to wear them.

Most of the families obtained their food on what they called the 'strap', a buy now, pay later arrangement with the local shopkeeper. Sometimes, when money was very scarce and bills ran up too high, ashamed to face the owner of the shop some families just had to do without. I can remember it happening to us, although it's hard to believe now. My mother's sisters and their husbands got together to bail us out. It was yet another blow to my dad's self-esteem.

Even though as children we were aware, we didn't quite appreciate the gravity of the situation our parents were facing day in, day out. For them it must have been a frightening and depressing experience.

My mind was concentrated on the Headmistress of the St Matthias Infants School, who was to me the tall, beautiful, slim, exquisite Miss Palmer with the blue eyes and flame-red hair.

I mentioned that the school was small and badly designed. She for example, didn't have a separate office; her desk stood in a place which had to be passed when leaving the classroom I was in. Every other day Miss Palmer would place fresh flowers in a vase on her desk. The day I really got to know this young lady, who up until then had been the subject of my unspoken affection, was when the airship R101 flew low over Birmingham.

We had been told that it would be flying over the city but hadn't expected that it would choose to fly over our humble school. When we heard the noise of the engines there was a fast exit from the classroom to the playground. Racing past Miss Powell's desk I knocked over her flower vase.

Standing in the playground, we looked up to see this huge airship sailing low over our heads. We could see the number written large on both its sides, and the capsule underneath carrying its passengers; it was so low we could see them waving to us as we waved back at them.

Returning to the classroom still spellbound by what we had seen, we were brought down to earth when Miss Powell called Assembly. Holding up the empty vase in one hand and the drooping flowers in the other, she demanded to know the name of the guilty party. In the excitement no one had the slightest idea but, like the young George Washington, I owned up to the crime. I think I must have been labouring under the misguided impression that I would be complimented for my honesty, to be held up as an example to the rest of the school. In the event I received four of the best.

My affection for Miss Palmer became more clouded with each whack of the cane. Rubbing my painful palms I began to reassess my feelings. Since then I have viewed beautiful women with a certain amount of circumspection.

The Headmaster, a kindly but severe-looking man, had a nervous tic which had him twisting his neck every few minutes. He had served as a captain in the infantry and his twitching, we were told, was brought on by his experience during the Great War.

As I have said, he was a kindly man who, it seemed, felt the need almost to apologise if faced with having to administer corporal punishment for some misdemeanour. He was also bothered about the conditions in which we lived and he tried to introduce a little culture into the lives of his pupils.

The school was badly underfunded, so he raised money to buy a radio so that we could listen to the BBC's school programmes. He entered our paintings or drawings in the Birmingham Schoolboys' Art Exhibitions. My brother Eric's work was chosen two years running, and Mr Knight, who included in his duties those of art teacher and sports master, approached my father urging him to send Eric to an art school. Knowing that my parents were in no position to fund it, he offered to pay the fees. Eric's pride wouldn't allow it.

I ought to add at this point that our pride, a disability shared by the family, has proved to be an affliction we could have well done without. As far as I am concerned it has, on even the most elementary overview of my past, cost me dear.

As for higher education, when any of us got through the Grammar School entrance exams, our parents simply couldn't afford to let us attend. We were not alone, by any means. Books and some materials had to be paid for, and then there was the cost of the obligatory uniform, blazer, shirt, tie, cap, socks, shoes and gym clothes. Most of us had to wear hand-me-downs, so uniforms were completely out of the question.

Although many passed the entrance exams I can only remember three or four St Matthias boys going on to Grammar School. They were from one-child families with parents who owned shops or fathers in full-time employment. So much for equal opportunity.

The exception was a boy in my class. Young Rafferty and his elder brother, who lived with their widowed mother; they were both naturally brilliant. The older boy had no chance; he had to go out to work as soon as possible. However, the Headmaster convinced Mrs Rafferty to let her younger son go on to King Edward's Grammar School. The boys in the school had a collection and the teachers made up the difference to buy him a present: a leather briefcase.

We were all embarrassed when the poor fellow was back with us after just one term. His mother simply could not afford for him to continue. It was enough to put the toughest of boys back on their heels; the effect it had on this sensitive and rather meek lad was devastating.

During a geography lesson, we each drew a map of Great Britain, zoning the industrial and rural areas along with the coastline, ports and well-known seaside resorts. The master, Mr Knight, asked for a show of hands on who had not as yet been to the coast. Only two out of the forty failed to put up their hands. A few weeks later, he had arranged a day trip to Rhyl, the North Wales resort.

He booked a cheap day rail excursion paid out of school funds, which I suspect was heavily subsidised by the teachers. Eagerly waiting to catch a sight of the blue glistening water he took us to the beach. The tide was out, and in Rhyl that meant a long walk over the sands to the water's edge.

Although the water turned out to be grey rather than blue, we stood in silence looking out to sea. Mr Knight left us to our differing images of what lay over the horizon. He would not have missed the contentment written on all our faces.

Before we returned home, he took us to a café for a bangers-and-mash tea. The importance of the café was that it was owned by one of Britain's greatest footballers of his day, Harry Hampton. He had played for Aston Villa and had more England caps than any other player at the time. It was a great occasion for boys from a slum school to be able to meet and spend a little time with this legendary football star. He allowed me to try on one of his precious International caps which were on display in his window.

Had Harry Hampton been playing football today he could have retired a very wealthy man, but there he was, having to eke out a living running a small café in the backstreets of Rhyl.

Mr Powell arranged for a number of us to attend a cultural event on what was called a 'Music appreciation day'. It rained as we were marched to the town hall and after we had been seated for about half an hour with the steam rising from our wet clothes, five men in white ties and tails walked on to the stage.

We were on the ground floor and they on the platform above us. The quintet were members of the City of Birmingham Symphony Orchestra. Holding his violin, the leader stepped forward to announce to his young audience, 'The flight of the Bumblebee' – and without further explanation they rattled through it, and so it went on until they had fulfilled their obligation.

They stood up, and without a word or a gesture, left the stage. Their treatment of a gathering of children, who in the main had little or no opportunity to understand or enjoy classical music, made a lasting impression on me. The memory of this occasion was one of the reasons why later in my life, I founded the Midlands Art Centre for Young People for whom I called 'The cultural orphans'.

Through the good offices of our Headmaster, both my brother Eric and I attended Vittoria Street School of Art which was situated in the centre of Birmingham's famous jewellery quarter. Sponsored jointly by the education committee and the Jewellers' Association, pupils with an artistic ability were recommended by their school. Eric and I sat an entrance exam and studied there but neither of us entered the jewellery trade.

My last contact with St Matthias School was at its centenary celebration. A number of the retired teachers and many old boys and girls who were still breathing turned up. Tea, sandwiches and cake was laid on and the memories, good and not so good, came flooding back.

The Rose twins, Teddy and Theodore, were there. Unlike many twins they were completely different; Teddy had ash blond hair, Theodore's was flaming red. Teddy was a bit of a tearaway, Theo was quiet; Teddy was as bright as a button, Theo was a little dull.

They were raised in a back-to-back house in Clifford Street. Having white and red hair and the name Rose, the jokes about the War of the Roses had worn thin by the time we met up again. I didn't meet Teddy after that day, but was to appear with Theo in a television programme hosted by a famous writer and broadcaster named Godfrey Winn.

I spotted Nana (short for banana) Clark. He earned his nickname because of his height, bent shoulders and lack of breadth. He still looked the same only much, much taller. When we first met in the Infant's he was a bit of a bully. He thumped me a few times until the day I decided to strike back.

Turning up with his mother, the teacher asked the boy who had blacked Nana's eye to stand up. When his mother saw just how small I was, she clouted Nana and walked out of the classroom.

In 1949, when I was knocking doors canvassing for votes in Bridge Street West during my first election campaign, I was surprised when Nana opened the door; he was still living with his mother. From his reaction, I realised that he remembered the incident; so I marked him down as a doubtful voter.

As I was reminiscing with Nana and the Rose twins,

Miss Palmer, the Headmistress with whom I had fallen in love twenty or more years before, came over to introduce herself in that lovely Welsh lilt she hadn't lost. She appeared to have shrunk quite a bit.

Addressing me, she said, 'I used to teach at this school,' and with a certain amount of deference added how nice it was that a representative of the city's education committee should take the time to honour the school's centenary with a visit. She obviously thought that no one educated at St Matthias School could have ever reached such dizzy heights as to become a city councillor. What was worse, she had forgotten me.

Placing both hands on her shoulders, this time looking down and not up into those blue eyes I remembered so well, I replied, 'No, dear, dear Miss Palmer, I am not a member of the education committee.'

I went on to tell her that one of the reasons I was there was with the fervent hope that she would be there too; that I wanted to meet once again the first love of my life who tossed it away on the day the R101 decided to fly over the school.

She was speechless, so I planted a kiss on both her cheeks and moved away. I stood watching her having an agitated conversation with Mr Powell. He looked across and wagged his finger at me, as he had done many times when I was in his charge.

I had been looking forward to meeting Mr Lamb and was disappointed to hear that they had lost touch with him. He had left the theatre to take up teaching but remained every inch a thespian. He had a rather long pointed nose which, like the rest of his face, was heavily pockmarked – brought on, my mother told me, by the heavy use of the stage cosmetics in those days.

Mr Lamb was totally bald, slim, and always immaculately dressed. I remember the dark blue suit he wore and the light blue shirt with the blue and white polka-dot bow tie. The blue cummerbund around his waist was seen when he was about to hold forth.

He would unbutton his coat, push it open, place his long manicured fingers on his hip and parade up and down the aisles between our desks, gesturing as he quoted the Bard. I was spellbound by his beautiful voice and the way he projected it, whispering and at times bellowing to give emphasis as if he was still on the boards playing a role in a Shakespeare drama. He came in to his own when quoting passages from his favourite, *The Ancient Mariner*. He had a sense of humour too. He was as I say, totally bald, and when we came to that passage describing the mariner 'and his head was as bald as a new-laid egg', he laughed with the rest of us.

Mr Lamb made everything come alive, opening up vistas to us that were broader and brighter than the streets we lived in. He coached us, putting on school plays for the first time. He tried so hard, battling against overwhelming odds trying to teach us how to speak 'proper'. Our Brummagem accents must have grated on his nerves, poor chap.

Mr Basil Belk, a rugby player from Bromsgrove who did his best to turn our heads away from football without success, was there looking the same as I remembered him. Mr Grunhill, another dedicated teacher, came over to say hello, an olive-skinned Norfolk man who I had heard had been a scratch golfer and had represented his county.

He was another who had joined the staff straight from college. I was surprised to hear that he was still teaching at St Matthias which, having been absorbed into the Birmingham Education Department was now a junior school. I enquired of Mr Powell why Grunhill hadn't progressed. 'He just doesn't interview well,' I was told.

This was confirmed by Mr Russell, the Chief Education Officer, of whom I asked the same question.

'But that seems terribly unfair,' I said, and Russell agreed. Within a few months Grunhill had his first deputy headship and in his last few years before retiring, became the head of his own school. Justice done.

Whilst I was still at school, my mother was taken to Dudley Road Hospital suffering from peritonitis, from which patients rarely recovered. After they had returned her to the ward from the operating theatre, the priest was called to administer the last rites. My father, who was still unemployed, was facing the probability of losing Mom and having to raise his four sons alone; he was in a bad way.

I came home from school just after he had returned from the hospital to see him sitting on a chair with his head in his hands weeping. I slipped out of the house and walked to the jewellery quarter.

The area was full of small workshops set up in what had once been, fine Victorian houses. I knocked on many doors asking for a part-time job, without success. In Spencer Street on the wall of one of these converted houses I saw a brass plate inscribed: CUTTS AND SONS, ENGINE TURNERS TO THE TRADE.

I entered the hallway and stood on my toes to press the buzzer. A small serving hatch door opened and out popped the head of one of the Cutts Sons. He opened his mouth and on his tongue rested what remained of a lighted cigarette.

'What do *you* want?' he demanded.

'Please sir, I want a job,' I replied, eyes firmly fixed on his cigarette, which had disappeared while I was answering him. It popped out again when he asked how old I was. In it went again whilst I lied, 'Thirteen, sir.'

The hatch was slammed to and I turned to leave. A door opened and he grabbed hold of me and took me into a shop full of noisy machines which cut patterns on gold and silver cigarette cases. He called for the attention of his workforce by yelling over the din, 'This cheeky little bugger has asked me for a job!'

They all laughed dutifully.

'Tell us, why do you want a job?' he asked, so over the noise of the machines I yelled, 'My mom is sick in hospital and my dad's out of work – we need the money.'

His workers stopped laughing. Embarrassed, he grabbed me again and hustled me into his office. He offered me a shilling. I looked at it and then at him and, handing it back, pleaded, 'Mister, I want a job.'

He started me on at half a crown a week, which he paid me in advance.

Every day after school I raced up there, fetched the tea and cakes for the boss and his workers from the coffee house on the corner of Warstone Lane and Vittoria Street, and swept the silver cuttings into one pile and the gold into another. When I had built up a sense in Mr Cutts of my reliability, he trusted me to deliver the precious sides of the cases which had been turned to other jewellers in the district.

I worked for Cutts and Sons, Engine Turners to the Trade, for the next eighteen months. I remember it as if it happened yesterday and I bless their memory still.

During my mother's illness, the neighbours and the nuns from the Catholic Church helped us through a desperate period. The doctors were amazed that she recovered; my aunts said that the thought of leaving her boys had given her the will to fight for her life. 'She has the Bayley spirit,' they told us with pride.

When she returned home, the neighbours banded together to buy her a large bunch of black grapes. We had never seen grapes before, other than through the window of the greengrocer's shop. We put them on a plate and placed it on the sideboard so that Mom, who during the day lay on the sofa could see them. They were there for two days before she could bring herself to disturb the bunch to eat one.

Her employer, Joseph Lucas, found out that she had broken the rules, that she was married. Nevertheless they sent her to their convalescent home in Weston-super-Mare. It was the first time that she had seen the sea. She was thirty-seven years old.

She returned home after a two-week stay, sorry that we had not been with her to enjoy the sea air and the three good meals a day. As she was still very weak, our neighbours continued to clean the house and wash our linen.

There was a shop near to the bottom of our yard owned by Mr and Mrs Birch. He was a small wiry man with a head of short-cropped hair and a waxed moustache similar to that worn by the German Kaiser Wilhelm. He never smiled and rarely spoke. I can't remember if he had a foreign accent, but a rumour started during the First World War that he was a German. It stayed with him until 1936, when they sold up and left.

His wife was also small, but plump. She had a very large lump on her right buttock which caused her to limp badly; they made a strange couple. They were quite mean and had an attitude of superiority that irked their customers. That and the fact that they were both active members of local Unionist Conservative Party didn't endear them to the locals.

Our member of parliament was Sir Austen Chamberlain, son of Joseph and half-brother to Neville. He had been, or was at the time, the Foreign Secretary, but unlike his father he visited his constituency rarely, and Great Russell Street only saw him during a General Election.

Most of those who lived in the street voted Labour. Sir Austen's visit to Great Russell Street to call on the Birches must have been an effort to assist them in trying to convert the locals. It was a wasted journey.

I remember well Austen Chamberlain's visit; it was during his re-election campaign. He was being driven in an open car, dressed in a morning suit, top hat, wing collar, silver grey cravat, wash leather gloves, spats, a monocle and a silver-headed cane. There was no doubt that our MP was a dandy and that Great Russell Street was not a suitable backcloth.

Mr and Mrs Birch stood outside their shop as if waiting to greet a member of the royal family. Chamberlain's car pulled up, his chauffeur jumped out and opened the door, and the great man stepped out.

In front of the large crowd that had gathered, the Birches bowed their heads and were presented. It didn't go unnoticed that the visitor failed to remove his glove when he shook their hands. Those watching may have been poor but they knew that this was a slight. Rumour went around that when he returned home he had his servant remove the gloves to be burned.

Even with the large business vote which ensured that he represented the constituency until he retired, he still needed to be seen among his poor constituents, even though he did little if anything to relieve the conditions in which we lived.

I remember helping to deliver poll cards for O G Willey, the Labour candidate who almost unseated Chamberlain in the 30s. The Conservatives held the seat until 1945 when Chamberlain's successor, Walter Higgs, a local manufacturer, came out with a classic comment which assisted the Labour Party for years. He said, 'Industrial peace depends on ten men looking for nine men's jobs.'

They haven't held the seat since.

Our street had six hucksters' shops, a greengrocer, and a fish and chip shop in our section alone. This unbridled competition meant that only the pawnshops and the pubs made a reasonable profit. Mr Scrivens, who also rented out the bikes I've mentioned, was a bit of an enigma. Although he only charged a pittance most of us thought he was *loaded*.

The shops were really converted houses, some taking in both the front and back, but they provided more interest to small children than their modern counterparts do today. Each shop had its own peculiar character in either its owner or what it sold, generally both. Mr and Mrs Gray closed their little shop across the street to buy out the Birches. The Grays always appeared to my young eyes to be a cut above the rest of us. It had nothing to do with their attitude, as they were always sympathetic and helpful.

Many families lived on what I've referred to as 'the strap' – buy now, pay later – and the Grays never pressed hard for payment when we were in deep trouble. I think that Mr Gray, a highly skilled electrical engineer holding down a well-paid job, was a Christian in the true sense of the term. His daughter, Lillian, had been seriously ill and I think that he felt blessed that she had survived.

He was overactive, trying many ways to build up the business his wife ran. Most of the houses had no electricity, only gas, and those who had a wireless ran them off a battery and an accumulator which needed to be recharged on a regular basis. Mr Gray bought a number of spare accumulators and a trickle charger and set up charging the accumulators in his cellar. Whilst the owner's accumulator was being charged he rented them one of his. It proved to be a profitable sideline.

He and his family were liked and respected; not so Mr and Mrs Blower, who were also shopkeepers in the street. Blower had lost most of the fingers on his left hand in an industrial accident and his compensation money enabled him to set up in business.

None of the kids in the street liked him. His bloated red face, tattoo-covered arms and surly manner created a bad impression. Whenever we returned an empty pop bottle to claim the penny deposit we were always cross-questioned as to whether we had actually purchased the bottle of pop from him.

A few days before Christmas, my younger brother Norman and I decided to take our revenge, not realising just how sweet it would turn out to be. We returned to Mr Blower three empty lemonade bottles and before he could question us, asked for checks – tokens – for the fruit machine. As we had asked for checks instead of the money, he handed them over without a quibble, unaware that we had lifted the bottles from his shed at the back of the shop. I guess he figured that the money would soon be coming back to him. He was wrong.

Norman placed the first disc into the slot at the top of the machine, pulled the handle and up came three cherries; four checks dropped into the cup. With the next pull, two oranges and a bar, eight checks came tumbling out; then three bells and sixteen; then, another eight; then another sixteen... and so it went on until the three bars appeared. Twenty-one checks plus the jackpot poured out of the machine and into my cap!

We were jumping up and down with excitement whilst Mr Blower stood behind his counter, aghast. The proceeds had to be spent in the shop so we loaded up with groceries. Bearing all these goodies back home singing, 'Happy days are here again' lifted all our spirits. We thought our luck had changed at last.

It must have because our mother's youngest sister, Emily, who worked for a small electroplating firm in Barr Street, had spoken to the manager about the plight of our family and he offered my dad a job in the plating shop.

It meant working over vats of chemicals used in the chrome plating process. Dad was issued with a rubber apron, rubber boots and a pair of rubber gloves to protect him from the burning acid, but there was no extraction plant and no masks provided to protect his lungs from the fumes. In those days, the safety at work act didn't exist. The wage was low but as there was no other job in sight he had jumped at the offer.

Within a week he had acid burn holes in his trousers and on some of his fingers but he felt himself lucky to be a breadwinner once again. The factory was precisely eight minutes' walk away from our house.

Home from school just after midday, I waited to hear the one o'clock whistles blow signalling the lunchtime break at the local factories. I would boil a saucepan of water, cut three pieces of bread and spread them with margarine and watched the alarm clock we had on the shelf. Four minutes before he was due to arrive I put an egg in the boiling water so that his lunch was ready by the time he walked through the door.

Once he'd eaten he would sit on the sofa and sleep. I would wake him fifteen minutes before he had to return to work, and me to school. This went on every day, except at the weekend, until I went out to work myself.

Manhood came early to a majority of the children born into working class families before the last war. My entry happened in the summer of 1936 when I left school at fourteen to go to work. I had to change my short trousers for long, so my mother bought a pair from Shepherd's, the pawnshop on the corner of our street.

They were black with a pinstripe, and as I was still quite small, they had to have a big tuck in the back and the legs severely shortened. They were so wide at the bottom that my feet disappeared from view. I was embarrassed to wear them but said nothing. I knew that my mother couldn't have afforded anything else.

The Education Department had obtained an interview for me with a local garage owned by an ex-racing driver named Pollitt. I was to be trained to be a motor mechanic, or so I was told. Presenting myself at 8 a.m. on the Monday after the August Bank Holiday week, I waited at the entrance to the repair shop. Standing there, I noticed the clock fixed to the wall and the box at the bottom with a lever. Alongside it was a rack with cards in it.

The foreman came out, and without speaking a word took me to the clock. He pointed to the rack full of cards with names and numbers on them and touched one which had my name on it, telling me to take it out of the rack. I had to stand on my toes to reach it. He then directed me to place it in the slot at the bottom of the clock and to press the lever down hard. I followed his instruction, a bell rang and he pulled out the card.

Pointing to the time clearly stamped on it, he asked, 'Can you read what it says?' then, not bothering to wait for an answer, he read it out. 'It says 8.05 a.m. You make sure that in future it reads *before* 8 a.m.' Still wagging the card at me, he went on, 'When you leave, you clock out *after* 1 p.m. and when you come back you clock in *before* 2 p.m. Tonight, when you leave you clock out *after* 6 p.m. – do you understand that, my lad?'

I looked up at him and said, 'You mean don't come late and don't go early.'

He obviously wanted me, a fourteen-year-old boy, to be quite clear that he was in charge. I looked up at him, then at the clock, and made up my mind there and then that the clock-in, clock-out card system was not for me. How and when I would be able to bring about a change in my circumstances which would release me from that tyranny I had yet to figure out.

I spent that week delivering or collecting car parts, pedalling a bicycle with a large wicker basket on the front. The bike was far too big for me. When not doing that, I was out on the car wash. Handed a spoke brush, a water hose, a wash leather, and a pair of oversized Wellington boots for protection, I was left alone to clean the vehicles presented to me.

At the end of the week I collected my first wage packet. Inside, I found a pay slip telling me that I had earned twelve shillings, less the cost of my employment insurance stamp. I realised that it would be a long time before I learned anything at Pollitt's garage, so without telling my mother I left to seek my future elsewhere.

One of my bicycle journeys took me past Restall's, a high-class furniture manufacturer in Great Hampton Street. They had become famous for their quality and design, and against strong opposition had won the contract to manufacture and fit some of the interior furnishings of the French luxury liner, the *SS Franconia*. I had spotted a notice on the door advertising for an apprentice mechanic so I applied for the job.

The fellow in charge of the garage, which took care of the Restall family cars – the vans were looked after elsewhere – wore a brown cowgown which, along with his hands, was spotless. He had a large white moustache, white eyebrows and a head of white hair, over which he wore a brown trilby hat with its brim turned up all round.

He took me to a clock and went through the same routine as the Pollitt garage foreman, the difference being that he didn't look as if he ever got his hands dirty. He gave me a pair of rubber boots two sizes too large, a rubber apron that touched the floor and a spoke brush, and there I was back on the car wash.

Two of the Restall brothers were mountaineers. Spike drove a Riley sports car and Harold a Morris sedan. I remember with a certain amount of pain that they both had spoked wheels.

The man in charge of the garage had to take Spike's car back to the Riley Company in Coventry, so I was left to look after the show for the day. Harold's car was green with green leather upholstery and on the back was a large leather-covered box the same colour as the car.

Peeking into it I saw an ice pick, climbing boots, crampons and climbing rope. Later in life I was to own climbing gear of my own. Unfortunately, a few months after I had joined the company, Spike was killed climbing in the Austrian Alps.

In 1964, twenty-eight years later, I was invited – as Lord Mayor of the city – to open an exhibition in Restall's showrooms. I was greeted by Mr Harold Restall, who seemed not to have changed. He was completely unaware that I had worked for him and as we walked into the building to be introduced to his directors and VIP guests. I asked what had happened to his Morris sedan with the box on the back. Telling me that he was still driving it, he asked how it was that I knew the car. Before I could answer we had reached the line of people waiting to be presented. A couple of hours later, with my task over, Harold Restall escorted me back to the Lord Mayor's Rolls.

Thanking me for agreeing to open the exhibition, he added, 'By the way, Lord Mayor, you didn't tell me how you came to know of my car.' I leaned into the Rolls and took out a brown paper bag. Holding it, I explained that I had cleaned it many times. I then opened the bag and handed him a new spoke brush I had bought. 'Here,' I said, 'this belongs to you, try cleaning those bloody spoked wheels!'

He was still laughing when we drove off.

Back in 1936, with so few cars and a lazy old mechanic, I had again realised that I wasn't going to make much progress at Restall's. Wanting to learn to be a skilled tradesman, I applied for a job at Moreton & Crowther's. They were general manufacturers with a factory just around the corner from my home. I was interviewed by, and then worked under, a Mr Crowther – one of the brothers who owned the firm.

It was in what was called the press shop that he patiently taught me how to forge chisels, which I was to work with for the next ten or so years. Along with a young toolmaker named Harold Faithful, he showed me how to set tools in the hand presses and introduced me to the mystery of making press tools.

The room in which we worked was long and narrow with thick wooden benches on either side stretching its whole length. The windows were small, and the ceiling low. To it were attached overhead camshafts and pulleys driving machinery which, as well as creating a horrific noise, dripped oil on the benches, the floor and sometimes our heads.

In one corner there was a lathe, a mechanical saw, an anvil and a small forge. Here we heated and then hardened the press tools that were made. The bench in the centre of the room was where Mr Crowther, Harold Faithful and I worked.

The rest of the benches had a large number of hand presses bolted to them. There were about twenty females sitting on stools operating the presses. Being raised in a family of boys and educated in a single sex school, I found being in a room full of young girls and women up to the age of sixty quite embarrassing. They were all local to Hockley, but none I recognised.

The girls sensed my shyness and were merciless in taking advantage of it. Conversely, if I was ill or when they found out it was my birthday, they became angelic. They worked for nine hours a day on these hand presses, singing as if they hadn't a care in the world. I had been there for about ten months and was looking forward to the Christmas break, when a few days before the holiday Mr Crowther allowed the girls to hang Christmas trimmings around this dismal workshop.

On Christmas Eve, an hour before we were due to leave, Mr Crowther turned the machinery off, wished us all a Merry Christmas and left. It was an unlikely place to hold a Christmas party, but with the boss gone and the room strangely silent, the ladies quickly spread paper tablecloths over the oil-soaked benches. Out came the home-made sausage rolls, pork pies and sandwiches. They had clubbed together to buy litre bottles of

Spanish Tarragona wine, popular because it was about as cheap as one could get.

As we were the only males present, Harold Faithful warned me to be careful. I hadn't a clue what he meant, but found out before we left the premises that night.

Harold was a tall, very thin young man in his mid-twenties. He was religious, a member of the Salvation Army, as was his young wife. They kindly invited me home to tea one Sunday. Realising that I was about to be recruited, I explained that all of my spare time was devoted to boxing, and excused myself. Even so, he was very helpful to me and suggested that it would be in my best interest to seek an apprenticeship.

Taking Harold's advice, I left Moreton & Crowther's and went to work for a contract toolmaking firm known as Turner Brothers. Contract toolmakers were not involved in manufacturing; they designed and made press tools for those who were.

In 1938, when the British Government began to wake up to the fact that war was inevitable, Turner Brothers began to receive orders to make tools for the aircraft industry. At this time, I was working under the tutelage of a couple of highly skilled men who could not have been more different in appearance and outlook.

One had been to Grammar School and, had he wished, could have gone on to university. He was married, owned a fine house in Handsworth Wood, was always well dressed and drove a car. In short, he was obviously comfortably off. The other, who earned the same, was as rough as old boots. He was more often than not unshaven and the collars of his shirts were usually soiled. He was a heavy smoker, and his teeth as well as his fingers were stained by nicotine. He lived on an estate in Kingstanding, which was almost totally devoted to council houses.

My tutors were both considerate and very kind to me; but what seemed incomprehensible to me at the time was to find that the fellow from Handsworth Wood was a rabid Marxist and the other guy who lived on a council estate a fervent Conservative. I learned a great deal during the lunch breaks listening to their some times fierce debates. I found myself privately siding with the Marxist.

It was he who introduced me to books as varied as *The Ragged-*

Trousered Philanthropist, about a kind, intelligent, left-wing plasterer, and *Following the Sun*, a book written by Alain Gerbault. He was a French First World War airman who'd been so sickened by the slaughter that he wanted to sail around the world alone. He couldn't afford to have a yacht specially built, so he scoured the south coast of France until 1923 when he found and bought the *Firecrest*. He continued to sail the seven seas single-handed until he died on an island in the Timor Sea twenty-one years later.

My Marxist tutor taught me to think for myself and to tell the difference between straight and crooked thinking. It was he who enrolled me in a correspondence course with the National Council of Labour Colleges. I took economics and at twenty-three won a place at Ruskin College, Oxford.

When the offer came through I was over the moon. At last I could break out, expand my mind and my horizons, create my own destiny instead of being carried along on a tide that was taking my compatriots and me nowhere. I'd also be able to free myself from the tyranny of the clocking-in system. It turned out to be just a dream.

I had been married for about twelve months and the war was over. I tried to explain to my wife the opportunities that studying in Oxford presented. How we could move to Oxford and rent accommodation; I would take a job in the evenings so that we could live until I obtained my degree. She refused to move with me. As a good working-class lad brought up to love, honour and obey, I stayed, and have regretted that decision ever since.

As a young man, listening to the debates at my workplace had given me a deeper insight into politics and to what was happening to democracy in Spain, Italy and Germany. In 1936, children had been brought from Bilbao to the nearby town of Sutton Coldfield to escape the bombing by German and Italian planes helping Franco's fascist revolution. I couldn't understand why the rest of the democratic countries failed to intervene. They must have known that Germany and Italy were practising for what was to come.

In Birmingham's Bull Ring, at the foot Nelson's statue – the first to be erected in his honour – open-air meetings took place. As a youngster I stood there to listen to the powerful orators of the day, among them a communist named Jessie Eden, who stirred something inside me.

Having watched my mother struggling against overwhelming odds to raise my brothers and me, and the indignities that my father suffered during periods of unemployment, Jessie Eden's message spelt out hope.

I had watched my dad quietly pressing his coat and trousers, polishing his boots, wash and shave and leave early in the morning to be up front in the queue for a job he had seen advertised. There always was a queue. It formed up outside the works office, and after they'd been waiting for two or three hours a clerk would come out and choose one man. When they asked why only one when the advert said ten, they'd be told that the advert was a mistake. Men were treated that way and I grew to hate the system that condemned my parents to it. I was ready-made for Jessie Eden.

Speaking with such passion about the Spanish revolution, she told us the reasons why right-wing governments were prepared to stand by and see the democratically elected socialist government of Spain be defeated by the fascists. She outlined the fear the ruling class had, that since the Russian Revolution socialism would spread and they would lose the power they wielded to keep the working class in its place. There was more than a modicum of truth in it.

With other powerful orators, she went on to explain to their ever-growing audience where the policy of the Nazis in Germany and the fascists in Italy would lead, warning us of the dangers that lay ahead for the working class. A few weeks later, without telling my parents, I joined the Young Communist League.

In the winter of that year I went out at night with other young fellows to paint slogans against the Nazis on pavements and walls in the area, taking care not to be spotted by the police or the neighbours for fear of my parents finding out. Once a week I attended classes in the local Communist Party offices in Birchfield Road, Aston. It was at one of these, which was instructing us on the basic tenet of communism, that I became aware that what they were actually trying to teach us was to accept the system as practised in the Soviet Union.

It was the night that Jessie Eden was our teacher that I saw the light. In 1945, she was to stand for parliament supported by the *Daily Mirror*. When she made it clear that we must obey without question the instructions issued from King Street, the British Communist Party headquarters in London, I remembered what my Marxist friend had taught me. He had introduced me to books, not all of which supported the ideals of the extreme left. He had urged me to question everything, that I learn to think for myself and not to be guided by others, however clever they appeared to be.

He warned me about people he called the 'pseudo-intellectuals' and those who had a power with words. However, I'm not sure he had in mind that I should question the ideological guidance of Jessie Eden. But on that night I had the temerity to question her.

I asked if she really meant that we could no longer have the luxury of thinking for ourselves, and she exploded. Taking me into an adjoining room she gave me the biggest verbal bollocking I had received up till then – or since. My membership of the Party had lasted less than six months.

My departure didn't diminish my hatred of fascism, nor my belief in the need for more equality in Britain. What it did was to enlighten me to the fact that what was called communism as practised in the USSR was as totalitarian as fascism, but under another name.

I began to understand that they, the Party hierarchy in Russia, had polluted the basic philosophy which in the end would destroy them but would also damage the chances of those struggling to bring about a fairer, more humane and truly Christian society, to win through.

I was later to discover how dedicated but misled communists operated when they infiltrated other movements, seeking positions of authority to use it for their Party against what they saw as a soporific we call democracy, and to take them on.

I read a great deal and was thankful to those enlightened City Fathers who set up the free public libraries. The one in Constitution Hill was the nearest to my home; it provided me with the opportunity to absorb knowledge of what was happening in other parts of the world. I read Steinbeck's account of the sufferings of the sharecroppers in America's Midwest. I read almost every thing Upton Sinclair wrote; the appalling conditions in the meat packing yards in Chicago; the methods used by Henry Ford and the steel kings in a country boasting that it was the cradle of democracy. The words, 'Workers of the world unite, you've only your chains to lose,' began to mean something to me.

One evening in the library I sat alongside a young man just a few years older than me. He was obviously worse off than I was. He was not too bright, but trying hard, he said, to improve himself. He lived in Hospital Street, which ran parallel with Great Russell Street, so when the librarian announced that he was about to turn off the lights, we walked back to the place where he lived with his aged crippled father.

His home – that was what *he* called it – consisted of a cubicle in a multi-occupied slum building. In the allotted space there was only enough room for a single bed, a chair and a small table. Where or how he slept puzzled me.

They rented this cubicle, furnished, for a few shillings a week. It was divided from their neighbours' space by half-inch thick plywood panels which fell far short of the ceiling. There were four cubicles to a room in this four-storey tenement building. The residents shared one single toilet, and the washing facility was a sink with cold running water.

This pathetic Dickensian accommodation was called a 'Furnished Wac'. The year was 1938 in a country which had an empire and was reputed to be one of, if not the, richest in the world. Just three years later the boy was killed fighting for it.

In 1938, I tried to enrol in the Aston Amateur Boxing Club. Their headquarters at the Holte Hotel, really a very large pub with an assembly room, was situated at one end of Aston Villa's football ground. Thursday was their night for training, so carrying my boxing trunks and plimsolls in a paper bag, which wasn't the smartest way to introduce myself, I entered the building.

The man in charge was Professor Hodder – professor of what I never found out, but he was a bald-headed, wiry little man who had built up a reputation as a trainer by producing a number of boxing champions. I didn't know it at the time but he only saw prospective members on recommendation.

I stood in the entrance, watching a number of boys skipping, shadow-boxing, punching bags and sparring in the ring. Hodder came up to me, looked at my paper bag and asked, 'What do you want?'

I summoned up my courage and replied in as firm a voice as I could muster that I had come to join his club.

He glared at me, almost shouting, 'Nobody comes to join my club unless I ask them!'

I apologised and, thinking fast, added, 'How do I get you to ask me?'

He looked like thunder, but after a few minutes decided to tell me to strip, and get weighed.

The club doctor examined me, and without further ado Hodder put me in the ring with a boy named Cuzick. I had seen him fight. At his weight he was one of the best in the Midlands; he was also a stone heavier than me. Having been allowed over the threshold I wasn't sure whether the Professor was testing my ability to defend myself or whether he thought that having taken a thrashing it would be the last he would see of me.

In the shower, my opponent said he thought I had done well. 'Don't let him put you off, kid, come again next week.'

I did. The following week I walked in, undressed and started to train on my own, and the week after that Hodder's assistant took care of me.

The first test to get through was the novices' contest. On some 'Fight Night' at the club, four novices competed against each other. The winners of their two-round contest fought each other and the one who succeeded was accepted as an amateur. This meant that you were good enough to represent the club in a preliminary bout, but it didn't necessarily mean that you would actually get a chance to do so.

I was sixteen when I first fought in the club team. The Prof then took an interest, telling me that it would help if I learned to dance. It was his way of telling me that my footwork was too clumsy. That weekend I visited the Palais de Danse in Monument Road. Plucking up courage, I approached a young lady and asked her for a dance. Once on the floor she soon realised that I hadn't tried before. The girl, whose name I can't remember, taught me to waltz, slow foxtrot, quickstep and rumba, so that many times in the ring I was able to dance out of trouble.

Weighing eight stone six pounds, broad-shouldered but small, I was in the bantamweight division. When I was due to have my first fight for the club I let my dad know that I was a member. I had acquired boxing boots, a gumshield and boxing trunks in which my mother had sewn a tiny St Christopher medallion.

After my first appearance, my father decided that I might make out, so he began to travel with me wherever I was due to fight. The programme was usually made up of seven contests: four of three two-minute rounds, and three of six three-minute rounds. Today, amateur contests are limited to three rounds.

Twelve months later I was unexpectedly called upon to top the bill. It was by accident, as many of the things that happened to me usually were. Our club was visiting the Bromsgrove ABC run at the Rose and Crown Hotel – really another pub – in Smallbrook Street near the city centre.

One of our senior boxers, a fellow named Burley, was billed to fight in the main bout of the evening – six three-minute rounds. When the doctor examined him, he found that he was suffering from an irregular heartbeat. Burley was pulled out, which meant that there would be no main bout.

Hodder, having had hurried discussions with his opposite number, asked if I would take on Burley's opponent. The problem I faced was that he was in a heavier division, meaning he was bigger than me; worse still, up to that time I had only competed in three-round bouts, but I agreed.

The announcement was made that Burley was being replaced, and the fight was now scheduled as 'catchweights', a term I hadn't heard before. I ducked through the ropes and caught my first sight of my opponent. He had on his trunks D A DALY. He was big, he was Irish and about ten years older than me.

The fight began and I thought I was doing quite well until he caught me with a standard straight left and right cross in the third round. I had no excuse, I should have seen it coming, my legs turned to jelly and down I went. It was pride more than the will to continue that forced me to grab the middle rope and haul myself up.

In those days, one good knock down and the referee called it a day, so despite my albeit half-hearted appeal, he stopped the bout. Now this had been, or was meant to have been, my first six-round contest, and I was anxious to prove myself, so I asked the Prof to arrange a rematch. It was announced from the ring, and two weeks later Mr Daly and I met again.

At four o'clock in the afternoon on the day of the fight the foreman came to my bench and told me to go home to rest. As I left the tool room all my workmates began to hammer the benches. Every one of them turned up to the fight, which took place at the Holte Hotel. Word had got around that it was a grudge match so the hall was packed to capacity by the time I ducked through the ropes.

In those days, during an amateur fight the spectators normally maintained a respectful silence whilst the round was in progress; but that night, despite appeals from the ring, they raised the roof. I had my opponent on the canvas twice during the fight, and he had me down six times. I was up and down so many times my brothers called me 'Sorbo' after the bouncing ball. The fight proved to be so exciting that the referee forgot to stop the bout, letting it go its full distance.

It was so unusual that the headlines in the *Saturday Sports Argus* read: ASTON BOXER TAKES SIX COUNTS. Although I had lost, they hardly mentioned the other fellow. From then on I was one of the team who regularly topped the bill.

Freddie Kirby, who came from a family of 'professional' boxers, also fought for the club. One memorable night, just after war had been declared, we were on the same bill against a team from a firm called Wright's Ropes, who had a factory in Tyburn close to a number of large factories producing armaments.

The ring was erected in their spacious canteen. Limbering up in the dressing room waiting our turn to fight, Freddie's famous uncle, Bert, came in to give him a few tips. We both won our bouts and were, as was the custom, presented with our prize. It was 10.30 p.m. when we left. The sirens had sounded and no buses were running so we walked home. There were no clouds in the sky, the stars were bright and there was what became known as 'a bomber's moon'; it was like daylight. It was early days, and we had yet to experience any serious bombing.

The local ARP (Air Raid Precautions) had placed empty oil drums, spaced out, along both sides of the Tyburn Road. These they filled with oil-soaked rags. Having received a warning of a possible air attack, they lit the rags and clouds of dense acrid smoke filled the air. There was no wind, and the smoke made it difficult to see. My father tripped, and up went the ceramic horses. We didn't bother to collect the pieces of the prize I had fought hard to win.

My father never offered me advice before or after a fight, but for some reason, on the night when I was due to meet a boxer who had represented Britain in the Empire Games, he decided to break with tradition. This was some time after I was established and fighting six-round contests.

We had boarded the tramcar in Newtown Row to take us down to the Holte. I had settled down with my thoughts about the forthcoming contest when he suddenly said, 'You know you're fighting Tony Clark tonight.'

'Yes, Dad.'

'You know he fought in the Empire Games.'

'Yes, Dad.'

'You know he punches more than his weight with both hands.'

'Yes, Dad.'

'You know you are a bit out of your class.'

All this about two hours before I was to get into the ring to face the guy. I began to appreciate the silence he had maintained up until then.

Although I had remained on my feet for the six rounds, I lost the fight by a big margin and was suffering from bruised eyes and a swollen right hand. On our way home that night, Dad resumed his pattern of silence. No word as to how I had performed, good or bad. Due to the bombing, the government banned public assemblies. I never entered a boxing ring again.

Chapter III

THE INEVITABLE

Before the war, from the age of fifteen I had followed what news there was about Nazi atrocities, but few people seemed to be aware of the menace Hitler was presenting. The government's policy of apathy and the warnings of Anthony Eden and the Ambassador in Berlin were ignored by them and given little publicity by the national press.

At an early age I was agitated by the wide gap in our society and more by the fact that we were treated as second-class citizens, which appeared to be accepted as an act of God. I believe that there are those in and outside parliament today who still believe that the lower orders should be satisfied to be drawers of water and sawyers of wood.

Pre-war, the run-up to a local or General Election brought the politicians to our street corners. There were no loudspeaker vans in those days and party activists would carry steps so that their speakers could be both seen and heard. As a child, I would stand as close as I could, fascinated by the oratory and their promises that 'something would be done to prise us out of our miserable living conditions'. The fact that nothing was ever done didn't stir the people to protest; they simply accepted that they were powerless. It still amazes me that the so-called 'silent majority' took their lot as inevitable.

By the time I reached my late teens I lost patience with both the politicians and their quiescent followers. Mentally, I became an old man before I reached my majority. I boiled inside, angry at the way those around me accepted the way things were.

The night that Neville Chamberlain returned from Munich, I was at home listening to the wireless with all the family and our cousin, George Hope. The commentator was describing the ecstatic welcome given to the prime minister when he landed at the airport and on his route back to Downing Street, and again from the balcony at Buckingham Palace. It made me feel sick.

We could hear the cheering crowds as Chamberlain leaned out of an upper floor window of Number 10 Downing Street, waving his 'Peace in our time' agreement signed by – he proudly announced – 'Herr Hitler'. It was grotesque. It was as if no one knew what the man had been up to during the previous seven years – or if they did, they were happy to forget and forgive.

No one seemed to give a thought about how the citizens of Czechoslovakia were feeling that night. That they had to swallow the fact that Britain and France had sold them out, that within hours German planes would be dropping bombs, that storm troopers would be crossing the border and thousands of innocent people would be on their way to concentration camps before the year was out.

The prime minister and his government knew this only to well, but neither they nor the cheering crowds gave a damn. It was a bad night for our Czech allies, Britain's anti-appeasers, and for democracy.

With my family listening to the reception being accorded the prime minister, I said, 'My God, listen to them! They are so shit-scared they are prepared to sell anybody out so long as they are safe.'

My father turned to me, white with anger, and slapped me across the face. It was the first and only time that he ever struck me. He cried out, 'You stupid young bugger, get to bed!'

He had been in a war and was aware of what it had done to him and millions of other men; I could understand how he felt, but not why he couldn't see what was inevitable. He was not alone.

On that fateful sunny Sunday morning in September 1939, returning home from the slipper baths, a public facility where people whose homes were without a bath – one hundred per cent in our area – could pay for the use of one, I found people standing on the street listening to neighbours' radios. When I reached the entry to Court 13, our neighbours were all outside, their doors wide open as Neville Chamberlain announced that we were at war with Germany.

Having read of the German's capability of devastating cities from the air, the men started digging trenches in the backyards to provide some protection. They didn't wait to get the landlords' permission; those days were over by the time Chamberlain had finished speaking. In the event they proved to be totally useless.

I was just seventeen and marvelled at men twice my age who hadn't stopped to think how badly we and the rest of the country had been let down. The government had been warned in 1933 by Phipps, our Ambassador to Germany, that Hitler would be at war in a decade – he was only three and a half years adrift – but the country was never informed. Worse still, in all those years nothing had been done to prepare us for the coming onslaught. Other than a belated issue of gas masks, there was no protection. My neighbours uttered not a word about this disgraceful situation. They just began digging up the backyards.

The government had recognised the Italian conquest of Abyssinia and as we now know, had pressed Eden 'to take a more understanding attitude towards the dictators and pursue a policy of appeasement'. So when I hear that oft-spoken request that when in company we must not discuss religion or politics because it might upset people, my mind goes back to those days and I dare to ignore the plea and risk being accused of 'making waves'.

The full story of the appeasers has yet to be told. Even today when I carry on about this, and as you can see I'm still at it, I'm told that 'it was the way it was, it was inevitable'.

When war was finally declared, I watched the reactions of those around me. The gung-ho attitude of the men, the quiescent reaction of the young women and the grim faces of those women who, old enough to remember the First World War, were able to comprehend the coming catastrophe. Those who had sons of military age slipped quietly off to church to pray. My mother went to St Chad's Cathedral, having visions of losing her four sons.

However, times had changed. Some lessons had been learned from the Great War, when every able-bodied man was encouraged to volunteer, and if he didn't was 'called up'. Subsequently it was found that there was a serious shortage of skilled men to assist in the making of armaments. The War Office had to call those they could trace back home.

In 1939, skilled men found that they were unable to volunteer. My older brothers were both in what were called reserved occupations, and Norman and I were not then old enough. As a toolmaker I was to be kept out of the armed forces. For me, who believed passionately that fighting fascism was akin to a holy war, the situation was unacceptable.

On 26 July 1940, the day I reached eighteen, I applied to join the air force. Flying crews were in short supply and I had heard that it was the only way I could obtain a release from my job.

I first called at the RAF recruiting office in Digbeth, filled in the necessary forms, took aptitude tests, one of which was for Morse code, of which I knew nothing but passed anyway. A few days later I was called to go before an examination board housed in some vacant apartments on the top floor of a new block of luxury flats known as Viceroy Close in Bristol Road, Edgbaston. I thought that I was on my way.

Sitting alongside other volunteers I was told, 'If they send you back to the desk you will know they have turned you down.' I got as far as the ear, nose and throat doctor who, after an examination, gave me a slip saying, 'Take it to the desk.'

I asked why, and he wouldn't answer, so I asked again.

'See your doctor,' was all he would say.

It turned out that whilst I was boxing my nose had been broken in two places. The septum was welded to either side, making breathing through it difficult.

Determined to get into the air force, I visited my doctor, who told me that the septum could be 'shaved' as he put it. He said, 'You realise that it would mean that even the slightest blow would flatten your nose to your face and you would be back to square one.'

I returned to work. Such an operation today would not be so severe.

My brother, Norman, was involved in war work like almost everyone else, but he was free to volunteer. He joined the 9th Dorsets just after his eighteenth birthday. Unlike me, he was then apolitical. It was whilst he was doing part of his training in Northern Ireland that his eyes were opened. When he came home on leave he asked about the Orange Order. He had been shocked by seeing signs hanging outside the dockyards in Belfast advertising jobs with the words: CATHOLICS NEED NOT APPLY. He began to wonder what he was fighting for.

Like so many people in Britain, even today, he couldn't understand how part of the United Kingdom could be acting in such an undemocratic manner, and worse still, why the British Parliament allowed it to continue. I could have provided him with an answer to that, but in 1942 what was the point?

Those of us who had to stay behind were obliged to join either the Home Guard, the Fire Service or the ARP (Air Raid Precautions). I had already enlisted in the Auxiliary Fire Service and was reporting to C1X, which, being so close to the city centre was termed a 'number one action station'. It meant that when the German planes were heading our way, we would be on first call.

C1X didn't look like a number one action station. It had been hurriedly housed in an old vicarage in Monument Road. The front gardens had been covered with corrugated metal sheds to house the engines, Beresford pumps and equipment. There was no sliding down poles when the call came; we bundled down the stairs. It was really pretty rough and ready but served the city well.

I was then working for the Cameron Tool Company in Great Hampton Street specialising in form tools used for the making of aircraft parts. During the week, we worked from 8 a.m. until 6 p.m. with a half-hour break for lunch, and 8 a.m. till 12 noon on Saturdays and most Sundays. During the period of the heaviest bombing which was in 1941–42, I reported to the station at 7 p.m. three nights a week. In the winter months the air raids started early but I was always on duty before the bells went down. I was involved in a number of conflagrations during the Blitz.

When the Docker paint works was hit, instead of going to the front of the building I was by mistake sent on to the fire barge operating from the canal which ran past the rear of the building. Once aboard, over the noise of the bombs, the leading fireman shouted a warning, 'If you fall into the cut, my lad, the chances of getting you out will be nil, so be bloody careful!'

Looking at the gear strewn all over the deck, I became more worried about tripping over it than about the bombs that were screaming down at regular intervals.

The decision to put me on the barge probably saved my life. The large tanks of paint and linseed oil inside the factory had been breached and the contents came flowing out of the building like a river. Our colleagues who were working from the street didn't stand a chance. They were stuck almost knee-deep in a mixture of oil and paint and couldn't move quickly enough to avoid the high wall that collapsed on them. We lost four men that night.

A few days later the chairman of the company, Sir Bernard Docker, called in at the station to thank us. I was told that he didn't perform very well. Having entered the station he went straight to the chief's office and stayed there until he left, failing to call in to the canteen where the men who had fought the fire were waiting.

His wife, the infamous Brummie, Lady Docker, who from working in a cigarette kiosk near New Street Station rose to such heights as to be banned from the casino in Cannes would, even so, have done much better than her husband. She was far superior in the field of public relations than was Sir Bernard. She was also easier on the eye.

When the Blitz was on, part-time firemen like me were not allowed to leave a fire under any circumstances until we were relieved. The reason being that too many fires had a nasty habit of flaring up again with disastrous consequences.

On the night when Birmingham was bombed for thirteen hours, I was for most of the time inside the blazing Reeves and Stedeford building near Spring Hill, lucky to be alongside an elderly full-time professional fireman. Part of the floor had collapsed and the basement was filling up with water. Although the fire was blazing away it was still dark inside.

The noise was tremendous, so I couldn't hear my partner shouting to me. He finally pulled me round and turned the hose down to the part I was advancing to. The jet hit the water where the floor was suppose to be. Had I taken two more steps I would have disappeared into the basement full of water with little chance of getting out.

During the night, a bomb came through what was left of the roof; luckily it failed to explode. We signalled for the water to be turned off and got out as quickly as we could. After a while the fire began to spread; so, as we had been in the building, the leading fireman had no other choice than to send us back.

We had no way of knowing whether the bomb would go off, but my partner, who had already won a British Empire Medal for bravery, patted my helmet and gave me a thumbs up sign – all meant to dissipate my fear. It didn't.

By daybreak the fire was under control; the all, clear had sounded and some time later, with the fire damped down, we were called out. We were unaware that the houses in the area had been evacuated in case the bomb decided to blow. An army disposal unit found it under the water in the basement.

Coming out, we saw crowds of people standing behind the roped-off area a block away. They knew that we had been inside with the bomb and they gave us a rousing cheer as we were taken to a refreshment van parked nearby for a welcome mug of tea. Back at the station we reported to the Chief and were given breakfast. I then left to return to work.

The owner of the firm I worked for was named Purnell; he was in his mid-twenties. His father, being the purchasing manager for Joseph Lucas, had set him up in the business just before war was declared. Most of the precision tools we produced were for the Lucas factories who were turning out aircraft components. Our production was therefore considered to be of national importance.

As young Purnell was the owner of the company he was also considered to be essential to the war effort; if he is still alive he would be in his mid eighties. As such he wasn't subject to call up, he also had the benefit of a special fuel allowance which enabled him to motor between the factory and his home in the heart of the Worcestershire countryside well south of Birmingham.

He generally arrived at the factory after 9 a.m. and was away by 5 p.m. – well before the sirens sounded. I mention this to underline a point – that of attitude. The morning after a thirteen-hour raid and my experience mentioned above, I turned up to work just after ten o'clock.

On arrival I was told, 'The boss wants to see you.' I climbed the stairs to his office and knocked on his door. He was sitting with his feet on his desk drinking tea. Without putting his cup or his feet down, he warned me that if I turned up late again, he would report me to the National Service Officer. He was appointed by the government and had powers to place a person before the courts for dereliction of duty.

I was standing bleary-eyed still in my wet uniform, part of which was a webbing belt with a holder for a fireman's axe. I looked at him dumbfounded. I think I said, 'I beg your pardon,' because he repeated his threat. I was too far gone to be worried about the National Service Officer. I slowly unbuttoned the holder, took out the axe and said, 'You would do what?'

He dropped his cup and rushed into his secretary's office.

Having heard the rumpus, she came out and patted my face, sat me down and brought me a cup of tea. She said, 'He has hightailed it down the backstairs.' I was nineteen years old at the time.

Birmingham suffered the loss of over 2,000 people killed, over 3,000 seriously hurt and 20,000 buildings completely destroyed or very badly damaged during '72 of the 'heavy' raids. George Street, which was were the slipper baths were situated, a few blocks from our home, was hit by a mine dropped by parachute. It wiped out a large, densely populated area and the people in it.

These mines floated down silently after the sound of the planes had gone. Once they touched a building they exploded, and being above ground they cleared vast areas.

In 1943, I had saved enough to be able to go to Bournemouth for my one-week summer holiday. I had booked a room in the Meyrick Mansions Hotel, which sounded posh but was only two stars. To get there I had to go by train, and the journey was excruciating. It took ten hours to get to Basingstoke, about ninety miles. There we were all tipped out to be put on another train which trundled on, stopping and starting in the middle of nowhere. I could have cycled there faster. It was no use complaining because we had all become adept at using a standard retort in such circumstances: 'Don't you know there's a war on?'

I had never stayed in a hotel before but made up my mind not to expose the fact to the other guests, most of them retired folk. I tried hard to 'put on the dog' and got away with it in the Meyrick Mansions, but when I decided to celebrate my 21st birthday having dinner in the five-star Royal Bath Hotel situated on the other side of the road overlooking the sea, I came unstuck. But that's another story. Otherwise the holiday was what it was meant to be – a break.

The period of bombing had eased and the government, sensing the need to lighten the days and nights of its war-weary citizens, removed the restriction on public gatherings. Along with my friends I visited the Casino, a popular dance hall in the centre of town. There I met up with a lovely girl named Joan Fletcher, whose uncle, Alderman Eli Fletcher, I was to come across some years on.

One night I had arranged to meet her inside the hall. I saw her sitting with her back to me as I approached. The lights were dim; I touched her shoulder inviting her to dance. I didn't realise until I put my arms around her that it was not Joan Fletcher! In the darkness, by accident I was dancing with the girl I was eventually to marry.

A few weeks after the invasion of Europe began, my mother received a telegram to say that brother Norman was missing in action. We were to find that he had been ferried to France to join the first Army on D-Day plus two. Four weeks later his unit was caught up in a fierce German counter offensive near Tilly-sur-Seulles. Many of his colleagues were killed, and he with others was wounded.

The medics found Norman in a shell hole, unconscious. He was brought back home with other wounded men on an American tank carrier. After a couple of agonising months we were informed that he was lying in a hospital in Preston.

Once released, he was given four weeks' leave and I was given a few days off so that I could spend time with him. We went to nearby Stourport-on-Severn, staying in a small wooden bungalow my mother had bought for £25, which she paid in weekly instalments.

As we were sitting by the river, fishing, it began to rain. There was a loud clap of thunder and when I looked round, Norman had disappeared. I found him in the bungalow hunched up by the bed; he was suffering from what his chums called being 'bomb happy'. Even so he was returned to his unit in France to help fight the rest of the war.

With hostilities over, the country got ready for a General Election but nobody dreamed the changes that it would bring. The Conservatives were confident that Winston Churchill's efforts during the war would sweep them back to where they believed they belonged. Although few people suspected the outcome, it really was inevitable.

The Labour Party enjoyed a landslide victory and the political landscape saw a change that has lasted till this day. Although the country had been left bankrupt by the war, the Attlee government set about keeping the promises that I had heard since I was old enough to understand.

They set about the task of clearing up the devastation left by the bombing and the neglect of past administrations and to try to rebuild a peacetime economy with our industries still working with pre-war machinery and equipment.

The problems facing the country were colossal. Having stood alone against the might of Hitler's forces and suffered greatly in consequence, the British were still enduring deprivation. I have often wondered what would have happened had the Americans been convinced that the Labour Government would cosy up to the Russians.

Would they have offered to help rebuild Britain's industrial base and assist us to re-establish our economic position in the world more quickly than we were able? To ensure that the Germans would resist the temptation, they poured millions of dollars of aid into that part of Germany under democratic control.

This is not a criticism; the Marshall Plan helped us a great deal, but hearing a young German doctor boasting to a mixed group on how his country had proved to the world just how clever they were, recovering and leaving Britain behind, got to me. We were sitting at a bar overlooking a harbour in Majorca. Although he was much younger and bigger, I threatened to throw him in the sea.

Chapter IV

HOCKLEY UNITED

In 1944, finding a place for newlyweds to live was difficult, so Maisie and I arranged to rent rooms from a widow who lived in a tree-lined road in Handsworth Wood. We had a bedroom to ourselves and shared the use of the kitchen and dining room with the lady of the house. I realised that our stay there would be short.

I was surprised to find that, like the home where I had lived, it too had no bathroom. We had to use the slipper baths, which were on a much grander scale than the one in George Street, Hockley. It was attached to the area's swimming baths in a large, well-designed complex, and the staff there treated their clients with more respect.

Although the towels and the soap were similar, the attendant gave us a little more time to bathe and didn't bang on the door. He must have thought that he was dealing with a different class of person.

My father-in-law found it hard to come to terms with the fact that his daughter had married a person from the slums and he didn't mind my knowing it. He was a member of the Handsworth Horticultural Society club. During a visit to their home, his wife pressed him to invite me to join him when he went off to the club. He didn't bother to introduce me to any of the members, bought me a drink and left me standing by the bar. As a visitor I was not allowed to buy a drink. I hung around for an hour and, as he was ignoring the fact that I was there, left.

In 1949, he invited me again. I only accepted to keep the peace. This time he proudly introduced me to the members saying, 'This is my son-in-law, Councillor Price.' He was surprised when I walked out the door.

Maisie and I were not happy with our accommodation. The

only private time we had together was in the bedroom or outside the house. We looked around but could find nothing suitable. When I returned home from work one night, the widow told me that Maisie had moved out. I went to her father's house to be told that she had gone to live with her sister in Great Barr.

We got back together when a house in the yard where I had lived until my marriage became vacant. The agent offered it to us and I was back in the slums. It was bad enough for me, but for Maisie, who had been raised in finer surroundings, it was traumatic.

I purchased a couple of touring bicycles and every weekend, rain or shine, we cycled out into the countryside, staying overnight in youth hostels, and began saving to buy a home of our own.

During those early years I got caught up in an argument between a very angry man and boys between twelve and fifteen years of age. They had upset him by kicking a ball in the street near his home. Knowing that they had nowhere else to go, I intervened, quietly suggesting that swearing at them wasn't going to get him or them anywhere.

He knew that there was no open space nearby and that their homes were not a place where young people could gather, but his response was predictable. He was lucky. Today there would have been no need for me to stick my nose in, he would have been 'sorted out' and the services of the police and a National Health hospital would have been called upon. But this was 1945; Hollywood had yet to educate young people in the use of knives, guns, martial arts and kicking people's heads in.

I spoke to the boys and took them home with me. Remembering what the Old Edwardians Boys' Club had done for me, I asked what they thought of the idea of setting up a club. They jumped at the idea. There were no suitable premises available at a rent I could afford, so we agreed that I should approach the Education Department to see if we could rent a room and the hall at a local school for two nights a week.

Subject to the caretaker's approval, the department offered Smith Street School which was central to Hockley and easy for the boys to get to. The caretaker obliged, and that was how the

Hockley United Youth Club was founded.

Although I had no experience of running a youth club I was able to draw on my memories of how the Old Edwardians had operated. Unlike my old club, *we* had no money and I had no one else to help me, but I knew that what I was about to start needed to be done. Seeking funds, I wrote to local firms hoping to prick their social conscience. Joseph Lucas, Swallow Raincoats and Smith and Wright's replied. It was with their kind help that we were able to buy a second-hand table tennis table and various items of equipment.

Such was the shortage of social facilities for young people in the district that the news that a boys club was opening spread like wildfire. Boys came from all over Hockley in the hope of being able to join. The membership grew so fast that within two weeks of starting the club I had reluctantly to close the list. It was heartbreaking to see the disappointment on the faces of those I had to turn away. The only consolation was to promise them that their names had been registered and when a vacancy occurred they would be made welcome.

With the help of the boys who had sparked this off, the club didn't take as long as I had anticipated to become operational, but it soon became obvious that if we were to succeed we needed to raise money. The Old Edwardians Club, long since closed, had their own building and was open five nights a week. There was no way we would be allowed, even if we could have afforded it, to use the school room and hall for that period of time. We had to be satisfied with the two nights we had been allocated.

Not having our own accommodation meant that we had the school caretaker watching over us, rightly so; but I had to convince the boys that he wasn't spying on us. Even so, it was a bit of a pain in the bum.

I needed to keep the boys both enthusiastic and loyal to the idea of Hockley United. I remembered how I felt when chosen to represent the Old Edwardians Boys' Club against others and realised that we needed to get into competition with other clubs. The quickest way was to form a football team and join the Youth League. Where to get the money to buy the gear – that was the rub. I was not earning enough to afford to carry the club so I sat down with the founder members and after a while came up with the idea of organising a Christmas Show.

Food was still rationed but I had heard that the club could apply for a ration book to buy certain limited food items. Using this, and with the help of some of the boys' parents, we were able to put on a reasonable spread. My mother and part of her family having been in the 'business' gave me the idea that I must have somewhere in my genes the capacity to organise and stage a reasonable variety show. All I needed was the nerve and the ability to convince some of the boys to ignore their inhibitions and take part.

Like a budding Ziegfield, I began rehearsing the boys. At first, the three I had chosen to imitate the Andrews Sisters, a popular American singing trio at the time, objected to being dressed and made-up as girls. After a little applied psychology – bullshit, really – they succumbed.

One of the mothers who was a seamstress made their costumes, and before they were to appear another applied the powder and lipstick. The wigs we made out of dyed mop heads. The boys came to my home to listen to records of the Andrews Sisters and to practise miming and moving with the rhythm.

On the night of the show, with the Andrews Sisters record blasting away, they mimed four numbers and were greeted with rapturous applause from a full house. Among the other acts, the boys did the Marx Brothers operating theatre scene behind a sheet illuminated from the rear. All in all the show went down well. I was pleased that many of the boys' mothers, and a few fathers, turned up to support them, and that my brothers and their wives came to support me. I thought, *At least, they will now realise that I'm not crazy*.

In addition to raising much-needed funds, it raised the interest of the boys' parents in what we were trying to achieve. We collected enough to enable us to buy the equipment we needed to enable us to enrol in the Sunday Football League.

We were too late to enter a division that year but the League arranged a number of friendlies. After a few disastrous defeats, we began to hold training sessions on nights when the club didn't meet. After that the team soon began to hold their own and to enjoy the game.

As the players' enthusiasm increased so did their competitive spirit and it wasn't long before other football teams paid us the complement of trying to poach some of our best players. I was happy to note that they had no success.

As is normal, we had one or two members who couldn't or wouldn't conform, so I suggested, in line with the club's policy of exercising democratic principles, that the boys draw up the club rules. I obtained a copy of rules of other established clubs which my boys used as a guideline to set down what they called 'Our Commandments'. They also decided, with a little help, to form a management committee to oversee the running of the club.

'Ginger' Green, so called because of his mop of thick ginger hair, was the first to fall foul of the commandments. He was fourteen years old and wore a permanent scowl on his young face. I couldn't figure out whether this was because he was small for his age, or that his flaming red hair embarrassed him, but he just wasn't fitting in. In common with most of the boys he came from a poor home, his father had been killed in the war and his mother went out to work trying hard to raise her five children in a small slum dwelling. Ginger was on his way to nowhere.

Came the day when he was caught walking out of the club with a table tennis bat under his jumper; why, I couldn't understand. Outside the club the bat was of little use to him, and as it had the club's name on the handle he knew that he couldn't have found a buyer.

The management committee had set up its own court to deal with Ginger or anyone else who broke the rules. He was represented by Kenny Hawker, the oldest and most respected member of the club. The prosecuting counsel was Walter (Wally) Atkins, probably the best football player we had and therefore highly regarded by his peers – and the accused. Despite Wally's pleas, Ginger was found guilty.

When the verdict was announced, all heads turned towards me for guidance. I said, 'It's really up to you, but I recommend that Ginger be banned from the club for a period of two weeks.'

They groaned. 'Is that all?' they shouted.

'Wait for it,' I said, and as an afterthought added, 'and dropped from the team for a month, but it's up to the jury.'

Ginger was a ball player and I knew just how much he loved to play football.

He suffered from a lack of self-esteem and felt honoured when chosen for his ability to play for the Hockley United football team. I knew that not being able to turn out would hurt him most, and it did. Standing on the touchline watching the team play was hard for him to bear. He gave us no further trouble.

In the slums, during late spring through to the end of summer, fresh air was a rare commodity. However long and bright the sun shone, it made hardly any difference to the pallor of our skin. Most kids rarely left the area and few had ever clapped eyes on the water that surrounded their homeland.

Watching them I had a recurring memory of my childhood. On the Friday night before August Bank Holiday week I used to sit on the steps of the house facing the street, watching young couples carrying their suitcases making their way to either Snow Hill or New Street railway station to go on their holidays to the seaside.

Every year at this time my mother's sister and her husband, who lived close by and were both 'working', would go to Torquay, Blackpool or Bournemouth, always bringing back a stick of rock with the name of the resort running through it for my brothers and me. I asked my mother why it was that we never had a holiday by the sea, not realising how much my plea hurt her.

My parents did the best they could. Every day during the Bank Holiday week they took us on a bus to picnic alongside the canal in Lapworth, a village some ten miles from home. One year we spent a whole week in Whittington, a village a few miles from the city of Lichfield, north-west of Birmingham. It was like Lapworth; we were in the country and the fresh air.

About three months after I began to write this book, my brothers and I paid a nostalgic visit to Whittington and the School House where we stayed. Posing for a photograph in the doorway of the house that brought back such happy memories, a lady asked my wife who we were. 'Just four old men recapturing their lost childhood,' she replied. Seventy years on and the house and the village seem not to have changed. Nice!

In my early twenties I used to cycle out of Birmingham most weekends and holidays touring the countryside, staying, as I mentioned, at youth hostels. I decided to try to encourage the boys of the club who had bikes to join us on a cycle trip to Barmouth, the nearest seaside resort about a hundred miles west of Birmingham.

For all kinds of reasons, of which I didn't embarrass them by asking, only seven of the boys could travel. I cleared the arrangements with their parents who, although pleased, thought that I'd gone off my rocker.

Kenny Hawker, Wally Atkins, Philip Grayson, Jimmy Doyle, his younger brother, Patrick, Johnny Hyde and Henry Maney made up the party. Johnny Hyde, an electrician's apprentice, was a lanky lad who had what is now termed as a laid-back personality – so laid-back that nothing, but *nothing*, appeared to alter his perspective on life. He just rolled with the punches. He asked whether he could bring an older workmate with him and as we were few in number I agreed. As it turned out, his eighteen-year-old mate came with a girlfriend and a tandem bike. They paid little attention to the rest of us.

Jimmy Doyle, who was less than 5' tall, wore a perpetual smile and had a laugh that brightened all our days, yet he and his brothers and sisters had very little to be happy about. Their father was a drunkard who, when inebriated, beat up their mother and them on a regular basis. He hit his wife so hard that she became permanently deaf.

The two Doyle boys pleaded to come with us; I wouldn't approach their father but spoke to the mother. She was pleased that somebody cared enough for her boys to take them for a holiday. The trouble was neither of them owned a bike. I couldn't face the prospect of leaving them behind so I scouted around to hire a couple of reliable machines that fitted them.

Wally Atkins lived at Number 2 back of 47, Great Russell Street, next door to were I had lived. His stepfather was a dour man, highly skilled and always in work, yet he spent little time or money on his family. He rarely if ever spoke to the neighbours, and once home from work he would change his clothes and go to a pub outside the area to do his drinking.

Mrs Atkins was a very sick lady who, after a long and distressing illness, was finally institutionalised. Wally's stepbrother, Charlie, was twelve years older and a born villain. How Wally turned out to be such an honest and decent individual was a miracle.

Kenny Hawker, Philip Grayson, Henry Maney and Johhny Hyde were from families who were not suffering financially like the parents of the others. They had a better chance in life but never acted in any way unkindly to their club mates – quite the reverse. I enrolled the boys in the Youth Hostel Association, and early on the Thursday evening before Good Friday, the beginning of the Easter holiday, we assembled in Great Russell Street.

Remembering the scene, and the variety of bikes the lads were riding, I wonder how I had the nerve to head them out on the journey into mid-Wales. We took a couple of Primus stoves and the necessary additional equipment to make tea, packing them along with sandwiches and biscuits into pannier bags which we and the elder boys strapped to our bikes.

I had suggested that they should bring something out of which to drink, whether it was the tea-brewing bit I know not, but we heard Jimmy Doyle on his hired bike approaching as he cycled down the street. The noise wasn't emanating from his machine, it was the tin kettle he had tied to his handlebars. We left it behind for him to collect on his return.

Our plan was to ride until we reached the other side of Shrewsbury, there to buy a fish and chip supper, brew tea and eat alongside the highway, and then ride through the night. By the time we arrived at our first stop we were already behind schedule but, thank goodness, just in time before the chip shops closed.

I realised long before we got to Shrewsbury that we had a problem. In the Black Country, cyclists have a word for the kind of fatigue followed by cramp one can experience when cycling. They call it 'the bonk'. Some of the boys had a severe attack of the bonk, so after the supper break I massaged their legs and decided we should make our way across the border into Wales to spend the night in Welshpool.

We arrived in the early hours to a town in darkness. I looked around for a sheltered spot, and the best I could find was under the town hall portico. We quietly parked our bikes against one of the walls and sat against another to nap for a few hours, hoping the local policeman was already in his bed. The lads were so exhausted, that despite the hard floor they were asleep in a matter of minutes. Awake at first light, I roused the boys, telling them to keep as quiet as they could, and we were out of the town before the good people of Welshpool were about and headed towards the Welsh hills.

Gradually climbing to 800 feet wasn't too bad but it was taking its toll. I knew that to reach Dinas Mawddy would be a long hard slog, so to keep their spirits up I promised that we would soon be seeing the sea.

On the steeper parts we had to push our bikes, which was most of the way, and from time to time we stopped to drink and wash in the ice-cold water of the streams tumbling down the mountainside. On reaching the summit at about 1,200 feet, we brewed tea and finished the remains of our food.

Seeing the sunrise over the mountains gradually changing the colour of the landscape was breathtaking. Feeling the warmth from the sun's rays cheered the lads up, but I thought that they would be too tired to appreciate the grandeur of the scene that lay before us. I underestimated them. I could see by the way they were looking around that nature was making an impression.

Encouraging them to start down the mountain, knowing that we had more to climb, I began to repeat, 'It won't be…'

Before I could finish, they chanted in unison, '…long before we see the sea.' At least they hadn't lost their perky humour.

They were shouting and laughing as we coasted down the hills into the pretty town of Dolgellau, where we stopped for a snack and then along the side of the Afon Mawddach estuary we made our way to our destination, Barmouth.

We were lucky; the Easter weather was perfection. The sun was hot, the sea a sparkling green and warm, and the sandy beach inviting. We parked our bikes against the sea wall and walked to the water's edge, taking off our shoes and socks and paddling in the warm water.

Jimmy Doyle placed his arm around his younger brother whilst they stood staring out for their first real look at the sea. We left them standing there allowing the tide to wash over their feet. If I had held any doubt about the wisdom of embarking on the trip, their faces dispelled it.

We all lay on the sand, dog-tired but happy, and soon fell into a deep sleep. When we woke up, the pale faces we started out with had disappeared, replaced by rosy red countenances – all but the Doyle Brothers. Their olive skins had a tan we all envied. We had a meal in the nearby beach café, using its facilities to wash and tidy up.

Once they were refreshed I got them to visit Panorama Walk with me. I wanted them to see the effect the setting sun had, changing the colours of the vast variety of wild plants on Cader Idris. It is one of the most dramatic sights to be seen in Britain.

On our way back we got lost and decided to drop over a wall into what proved to be the gardens of a large estate. We found ourselves in a forest of huge rhododendron bushes in full bloom. Carefully picking our way we ended up walking through what seemed like acres of beautiful gardens without seeing a house or bumping into another human being. Jimmy piped up, 'It's a bit better than Burbury Park, Frank.' The understatement of the year!

We finally got back to the beach and I went in search of a place to put our heads for the night. I was lucky to find bed and breakfast boarding house with beds enough for us all. I asked the lady of the house if she could lay on an egg and chips supper, which she provided in abundance.

After a good night's sleep we came down to a gargantuan breakfast. As we got up from the table there wasn't a crumb to be seen. One by one the boys thanked the landlady as we wished her goodbye. We then rode along the coast road through Llanaber, and from Llanbedr up to Harlech with Cardigan Bay and then Tremadog Bay below us. The view, as always, was a moving feast.

Along the way we diverted into Portmeirion which, years on, became famous through a television series called *The Prisoner*. We booked in to the Harlech youth hostel and after looking around the castle and the town returned to the hostel for dinner.

We got an early start the following day and rode up to Ffestiniog. I didn't take them to see the slate quarries of Blaenau; its depressing landscape would have put a blot on their trip. Instead we turned right and rode down to Lake Trawsfynydd then left and on to Bala Lake. After a short stay in the pretty village of Bala we set out for Llangollen.

It proved to be too ambitious. By the time we reached Corwen it was getting dark, and seeing a CTC – Cycling Touring Club – sign on a large house we stopped to enquire whether there was room for us all. Meeting the lady of the house should have been enough for us to back off, but we were tired and the CTC sign signified that the accommodation had been cleared.

The rooms were lit by candles, which added to our concern. After a couple of hours sitting in chairs, Maisie and I crept downstairs to find that our group had beaten us to it. Very quietly we let ourselves out, mounted our bikes and rode. Having taken another look at the sign I realised that it was pre-war.

We rode down Horse shoe Pass, arriving in Llangollen in the early hours, and slept on the benches in the garden of a café, waiting for it to open. About 7.30 a.m., we were woken up by the angry owner but before he could remonstrate with us further I asked, putting on my best Welsh accent, 'Would it be possible for you to provide us all with a cooked breakfast, boyo?'

He cooled down immediately and we were soon called in, to sit before a bacon, sausage and egg breakfast with as much bread and butter and tea we could consume. Llangollen is a lovely place in which to be, but not during holiday periods. Having breakfasted early, we were able to show our small group the sites without too much hassle and then head off towards Shrewsbury and its youth hostel. Other than the fact that we ran out of money, our trip back to Birmingham was uneventful. We returned our charges tired, suntanned and happy.

The club was growing from strength to strength, some of the older boys who were quickly turning into men stayed on to help run the club as younger boys were taking their places. Some were called up to do their National Service and, when on leave, came in to see how things were going. That in itself was proof enough that the club had succeeded in achieving what I had set out to do. Once I had entered public life, the demands were so heavy on my spare time that I had to hand over the reins to someone else.

One thing above all is clear to me, that in today's affluent society there is a need, may be even greater now than then, for clubs like the Old Edwardians and Hockley United.

Chapter V

BACKED INTO POLITICS

Doctor Smith was a Scot, who as a newly qualified MD had come into our midst in the late 1920s. He came to a practice on what he thought was a temporary assignment but never got round to leaving.

His broad Glaswegian accent, coupled with the fact that whilst in his surgery he never removed the pipe from his mouth, meant that most of his patients found it difficult to comprehend his words of advice. Years later, he told me that the pipe was there to ward off the germs. There must have been something in it because I can't remember him ever being off sick.

He was a brusque, small, tidy man with a head of thick – almost black – hair. His serious countenance was relieved by his twinkling brown eyes. His panel of patients were suppose to pay for his advice, but from the time he came until 1937, when things began to look up and men were finding employment, not many could afford to pay the full amount. I don't know how he managed but it seemed the good doctor just forgot to ask; consequently his not too salubrious surgery was usually full. I think the Health Service meant more of a blessing to him than his patients.

As I was sitting in his surgery in 1947, the man next to me asked whether I was the one he used to watch box at the Holte. It was his enquiry that got us talking. It led me to hold forth on the conditions we had to suffer, especially the women, and of all those broken promises that something would be done. He asked where I lived and if I knew Denis Howell.

He was speaking of a young fellow who had just been elected to the city council. He was a couple of years younger than me and had already made an impression on its members and the St Paul's Ward electors.

The man must have spoken to Denis, because about a week later he knocked on my door. It was long past 10 p.m. He introduced himself and I invited him in for what turned out to be three hours of conversation. I was to learn that he was still a single man and a bit of a night bird. Time didn't seem to matter to him.

He knew that my family had been members of the Labour Party for a long time and urged me to attend the Ward Party meetings. For some reason I have never been able to figure, he had made up his mind that I should stand for election to the city council.

Denis was later to be elected to parliament. He went on to become a Minister of State, a privy councillor and a member of the House of Lords. He pays me a great compliment in his memoirs; however he repeats that we first met on the terraces watching a Birmingham City football match. I have no idea why he should have thought that, but nothing I could say would convince him that he was mistaken. However, there is no doubt that had it not been for him I would never have stood for elected office.

After a number of meetings with him he talked me into putting my name forward for the panel of local government candidates and then coached me sufficiently to successfully pass through that ordeal. Without him I doubt I would have made it. His encouragement and dogged determination led me to become the Labour Party's municipal candidate for St Paul's Ward.

The night in 1948 when the Ward Party met to select the one who was to contest the election on their behalf is etched on my memory. The ward committee had invited three potential candidates: Jim Meadows, Aston Divisional Labour Party's political agent and adviser to its member of parliament, Woodrow Wyatt; Bob Merry, a well-known and much-liked member of the Party; and me. They had both fought seats which were either marginal at best, or solid Tory.

The three of us were sitting in a side room – they seasoned performers, me a novice – waiting to be called individually to face the Ward Party members. This thing Jim and Bob had done on a number of occasions, me never. Having each made speeches and answered questions from the floor, we were sent back to the room to await the committee's decision. An hour went by and we were then called in collectively to hear who had been chosen.

The oldest member of the St Paul's Ward Labour Party, a lady who had a reputation for speaking her mind regardless of whom she offended, spoke up before the chairman had a chance to open his mouth.

'He hasn't had the experience of the other two and he isn't as bright, but something tells me that Frank Price is our man.'

With that questionable recommendation we were informed that I had been selected to fight the forthcoming election on their behalf. She and Denis Howell had backed me into the world of politics. I wasn't sure whether to laugh or cry.

Calling in to tell my parents that I had been selected to stand for the council, my father commented, 'You – what do you think you can do, even supposing that you are elected?'

His reaction was typical. I loved him dearly, but as far as I was concerned, he was a professional 'wet blanket'.

I was to face the challenge in May 1949. The Labour Government had been in office for just over three and a half years, and the majority of the people who had rejoiced at the time still didn't realise that the country was not only broke, but deeply in debt. We still had food rationing and the government was having a rough time.

John Strachey, the Minister of Food, was forced to cut the bacon ration. He couldn't have been much of a political strategist because he did it two days before the 1947 Municipal Elections. The women were so incensed they poured into the polling stations and the Labour Party lost control of the Birmingham city council, along with many other town and cities in the country. I was to learn that when it came to being concerned for the future of their colleague's seats in local government, members of the Parliamentary Party appeared to turn a blind eye.

During the winter of 1948, a few months before my election, Hugh Dalton, Richard Crossman, Jim Callaghan and Woodrow Wyatt – all considered to be political giants – held what was called a 'Brains Trust' in the Birmingham Town Hall. They spoke and then answered questions from the large audience who had gathered to hear these famous parliamentarians.

Jim Meadows, Wyatt's agent, kindly invited me to a dinner he had arranged for them after the meeting. For a young budding politician it was quite an honour. It was held in a private room at the Burlington Restaurant in the city centre. Jim placed me next to Richard Crossman.

I had heard that he suffered with a gastric ulcer and had been ordered to be careful with his diet. That night he ordered a large Wiener schnitzel. More surprising to me, a babe on the political scene, was the banter between the great men.

It has never been easy for me to hide my feelings and Crossman noticed. He said, 'Does this shock you, lad?' Before I could reply, he went on, 'Let me tell you how the Parliamentary Party is made up. It consists of men of genius like Nye Bevan and me, carpetbaggers like Jim Callaghan, and don't-care-a-fuckers like Woodrow Wyatt. If you are to make your way in politics you had better get to recognise the difference.'

This shook me, but not so much as the fact that those he had so caustically criticised simply laughed.

I never had much time for Dick Crossman, and I was not alone. He was an intellectual, an Oxford don and a member of All Souls, but many who admired him began to recognise that he was an intellectual bully. I didn't know it then but I was to take issue with him on a number of occasions in the future. I took note of his advice that evening, and it was to help me in my public life.

I stood for election on 12 May 1949. My Unionist Conservative opponent was a Commander CVG Simpson RNVR, who had already served on the council. He was a formidable opponent who didn't pull his punches. The local Labour Party were still in opposition and we knew that we were in for an uphill struggle.

The weather during that May was kind to us. It was very warm and most people living in the cramped airless houses in St Paul's Ward sat outside until quite late. Canvassing normally ceased at 9 p.m. but my brother Eric and I decided to carry on well after hours, helping to canvas every house in the Ward.

Alderman Sir Ernest Canning, who controlled the West Birmingham Unionist (Conservative) Association, owned the largest wholesale industrial chemical company in the Midlands and it was situated in St Paul's Ward. His staff, cars and vans were at the disposal of his Party's candidate.

Ernie Canning, as he was known to all and sundry, had been educated at King Edward's Grammar School, Aston, but didn't go on to university. On the surface he appeared to be a bit of a hard-nose, but for all his bluster he really was something of a pussy cat, although I didn't know it then. The odd thing was that unlike any of his contemporaries, Ernie had a very broad, grating Birmingham accent.

Fifteen years on, I was asked to propose the toast to King Edward's School, Aston at its centenary celebration dinner. It was attended by leading members of the city's society, and of course the 'old boys', including Sir Ernest. He sat at the top table not too far from me. During the toast I told the story of the day in 1937 when it was announced that Mr Canning, as he was then, had been selected by his peers to become the Lord Mayor of the City.

Having heard the news of the honour being paid to one of his pupils, his English teacher, long retired, phoned him. He said, 'Ernest, when you become Lord Mayor you will be meeting important people from all over the world and it is your duty to represent your city properly. You simply must do something about your appalling accent.'

To his surprise, Canning agreed to take elocution lessons so long has he would agree to be his teacher. He accepted the challenge and advised that if they were to succeed they should get right away from the city. He recommend that they travel to Switzerland. This agreed they spent three weeks in Davos.

On their return to the city after three weeks of intensive instruction, the only noticeable change that had taken place was that the teacher had developed a broad Birmingham accent.

Sir Ernest laughed along with the rest of the guests calling out, "'e's right, yo know!'

For all that, Canning was an astute politician, and during my first election poured his efforts and a considerable amount of money into his Party's campaign to beat me, and in the process gave me a very tough time.

My Party colleagues, Albert Benton, Dennis Williams, Denis Howell, his sister, Beryl, and brother, Stan, Wal Smith, Ray Millerchip and others, having worked all day, turned out to help every evening and at weekends. They tried to keep cheerful but few if any thought that we stood a cat in hell's chance of winning the seat. It was a time when anybody with business premises had two votes, one in the Ward where their premises stood and another where they lived. As St Paul's was full of small workshops in the jewellery quarter, the gunsmiths' quarter and elsewhere, we knew that the Conservative candidate could count on almost a thousand votes. However, I didn't know at the time that we had a secret weapon.

Three weeks before the poll, and without my knowledge, my Hockley United boys rounded up most of the 'kids' in the area, pinned our Party colours on them and gathered in their hundreds to cheer me wherever I went.

Knocking doors to canvass votes was like opening Pandora's box. In a little backyard behind a factory with just two houses in it, I tapped on the one with the lights on and curtains drawn. The call, 'Come in,' was light and cheery. I popped my head round the door and there, standing naked in a tin bath in front of the fire was a young women in her twenties. I had obviously arrived before the lucky fellow she had been expecting; I didn't stop to ask if I could count on her vote.

On a Sunday morning, an old lady who was scrubbing her step assured me that she had already been out to vote; it was five days before polling day. Try as I might I couldn't convince her that she was wrong. 'If you think I'm going there again,' she said, 'you're mistaken, they will think I'm crazy.'

It was all I could get out of her. Then there were those clever fellows who invited me in for a cup of tea to discuss politics, a delaying tactic Conservatives used, but one well known to us. There were some others who hated politicians and anyone else, and set their dogs on me.

Unlike the opposition we had very few cars at our disposal. We needed them to take old or disabled people to the polling station. I heard that we had a car-owning member who practised with a brass band at a local church hall every Wednesday night. I called in and innocently enquired of the bandleader, 'Where do you usually play?'

'Play?' he replied. 'Play? We rarely get the chance to actually *play*, we only practise!' It was heaven sent.

I convinced him that if his band met outside the hall at 7 p.m. on Thursday the 12th – polling day – I guaranteed that they would play before the biggest audience he could ever imagine. In his book, Denis Howell claims that it was he who got the band; it's a small point, but again he was mistaken.

The following days we went around telling the kids to meet at the hall, and for two hours before the polls closed, they paraded around the streets behind the band creating a festival atmosphere, bringing people out and making it easier for us to encourage them to go to vote.

As I entered the Constitutional Hill library, where the votes were being counted, Commander Simpson's election agent, a director of Canning's company, beckoned me over. He had a copy of the law on the conduct of elections and took joy in pointing out that we had forfeited the election by employing a band.

The Returning Officer was called, and Denis Howell informed him that the band members were in the musicians' union, affiliated to the Labour Party, and that no money had been passed. The officer smiled and walked away. Denis was right about not paying the band, but neither he nor I had checked whether they were card-carrying members of the union.

Commander Simpson's agent, a large man sporting a Churchill-size cigar, bellowed, 'It makes no difference, you've lost anyway!' As an afterthought he said, between blowing clouds of smoke over my head, 'You are young enough to fight another day.'

At midnight the count was completed and the St Paul's electorate had proved him to be wrong. I had won the seat with a majority of 625 votes.

My ecstatic supporters carried me out of the building, shoulder high, to be greeted by a huge crowd of well-wishers. They carried me, cheering, down the street where I was born. People leaned out of their bedroom windows to join in shouting words of encouragement. I looked back over the heads of the crowd and there I saw my mom and dad walking and cheering with them. It was for me a very moving and memorable night.

During the election I undertook to keep those promises that

had been made by my predecessors over the years: to plant trees and grass where none had grown for a century, to open up the area to fresh air and to replace the slums with houses which had inside lavatories and a bathroom. I didn't realise that only a few years was to pass before I would be placed in a position to actually assist in bringing this about.

That night, as we had suspected, the Labour Party lost a number of seats. Jim Eames, another new boy, and I were the only new members to be elected. I didn't know it then but on 12 May 1949, my devoted colleagues and the good people of St Paul's, had pushed me up and out into the light.

A nice end to the story was that Simpson's election agent wrote to me after I had been on the council for some years. His letter said that he had watched my progress and although he hadn't changed his party allegiance, offered his congratulations and best wishes. I remembered this when I became Lord Mayor and invited him, now long retired, and his wife to dinner in the council house. He told me that although he had been a Conservative Party agent for years, helping to elect many of its members to the council and to parliament, it was the first time that he had been invited to a function in the council house. 'And it had to be a by Labour Party member,' he said with a sad smile.

On the morning after the election a brown envelope was lying on my doormat addressed to Councillor F L Price. It was too early for the postman so it could only have come direct from the council house. They must have these ready prior to the election sending them out by courier to the successful candidates, dropping the others into the waste paper basket. If it was meant to impress, the town clerk had succeeded in my case.

It was an invitation to meet him in his office to go through 'the usual proceedings' it was to be sworn in, choose one of the vacant seats in the council chamber and be handed a copy of the municipal diary.

Having observed the town clerk closely, I gained the impression that the meeting was really to give him a chance to size-up the new intake. I suddenly remembered the advice of Dick Crossman about politicians; it seemed also to apply to some public officials. My relationship with this town clerk proved not to be a happy one. I was soon to realise that the envelope containing his invitation didn't include an extra piece of 'grey matter and if I was to be worthy etc.' I would need to apply myself. What I hadn't realised was that there was a price to pay. At times it turned out to be a very bitter price indeed.

At the time of my election I was working for the world-renowned manufacturer of scales, testing and measuring equipment, and petrol pumps; W T Avery. Their factory was on the site where the famous engineers/scientists, Boulton and Watt, had worked together in Smethwick, on the borders of Birmingham. The town was later made infamous by a little-known Conservative councillor who, in a parliamentary by-election, defeated Labour's ex-Foreign Secretary, Patrick Gordon Walker.

He had won what had been a safe Labour seat by cynically exploiting the colour prejudice prevalent at the time. As the men took his seat in the House of Commons, the prime minister, Harold Wilson, took the unprecedented step of labelling the new member 'a parliamentary leper'.

Being naive enough to believe that I was living in a truly democratic state, I explained to my immediate superior at work that I was to be a candidate at the forthcoming Municipal Elections, that as it was a large authority the meetings took place during the day time and that if I was successful I would require two half days a month off from work to attend council meetings.

He congratulated me and asked for which Party I was standing. When I replied, 'The Labour Party,' he smiled and asked if there was anything else. Thinking that he might be under the misapprehension that I expected to be paid for the time I was away, I hastened to assure him that it was not the case, thanked him and left his office.

Twelve days after my election I answered the summons to attend my first city council meeting, leaving my workplace at the lunch break and returning the following morning. On arrival, I was told to present myself to the manager, who greeted me with, 'What the hell do you think you are doing? You can't simply walk out on your job like this.'

Surprised, I replied, 'But you agreed.'

'Yes but I didn't think that you, a Labour man, would get in,' he spluttered.

I now understood the reason for his smile when I answered his query about my Party allegiance.

Regaining his composure, he placed his hand on my shoulder and asked me to sit down. He walked around the office and, looking down, told me that a bright young man like me could have the opportunity of going far in the firm. He described 'opportunity' as a wall which had in it a carefully camouflaged door which only bright people would find and go through to become managers like him. Then he said, 'Take my advice; give up this councillor nonsense.'

I couldn't believe my ears.

At this stage I should tell you that my parents demonstrated unusual foresight when they christened me Frank. It's the way I am, and it as got me into all kinds of scrapes. This was one. Listening to this load of old rubbish from my boss I couldn't hold back.

'Who do you think you're kidding? My two brothers have worked here for the past fifteen years. They are a bloody sight brighter than me and they are still working on the shop floor.'

He was taken aback but I continued. 'They haven't had the good fortune to be standing by one of your camouflaged doors when it opens and unlike you, had they been, they didn't have the general manager of the company for a father to yank them through.'

It was my undoing. He kicked me out of his office and on the following Friday I was handed a week's notice to leave.

On the Sunday evening I was speaking on the same platform as the local MP, Woodrow Wyatt. I was asked if I thought that Britain was a truly democratic country, and in answering mentioned what had happened to me. The meeting over, Woodrow asked where I worked. On my telling him, he asked, 'But isn't Sir Percy Mills, the chairman?'

Frankly I hadn't a clue. Evidently, Woodrow, who was a junior minister in the defence department, sought him out to tell him my story. Before my week's notice had expired, Sir Percy travelled up from London and I was called into his presence.

His secretary said that the chairman was expecting me and asked me to take a seat. Disappearing into what I rightly presumed was his room; she returned and sat down at her desk. I waited for about thirty minutes and enquired whether the chairman knew that I was there; she nodded. A further ten or so minutes elapsed when the phone rang. She answered, and putting her hand over the mouthpiece said, 'You can go in now.'

I walked to Sir Percy's desk and stood whilst he continued to read his papers. After a while he looked up, asking, 'Who are you?'

I was stumped for a moment but replied, 'What?'

When he repeated his question, which I took as his way of putting me in my place, I replied, 'My name's Frank Price, I was sent for by Sir Percy Mills, so who might you be?'

Not the best way to win friends and influence people, I'll admit.

Sir Percy wasn't blessed with a kindly face. His eyes were small and close together, one being slightly out of line, and set in a ruddy, lived-in kind of face. With a small, thin-lipped mouth he looked what he was – very hard and unsympathetic.

He turned his head slightly to one side, looking at me with what I can only describe as contempt.

'I know who you are!' he shouted. 'Now let me put you straight. Wyatt has had a word with me on your behalf. You can stay at your job, but the first excuse we have of getting rid of you, out you go. Now get out of here!'

A few months later, the Labour Government raised the tax on petrol. I was working on the Avery and Hardoll petrol pump unit, and out of almost a thousand employees, as good as Sir Percy's word, I was the one that was made redundant. For the first time in my working life I found myself unemployed. However, I was to meet Sir Percy again.

Being a councillor – on the left – I found it difficult to obtain a job. The jobs were there but when I told my prospective employers that I was a local government representative they found that I was unsuitable. I was asked many times, 'Why don't you resign?' I could only reply that I was elected to serve some twenty thousand constituents to whom I had made promises that I wanted to keep. To be truthful, I also felt that my destiny was tied up with being there. I wanted to stay the course and I wasn't about to let the bastards beat me.

But to complete the Avery episode. The city council had commissioned a life-size statue of Boulton-Watt and Murdoch. Finished off in gold leaf, it had been erected on a prominent site in Broad Street. It still stands there. It was decided that because of the Boulton, Watt connection with the Avery plant, the most appropriate person to perform the unveiling was the chairman of W T Avery's, Sir Percy (by then Lord) Mills, a personal friend of Harold Macmillan, the then housing minister.

By this time I had become the chairman of the Public Works Committee, which, among its many responsibilities, looked after statues and public buildings. Before the ceremony, the VIPs gathered in the Lord Mayor's parlour and the Lord Mayor thought it appropriate that I should be presented to Lord Mills.

Remembering the months of unemployment, the misery and the indignity it brought, I had to say, 'We have met before, my Lord.'

'Oh really, and when might that have been?' he enquired with a broad smile.

'You invited me to your office when I worked for your company. Surely you remember your prediction. You were right, I was fired a few months later.'

The Lord Mayor meanwhile choked on his drink. Without blinking an eye, Lord Mills replied, 'Ah yes, and how are you?' Whether he remembered or not, I knew that he couldn't have cared less about what had happened to me. In the circumstances, his was a classic reply to someone he considered not worthy of his honest concern.

I had remained jobless for near on twelve months and all I had saved had gone. None of my colleagues enquired as to my welfare; the only one who mentioned his concern, and that was much later, was Sir Herbert Manzoni. He told me that he watched as I became less and less buoyant and wanted to say something but couldn't bring himself to do so. I was pleased he didn't.

Every time I applied for a job for which I had been trained, I had to inform them that I was on the city council. 'On the Labour side?' they always asked, and my reply always meant no job.

I finally landed a position with British Rail as a clerk. The wage was far lower than that which I had been earning, but I had no other choice. In those days councillors received no remuneration, so it was a case of any port in a storm. As it turned out it was to lead me to better times. I'm not sure whether I believe in fate but at times, and in this particular instance, it appears to have played a significant part. Joining British Rail led to a series of remarkable events in my life.

My new employer decided to place me in a little-used station about a mile from the city centre. It was built over a railway tunnel in Monument Road, Ladywood. The stationmaster took me into the booking office; looking around I couldn't under-stand why it was so filthy, that is, until the first express train came thundering underneath heading north, shaking the foundations.

We were still in the steam age then, and as the smoke poured through the floor boards, the clerk, who was about eighteen, sprang to the sloping desk spreading his body across the papers in an effort to stop them falling all over the floor. This performance was re-enacted every thirty minutes or so.

The office was kept reasonably warm in winter by a small open coal-burning fire. The station was so old that the rail tickets that filled the racks were for excursions that had been cancelled for a decade or more. There was little or no passenger traffic, but parcels were brought to the station and a few goods trains heading north or on their way to New Street Station would stop and collect them.

Part of my job was to weigh them, work out the costs, stick on the appropriate number of stamps and take them via the goods lift – which was operated by pulling on a rope – down to the appropriate platform. This less than mind-stretching exercise was taught to me by the clerk. Neither of us could claim to be overstretched, so he didn't miss me when I was out on council duties.

I had been there just over a month when he disappeared. I asked what had happened to him and was told, 'He blotted his copybook.' With such a limited scope for mischief, I couldn't imagine how it was possible, but whatever his misdemeanour the taciturn stationmaster never let on. I was left in charge, on my own, rarely seeing him. I heard that he spent almost all of his time in the marshalling yard arranging goods trains – not as easy an exercise as it sounds.

The station was one from which homing pigeon fanciers despatched their birds to distant parts. On reaching their destination the baskets were opened by a British Rail employee, freeing the birds to fly back home. The empty baskets were then placed on the next available train to return from whence they came.

A well-mannered, intelligent little girl of about twelve collected her father's basket twice a week. She would tell me of her friends, her school and how she was progressing with her education. If I happened to have chocolates or a few sweets, I would share them with her. One winter afternoon, just as it was getting dark, a lady came into the office and introduced herself as the girl's mother.

She thanked me for the kindness shown to her daughter – unfortunately, nowadays my actions would have been automatically misconstrued – and told me that she had come to collect the basket. She decided to accompany me down to the platform to collect it. Not thinking that anything was amiss, I went to the storeroom and she followed.

The station was old and not well lit, having gas not electricity, so it was quite dark. Once in the room she closed the door and pressed me against the wall, unbuttoning her blouse. Staring at her ample bare breasts, I thought of my predecessor. *Was this how he had 'blotted his copybook'*? I wondered.

Although she was quite a handsome women, the fact that I was now a public figure and, just as important, needed to keep my job, helped me curb my instincts. I decided to turn down the opportunity that had presented itself. Turning her to the wall and taking a last look at what I was passing up, I beat a hasty retreat in search of the stationmaster.

Telling him of my experience he chuckled, 'Oh, she's been at you already, has she?'

Without a word to me he arranged that on the following day I be transferred to the passenger parcels department attached to New Street Station.

Because of the time I needed for my council duties they put me on split shifts. It meant reporting at the Main Station at 6 a.m., working until 10.30 a.m. checking off the perishable traffic, then reporting to Suffolk Street Passenger Parcels Depot from 5 p.m. until 8.30 p.m. This was where we received parcels for onward transmission. Most of my free time between shifts was involved in my council work.

On an afternoon just before Easter, Alderman Sir Charles Burman, head of Burman Industries and a previous Lord Mayor, came into the small office on the passenger parcel deck where, during what was usually a quiet period, I was the only person present.

Charles Burman was generally recognised as being rather pompous and not popular among some of his own Party members. He had a tendency to treat the members who were less well established – socially – as he treated all of us in the Labour Party, namely, with complete indifference. It took some years before I realised that it could have been due to shyness. If that was the case I can only feel sad that he missed so much.

Standing by the door he called out, 'I say, you there! My son's luggage has gone astray. It was put aboard at Harrow Station – find it, will you.'

There was a deck where mislaid luggage was placed in bays. At holiday times they were overflowing.

As there were no porters about I suggested that he accompany me. We walked some distance to reach the appropriate bay and with difficulty I was able to retrieve his son's trunk. Not having a trolley, I suggested that he took one handle and I the other. He hesitated and looked around to find someone to assist me. I stood waiting for him to make a move. He wasn't at all pleased that no one appeared and had no choice other than to agree.

We carried the trunk to his Bentley; he opened the boot and we placed the trunk inside. This done I watched him as he searched his pocket and then proffered me a shilling. I stared at it and then at him and declined.

'Part of my job, sir,' I said.

He sniffed, got into the car and drove off.

Although I sat not too far from him in the council chamber, he simply hadn't recognised me. About two months later after I had spoken in a debate, we passed in the corridor.

'I say,' he murmured, 'haven't we met somewhere?'

There was no answer to that other than to ask him to wait a moment. I searched my pocket and offered him a shilling. He turned and walked away without uttering a word. It wasn't very nice of me but in those days I was still carrying a chip on my shoulder.

During the bitter winter of 1950–51, standing on an open platform in New Street Station at six o'clock in the morning checking off the fish boxes from Fleetwood was debilitating. It was considered to be the most unpleasant job of any in the clerks' department, but I had no choice.

After suffering this for four bitterly cold months, the head of the accounts department stopped by to ask me how I liked my job. Rubbing my frozen fingers there was only one answer. He smiled sympathetically and disappeared into the station.

Some days later he stopped by again and surprised me to ask if I would like a job in his department. I told him that I knew nothing about accounts, but this didn't seem to deter him. The following week he arranged for my transfer and asked me to be outside the accounts office at 9 a.m. on Monday morning.

Promptly at 9 a.m. he arrived, and before removing his topcoat led me in to be introduced to his minions. They were sitting on high stools leaning over their books like an army of Bob Cratchits. Tapping the handle of his umbrella on the nearest desk, he called out, 'Let me introduce Mr Frank Price, who will be working with us. He knows nothing about our accounting methods; you will teach him.'

With that he turned to leave. Turning back, he added in a somewhat lower tone, 'By the way, in case you are unaware, he is a member of our city council, and from time to time will be absent, attending to his civic duties. I will ignore the fact and so will you; I trust you understand.'

It was clear that he was acting out of concern for me and I have never forgotten his kindness. Despite his instructions, it was not too long before one or two of my new colleagues began to complain among themselves that I was away from my desk leaving them to carry my burden. It wasn't the first, nor the last time that my position and means of earning a living was threatened by jealousy or malevolence among those who, above all, should have understood.

Chapter VI
LEARNING TO SWIM

Before the monthly full council meeting, at which the various committees reported on a rota system, the political Parties met separately to discuss the agenda and their attitude to it. The Labour Group met on Friday night, the Tories on Monday. The council meetings were on Tuesday beginning at 2 p.m.

After each municipal election, the leaders and secretaries of the two main parties met to decide the split in representation on council committees, which depended upon the numbers of elected members of each party. Once agreement was reached, they reported to their respective group officers, who then decided which of their members they should recommend to represent their party on the various committees.

The annual meeting of the groups was therefore important to the members, especially those who harboured political ambition. The first business on the agenda was the officers' recommendations in respect of the allocation of committee seats and, if in power, the chairman – in today's parlance 'Chair', which I still think is a nonsense.

This completed, the members then had an opportunity to re-elect or replace the group officers for a period until the next election. These were made up of the leader, two deputy leaders, a secretary and four officers along with a chief whip and a junior whip – positions much sought after by some members.

When I arrived, the leader of the Labour Group was Alderman Albert Bradbeer, a total abstainer, vegetarian and a Quaker. He was the secretary to the board of the Cadbury chocolate company in Bourneville. A striking-looking man in his early sixties, he was quite thin, about 5'10" with pale, pleasant and eternally calm features. With his long white hair he had the appearance of an ascetic.

Alderman Bradbeer had a wry sense of humour, and on his day was a compelling orator; his kinds are in short supply nowadays. Although the group had a very competent secretary, during the meetings he was in the habit of keeping his head down making copious notes. He rarely sat looking out at his fellow members and only raised his head to call on the next member wishing to speak, or to speak himself. I often wondered just how much attention he was paying to whatever was being said and what the hell he did with all those notes.

He was kind to me, but then he was kind to everybody, but as long as I knew him I felt that he never quite understood me. Yet it was he who was to propel me into the most important job on the city council.

The Labour Party had lost a number of seats in the two previous municipal elections so I was lucky, they told me, to be appointed to the much sought after Parks, Public Works and Estate Committees. As I was elected in mid-May and the council and its committees went into recess during the months of August and September, I had little time to 'get my feet wet'.

During the rest of the year the committees and their sub committees met monthly. Due to the enormous workload of the Public Works Committee, it met every week. Council members were not paid in those days, but if you could prove that by attending a meeting pay had actually been lost, members could apply via the town clerk for what was called 'lost time allowance'.

A form had to be completed and sent to the town clerk, who had one of his minions check its validity. The allowance was not based on what was actually lost; the maximum was based on four hours a day at a fixed rate, regardless. The sum allowed being so paltry, coupled with the fact that claims were scrutinised by some junior clerk, meant that many members didn't apply.

Birmingham had a reputation of being the best-governed city in Britain, and it attracted officials who were usually of the highest calibre and among the best in the country. It also attracted dedicated, intelligent men and women to serve on its council.

It annoyed me to hear critical comments from people, usually from those who had never given up any of their time for the benefit of others. The most common was that 'they only do it for what they can get out of it'. It's true, but not in the way they meant it. Most of those – on all sides – with whom I served, were in it for what they could contribute to further the welfare of their city and those who lived in it. What they and I got out of it was the deep personal satisfaction of being able to do just that.

Long before the Conservatives' disastrous 1974 reorganisation of local government via an act which carved up a number of authorities and also brought in payment to elected members, people served long hours without remuneration. Some of them, whom I knew personally, suffered in silence, having too much pride to ask for help. During my first twelve months on the council, I was numbered among them.

To those who have never had the inclination to get involved, it doesn't make sense, and so it's difficult to convince them that there are selfless people who are prepared to give of their time and energy to serve in local government. I'm not foolish enough to suggest that there are no black sheep, but they were few in number in Birmingham.

The citizens elected some remarkable men and women in the past. During my twenty-five years on the city council I served alongside a few of them. Unlike today, there were no microphones in the large semicircular council chamber, which seated 160 members. It was a case of speak up or go unheard, a sure way to make one become an able public speaker. We had a number of truly great debaters who would have outshone many of those sitting in the Houses of Parliament today.

At my second full council meeting, Denis Howell, who was then Group Secretary, came down from his seat on the back row of the Chamber to ask when I was to make my maiden speech. I replied, 'When I have something meaningful to say.'

Each meeting he asked the same question. On the day I informed the Lord Mayor that I wished to speak, Denis asked me again, and I told him, 'Today.'

It was a mistake. He asked what I was going to deal with and I gave him an outline. Before I was called, Denis had jumped in to speak and mentioned, as if in passing, that his colleague from St Paul's would be making his maiden speech, and then briefed the council on what I was about to cover. It was bit disconcerting for a new boy, but when I got to my feet I was able to get through it reasonably well. I had however learned another lesson. Don't let even a close friend know your thoughts, that's if you want to progress in politics.

Sir Theodore Pritchett, who had won the Military Cross during the First World War, was the senior partner of a law practice in the city and leader of the Tory Party at this time. He had the appearance of the cartoon sketches of pre-war Ministers of the Crown: a strong large handsome head with white hair and moustache to match. He had a straight back and was always attired as if he were in court. With his black morning coat, striped trousers, white shirt and grey silk tie, he never looked other than an elder statesman.

Pritchett was a powerful debater and had a way of taking apart other members' arguments in a friendly yet cutting way. He bowled me over a few times but I could never feel aggrieved. I decided that if I was to learn the art of debate I needed to pitch myself against him. This I did, to the amazement of *my* colleagues and the amusement of his. He verbally brushed me aside time and again, but I ignored the sniggers and kept after him.

The day came when I pierced his defences, having followed him after he had made yet another powerful speech. By the time I resume my seat both he and the council knew that I had bested him. I thought, *It must be one of his off days*. I looked across the Chamber at him, he nodded his head and signalled to me as he rose to leave. We met in the ante-room.

Expecting something of a blast I was taken aback when Sir Theodore said quietly, 'Let us take a walk, young fella.'

We strolled down the main corridor past the life-size portraits of famous men who had been members of the council, such as Joseph Chamberlain and his son, Neville.

He stopped and turning to face me he said, quite quietly, 'You did it to me today, my lad.'

Acting as if I didn't know what he meant, I asked, 'Did what, sir?'

He looked hard at me, saying, 'Come off it, you know perfectly well what I mean!' He turned to face the way we came and then back at me. 'I want to say this. If you keep at it, young

man, you will be one of those who will make a difference here.'
And with that he walked back to the council chamber.

It was the first compliment I had received from either side and
one which I have never forgotten. Although we were politically
opposed and were to cross swords now and then, I was to learn
much later that he had protected me from a vengeful town clerk.

Before the end of the war, the 1944 Blitz and Blight Act was
placed on the statute book, and I believe that Birmingham was the
only local authority that took full advantage of it. It came about
because Winston Churchill had never been allowed to forget that
whilst a minister during the 1914–18 war he and Lloyd George
had promised the serving men that they would return to 'homes
fit for heroes to live in' – a promise that was never fulfilled.

It must have burned into him, for at the height of the 1939–45
war he set up a committee which brought forward the Blitz and
Blight Act. Fortunately for Birmingham, Herbert Manzoni played
a leading part as a member of that committee.

Believing that the government would accept their recommendations, he began preparing plans for the city. His belief was
justified, and when the act became law Birmingham – which had
a Labour-controlled council for the first time – accepted his
advice and applied for the powers set down in the act: that of
clearing the slums. It was a momentous undertaking and it meant
that the promises made by so many, for so long, could at last be
honoured.

We began to take over all the properties and the land upon
which they stood within five large designated areas around the
neck of the city. It was a tremendous act of faith by the city
council.

Within this huge estate there were over 30,000 back-to-back
slum dwellings which stood cheek by jowl with small workshops,
factories, schools, churches, cinemas, and lots of pubs. Even
before the war, other than the pubs, most of the properties had,
not been too well cared for. During the war years nothing was
done to either maintain or to improve the conditions, so we were
faced with a crumbling mass of bricks and mortar, most of it
occupied.

There was no way that the council could carry out wholesale

demolition, so we staggered the takeover. It meant having to leave families in sub-standard accommodation for longer than they or we wished. In some cases the properties remained in the ownership of avaricious landlords until we were able to acquire them.

I was disgusted at the greed shown by some of the private owners who fought to keep hold of these pathetic hovels, collecting the rent and failing to carry out repairs until the Health Department threatened to take them to court.

The Estates Committee, given the responsibility of managing the Estate, formed a special committee to handle it. I became a member of its Central Areas Management Committee which managed and maintained this jungle of dilapidated property until the Public Works and Housing Committees were in a position to rehouse the families and demolish and replace the properties with modern housing.

Having surveyed the conditions, our first priority was to make those houses under our control windproof and watertight. We then began the process of putting them into a reasonable state of repair until the time came for their demolition. The tenants of those still in private ownership, seeing repairs being carried out on those that were under council control, became quite agitated.

Labour lost control in 1947, and when I was first elected the Conservatives were still in power. The private landlords leaned on the then chairman of the Estates Committee to delay the takeover on the basis that their property was, as they put it, 'in a fit state of repair'. He succumbed and ruled out, among others, one hundred houses in my Ward of St Paul's. This was despite the fact that he was an estate agent and represented some of the owners.

Incensed by this coercion I asked a qualified surveyor to inspect each of the hundred houses occupied by my constituents and to prepare a detailed report on their condition. As I expected, his report proved to be devastating. I gathered a petition and presented it to the first available full council meeting.

Petitions were referred to the appropriate committee, in this case the Estates. When it came before us, I was surprised to see that the Lord Mayor, Alderman Yates, a member of the

Conservative Party, was in attendance. This was very unusual. The petition was read out by the clerk, and the chairman, Councillor Cross, supported by his political colleagues, immediately dismissed it. The Lord Mayor, a lawyer by profession, intervened, suggesting that as I had presented the petition I should be allowed to speak.

Thanking him, I explained that I had visited each of the houses and was well acquainted with the conditions in which the tenants were living. I then read out extracts from my surveyor's report. Finally I questioned the right of the chairman, who as an agent for some of the owners had in my view a pecuniary interest, to vote on the issue.

The Lord Mayor leaned over to the chairman. What was said I know not, but whatever it was, he left the Chair and the Lord Mayor then presided. I passed him my surveyor's report and having read it he counselled the committee to accept the petition and to agree to instruct the officials to take the properties over.

It was my first battle with authority and I had won. It was obvious why the Lord Mayor had taken the unusual step of attending the meeting. He had realised, or had taken counsel from his leader, Sir Theodore, that one of the party's members was about to create an embarrassing problem.

The outcome was reported widely in the local press as 'The battle of the hundred houses'. It was a famous victory, earning me more than a little respect from my colleagues and the gratitude of a hundred families in my Ward, which to me, was important. I was learning to swim.

Seeing improvements carried out to adjoining property naturally gave rise to demands from neighbours and the department was overwhelmed. Trying to work on a priority basis was almost impossible as almost all these very old, neglected dwellings were in need of urgent repair. It made the task of managing this huge slum estate, ranging from dilapidated small hovels to large factories, a constant headache. Reginald Ross, the Estates Department chief, and his deputy, Edward Knight, were outstanding. Without them and the other capable, hard-working and sympathetic officers in the department, I doubt that we could have succeeded.

My second joust with authority came about by a near accident. Whilst working for British Rail, I had to cross from

New Street Station to the parcels depot in Suffolk Street every day. The street is now part of the inner ring road renamed Queen's Way. It was a steep cobblestone incline leading from the city centre proper. Traffic heading out of town made its way via Paradise Street into and down Suffolk Street. On the left-hand side stood the Boulton and Watt Technical College, and in front of it there was a long line of covered bus shelters which stretched almost down to a busy intersection, at which there was a pedestrian crossing.

It was on this crossing that I almost came to grief with a sliding car. It was no fault of the driver; it was wet and his view of the crossing had been obscured by the line of double-decker buses parked alongside the shelters. Applying brakes on this cobbled surface at any time was tricky; after even the slightest rainfall, it made a hazardous exercise for driver and pedestrian alike. Having been forced to jump out of the way of the skidding car I took the trouble to look into the problem.

It didn't take much imagination to figure that the shelters needed to be moved further up the hill, away from the crossing. Simple it was, but to achieve it against the all powerful and profitable Birmingham Municipal Omnibus Department proved to be a mammoth task. It was my second brush with authority since being elected.

I made an appointment with the general manager. I was ushered into his office but he didn't bother to come from behind his desk or even to rise out of his seat. It registered. He greeted me by saying that he was very busy and could only spare me a minute or two.

As I was a new boy, young, and as far as he knew, only possessed an elementary school education, he made it clear by his greeting that I wasn't important enough to concern him over much. I explained the problem and the way it could be easily solved. He rose from behind his desk, took my arm and guided to the door, saying he would look into it.

Having heard nothing for a month, as a matter of courtesy, I informed his chairman, Alderman Goodby, 'If nothing comes of my approach to your chief officer, I will raise it on the floor of the council chamber when you next report.'

This I was forced to do. From the rostrum, Goodby also agreed to look into the matter.

The *Birmingham Mail* municipal reporter, Roy Smith, picked it up and after the meeting had a word with me. If the transport manager didn't see the point, Roy Smith certainly did. He had pictures taken and the resultant publicity brought me a number of letters from people who had suffered close encounters with sliding cars whilst on the crossing.

Still I failed to hear from the department, so I tried again. This time the general manager became quite angry, telling me, 'You simply do not understand, Councillor! You have no idea of the problems entailed in moving the shelters.' In other words he was telling me to drop it.

It occurred to me then, that if an elected member of the council received such arrogant treatment, what chance had the man in the street? I decided to take on the powerful department, its general manager and its chairman.

My first step was a visit to Police Headquarters. I asked if they kept records on accident black spots. 'Yes,' was the reply. Did they consider Suffolk Street a black spot? 'Yes,' again. Would they provide me with information and figures in respect of this particular black spot? 'No problem.' Within days I had enough ammunition to blow the department out of its lethargy.

I thought hard as to my next move. Should I present my findings to the general manager? No, he'd told me he was too busy, so chances were that he wouldn't make time to read it. Should I raise it with the chairman? No, he too hadn't had the courtesy to follow up a councillor's genuine complaint. Although considered to be one of the powerful members of the council, he was clearly under the influence of his chief officer. I decided to hit them in open council.

I waited for the day that the committee was reporting, informing the Lord Mayor that I wished to speak on the motion for the approval of its report. With the press corps there and the public gallery full, the Lord Mayor called me.

I repeated the reasons why I thought the shelters needed to be moved. I spoke of the approaches I had made and the manner in which these had been summarily rebuffed. I asked what chance an ordinary citizen had if one of their elected representatives received the treatment that had been meted out to me. This brought cries of 'Hear! Hear!' from all sides of the Chamber and applause from the Strangers' Gallery, for which they were admonished by the Lord Mayor.

I then produced the statistics of accidents, fatalities and near fatalities provided by the Police Department, updated since I had first raised the issue. I also produced the statement from the police that the position of the bus shelters was in their opinion a prime factor.

It was time for a bit of histrionics. I pointed my finger at the chairman. Speaking in a voice slow and low, I said, 'It's raining outside. It is dark and it is peak hour. At this very moment cars will be travelling down Suffolk Street and your buses will be standing at the shelters obscuring their view.' I paused to let that sink in and then added, 'What, Mr Chairman, will you say tomorrow if yet another person gets struck down when you and this council know that had you acted on my request many months ago it could have been avoided?'

With that I resumed my seat.

The chairman and his general manager waited for me in the ante-room.

'You bastard, who the hell do you think you are dealing with?' the chairman whispered in my ear.

I put my face close to his and said in a menacing tone, 'I should be asking you that. Very soon, my friend, you will find out.'

The next morning as I was making my way to my job I saw workmen moving the shelters further up the hill. That day I joined the band of iconoclasts. I recognised that too many of those we admire and wish to follow have feet of clay. I began to understand that the only way to beat the bureaucrats, elected or appointed, even if they are people who I thought share the same ideals, was to fight them when you know that you are right and they are wrong. I had learned to swim.

Chapter VII

WHEN IGNORANCE LEADS TO BLISS

At my first meeting of the prestigious Public Works Committee in May 1949, a kindly old Labour stalwart, Alderman James, indicated that I should sit next to him at the bottom end of the long committee table. He had a deadpan look and was the image of Stan Laurel. He had a habit of sucking sugared almonds and then cracking them with his teeth.

He whispered so loudly that all those sitting in this long room could hear every word. So much so, that when he whispered, 'You are the youngest fellow ever to sit on this committee; my advice is to sit quiet and learn,' the chairman, Alderman Griffith, sitting at the other end of the room called out, 'that's good advice, young man!'

Griffith was a long-time member of the Conservative Group. An accountant with a rather pompous attitude, he was lacking in both personality and common sense. I did sit, I did learn, but I didn't stay quiet for long.

Other than me, the committee was made up of leading members of the two main parties. Having sat as advised, I found myself voting with my Party without fully understanding the reports. After a couple of months I knew that if I was to be honest with myself and to my elected position, I would have to expose my ignorance.

At the next meeting, before the vote was taken on one of the reports, I interjected, 'I'm sorry, Mr Chairman, but I would like the report further explained.' All heads turned towards me. He responded, 'The report is quite simple, Councillor.'

'Not to me,' I replied.

'Well, it is to everyone else, so let's get on,' he retorted.

I thought, in for a penny in for a pound, so I interrupted once again. 'Well, I'm sorry, sir, but I want to understand that which I am expected to vote upon.'

At this point Sir Herbert Manzoni, the Chief Officer, butted in. 'May I, Mr Chairman?' He then proceeded to simplify the details.

I repeated this exercise at the following meeting, to the annoyance of the chairman and some of the committee members. Sir Herbert passed me down a note which suggested that I see him in his office after the meeting. Preparing myself for a head-to-head confrontation with an irate officer, I knocked on his door.

I was surprised when he said, 'I admire your persistence, Councillor.' He continued to look hard at me, adding, 'Did you notice how attentive some of the other members became when I explained in more detail the report you said you didn't under-stand?'

Not waiting for an answer, he went on to suggest that I arrange to see him a day before the meeting to go through the agenda so that he could explain anything that I felt I had difficulties with. I thanked him and agreed so long as he didn't expect me to agree with everything he was putting forward.

Over the next few months the other members became aware that by the questions I was asking and amendments I was putting forward I had not just mastered the agenda, I had discovered enough to question or debate its contents. Another lesson learned.

This was at a time when Britain was suffering from the burden of neglect of past decades coupled with the destruction brought about by the war. The newly elected government had promised to alter the social imbalance and their far-reaching policies needed money – lots of it – but they had taken over a country that had bankrupted itself to win the war.

In addition to the bringing in the National Health Service and nationalising the railways, electricity, gas, the docks, steel and the coal industries, they passed the Lewis Silkin 1947 Town and Country Planning Act. Its aim was to bring order to the chaos of land use planning in Britain.

The Act placed on every local authority the responsibility of preparing a land use development plan. In essence it meant that every square yard of its area required to be zoned for specific uses.

In a city which covered eighty square miles, this was no mean task. The Public Works Committee was allocated the job, resulting in extra meetings, some times two or three a week.

The Labour Party became the majority party on the Birmingham city council for the first time in 1945 but lost control in 1947. They were still in opposition when I was elected. The Conservatives were back were they always believed they belonged.

When I walked for the first time into what was called 'the round room' – the anteroom to the council chamber – Alderman Sir Ernest Canning was chatting to a couple of his colleagues. He was deaf and had a tendency to shout when conversing with others. I couldn't but help hearing him shout, 'If that young sod Price gets elected next time, I'll resign!'

I stopped to tell him, 'I *will*, Sir Ernest, and I hope you *do*.'

I was re-elected three years later, and he did in fact retire. It was sad really. Although he was on the right of his Party, he was one of our 'characters'.

During the three years we shared on the council I must have earned his respect, for years later, he contributed generously to a number of causes I was sponsoring. He would phone me and say something like, 'Is that yo, Frank Price? This fund yo'm raisin' – tell me about it.'

I would go into some detail and promise to write him.

'Yo don't need to do that. If yo'm recommending it, I'll send a cheque.' And he always did.

'Characters' tend to upset some people, but once they're recognised for what they are, you know they're a blessing in a world too full of stereotypes. Only fools dismiss them.

Attending a political meeting in 1950, I sat next to a fellow a few years younger than me. Over 6' tall, which accentuated his lack of weight, he had tight, fair, slightly wavy hair and a thin, well-shaped nose, under which he wore a clipped military-style moustache. Wearing a black morning coat, striped morning trousers and a grey silk waistcoat with pearl buttons, and sporting a thick gold watch chain, fob and pocket watch, he had the appearance of a solicitor with a thriving practice.

His ensemble was somewhat Victorian and would have been impressive except that on closer examination I noticed that the cuffs of his sleeves, the edge of his waistcoat and the bottoms of his trousers were frayed. I had no doubt that he was aware of it, but it didn't appear to bother him one jot. When he stood erect, he had a military bearing and with an upper-crust accent and a slight lisp, he was bound to impress the lower orders.

After the meeting, we had coffee together in a local café were our friendship began to blossom. His name was Roy MacGregor-Hastie. He was a linguist, capable of speaking, reading and writing in half a dozen languages. He had a public school and university education followed by a period in a Guards regiment and then, disappointing his family, he joined a travelling circus. He baled out when playing in a town near to Birmingham and at the time we met, was working for the Smethwick Treasurer's Department.

Hearing that I was a humble British Railways clerk shocked him. He urged me to take a course and seek entry into the Institute of Secretaries. He was quite serious and undertook to assist me in my studies. I was heavily involved and had too few hours to study, and as on many other occasions, I passed up the opportunity.

That night over coffee we were discussing the defeat of fascism. He said quite casually, 'I can't believe you've fallen for the crap the Establishment is feeding out to the rest of the plebs.'

He went into some detail about Nazi scientists, some high-ranking SS officers and members of the German aristocracy who, all members of the Party, had been allowed, even assisted to escape by the Allies. Some went to France, Switzerland, America, Britain and even to the USSR.

It was hard to believe, but he was quoting it chapter and verse. In the last few years it has been revealed that the American CIA, in its paranoid battle against communism, along with other Allied countries, assisted the Nazi 'Odessa' under-ground movement in getting high-ranking members and their loot out of Europe.

'If what you are saying is true, shouldn't we be doing something about it?' I asked.

Before we parted that night we decided to start the Birmingham Movement Against Nazi Resurgence. We booked a room at the Arden Hotel in New Street and advertised the meeting, having no idea if anyone would appear.

As it turned out the room wasn't big enough to hold those who did. A number of Jewish business and professional men were in the audience; among them Josh Horn, the senior surgeon and Simon Sevitt, the pathologist, both of the Birmingham Accident Hospital.

They were to become deeply involved, suggesting that we should write to various bodies who might be sympathetic to our cause, and to offer to send a speaker. They volunteered their services. It wasn't until I called in at one of the meetings which Josh was addressing that I began to suspect that he and Simon were card-carrying communists. It was the things that Josh was dropping into his speech that made me aware that it might be the case. Challenging him after the meeting, he admitted it to be a fact.

Both of them were fun to be with, and I thoroughly enjoyed being in their company, and though we remained friends it was clear that they were using the movement for the Party. There was a mitigating circumstance; they were both Jews.

As with so many organisations set up to try to alter wrong into right, the members of the Movement Against Nazi Resurgence drifted away. Later, I am sad to say, Josh took his wife and children to China where he set up an accident hospital in what was then known as Peking. He began to lose his sight and died in China a broken man.

Roy MacGregor-Hastie took up with a beautiful girl he had met at university. They rented an apartment in Hall Green on the outskirts of the city and he became Labour's parliamentary candidate. The constituency was, and I believe still is, a solid Conservative seat. Roy went down with tuberculosis and left the area without leaving a forwarding address. The postman delivered to my home two large parcels with a note from Roy asking me to keep them for him, and would I be good enough to pay the postage.

He reappeared about three years later, unannounced. I gave him the parcels, which he had forgotten, and on opening them he found that one contained a pile of soiled laundry and the other past issues of *The Tribune*. He dumped the lot in the bin.

Roy explained his hasty departure from the city. Having developed tuberculosis, he left his girl and Hall Green and headed for the dry climate of Spain. Somehow he introduced himself to people close to Generalissimo Franco, and such was his personality that he gained access to the dictator. It helped him write a book about his life and times. He also wrote a book of verse with a foreword by the British Ambassador to Spain.

Back in Britain he was editing and acting as commentator on a magazine-type programme made for American television audiences. He also became a joint producer of the successful programme, *This Week* for ITV, He had become quite prosperous. Without a word of farewell, he was to disappear from my life yet again.

Some years on I was half listening to a Sunday morning weekly religious programme hosted by the Canadian broadcaster, Stanley Maxted. He became famous when he was dropped with the Paratroop Brigade on its ill-fated attempt to capture Nijmegen Bridge.

Maxted introduced his guest for the day. 'I have with me,' he said, 'a world traveller, a syndicated columnist and broadcaster who has written many books, among them the life of Pope Paul. He has lived in Spain, Russia and Italy, and is a devout Christian. May I introduce Mr Hastie – which he pronounced "Hasty".'

The penny didn't drop until I heard that lisp. I gasped, to those who were listening with me, *Devout Christian be buggered*! I couldn't believe my ears! My outburst was justified because some months before I had received a call from a lady with a foreign accent saying that she was Olga MacGregor-Hastie, phoning from New Street Station. She asked if I could collect her and hung up.

I met this petite, olive-skinned brunette standing outside the station with a trunk, a number of suitcases and a small blond-haired boy. Introducing myself, I asked how she had come to call me. Roy had dropped them off in New Street Station on his way to Hull, where he was to take up a post at the university. He had left her with instructions to contact me. She said that he wanted her and their son to settle in Birmingham because he knew that his friend Frank would watch over them. The experience of the parcels he had left with me some years before came to mind.

They had no accommodation; so I booked them into a local hotel and within the next two days helped to find a suitable furnished apartment. Olga was highly qualified and, like her husband, a talented linguist. I was able to find her a post at a school in Moseley, not too far from the city centre.

Anxious to ascertain how Roy and Olga had met and the background to this bizarre situation, I took Olga and the boy out for an early dinner. Apparently Roy had worked for a number of newspapers and turned up in Moscow as a syndicated columnist. As such he had access to some of the highest in the land.

He became friendly with Kruschev, and drank and played billiards with him in his dacha; this was before Kruschev became Secretary of the Party. With a talent for holding his liquor, Roy became quite popular with the Moscow apparatchiks and was allowed to travel widely.

During his stay he wrote a number of books. His *Don't Send Me to Omsk* sold quite well. Olga said that when the time came for Roy to leave his Moscow post the press corps took him on a week-long binge and poured him into an empty compartment on a train bound for Paris. They drew the curtains, closed the door and left him to his fate.

Olga boarded the then crowded train in Berlin. A porter carrying her luggage opened the darkened compartment. She said the smell emanating from it was no doubt the reason why it had stayed empty. Empty, that is, apart from a very sick Roy. She held on to the porter, who by this time had dropped the luggage and was about to beat a hasty retreat, and offered him a healthy tip to get a doctor. She opened the windows, closed the door and stood outside waiting for the medic. His prognosis was not good.

By the time they reached Paris, she had cleaned up both Roy and the compartment and with the help of the kitchen staff on the train had fed and watered him. She decided to take him on to her father's vineyard in the then depressed rural heartland of north-west Italy.

With the sun, fresh mountain air and tender care from Olga, he recovered. Had Olga decided to close the compartment door and do what the other passengers had done, Roy would most probably not have survived. Knowing this, he decided to stay in this rural backwater. He concentrated on writing and soon became emotionally and politically involved with his peasant neighbours.

Realising that the area had been denuded of its youth and that the local communities were by then in desperate straits with no idea on how to reverse the process, Roy set out to become their saviour – whether they liked it or not. To placate her parents, who couldn't quite understand this motivated blond foreigner their daughter had wished on them, she married him.

Annoyed by the authorities' lack of concern for the locals, Roy began a lone crusade, writing articles for the regional and national press, drawing attention to the plight of the region and its citizens, underscoring it with vitriolic attacks on the Government of the Province and the powerful local religious leaders.

By organising the reluctant peasant vineyard owners into forming an agricultural cooperative, begging or borrowing modern agricultural machinery and equipment, and getting the suppliers to teach the peasants how to use and maintain it, he began to improve the economy of the district. Through his press articles he nagged the Provincial Government into improving the roads.

In turn, tiring of his attacks the authorities hauled him into court on a charge of 'writing articles likely to provoke public disorder'. Representing himself, he notified the national media and before them pounded the authorities' case into the ground. With nationwide media coverage of his win, he boosted his position with the local peasantry. Having fought the recalcitrant farmers, town halls and the Church, in the end he received the blessings of all three.

The roads were improved, they built a clinic in the village, they funded and opened an Agricultural Technical College and helped him develop a thriving tourist industry. Before he left the area, Roy MacGregor-Hastie was awarded the European Citation by the Lane Bryant International Volunteer Award Committee and won the Christian Herter Prize. As I say, he was a character.

The last time Roy and I met was in the Reform Club. Over lunch, he told me that whilst in Paris many years before, he had tripped over a drunk who was lying on the pavement. The fellow was in a pretty bad way, and remembering the help he had received, Roy got him to his feet and took him back to his lodgings. It turned out to be the Romanian poet, philosopher and close friend of Picasso, Tristan Tzara.

Roy and he became close friends, and Roy translated the Romanian's work into English. Tzara died in 1964. Having been so taken with the man, Roy approached his publisher to see if they would commission him to write a book about him. They suggested that they and he would be better served if he wrote a book based on the information he had garnered from Tzara about his close friendship with Picasso.

Twenty-four years after Tzara's death, Roy published his book *Picasso's Women*, and in dedicating it to Tzara wrote of him:

> Poet, troublemaker, founder of Dadaism and inspiration of much else, who was my guide, philosopher and friend. He encouraged me for a quarter of a century to wrestle with UNESCO. He was an almost bottomless pit from which I mined Picasso tales, long before I thought of writing this book.

Like many nonconformist people on the political left, Roy attracted the attention of Lord Beaverbrook. According to his version of the event, he received an invitation to visit the press baron at his country home. He informed the secretary of the time his train would arrive, expecting to be met at the station. He was unlucky and had to make his own way to house. As he was walking up the drive he saw His Lordship in the gardens some distance away.

Reaching the main door, he was greeted by Lady Beaverbrook, who took him into a large room where they stood looking through the window. They could see Beaverbrook relieving himself.

Lady Beaverbrook said, 'It's his birthday and he hates it so, he's out there pissing on his birthday cake.'

Before we parted, Roy, then the Professor of Languages at the Osaka University in Japan, told me of his marriage to a local girl and of the three daughters he had sired. He said they doted on him. His in-laws, it seemed, didn't share their enthusiasm for this behaviour, which for him was 'par for the course'.

Olga Hastie moved from Birmingham to teach at a private girls' school in Lichfield and then to another in the south-east. I lost track of her.

MacGregor-Hastie was – I say *was*, because I haven't heard from him during the last ten years – a character. He appeared not to care for anyone but himself and yet he went to great lengths to help many people with whom he had little in common. Although he failed to keep in touch with those who became his friends and lovers – which gave some a reason to think him selfish and uncaring – I know of no one who wished that he had not crossed their path.

Chapter VIII

ONWARDS AND UPWARDS

In May 1952 I won a second term. The Labour Party had already regained control of the city council but with a small majority. The Group elected me to be an officer; a Junior Whip, the lowest post on offer. I was soon to be knocked off this bottom rung of the ladder for telling the public what they needed to know and later to go up a few more rungs for the same reason.

Bernard Watson, a qualified chartered surveyor, was appointed chairman of the Public Works Committee, of which I was still the youngest member. Bernard rarely mixed with his colleagues and possessed a rather dour personality; nevertheless he was quite popular. He was also extremely efficient.

Having a paper-thin majority made it difficult for any chairman. The Public Works Committee, with its multifarious responsibilities, was no sinecure and Bernard needed support more than most of the other chairmen. He required his party members to be in their seats at the beginning and at the end of every meeting.

There were some who considered that this was not always necessary, and as the new Junior Whip I had the job of remonstrating with recalcitrant long-serving older colleagues. Being also junior in age, I was bound to upset a few. Coupled with the fact that I was considered to be 'middle of the road' by the left of the Party, my future wasn't too secure.

While speaking at a public meeting just before the 1953 municipal elections, I was asked my view on the desperate housing situation. I outlined the problems facing the council: the shortage of land, the need to rehouse more than 35,000 families from the slums in addition to the 60,000 families already on the housing waiting list, the shortage of land and the refusal of Whitehall to commission a New Town in the West Midlands.

The fact was that we were faced with an almost insoluble situation.

Asked what I would do in the circumstances, I replied, 'My personal opinion is that the city council should let people know that they don't stand a cat in hell's chance of getting a home in the city unless the government changes its policy and allows us to expand our boundaries. At least it may stop people making their way here hoping to get a house as well as a job.'

My comments were widely reported in the local press.

Although we had gained more seats, at the annual meeting of the Labour Group, Councillor Ted Haynes, a left wing organiser of the then communist-controlled Electrical Trade Union, supported by other members on the left of the Party, complained about the speech suggesting that it could have jeopardised the Party's chances at the election.

I decided to put my neck on the block by informing the Group, 'If telling the people the way it is – I mean, telling them the truth – is considered a crime against this Party, then I should tell you that I will continue to be a criminal.' The left-wingers, joined by those I had upset when hustling them into attending their committee meetings, voted me out of my junior office.

At the time I was attracting a great deal of media attention and dismissal from this lowly post was treated as something of importance. It was mentioned the following morning on radio's *Midland News*.

My dear mother, always concerned for her son's future, heard the broadcast. She was waiting for me as I turned in for work. Very worried, she asked whether the Party had sacked me from the council. I took her to a local café and over a cup of tea explained that I had just been knocked off the first rung of the ladder.

Without altering my approach of 'saying it as it was', the following year the Group elevated me to a much higher station, a Group Officer no less. Soon after, I would become deputy leader and later be its leader.

On regaining control, Councillor Len Chaffey, an intelligent, gentle man from South Wales, had been selected to Chair the Parks Committee. He asked me to head one of the sub committees. I grabbed at the chance of gaining the experience even though it was only the chairmanship of the Cemeteries and Crematoria sub committee.

In 1952, there were not many young members on the council, and at thirty years of age, being the chairman of the committee which dealt with the end product, as it were, was thought to be a bit of a joke. Of course I had to put up with comments such as, 'How are you handling the burning question?' and 'Don't get too buried in the subject.'

I absorbed all the banter. Having lost the opportunity to attend Ruskin College, Oxford, I decided to absorb as much knowledge on any and every subject that came my way. I made up my mind to use the city council as my university, and this minor chairmanship was a stepping stone.

I concentrated on the burning question and buried myself in the subject and was soon to discover just how interesting it all was. I *was* appalled at the cost of running the cemeteries, the air of desolation in parts of these walled estates, and the amount of land these repositories for our departed citizens absorbed in a city short of land for the living.

Before I gave up the job we had turned many of them into garden cemeteries and with the help of my new-found friend, Roy MacGregor-Hastie, saved the city a considerable amount of money.

Soon after my appointment, Colonel George Ross, the popular general manager of the Parks Department, informed me that the town clerk had been negotiating with his opposite number in Smethwick, an adjoining small town. They had offered to pass on to the city a large tract of land next to our Quinton cemetery for the sum of one pound. It was then that I realised how important to a budding politician was the word 'why'?

Asking the question, Ross told me that the town clerk had agreed that, as a quid pro quo, from the date of the agreement we would undertake to accept the internment of Smethwick's expired citizens. He was of the opinion that we were on to a good thing and went on to tell me that the two town clerks had already drawn up the deeds ready for me to sign.

I called my friend, Roy, who was at that time still working in

Smethwick's Treasurers Department, to find out the town's average annual internments, and how much burial land they had left. I don't think that anyone had taken notice of the annual cost to the city of burying its dead. It was this proposal that made *me* look into it. I found that that taking into account the overall costs of maintaining the cemeteries, every burial was subsidised to the tune of £10 or more, and costs were rising.

Roy's information was interesting. Simply by multiplying Smethwick's annual burial rate by the subsidy we paid, I realised that the town clerk of this small authority was outwitting his opposite number. Added to this was the fact that they were running out of land. I informed our town clerk that I wasn't prepared to sign the agreement.

Still under the impression that this young uneducated socialist had difficulty in understanding who was really in charge, he went on with the arrangements for the signing ceremony. He just didn't know me.

At the meeting, the leader of Smethwick Council headed his delegation. I waited for the end of the our town clerk's preamble before announcing that there was no way I would sign on behalf of Birmingham and spelt out my reasons. The town clerk intervened, saying that he had drawn up the agreement, that it was acceptable to Smethwick and that he would be recommending it to the city council.

Ignoring him, I looked across the table at the leader of the Smethwick Council and asked, 'If the boot was on the other foot, how would you explain to your ratepayers, that on their behalf you had taken a piece of land in exchange for services to be rendered, which would cost them thousands of pounds annually, in perpetuity?'

The look on his face made it obvious that he knew the score. He replied slowly that he wouldn't be able to sell it to his council, let alone the electorate.

He was an honest politician. I thanked him and at the conclusion of the meeting took him to one side. I sympathised with his council's position and agreed that we would offer them a fair price for their land and undertake to accept burials, on the understanding that Birmingham would not bear the subsidy. We shook hands on it and so it came to be.

Through this minor incident the Parks general manager began to realise, as many more would, that I took my responsibilities as a councillor very seriously. My relationship with the town clerk didn't improve.

In respect of 'the burning question', I mugged up on cremation and found that it was a Welsh doctor by the name of Price who, as there were no facilities available had followed his beliefs by cremating his son's body on the top of a Welsh mountain. It was against the law but it opened up the question of cremation as against burial. Having in my line of duty walked around our cemeteries, I became a convert to his cause.

We had two crematoria and as the chairman of the committee I accepted an invitation to the annual conference of the Cremation Society. It was held in the seaside resort of Margate, where I was to meet Lord Horder, the President of the Society.

He had been one of King George V's physicians and was in the Chair when I was called upon to speak. He must have been reasonably impressed because he invited me to have dinner with him that night. Colonel Ross was also impressed, not by the speech; more the fact that Lord Horder had invited me to dine with him.

He hadn't bothered to change for dinner, which surprised me; he was still wearing his morning coat and striped trousers, flannel shirt and starched wing collar. He must have been in his eighties but still as bright as a button.

During the meal he quizzed me on my background. Having been given a short version, he asked whether it was that that had made me into a bit of a rebel. Replying, I said that if not being happy with the social system and wishing to correct the imbalance made me a rebel then I would plead guilty.

He smiled and told me that he was considered to be something of a rebel too. 'I do so hate being told what I should or should not do,' he said. He instanced this by saying that a hospital where he had been a consultant for many years, decided, without referring to the staff or him and his fellow consultants, to put up signs instructing them on how they should drive into the grounds. 'They placed IN and OUT signs on the gates. I ignore them, of course.'

I thought, but didn't say, *I'm not that sort of a rebel.*

I was suffering with a boil on the back of my neck and was, and must have appeared to be, uncomfortable. Although he was getting on in years Horder had noticed my discomfort. Before we parted he asked if I usually suffered with boils. I told him that it was the case and asked if he had any advice.

With a twinkle in his eyes he told me, 'My boy, even if we were in Harley Street at this moment, I think my fee would be too much for you. Being here in Margate, miles from my consulting rooms, I *know* it would.'

Two weeks after the conference I received a parcel from the Park Royal office of the Guinness company. It contained a box of fresh brewer's yeast with a note saying that it had been sent at the request of 'Your Physician, Lord Horder'.

The Conference was an education in many ways. I was sitting at the bar in the dimly lit cocktail lounge quite late, when the fellow next to me asked whether I was in the business.

'Cremation, you mean?' I asked.

Before I could tell him that I was just a chairman of a public facility, he said, 'It's diabolical what we charge, you know. Sometimes I feel quite ashamed.'

I could tell that he had taken a few drinks but, intrigued, I asked him to elaborate.

'Well, it's what we charge for the urns and the rent for the alcoves, the plaques, the dedication signs beneath trees and bushes and every other bloody thing... Don't you?' he enquired.

I replied, 'No, as a matter of fact we don't, but if people are prepared to pay maybe we should.'

He sat quiet for a moment and then turning to me said, 'Christ, what kind of a business are you running?' Then he added, 'Hold on, you are the chap who spoke yesterday. You run a municipal crematorium – you're letting the side down, you know.'

'Yes,' I replied, 'that may be, but I'm not sitting here feeling ashamed.'

He grunted and bought me a drink out of his profits.

Most of my colleagues were under the impression that my

position as chairman of the cemeteries and crematoria sub committee was the most boring and uninteresting job on the council. They were so wrong. Like them I thought that those in the undertaking business were a sombre and depressing lot, but that was before I attended my first Undertakers' Ball.

It was a perk which came with the job. An envelope, not black-edged, I noted, dropped through my letter box containing an invitation to their annual jamboree, which they held in the attractive surroundings of the Botanical Gardens Banqueting Suite in Edgbaston.

My inclination was to decline, but Colonel Ross rang to say that the chairman of the full committee would not be attending and as it was customary for the council's representative to reply to the main toast, he trusted that I would be there. I was glad I was.

The first surprise was to see some of the members of the undertaking profession arriving with their wives and friends in the cars normally reserved for mourners. The next was the sumptuous meal laid before them and their guests, followed by after-dinner speakers whose patter would have gone down well from the stage of the London Palladium.

They had booked one of Britain's premier dance orchestras so that there would be no doubt that the dancing which followed would go on well into the early hours and would be enjoyed by the most fastidious among them. For me, the Undertakers' Ball turned out to be the best 'do' of the year.

Although most, if not all, would never have supported my political views, they always showed me the greatest respect, even when I took issue with them over the charges made for their services. In my efforts to create garden cemeteries, we clashed. It meant reducing the size and shape of headstones and forbidding kerbstones. They said that I 'was taking bread out of their mouths'.

I had to underline the costs of maintaining the cemeteries which I was trying hard to reduce. I thought that as ratepayers they would applaud my efforts but they were not impressed. My claim that it would beautify the places to which they were regular visitors left them as cold as those they took with them.

Our meetings were always good-tempered but I left them under no illusion that we were also in the business of serving the community, and that what I had put forward would not ruin them as they suggested. *Garden cemeteries there will be* was my last word.

I reluctantly gave up the chairmanship of this absorbing committee in order to concentrate on the unexpected challenge with which I had been presented by the leader of my party.

Chapter IX

THE BIG CHALLENGE

The 1947 Town and Country Planning Act placed a heavy burden on local authorities. Its aim was to bring some order to the chaos of land use planning in Britain. Local authorities had the responsibility of preparing plans which would then be subjected to public inquiries and finally government approval. This mammoth task was passed to the Public Works Committee.

The Labour Party had regained control of Birmingham city council with a small majority and Councillor Bernard Watson, a chartered surveyor, was elected to Chair the Public Works Committee. Just seventeen months later, his tenure of office was to be tragically cut short. Returning home one night he found his young wife lying by their bed in a pool of blood; she died on the way to hospital. The effect on him was devastating. He resigned from the council and shortly afterwards left the city.

With a small majority in mid-term, losing a valuable chairman of a main and at the time the most important council committee, created a difficulty. The other members were already overburdened and the leader, Alderman Bradbeer – who had been knighted by this time – called me into his office at the council house.

He surprised me by asking whether I felt capable of handling the post vacated by Bernard Watson. I couldn't believe that I was the first he had approached but didn't want to embarrass him by asking. It was one hell of a challenge but an opportunity too good to miss. I agreed to do my best and waited anxiously for the next meeting of the committee.

With our small majority and the loss of Bernard, we needed our members to be on parade when I was nominated. They were not. The Conservatives pounced on the chance and nominated Councillor Albert Shaw, the owner of a local plumbing, heating and engineering company. This was carried and he took the chair.

At the following meeting, Bradbeer, with the help of the Whips, made sure that we were at full strength. Shaw was voted out and I took over. Albert was a nice fellow and took it all in good part.

Since told that I was to be appointed, I swatted up Sir Walter Citrine's book on chairmanship, the best of its kind on nuances of mastering the art of controlling a committee. It proved to be a blessing, giving me the confidence to handle any minor skirmishes that might break out from time to time.

At the conclusion of my first meeting in the Chair, Sir Herbert Manzoni guided me into the chairman's office, which led off the committee room. It was the first time I had seen it. He congratulated me on my elevation. I looked at him saying, 'Sir Herbert, it's nice of you, but you and I know that the committee has had, until today, a chairman chosen from the elite, and here you are, with a wet behind the ears nobody who has no sway with the council. You can't be too happy about it.' I then asked if he had an hour to spare.

We walked down the steps of Baskerville House, the head-quarters of the Public Works Department, to a vintage Daimler and an equally vintage uniformed chauffeur. Manzoni introduced Mr Bayliss, explaining to me that this was the chairman's car – something else of which I was unaware. I directed Mr Bayliss to Court 13, Great Russell Street. He didn't try to hide his feelings; it was obvious that I didn't quite fit his idea of a chairman.

Standing in the middle of the backyard where I was born, surrounded by tightly packed slum dwellings, outside lavatories, wash houses and miskins, I raised my arm and gestured to the City Surveyor.

'Sir Herbert, you may not realise it, but you are now standing on my university campus.'

I paused, hoping for a response. I think he was too confused to speak. I went on, 'This is where I earned my degrees in philosophy and psychology.' He looked puzzled. 'Sir Herbert, think about it. To survive in these conditions and to still have the hope and aspirations that burn in me, I needed to be a philosopher. As to psychology,' I continued, 'living so close to people for the greater part of my life, I became schooled in knowing and understanding what was going on in their heads before *they* had even figured it out.'

Taking a deep breath, I continued, 'You see, I know my colleagues believe that come May they will dump me. Not because they are vicious but because they don't really know me, and if I may say, nor do you.' He didn't move to interrupt my flow. 'I know that you need someone in the Chair who commands the respect of the council, and that until now the position has been filled by a long-serving established member who has been able to do this. But, Sir Herbert, let me tell you now that whether you believe it or not, I know that with your help I will be the best bloody chairman the Public Works Committee has ever had. But make no mistake, if needs be, I will be so without it.' I then added softly, 'But it will take me a little longer.'

Looking back, it really was outrageous, but I needed to put my marker down.

No words were exchanged as we left Court 13. He waited for me to get into the car but I said, 'You carry on, I belong here.'

I had questioned older members about Sir Herbert and had watched his demeanour in committee. As a new member I had been helped by him but circumstances had changed; I wasn't sure how we would get on together.

His Italian father had been a sculptor who sailed to England to escape persecution. Landing in Liverpool with his young family he settled near Ellesmere Port, where the young Manzoni grew up and trained to be an engineer. He applied for a job in Birmingham's Public Works Department and soon realised that his destiny was tied up with its future.

In 'The Settlement' – a social centre housed in an old converted vicarage at the corner of Tower Street and Summer Lane, a few blocks from my boyhood home, was a youth club of which my brother, Eric, was a member. He came home one night to tell us of this young civil engineer with a foreign-sounding name who had come to give a 'talk' to the club.

Eric bubbled over with admiration for this fellow, who had spoken of his ideas of clearing the slums, of bringing light and fresh air into the dark corners. Of building a brighter, nicer city which would make all its people proud to be its citizens. That young engineer was Manzoni. It was a long time before he occupied the top job, and twenty-five years before I joined him to help make those dreams come true.

At the end of the 1939–45 war, like so many cities Birmingham was faced with the massive problem of clearing the bomb sites and getting rid of its jungle of overcrowded, dilapidated and unsanitary Dickensian dwellings. Guided by Manzoni, we embarked on the most comprehensive slum clearance and redevelopment programme in the country.

Without his vision, drive and love of his adopted city I doubt whether the council would have started out on this gigantic project. I am not sure how many members of the city council, to say nothing of its citizens then or now, are aware of the debt owed to that man.

It's hard to believe that when his name was proposed to succeed Herbert Humphries, the retiring chief engineer and Surveyor, Humphries warned the committee, 'If you decide to give Manzoni the job, the city will come to a standstill within a month.'

By ignoring that piece of gratuitous advice they did the city a great service.

To embark on the mammoth task of clearing away thousands of occupied slum properties was courageous to say the least. It was to be the biggest comprehensive redevelopment programme ever staged in Great Britain. Faced with a shortage of land to house the thousands already on the waiting list and having to build homes for the 30,000 or more families in order to demolish the slum properties they occupied was enough to deter the bravest among us, but not a voice was raised against going ahead with Manzoni's plans.

In addition to being the finest engineer in the country, Sir Herbert had style.

He was admired international for his ability and his charm. After what must have appeared to him to be a shaky start, I believe that before my term as his chairman was over we had built up a mutual respect and friendship, although we never addressed each other by our given names until the day he retired. I was taken aback hearing him say, 'Frank, I would like you to come to my home for dinner.'

It was some years after I had resigned from his committee and I was the only guest. Over coffee, Lady Manzoni told me that when he got home after his visit to Court 13, Great Russell Street on the day I became his chairman, he repeated what I had said to him. She said, 'I told Bert, you hang on to that young man's coat tails, because I have a feeling that he will help you to realise your dream of changing the face of Birmingham.'

I was quite moved and have never forgotten it; and she was right, we did.

I remember the day we had a visit from an American Senator who had heard of what we were doing. When he enquired as to how we were getting control of these vast tracts of land and the properties that stood on them I described the procedure. Namely, we placed an advert in the local papers spelling out the boundaries and that it was in law a notice to treat. We took over and sorted out the compensation with the district Valuer at a later date.

'Good God!' he exclaimed. 'That's unadulterated communism.'

'Yes,' I agreed, 'and it works.'

Manzoni taught me a lot about planning. He was a diplomat, but I must admit in that direction I proved to be a very poor student. But I must return back to the beginning of my role as the chairman of what he called 'his committee'.

My first few meetings went so well that I began to feel that I had grasped the details and gained the respect of the members. That was until the day it blew up in my face. Suddenly, a fierce argument broke out between the two party leaders who, facing each other across the committee table and ignoring the chairman, were exchanging strong words, culminating in Sir Albert Bradbeer saying, 'I warn you, if necessary I will use the mailed fist!' I had lost control of the committee.

Sir Albert's remarks spurred me into action. I stood up and slammed my fist on the table. The startled members stared at me in disbelief. I said in as quiet a tone as I could muster, 'If it ever becomes necessary for anyone to use the mailed fist in this committee, it will be me. I think that you had better understand that now. This meeting will stand adjourned for fifteen minutes.' With that I left the room.

A minute later, Sir Herbert tapped on the door of the

chairman's room and, closing it behind him, held out his hand. 'Forgive me, but can I *now* congratulate you, *Mr Chairman*.' And with a smile he ducked out.

I sat for a while thinking that my days would soon be numbered, but although the council's standing orders laid down that a committee chair could only be occupied for three successive years without a special resolution of the council, I was to be re-elected for a further six years and could have stayed on, had I so wished.

Other than the preparation of the city development plan – the planning and redevelopment of the five designated areas – we had a major traffic problem. Twenty years before I was elected, the city council had submitted to the government a plan to construct an inner ring road. It was just one part of an overall plan to construct three ring roads: an inner, intermediate and outer ring featuring limited access double carriageway roads with three lanes in either direction.

They were to be linked to the thirteen main roads already leading into the city. We aimed to make them limited access arterial roads leading from the city boundary to the centre like spokes on a wheel. They were planned so that traffic could go around the city instead of having to go through its centre. Had we been able to achieve it, along with the other ideas we put forward, Birmingham would have no traffic problem today.

Central Government control and the overbearing interference from Whitehall kept our city – and no doubt others – from adequately dealing with its problems. Over the years there had been numerous visits to the Ministry of Transport to obtain approval to make a start on the inner ring road, but no permission had been granted.

As an interim measure, in order to avoid the centre being completely snarled up, Manzoni designed and activated a one-way traffic system, the first of its kind in the country. It was simple enough when one got used to it. Based on the principle of interlinked cogs, the system kept the traffic moving.

However, not being familiar with the system, visitors found it difficult. So much so that it became a music hall joke. 'Driving into Birmingham I was stuck in their one-way street system for two days and nights. I asked a local, "How do I get to Coventry?" He said, "Yo cor get ta Coventry from here, mate."'

Traffic engineering was common enough on the Continent and in the United States but hardly understood in Britain. In the Fifties *The Daily Telegraph* commissioned an American traffic engineer to examine and write about the increasing problems created by traffic in Britain's major cities.

He came to Birmingham and in the course of his investigation interviewed me. He outlined his remit and asked, 'In the light of the failure to obtain permission to embark on your road schemes, how are you dealing with the traffic?'

With a plan in front of me, I explained the one-way system.

'How long has this been operating?' he asked.

When I told him that it had been working since before the war he gasped, 'Are you telling me that this traffic control system has been in operation for ten or more years?'

When I answered in the affirmative, he cried out, 'But that's traffic engineering, man!'

I replied quietly, 'Yes, I know.'

When I first joined the committee, the Minister of Transport was Lennox-Boyd, a cheerful fellow who, being a member of the Guinness family, had a lot to be cheerful about. The town clerk organised a delegation to visit him to plead, yet again, for permission to start building our inner ring road.

On the return journey the members of the delegation all commented on how pleasant the meeting had been. As we were going home, not for the first time empty-handed, their attitude was puzzling to say the least.

Shortly afterwards, Mr Boyd-Carpenter replaced Lennox-Boyd, so another visit was arranged. The gain, if it could be described as such, was that he had agreed to pay us a visit. His short time with us was again described as pleasant but we still had no idea *if*, let alone *when*, we would get permission to build the road. In the meantime, our peak-hour traffic jams were getting worse.

I asked Manzoni, 'Why the hell does a city the size of Birmingham have to toady to Whitehall?'

'Seventy per cent grant towards the cost,' was his reply.

I suggested that had the city ignored this and floated a loan twenty years before, the work could have been completed for a great deal less than the thirty per cent that we would be faced with once we got a start.

'I wouldn't argue with that,' he sighed.

Eighteen months after my election to the Chair, in control of the biggest redevelopment scheme in Britain and a multimillion pound budget, I was still working as a British Railway clerk on a pitifully low salary. With my wife working and a mortgage to pay, I was having second thoughts about the wisdom of my continuing in public service.

Just in time, Councillor Doris (now Baroness) Fisher, one of my more caring colleagues, drew my attention to an advert in the local press. The Birmingham Co-operative Society was setting up a new section, a hire purchase department, and wanted to engage a supervisor. It stated that he or she must have some accounts experience and knowledge of hire purchase law. The salary offered was attractive.

Although, thanks to the BR accountant, I had a little experience in the former, I had none in respect of the latter. Nevertheless, I applied for the job. I called to see Harry Parkinson, the jovial deputy town clerk. Outlining the job and the fact that I knew nothing of hire purchase law, I asked if he knew of a lawyer who did. He put me in touch with Glaisyer, Porter and Mason making an appointment for me see the senior partner, Mr Glaisyer, in his Colmore Row office.

I explained my predicament, that I was totally ignorant on the subject of the law on hire purchase, and asked if he could help me.

'You expect me to educate you on hire purchase law?' he almost shouted.

My quickly mentioning that I intended to pay for his service only made matters worse. He picked up the phone and called Harry, demanding to know what he meant by sending me to see him.

I had had a very rough time both physically and financially since entering the council, and of the two officials who knew and sympathised, Harry Parkinson was one. I guessed that he did a bit

141

of special pleading on my behalf, for as Glaisyer put down the phone, he agreed to spend an hour with me every night after office hours until he was confident that I was capable of putting up a show.

During our meetings he began to warm to me. He was a staunch Tory of the old school, but when the time came for my interview and I asked him for the bill, he just smiled and patted me on the back, saying, 'Have this on me, and good luck to you, my lad.'

I had been told that the son of the President of the Society was in for the job, so I wasn't at all sanguine about my prospects; but I hadn't counted on the quality of Mr Glaisyer's tuition.

Having sailed through the interview so far, the President, reading from a prepared list, asked a question on a particular section of the law covering hire purchase. I answered and he looked at me. Taking off his glasses he told me that I was very much mistaken.

I asked him if he would be kind enough to repeat the question. When he read it out again I said, 'With respect, sir, I believe that my answer was quite correct.'

I was able to tell him and the interviewing panel that the section he had referred to had been overtaken by what was known as the Helen Wilkinson amendment. During an awkward silence whilst I was saying a prayer of thanks for Mr Glaisyer, the Secretary of the Society proceeded to consult his law books. With every head turned towards him, he looked up to tell the President, 'I'm afraid Mr Price is quite right, the law was amended has he says.'

Afraid, I thought, *what a bloody nerve!* After that they couldn't turn me down.

Two weeks later I reported to the departmental manager, who I suspect was rather relieved that it was me and not the President's son. He showed me my office and told me where I was to collect the car that went with the job. I had to tell him that I couldn't drive a car. Answering the question on the application form which asked, 'Can you drive?' I had indicated, yes. I owned a motorbike. He picked up the phone, called the Co-op's garage manager, saying, 'Joe, I've got a problem, I need you to teach my new supervisor to drive a car, and bloody quick.'

He directed me to the garage in Duddeston where I was introduced to one of the funeral department's drivers. In between attending to his normal duties, he spent every other working hour and some of his own time on teaching me to drive. I passed my test and was handed a new Morris Minor.

My standard of living was improved, and the Society, particularly the head of the department, was very kind to me. Although the policy was one of allowing elected members time off to attend to their council duties, I tried to repay them by working late, and on many weekends to help make up for the time I lost. I helped to built up the hire purchase section and when I left, regretfully, four and a half years later, it was one of the most successful departments in the Society.

Chapter X

ROAD RAGE

The traffic snarl-ups in the city were increasing and drivers were getting angrier with each other and with the council. They blamed us for not being able to deal with the problem, having little sympathy even when we pointed out that the answer lay with Whitehall.

The numbers of cars on the roads was growing daily, and as the main arterial roads were grant-aided, Whitehall controlled which, where and how they would be improved. The Ministry of Transport was, and in too many other respects still is, too slow to react to the obvious. When they did, many of their efforts were totally inadequate.

Successive ministers, through ignorance or arrogance or both, didn't seem to see the need to grasp and deal with an escalating problem of traffic management. As long as Whitehall insists that they control the way money for urban roads is raised and allocated, local authorities will be left with problems. Ministers act on the advice of their officials, who are no better, and in too many cases far worse, than those who are employed by the larger cities.

Birmingham city council and the business community continued to press the government to allow the city to get on with its highway and off-street parking plans but this was ignored. One of the things that bugged me was the manner in which they dealt with our visits to the Ministry headquarters.

The officials on both sides were always courteous but we were getting nowhere. It became patently obvious to me that each time a delegation visited the Ministry, the Whitehall civil service were ever so politely, kicking us into the long grass.

When Harold Watkinson became the new minister, I suggested that we arrange to see him. The make up of our party was as usual: the town clerk (protocol meant that he arranged meetings with Whitehall); the chairman of the general purposes committee, a fiery little Welshman named Tegfryn Bowen; the City Engineer Sir Bertram Waring, chairman of Joseph Lucas, who was also representing the Chamber of Commerce; and myself.

Bowen had served on the city council for many years and had been Lord Mayor. A long-serving Labour Party member, he had a powerful way with words. His command of the English language was such that at times few amongst those who he was addressing understood all the words he used, although we never gave him the satisfaction of knowing.

He was fearsome in debate and if provoked dipped his tongue in vitriol, lashing out at friend and foe alike. As chairman of the all-powerful general purposes committee, he laboured under the impression that he could treat the chairman of other main committees as if he was their superior, a kind of president of the council.

A compartment was reserved on the London-bound train and when we had settled in, the town clerk, as was his usual practice, outlined how we should proceed at the meeting with the minister. I had heard it all before. When he had finished I suggested that as we had followed this procedure so many times over the years without success, this time we should change our approach.

Bowen glared at me and with pointed sarcasm asked, 'And how, with your wide experience, would you propose we proceed?'

I let it pass and recommended that after we had gone through the usual formalities I be allowed to lead.

Bowen, who had little time for the younger members of the council, began to bristle. I waited for his verbal onslaught, but Sir Bertram Waring interjected, 'This is my third trip to the ministry on this matter and although they are always very pleasant, I'm bound to say I always come away feeling that it was a total waste of my time.' He added that if I was prepared to put the straight question – 'Will you or won't you?' – we should get a quick reply and could all get back to our business. Although it wasn't quite what I intended to do, Bowen and the rest agreed.

We were shown up to the first floor of the ministry and into a very large room with an enormous coffin-shaped conference table. We were directed to sit facing the windows. After a short period, the double doors opened and in walked the minister, his permanent secretary and numerous other civil servants.

Harold Watkinson, who rarely smiled, had the reputation of being a no nonsense minister who didn't suffer fools gladly. He took his seat, which happened to be directly opposite to, where I was seated, greeted the town clerk and Sir Herbert Manzoni, and nodded his head to the rest of us. Whilst coffee was being served he looked across at the town clerk, who introduced our team.

The minister then sat quietly sipping his coffee. The permanent secretary, who sat next to the minister, gestured to the town clerk expecting him, in time-honoured form, to make an opening statement. As nothing was forthcoming, the minister looked at Sir Herbert, who quickly reintroduced me.

Looking at Watkinson, I thanked him for seeing us and added, 'Minister, you must be aware that over the past twenty years the City of Birmingham has sent many delegations here, so I am sure that you have been well briefed. As much as it is to have the pleasure of meeting you, I don't want to waste too much of your valuable time going over old ground. Would you therefore give my colleagues and me a straight answer to this unambiguous question?'

Surprised, he nodded his head.

'Will you agree to arrange for my city to start work on its inner ring road during this financial year?'

Watkinson – now Lord Watkinson – whilst thanking me for my brevity, didn't take his eyes of me and replied, 'I will be equally brief, Councillor. The answer is no.'

The silence was such that it was almost embarrassing.

I had ascertained that the minister was to open a number of conferences to do with transport at which he would normally give a short address. The first one being an International Roads Congress to be held in London. Hearing his reply, I smiled and then took out a sheet of paper from my inside pocket and slipped it across the table.

'I expected your answer, sir, and appreciate you for being

frank.' Pointing to the paper which he had picked up I went on, 'Minister, you will see that it is a list of conferences that you have agreed to attend. I have also been invited, so I may be able take the matter up with you at one or the other.'

He glanced at the paper and glared at me, responding in a sharp but quiet tone, 'Councillor, that sounds very much like a threat.'

I replied equally softly, 'Yes, I suppose it does.'

He rose from his seat, thanked us for coming, and proceeded to leave – followed by a bewildered permanent secretary and assorted civil servants. My colleagues stood up in a state of shock.

Standing on the steps outside the ministry building, the town clerk turned to me, and said, 'Congratulations, Councillor. For many years the council have had a very good relationship with the ministry; you've just tossed it out of the window.'

With that he walked off to return to Birmingham alone, I presumed. I was in no doubt that he would spread his version of the meeting among members of the council. Sir Bertram Waring, who I suspect had little time for politicians, smiled and shook my hand.

The opening session of the International Roads Congress, the one I referred to, was to be chaired by Lord Derwent. There was no way that I could have got to meet him so I asked Manzoni if he could fix for us to have lunch with him before the conference opened. This he did.

During the meal, Derwent explained how frustrated he was that so little progress was being made to bring our road system up to date. He said he was embarrassed because most of the other countries in war-torn Europe who had sent representatives to the Congress, were, as he put it, 'steaming ahead'.

Agreeing with everything he said, I asked if the minister would be taking questions after he had officially opened the conference. Derwent said he thought it most likely.

'If he agrees,' I asked, 'would you be kind enough to call on me?'

Having just enjoyed luncheon on us, how could he refuse?

The minister made an outstanding address of welcome to this large international gathering, during which he told of the many plans his government had to improve traffic flow in Britain. After he sat down, Derwent announced that the minister had kindly agreed to take a few questions. I can still recall the astonished look on Harold Watkinson's face as I walked to the podium.

I thanked Lord Derwent, and then the minister, for graciously agreeing to answer questions. When I added, 'You really are on dangerous ground, Minister,' there was a roar of laughter and applause from the British delegates. I went on to tell the audience how pleased we all were to hear of the government's commitment to improve traffic flow. 'Minister, it will be music to the ears of industrialists in my city, because as I speak, traffic is grinding to a halt there and the cost to them is crippling.' I added, 'The problem is, minister, that they don't blame you, they blame *me*.' I turned to look up at him. 'I think that for a city which has rightly been described as the workshop of Britain, a twenty-year wait for permission to start work on its inner ring road is long enough. Don't you?'

My remarks brought a long round of applause.

The minister joked at my expense, saying that it was I who was on dangerous ground and didn't bother to answer my question. I admired him as a man and knew that he was just another prisoner of the system.

A short time after the Congress, whilst on the rostrum in the council chamber, placing my committee's monthly report to the members, I was handed a telegram. I read it, and handed it to Sir Herbert who was sitting behind and to the right of me. Looking back at him I swear he had a tear in his eye as well as a smile on his face.

The council having voted the approval to my report, I asked the Lord Mayor if I could read out the telegram I had just received. He asked if it was relevant to the city's affairs and I replied, 'Not half, sir – it is from the Minister of Transport.'

I read out the contents, announcing that we had, at long last, been given permission to start work on the first phase of the inner ring road. Order papers were waved in the air and the members stood up and cheered as I stepped down from the rostrum to leave the Chamber.

Outside, Sir Herbert clasped my hand. 'Congratulations

Mr Chairman, I'll never doubt your method of approach again,' he said, and went off with a spring in his step. Even so, I was to regret the fact that the Ministry of Transport, because they held the purse strings, gave cause for a number of fundamental mistakes to be made in the design of the road.

I wrote a personal note of thanks to the minister and expressed the hope that he would come to Birmingham to commemorate the start of the work. He kindly agreed and it turned out to be an event that those present would never forget. Even the Goons rewrote their radio script for the week that followed, based on 'the happening'.

The start of the road gave us an opportunity to improve the city's fortunes. Over the years the council had acquired most of the properties along the line of the road, renting them out on short leases awaiting the go ahead. After twenty or more years of little maintenance, the buildings could hardly be described as 'prime' so we began to clear away the properties in Smallbrook Street for the first phase.

Discussing the arrangements for the inauguration ceremony, it was suggested that we leave a wall standing for the minister to demolish as a symbolic gesture. A fellow in the Engineer's Department who had served as a demolition expert during the war was delegated to prepare a charge that would ensure that the wall was brought down neatly.

My department had agreed the day's proceedings with the Ministry, which included the minister pushing a plunger that would explode the charge and demolish the wall, signifying the beginning of the construction of the inner ring road. As the event was to be covered by the national media, I needed to be assured that the whole wall would come down. I had a chat with our expert, who made it clear that he shared my concern and was confident that there would be no foul-up.

On the day, an elevated stand covered with a gaily-coloured awning had been erected near to the corner of what was then called The Horse Fair. The minister arrived at the council house to join other VIPs for coffee, after which they moved in a procession of cars to the site.

Arriving just before the minister in order to greet him, I was pleased to see that a massive crowd had gathered to witness what was for us a very special occasion. I escorted the Lord Mayor, the minister, the town clerk and Sir Herbert Manzoni onto the dais. Speaking into the microphone, the Lord Mayor addressed the people and then invited me to introduce the minister.

I uttered a few words of thanks to the minister and invited him to address the citizens who had gathered to see and hear him. He made pleasant and humorous references to my efforts, and with the other members on the dais standing at the rear, I moved to the front to join the minister, inviting him to inaugurate the work. He stepped to the plunger set on a table near to him and pressed it down... and all hell broke loose.

Large stones came flying through the air; the minister never moved, he just stood there with his hands still on the plunger, completely dazed by what was happening. I thought, *I must have overemphasised my concern to the expert.* When the dust settled I could see that a number of cars parked in the area had been damaged, as were a number of the people – but only slightly, I was pleased to note.

Everything went quiet and then suddenly the minister, not known for his sense of fun, began to laugh. With the public address system still on his laughter resounded around the area and gradually everybody joined in. Instead of a disaster it turned out to be quite hilarious.

The official party returned to the council house for lunch. A note was slipped to me saying that the 'expert' wished to speak to me. I left the table to see him standing outside the Banqueting Room, looking very pale and in a state of great agitation. He explained that my comments about making sure the wall came down had him so worried that he had increased the explosive charge. He had then asked the workers on the site to fill the sandbags he handed to them to cover the extra dynamite. He didn't supervise the fill, and Murphy's Law prevailed.

The stones that had rained down on us were those that had been put in the sandbags. He proffered his resignation. I got him a stiff brandy, told him that it would give us more publicity than we could ever have hoped for, and that he should take a couple of days' leave and forget it. He didn't forget it, and neither did anyone else who was present. The story was broadcast and the world's press reported it. Three days later the *Goon Show* radio series, popular at the time, devoted their whole programme to the event. Thanks to our 'expert's' mistake, the rest of the world heard about our inner ring road.

We had waited a long time to get a start on the first of our planned ring roads, but if we were to handle the ever growing number of cars and lorries coming onto our roads, we needed to get on with our plans to construct the double carriageway intermediate and outer ring roads. I didn't want the fact that we had won the battle on the first part of our plan to blind us to the need to press on with the rest. However, what we got from the Ministry was – their – Spaghetti Junction.

It made access to the city centre easier, which increased our problems. Had this been foreseen, the inner ring road would have taken a wider circle. People who point this out today forget that the road was planned over sixty years ago. Had we been able to construct the intermediate ring road link-up to match Spaghetti Junction and then the outer ring road, today's problems would have been reduced. But had Watkinson not helped with getting the inner ring up and running, the traffic emanating from Spaghetti Junction could never have been handled. As it is, even in off-peak hours it is in danger of being choked with traffic.

The priority, so far as the city was concerned, was to improve the thirteen arterial roads leading from the north, east, south and west, and the ring roads which would have allowed traffic to move easily around and away from the city centre. Added to this, had we not been forced to seek parliament's approval to allow us to sell services in municipally owned car parks, we could have had a number of multi-storey facilities around the ring road.

However, the new road gave us an opportunity to expand the shopping, commercial and entertainment core, which for a city the size of Birmingham was pathetically small. With the improvement of the residential areas close to the centre we were able to sweep away the outdated, not too pleasant part of the south and west sides of the city centre and to provide much improved facilities for both our citizens and visitors.

The Bull Ring Centre was just a part of the improvement.

Although heavily criticised today, at the time it was hailed as a model for the future. It provided almost 400,000 square feet of air-conditioned retail shopping in covered malls along with the most modern food markets in Europe.

Birmingham is known as Britain's second city, and was at the time its biggest manufacturing base. It was and still is the capital of the Midlands; its conurbation has a population in excess of five million and I took every opportunity to try to expand its attractions in order to make it a capital city in the way that Lyon, Hamburg, Barcelona and Amsterdam have become. I'm happy to see that Birmingham has now achieved that status, thanks to an ambitious council and the European commission.

The start on the inner ring road and our redevelopment programme had caught the imagination of planners and developers, not only in Britain but in many other parts of the world. It was the time to start campaigning to attract those quality stores who were not represented in the city. The improved highway system was to help.

Chapter XI

A NEED TO EXPAND

Sir Herbert Manzoni and I were inundated with invitations to speak at one conference after another. We had no reason to complain. It gave us a platform to underline the benefits our schemes would bring to the city for those who lived, visited or traded in it. We took every opportunity to extol the value and the opportunities that Birmingham's redevelopment and road improvement schemes presented.

Speaking in London, I mentioned Broad Street, which linked the high-income residential area of Edgbaston to the city centre. It had once been an attractive shopping street but during the war and afterwards had deteriorated into a third-rate mixture of cafés, fish and chip shops, and seedy pubs. It had just a couple of decent showrooms to commend it. I outlined our plans to turn Broad Street into the equivalent of London's Regent Street.

The following week I had a call from the Public Works Department to tell me that Sir Richard Burbidge was in the office asking to speak to me.

'Who is he? Has he got an appointment?' I asked.

'No he hasn't,' came the reply, 'he's the chairman of Harrods.'

I dropped everything and rushed to meet him. I answered his questions as to our plans and my views on the city's future. He asked to see the street that we were to turn into a Regent Street.

The city had owned the Gas Department before it was nationalised. Its offices in Broad Street had not been taken over because it had been one of the first casualties of the war. Behind the site on which it had stood was an equally large corporation depot. Put together the sites were of a size Harrods would require. Occupying a long frontage on the opposite side of Broad Street stood the Orthopaedic Hospital.

Sir Richard was enamoured by the site I had shown him but

enquired whether the hospital was to be replaced. I had to tell him that there were no plans to do so. It was relocated thirty years later. He looked genuinely disappointed when he told me that Harrods wasn't likely to build opposite a large non-commercial property. He got into his Rolls, asking if he could drop me anywhere.

Feeling disconsolate I declined, but just as the car was drawing away, I had an idea. It was a long shot but I tapped the window asking him if he would drive me into town. Sitting next to him I asked if his man could drive into Corporation Street, where I could show him Rackham's Store. I had heard two days before that it was about to go on the market.

The reason I raised it was that the city owned part of the frontage and adjacent buildings at the side and the rear of the store and it was in the heart of the shopping area. We got out of the car and I walked him round the block, suggesting that if he was interested and decided to buy Rackham's, I would arrange for the city to come to some arrangement with him to merge the sites.

My hopes rose when he suggested that I walk him round the site again. Whilst we circumnavigated the area I gabbled on about the prospects like an overzealous real estate agent. He asked if I could guarantee the council's cooperation if Harrods decided to take up my suggestion. I was flying by the seat of my pants. Anxious to secure such a prestigious store for the City, I said, 'Yes, I can.'

A few weeks later I read the news that Harrods had bought Rackham's.

Sir Richard called me and I was able to tell him that I had convinced the council to open negotiations with his company. Having landed Harrods, I hoped the news would bring in many other quality stores which had yet to be represented in the city and would help our plans towards expanding the size and quality of the central shopping district.

I had vacated the Chair of the Public Works Committee by the time Harrods had completed the construction and fitting out of the store. Nevertheless, the week before it was ready for the opening ceremony, Burbidge phoned me.

'I thought you should know that an announcement is about to be made that the House of Fraser – a Scottish-based store group – have bought Harrods.'

He was not a happy man, and neither was I. He told me that the arrangements for the opening he had planned would go ahead but that Sir Hugh Fraser, the new owner, had made a few changes. He was to preside at the opening and had altered the guests list and seating plan. He added, 'Although the chairman has been made aware of the part that you personally played in bringing the store to Birmingham, I am embarrassed to have to tell you that you will no longer be sitting at the top table where you belong.' As if as a consolation he added, 'And neither will I.'

As I entered the door on the top floor of the building where the official lunch was being held, Burbidge was waiting for me. I wasn't surprised that the new chairman had ignored his advice but was, pleasantly so, when I found that Burbidge had kindly arranged for me to sit next to him at a table lower down the room.

I was aware that Sir Hugh Fraser had an aversion to socialists. During his speech when he was making generous comments about the Lord Mayor, Alderman Garnet Boughton, I whispered to Burbidge, 'The joke's on him, he obviously doesn't know that the Lord Mayor is a long-time member of the Labour Party.'

Fraser didn't name the store Harrods but kept the Rackham's title, which led me to suspect that he had no intention of it being a replica of the famous London store. From a business viewpoint, I thought it a mistake. Sir Richard soon left the company to become the chairman of British Home Stores. He improved its merchandising, the quality of its numerous outlets and its profitability and began to seriously challenge the House of Fraser.

As the city had purchased the land on either side of the inner ring road, I aimed to see that it was developed quickly but well. We recognised the difficulties we were faced with in trying to attract developers and store groups to invest whilst a major road scheme was still under construction. Nevertheless, my committee unanimously agreed to set conditions in respect of the quality and design.

Enquiries were few and far between, but we stuck to our

policy. On the Thursday that the committee decided to turn down a scheme put forward by Jack Cotton's City Centre Properties to develop land on the south side of the road, the 'Opposition' Party began to voice their objections. This was the way of politics but when the objections were coming from their members on the committee who had endorsed the policy, I found it unacceptable.

They knew that the proposal failed to meet the standards we had set but briefed the press, and newsvendors' boards were carrying in large letters: WHITE ELEPHANT RING ROAD.

I rang the editors of the *Birmingham Post* and *Mail* and they agreed to publish my reactions. The BBC Midlands news programmers pulled me in to discuss it over the air, and during the months that followed I found myself under constant attack.

However, my day came when I was able to announce that we had agreed terms for the Albany – the first hotel to be built in the city for at least thirty years – whose owner had chosen a site on the inner ring road. It was followed by the Holiday Inn and the Angus hotels, all situated along the line of the road. Our efforts had been rewarded and the doubters converted.

I hadn't bothered to take too much interest in the design of the road until we were given the go-ahead by Whitehall. Once I knew that it was on, I began to concentrate on the 'plans' which had lain in council cubbyholes for more than two decades.

Woodrow Wyatt, who represented the Aston Division in Birmingham, urged me to retain the fine Regency houses which stood in Easy Row on the line of the new highway we were about to construct. I had to explain that we had already proposed to the Ministry that we put the road in tunnel from its junction at Bristol Street to the bottom end of Snow Hill. This would have allowed us to retain these houses along with a large number of equally fine early Victorian buildings which, at the same time, would have vastly reduced the cost of their acquisition. The Ministry wouldn't agree.

Among them was the Midland Institute, the Royal Insurance offices, King Edward's School in Edmund Street, the West End Theatre and Ballroom complex, the Central Library, and the Woodman. This very special pub was full of fabulous woodcarvings and was where, over 150 years before, local businessmen agreed to form the Birmingham Canal Navigation Company.

I also told Wyatt that Manzoni and I wanted the planned underpasses to be for traffic and not pedestrians, but the Ministry of Transport were adamant on this point too. As they contributed seventy-five per cent of the cost, they insisted on having their way. There was nothing that we could do about it. Whitehall ruled, I told him.

Ironically, after the buildings I've mentioned had been demolished, newly appointed engineers in the Ministry brought about a change. The road is now in tunnel on the section we had pressed for, but the pedestrian underpass design remained the same and the council, and me in particular, have had to bear the brunt of justifiable complaints.

Conversely, the Market Hall, standing at the entrance to the Bull Ring, which to put it mildly was not in the best of shape even before the 1940 incendiary attack left it with four walls and no roof, was to remain.

Built laterally across a hill, the floor of the market was elevated on three sides; the area below was used as storerooms by fish traders and others. It was unsanitary, rat-infested, and when it rained, awash with water. Added to this it was of a size one sees in small market towns. Although many felt that it represented 'the good old days', it continued to deteriorate and present standards would have forced the council to close it.

On the plans the Hall stood on an island smack in the middle of the planned dual carriageway. I asked Manzoni why the road was diverted at this point, and whether he was happy with the idea of having a dilapidated roofless building sitting on high ground in the middle of this major highway, which would make our job of attracting promoters all that more difficult. He raised his hands saying, 'No, of course I'm not pleased with the idea but the Markets and Fairs Committee simply refused to budge.'

Although it may have looked good in its time, in its condition it had little to commend it. In addition it was far too small to cater for future demand. I outlined the problem to Councillor Ivor Thomas, a Welshman who, like so many of his countrymen, had a silver tongue. Once in full swing he could charm the birds off the trees. He and I walked around and through the building. He suggested that he raise the matter with me when I next reported to the city council.

As good as his word, he rose to speak and in his inimitable style described the hall as a dinosaur, an architectural abomination made worse by Hitler's bombs. He demanded to know why my committee was prepared to allow such a dilapidated building to remain standing on such a prominent site.

'Unless the council is prepared to waste ratepayers' money to put it in good order it should be removed,' he declared with a flourish.

His remarks were received favourably by the members, so I undertook to meet with the committee to ascertain their views.

The general manager of the Markets Department asked to see me. The markets in the very heart of the city, in addition to the roofless Market Hall, comprised a number of building he described as nothing more than very large sheds. He didn't need convincing that we needed a market complex capable of meeting the needs of a modern city. A few weeks later his committee asked the council's permission to demolish the building. It was given without a division.

Unfortunately, the plans for this section of the road had been approved by the Ministry, and had we wanted to change the line would have meant an interminable discussion with the Ministry and in consequence long delays. The city had waited long enough, so whilst the building disappeared, the island site had to stay.

A believer in consultation, I was under the mistaken impression that the Fishmongers and the Market Hall traders would welcome a discussion on alternative arrangements so that they could continue in business. I offered to rehouse them in a building in the immediate vicinity but, thinking that they might be in line for compensation, they protested that they would lose trade. It was a nonsense.

It was to be a temporary measure until the new Market Hall was finished where conditions for them and their customers would be vastly improved, and it was meant to be helpful. They were adamant and threatened to hold up the work on the road.

As the road works got closer they held a press conference

stating that, come what may, they would not be moved. I tried to convince them that they had no case, but thinking that they were on strong ground they became offensive. It was time to spell out the council's position. I gave them notice that if by their obduracy they held up the road contract for only one day the cost would be charged to them.

'I will not allow the ratepayers to foot the bill for your obstinacy, but I will make sure that you will,' I said emphatically.

Their lawyer, who was present at the meeting, took me on one side and suggested that I leave it to him. He advised them to back off.

When the new Market Hall was nearing completion they threatened not to move into it. When asked why, they told me that they were very happy with the temporary accommodation. I thought that they were kidding me. They seemed to have forgotten how they so vehemently criticised having to move into it a few years before.

The Bull Ring Centre, with its new and enlarged Market Hall, was finished and the fishmongers moved in. It was amusing to see one of the most vociferous among them shaking hands with Prince Philip when he came to open the Centre in May 1964. I was then the Lord Mayor and was standing alongside the Prince when he asked the leader of the dissidents, 'How do you and your colleagues like trading in this new Hall – are you making money?'

'Yes, sir,' he yelled over the noise, 'it's bloody marvellous!'

He smiled when I gave him an old-fashioned look; he obviously knew what I was thinking.

When the scheme was completed it was heralded as being ahead of its time and the finest in Europe. The new market development covered one million square feet, just under a third being devoted to retail shopping. Since then it has been heavily criticised by those who with the benefit of hindsight knew better. Thirty-five years later it is to be redeveloped and I am looking forward to seeing the result.

British Rail saw the opportunity of cashing in on the 'new' Birmingham we were trying to create, and began to investigate the possibilities of developing the air space over New Street main line station. The only sad thing about the scheme they produced was that it meant the demolition of the Queens Hotel which was then the finest hotel in the city. The good part was that it had a threefold effect. It extended the covered shopping facilities in the heart of the city, it linked up with the market scheme, and it provided a finer Central Railway Station. Over the succeeding years a number of covered shopping centres have been introduced, adding a variety of stores and architectural interest to the city.

Mentioning the Queens Hotel brings back the memory of an invitation I received to dine with Dr Beeching, who was then the chairman of British Rail. He had been brought in by a Conservative Minister of Transport to make the railways profitable. Beeching's experience had nothing to do with transport; he was a director of the chemical giant, ICI. The dinner was an all-male, black-tie affair.

A large man in every sense of the term, and jolly with it, Beeching had me sit next to him. The table was occupied by about twenty chairmen of the top industries in the Midlands. The dinner over, Beeching began to discuss his future plans for Britain's rail system, and the longer he spoke the more depressed I became. When he had completed what I can only describe as a lecture, he asked his guess for their observations. Faced with such a galaxy of talent I kept quiet.

Halfway through the discussion he turned to say to me, 'I'm disappointed, I was given to understand that I would have trouble with you.'

I looked at him and then round the table at the other guests, most of whom had made a contribution which left me wondering whether they had any real notion of what closing down so much of the system would mean to ordinary people.

I replied, 'I'm not a troublemaker, just an observer. Having heard what you had to say about the future of our railways, it appears to me that in order to make a profit you would be prepared to concentrate the railways and industry in the South-East of Britain and turn the rest of the country into a grouse moor.'

For a moment there was silence and then Beeching burst into a gale of laughter and said, 'It's an idea.'

I think he must have meant it. He tried hard enough.

Now that the need for an efficient, reliable, fast and cost-effective public transport system has again been recognised, the then government's decision to let Dr Beeching loose is seen for what it was – a costly mistake.

Today, one hears members of parliament noisily expressing their concern for the countryside and the transport needs of those who live in it. Those crying 'wolf' have forgotten who was responsible for closing down branch lines and what it has done to reduce the quality of life for country people. They hope that the public have forgotten, and of course they have.

I have mentioned that Birmingham has a habit of breaking out with sudden bursts of energy, enthusiasm and enterprise. There was such a period during my years on the city council. The decision to build the National Exhibition Centre, in which I was able to play a leading role, was as courageous as it was enterprising. Forgotten is the battle we fought against the London lobby, who tried hard to steal the idea and have it built on the site of Northolt Airfield.

In addition to the NEC there was our decision to build a much grander replacement for Sir Barry Jackson's repertory theatre and to construct a larger Central Library which extended the services of its predecessor. We encouraged the arts generally by building one of the finest Concert Halls in Europe along with a massive Conference Center.

Added to this the Council built an Indoor Sports Center, which was the biggest in the UK if not Europe. With the help of the British Waterways Board the canals that run through the city center were transformed from virtually unused, dilapidated and dirty watercourses into a fantastic and envied tourist attraction. The council's outdoor stadium, which is so good that the British Olympic trials are held there, has brought worldwide publicity, but it's a small part of the City's achievement in expanding, thereby helping to make Birmingham a more interesting place in which to live.

Chapter XII
VISITING THE NEW WORLD

In 1955, we were to start the biggest major road improvement the city had ever embarked upon, and the council began to concern itself with modern traffic planning and management. They decided that we could learn from the American experience. The General Purposes Committee was asked to decide who should visit the United States to study the methods applied in some of their major cities; not an easy task.

Past experience had taught me that competition to join the delegation would be strong among the various Heads of Departments and their chairmen. It was understandable. To be members of any delegation chosen to travel to foreign parts, something that the war and austerity had made impossible for a very long time, and to visit the New World was naturally appealing, but it was not meant to be a pleasure trip.

The chairmen and chief officers of the major committees met to discuss the merits of the various aspirants. Being by far the youngest among them I thought it wise to keep quiet. The town clerk, through Alderman Bowen, the chairman of the all-powerful General Purposes Committees, made a bid because he had suggested that the city should invest in an underground rapid transit system.

This aroused the manager of the Public Transport Department, who argued that if this was the case he and his chairman, being in charge of public transport, would be best suited to go. I looked across the table at Sir Herbert Manzoni and gave him a knowing smile; he like me, kept quiet whilst the rest wrangled.

The meeting dragged on, but when the chairman of the Education Committee tried to jump aboard, it brought the members down to earth. Having kept out of the struggle,

Manzoni attracted attention by his silence. He was asked for his opinion. Being the diplomat he was, he said that he thought all those who had so far expressed a desire to be part of the proposed delegation would, if chosen, be admirable representatives of the city.

'If called upon, my chairman and I would be happy to set out the names of the cities they should visit and the people they should meet who could advise them on traffic management, the kinds of roads we should or should not be building to deal with the increasing number of vehicles coming on to our roads.'

He added that with his chairman he would be happy to prepare the questions which needed to be answered to help us with the problems that would face the city in the future. It was masterful.

After a period of silence the committee decided that the delegation should be made up of the city engineer and surveyor, the chief highway engineer and the chief planning officer, and led by their chairman. Later, at my request, they added the chairman of the Town Planning sub committee and the clerk to the Public Works Committee. I was over the moon.

Appointments were made in advance, for us to meet with officials in the cities of Chicago, Washington, Pittsburgh, Philadelphia and New York. The visit would be short – from 26 March–5 April 1956 – and busy. The delegation met to set out our programme and I made it clear to them that as the ratepayers were picking up the bill we must be prepared to make a full report on what I hoped we would see and learn. We decided to take a camera to film the more interesting parts of our visit so that when we returned it could be shown to those who wish to see it.

In the event, after the members of the city council had viewed the film, thousands of people took time off to view it during a two-week screening in the town hall. They also collected a fifty-five page illustrated booklet we wrote and printed. My insistence on this had a dual purpose. It was right that the citizens should see how their money had been spent and it would open their eyes to just how far we had fallen behind in dealing with traffic in Britain.

Our report demonstrated not just how much we had to do to catch up in the field of traffic management, but what the growth in car ownership would mean. This was way back in 1956.

The start on our journey was unpropitious. Having taken off from the airport in London the pilot announced that we were over Manchester and unfortunately had developed engine trouble. He was forced to fly in circles whilst he dumped six tons of fuel over the English countryside. We finally left London at midnight. Our plane flew via Iceland to Idlewild – now Kennedy Airport – outside New York.

This was before aircraft were fitted with jet engines, and flights to New York normally took about nine hours. Somewhere over the Atlantic a passenger went wobbly on us. We were told that her flight from India to the USA via London had been delayed, which meant that she got off one long flight to be immediately put on to another. It was little wonder that she went out of control. A doctor on board advised the captain to land the plane at the nearest airport. He put down in snow-covered Halifax, Nova Scotia.

We disembarked and were taken to an unheated building to remain there until the luggage had been unloaded in order to find that owned by the sick passenger. The stopover lasted for four very cold hours.

It scuppered our plan to travel into New York City for a brief meeting with the Head of the Port of New York Authority before continuing our journey. Landing in Idlewild, we were informed that our plane in La Guardia, some miles away, was waiting to fly us on to Chicago. Having already travelled for far too long, the further three-hour flight almost sent me berserk.

The plane had a number of ladies undergoing their stewardess training. One after another they woke me up to offer newspapers, magazines, drinks, biscuits or nuts, and always hoping that I would 'have a nice day'.

It was 6 p.m. on the 27 March when we arrived in the city famous for its jazz, the smell of its meat packing yards, the constant wind blowing across Lake Michigan, its violent history, the Mafia and Al Capone. We were met at the airport by a 6'3" Texan who loaded us into a Cadillac and drove to the forty-storey Morrison Hotel in downtown Chicago. Mercifully, he left us to our own devices: for me, a hot bath and bed.

All the rooms had an outer steel door and an inner heavy timber door, both with double locks. The outer door had a grille through which, by sliding an inside panel, a visitor could be inspected – a throwback to the days of Prohibition, I was told. My room was on the twenty-seventh floor so I was surprised to be woken up by church bells. I hadn't left the television on so looking out of the window I could see the source: a church across the street on the roof of the tall building a few stories below me. I tried to conjure up how its clergyman dealt with funerals. I knew this could only be America.

I phoned room service. Unable to find a menu I asked what they had got. The reply was, 'You name it, we've got it,' so I ordered grilled kidneys, egg and bacon.

The waiter asked, 'Kidneys – you want kidneys?'

'Yes,' I answered.

'That's offal, we don't serve offal,' he said, and hung up.

I began to get ready to go down to breakfast. What seemed no more than a few minutes after putting down the phone the doorbell rang. I opened the doors having first peered through the grill, and the waiter wheeled in a tray of bacon, eggs and kidneys. He said, 'I'm told you're a Limey; you forgot to order a drink so I've brought you tea.'

I was told many times how Americans hated our coffee; I didn't bother to tell him that I felt the same about their tea. But it was the courtesy that he extended that impressed me most. It was to be echoed by the rest of the people we met in that great city during our all too short stay.

For the next three days we were ferried around by our Texan escort. On the 28 March we met George de Ment, the Commissioner of Public Works, and his Chief Engineer, Dick Van Gorp. They said that they too tried to get financial help from their government, but to cut down delays they financed their expressways through the city, the county and the state, each authority bearing a third of the cost. There was no central government assistance and no interference.

Income from the fuel tax which was levied by the state, not the Federal Government, was shared equally by the three parties. The city raised a bond issue against general city taxes and devoted its share of the fuel tax to carry out their roads programme. The only control the county had in the affairs of the city was in the levy of tax; Washington had no part in the decision making or the planning process. We told Messrs de Ment and Van Gorp that they didn't realise how lucky they were.

They took us to meet the Cook County Highways Superintendent, James Kelly, who informed us that as long ago as 1924 they foresaw the effect the car would have in the future and started a five-year construction programme which was revised and extended every five years. Part of the fuel tax, which was first imposed in 1927, had also been devoted to traffic management programmes.

Our meetings with these city officials, especially their engineers and transport executives were illuminating. Mr Werner Schroeder, the vice chairman of the Chicago Transit Board, took us through their metropolitan transit research report. It stated that urban traffic congestion was the greatest single problem that most large cities faced and it has not, and cannot, be overcome solely by the construction of new highways, expressways or the widening of present streets.

I would remind you that they had already built huge highways, massive car parking facilities, and yet they had concluded this in 1955 – some forty-five years before our own Ministry of Transport cottoned on.

'Cities were not planned to cater for millions of automobiles, which have become an indispensable part of American living,' said the Mayor of Chicago in January that year.

When we returned home we trumpeted this message loud and clear. In 1956, I said publicly that we needed to prepare for the two or three car family and needed urgently to provide alternative means of transport which must be fast, clean, attractive and cheap. I was ridiculed, but the cynics hadn't seen the future; I had.

The policy of the Chicago officials was clear. City streets should not cater for parking. They took us to see multilevel car parks above and below ground, one of which, called Grant Park, had two floors under Michigan Avenue with a capacity to garage 2,359 cars. Drivers could park themselves or leave it to an attendant.

To me the most intriguing off-street car park was called 'Facility Number One' – a simple enough name for a park on twelve floors above ground and two beneath. It was really a series of shelves connected by lifting equipment which operated in a central well. The building was only 21' wide and 148' long; it housed 115 cars.

There were five lifting arrangements operating vertically and horizontally, and – surprisingly – run by a single attendant. In most cases he could park or retrieve a car in a few minutes. The driver-waiting lobby was the kind you would see in a four-star hotel.

According to James Kelly, the Assistant Superintendent of Cook County Highways Department, 'Thirty-two years ago, Chicago carried out a study of the use of automobiles which resulted in their five-year road construction programme. In order to defray the cost, a motor fuel tax was introduced.' This was in 1924. He told us, 'We, the city, the county and the state don't have to bend to the will of Washington officials. Had this been the case we would have been dead in the water.'

I murmured, 'Amen to that.'

The country, as we all know, is divided into states and the states into counties. From what we were hearing, there was little if any interference from the National Government. I have been and still am advocating this kind of arrangement in Britain. As a parting shot, Kelly came up with a most amazing statistic.

'You may not know it, but more freight is carried into Chicago than New York and St Louis combined.'

We began to understand the size of their problems. The following day we were taken to the twelve-lane Lake Shore Drive.

Standing on a bridge at one of the interchanges, we were shown the mechanically moveable kerbs which allowed them to limit or expand the flow of traffic according to the amount on a particular section. To have the ability to use a permutation, reducing or expanding the number of lanes on either side from a control tower, seemed to us very advanced; to them it was simply an essential tool that had been operating for some years.

I repeat, we saw these forty-six years ago. It underlines the fact that our nationally controlled transport authority hasn't *even yet* scratched the surface.

In order to reduce the load on the public highways they were also in the process of constructing a rapid transit system. They didn't have to ask for grants or permission of Central Government; they obtained financial support from the county, the state and the private sector. The Chicago Authority provided the land, the rail and the rolling stock, and a private company ran the system, carefully monitored.

Their approach to car parking also opened our eyes. We were taken to see the numerous and diverse off-street facilities, some run by the city, others by private individuals or companies, some on a joint enterprise basis. Companies owning a number of parking facilities in downtown Chicago ran a courtesy car system which travelled between their facilities. If a client found his chosen park full he would travel on to the next. He would park and then be driven to the car park he had wished to be in. To collect his car the process was reversed. He would be driven to where his car was stationed. At no extra charge. He was happy, and the owners had retained a client. A smart piece of marketing. Britain still hasn't caught on. Although we in Birmingham tried and you will see later how central control made it impossible.

We questioned the car park owners in respect of their pricing policy. In order to fill their spaces they had to keep parking charges down; to make it viable they provided ancillary services such as car valeting, maintenance, tyre change and a fuel service. It convinced us that if we adopted this approach we could free our central streets of parked cars and cut down congestion.

We came away determined to build multilevel facilities around the inner ring road, copy the courtesy car system and to keep down the parking fees, put in the services and endeavour to do this in conjunction with the private sector.

Manzoni tempered my enthusiasm by telling me that to be able to get ahead with building these kind of facilities, the council would need a Parliamentary Bill – in short, permission from parliament. The fact that our hands were tied by Whitehall seemed crazy to me then, and still appears crazy to me today. It's little wonder that our country just staggers along.

I made up my mind that as soon as we got back home I would urge the city council to add a clause in its next Parliamentary Bill so that we could get on with the job. The city council agreed, and what was to happen proved the wisdom of the words of advice which Robert Moses – the Head of the Port of New York Authority – gave me when we met him at the end of our tour.

Our visit to Chicago was both fascinating and impressive. We started out at 8.30 a.m. and ended our day when the moon came up. Being driven around by our Texan friend in his huge car I watched the fuel gauge moving down rather fast. As he gave us the impression that he was in complete command I didn't dare mention that it appeared that we were running out of gas.

We did so in what was the busiest part of town, known as the Loop. He was white and from the South, and this was 1956. During his non-stop commentaries he left us in no doubt that he wasn't partial to America's black community. It disturbed us but we were not surprised. Being guests in his country we kept our feelings to ourselves.

It was somewhat unfortunate that when the car finally began to splutter and come to a halt it did so in front of a popular bar. Unfortunate, because the policeman who was at that moment exiting from the said bar was big, broad and black. The Texan explained our predicament in a manner which we, and the police officer, noted. Twirling his truncheon, the officer looked our man in the eye and speaking in a tone which left no doubt in our minds that he meant business said, 'Buster, get that heap out of here, and I do mean now.'

Three of us leapt out of the car and began to push it down the street, thankful that a gas station was in sight.

Being in a town which was famous among other things for its music, I decided to slip out that night to sit and listen to some Chicago-style jazz. It was around eleven o'clock and I thought the place would be packed. I sat at the horseshoe-shaped bar with a few men who appeared to be locals. I asked the barman why it was so quiet.

'It's Lent, man,' he told me.

A well-known jazz joint in Chicago, empty because it was Lent... I found it hard to believe.

The night before we left Chicago, Mr Germanson, who was, if my memory serves me right, the President of the American Cement and Concrete Association, invited us to dinner at the Palmer House.

The Palmer House was one of the most famous multilevel restaurants in the Midwest and had quite a history. When the city was virtually run by Al Capone, he and leading members of the Mafia were regular visitors. We were told that it hadn't changed. It had a splendid turn-of-the-century look, with numerous huge decorative chandeliers hanging from high ceilings, great velvet drapes and private booths against the walls.

The main dining room, with an orchestra playing and guests dancing on a sizeable dance floor, was to me very impressive. A further pleasant surprise was that we were to be treated to a cabaret, which that night was an internationally famous troupe, José and his Spanish dancers.

Our host was what one might call, 'a strong silent type'; I guessed that he was in his mid-sixties. About 5'10", broad shoulders and a head of tight curled blond hair over a pale face with very pale blue eyes under rimless glasses, I imagined that he originated in Northern Europe. During the time we were in his company I can't remember him ever smiling and, other than his initial greeting, he hardly spoke a word all evening.

His wife, who was still quite pretty and must have been a great beauty in her time, appeared to be a rather gentle, lonely, nervous person. I sat next to her trying to hold a conversation but she kept glancing across at her husband as if worried that she might be saying or doing something that would meet with his displeasure. I found that very sad.

Whilst we were studying the gargantuan menu, he recommended as a main course the porterhouse steak, and dutifully we all agreed. Without reference to the menu, he ordered for himself a king-size Wiener schnitzel and for his wife lamb chops.

Having lived on a small ration of meat for almost ten years, during and after the war, to us the sheer size of the steaks was unbelievable. I was able to consume about a quarter of this delicious meat before reluctantly giving up. The waiter who was hovering around the table grinned when he took away the plate.

Within minutes a large, rotund, red-faced chef stood over me. 'What's da matter wit' da steak?' he demanded.

The waiter, who was of Irish descent, was standing behind him still grinning. I suspected that when he returned my plate to the kitchen with most of the steak left on it he had wound the chef up about his cooking.

I apologised, telling him that I had enjoyed that which I had been able to eat. Hearing my accent he asked, 'You a Limey?'

I answered that I was English.

'Oh,' he replied, 'dat's okay den, dat's okay den.' He was no doubt aware that the stomachs of most Limeys had shrunk doing the war years. His pride restored, he returned to his kitchen.

This somewhat embarrassing incident was overtaken by the effect that José had on the diminutive Mrs Germanson. The coffee had been served when the lights dimmed, the music struck up a Spanish Paso doble, and the cabaret was under way. A spotlight picked out José. Tall, slim, dark-skinned and handsome, his tan-coloured, tight-fitting outfit consisted of a bolero-style jacket, very tight flared trousers – so tight I thought his bottom would burst out at any moment – legs set in high brown leather riding boots, a cummerbund around his narrow waist, a frilly shirt, and a sombrero on his handsome head.

He stood with hands held high, one holding a riding crop. He danced across the floor slapping it against his thighs. The girls, in typical flamenco dress, danced around the centre of the room, whilst José, acting as a horse trainer, gyrated across the floor, at times dancing between the tables.

Our table was on the edge of the dance floor, so he careered around us from time to time. On each occasion, as he came close to Mrs Germanson she shuddered, holding a handkerchief to her mouth and muttering – well, more like gasping – again and again, 'Ooh, what a gorgeous man, what a gorgeous man!'

She appeared to be about to swoon as he brushed by her. I looked across the table to see the effect this was having on her husband; he batted not an eyelid.

Our next stop was Pittsburgh, a steel town like Sheffield. The locals tell that in the past, if you had on a white shirt when you left the house it would be black with soot before the day was out. Times had changed; with pollution control, Pittsburgh, sitting astride two rivers, was a model city.

The Mellon family were the owners of the steel mills and much else. Like the Cadbury family in Birmingham and the Rowntrees in York, they were great benefactors. The Museum and Art Gallery, the Central Public Library and a number of parks were the result of the benevolent attitude the family had towards the city in which their fortune had been made. 'It's called "Putting something back",' we were told. There are too few people around who do that.

The purpose of our visit to Pittsburgh was to see, among other things, the Squirrel dual tunnels cut through the mountain of the same name. It was built to ease traffic congestion and at the same time to preserve the environment, sorely needed on both counts in this large industrial city. We wanted to put a section of our inner ring road in a tunnel, as I have mentioned. It came about, but too late to save many buildings of merit.

We asked to see the large and colourful Mellon Square in the centre of the city underneath which they had constructed an eight-level car parking facility.

Leaving Pittsburgh, we flew into Philadelphia. Coming out of the airport there was not a taxi or bus to be seen. It was too far to walk and we had no other means of transport available; we waited hours to be taken into the city. We discovered that we had arrived just as Miss Grace Kelly was leaving to marry Prince Rainier of Monaco and everybody in town, it seemed, had gone to wave her farewell.

Ten years later, along with the Begum Aga Khan and Princess Grace, I was a guest of honour in the city of Lyon. The Princess invited me to sit next to her and I became involved in an interesting conversation with this beautiful lady. But that's another story.

After two days in Philadelphia we pushed on to Washington to spend the Easter weekend. Apart from the monuments and grand open spaces, I found Washington a rather disappointing place.

The Federal Administrative area was reminiscent of London's Whitehall, but on a much grander scale. Although the buildings were much cleaner, more spaced out and not so old, many of them to me at least, were architecturally unattractive.

A plus factor was the profusion of flowering trees; they were out in all their glory doing their best to help to beautify the area. We took time to visit the impressive Lincoln and Washington Memorials, but on the Sunday morning I left the hotel early and alone. Walking around the city for some three hours I found myself in a district which appeared to be solely occupied by the black community; it was 1956, long before the race riots broke out in America.

Camera in hand, I stopped at a large church where the congregation was gathering for their Easter service. The three small children dressed in white standing with their parents on the steps of the church looked so happy that I asked if I could take a photograph. The mother agreed and then invited me to join them at the service.

She turned out to be one of the ushers and placed me on the back row of the church with the youngest of her daughters, who was about five years old, I guess. The choir was made up mostly of women all cloaked in red cassocks who, with their voices raised, swinging, joyous and reverent, made it the most exciting and moving singing I had ever heard.

The Pastor stood at a lectern and opened the service by welcoming his flock. He then asked all those who were visiting his church for the first time to stand up and introduce themselves. I sat tight. The little girl looked up at me, tugging my sleeve.

'The Pastor says you gotta stand up and give your name,' she said loudly.

'I can't,' I whispered.

'Why can't you? The Pastor says you gotta!' she insisted loudly.

'I am too shy,' I told her.

She giggled and called out to her mother, who was standing behind our pew, 'Momma, he says he's too shy to give the Pastor his name.' At this those around me began to giggle.

Thankfully, Momma said, 'Hush there!' and I breathed a sigh

of relief. Not only was I the only white person, I was almost certainly the only agnostic sitting in that church during their Easter service.

After the Pastor wished us all a peaceful and happy Easter, the family invited me to join them for Sunday lunch. It was sad that I had to decline. We were due to leave Washington at five and I was some distance from the hotel. I could only hope that they believed me when I gave them my reason for not joining them.

That afternoon we travelled to New York by train. For me, this was to be the most memorable part of the trip. I was for the first time to meet my mother's elder brother, Jack, and his daughter, my cousin, Polly, and her family. My knowledge of her was through stories my mother told, and from the letters, food parcels and clothes she sent us during the war.

Although she had lived in the United States since she was a young child and was married to an American, Polly was deeply proud of her English roots. On the barbecue in her garden there was a Winston Churchill plaque and she still held a British passport. I found it hilarious when she described how her neighbours and friends admired her English accent. Having lived in New York for as long as she had, to my colleagues and me she sounded every bit a New Yorker.

Polly had met her husband, Harry, in Hollywood whilst she was filming. Harry had made his fortune designing and making furniture for the stars, with factories in Los Angeles and New York.

On the evening we arrived they entertained us at the famous Coconut Grove, and before we left Polly insisted on hosting a dinner at her home in Westchester County, well north of the city they knew as New York, New York. She prepared for us what she called 'a typical English meal' of roast beef and Yorkshire pudding, and was devastated because the pudding sank.

We had travelled to her home by rail via Grand Central, the most magnificent railway station in the world, designed like a huge cathedral. In its vast covered concourse there stood a circular enquiry office with a three or four staff who continually dispensed a vast amount of information without having to refer to any schedules and, it seemed, without stopping to take a breath. It was interesting to watch.

A few years later I was to return to Grand Central to discuss what turned out to be the development of the PANAM Building, to be constructed over part of its airspace.

Our main objective in New York was to meet Robert Moses, who was in charge of the powerful Port of New York Authority. Its powers covered, among other things, planning and transport for the New York metropolis. The difficulties facing them then were probably more difficult than in any city in the world.

We were due to meet the legendary Robert Moses when we first landed in the States, but the delay to our flight made it impossible. His advice was sought by traffic engineers and planners the world over, and we felt ourselves lucky to be squeezed into a seminar he was addressing that day in the boardroom on the top floor of the Authority's headquarters.

A tall, slim, distinguished fellow, honoured internationally by civil engineers and planners, he looked exactly as I had pictured him. He was discussing the problems created by vehicular traffic and at one stage stopped to ask, 'Are their any questions so far?'

As no one seemed to raise a point, I piped up, 'Sir, if you have the answers to the problems, why is it that the traffic outside is so snarled up?'

My intervention caused my colleagues to shuffle with embarrassment; they all looked as if to say, 'He's not with us.'

Mr Moses looked up and went over to the window, asking if I cared to join him. I did, not knowing what to expect.

He put his arm around my shoulder, asked my name and from whence I came. He then bade me look at the mass of traffic below us and said, 'When the boys returned from the war the first thing they wanted was a combustion engine underneath them. The problems of raising the means to provide adequate road space for them and their vehicles didn't bother them then, and doesn't seem to bother them now.'

He sighed. 'You see, it's low on their agenda and it's a problem that you, me, and all those who are sitting here share.' Still with his arm on my shoulder he turned to his audience. 'This young guy's question needs an answer.' He went on, 'You see, the three main talking points in America today are, who's going to win the

World Series, who's going to win the Super Bowl and... Marilyn Monroe. When the problem of catering for traffic becomes such that it numbers among these three, the general public will see to it that we are given the funds to physically provide the answer to traffic chaos.'

Robert Moses turned to me, 'I understand that you're in politics. If you can get your citizens to put traffic at the top of their agenda I'll come over to see how you are doing; if you can't, I won't bother.'

His audience applauded. Robert Moses was right, of course. Over half a century after the end of the war, British governments are still playing with the problem because there were no votes in transport. It didn't figure in the minds of the voters as being a priority. Although, the manner in which British Rail was privatised and the chaos it has caused, I sense that it is changing now.

One of the biggest problems Moses had to face in downtown New York was the pressure on space. The cost of land was so high and so were the buildings. Demolishing skyscrapers to make way for traffic became too prohibitive in cost; so the authorities were forced to construct both rail and road facilities over the streets.

We were driven on a dual carriageway three or four storeys above ground, running between blocks of high-rise tenements. The pollution and noise from motor traffic and trains regularly passing their windows must have been unbearable for the tenants. They vacated, and in the process turned the properties into multilevel slums.

I said then that there was no way that this would be tolerated in Britain, but the Ministry of Transport was to prove me wrong when they built Spaghetti Junction near the heart of the City of Birmingham. To be fair it is nowhere near as bad as New York, but bad nevertheless.

The visit to America made me realise that if we failed to face up to the task of dealing with traffic and vastly improving public transport, it would inevitably lead to the development of out of town shopping malls, which would have a deleterious effect on both the economy and appearance of town centres as we knew them.

The American experience should have given the British planners in Local Government and Whitehall notice of what was in store if they followed the trend. Unfortunately, they had their heads in the sand.

During my New York visit in the spring of 1956 the air conditioning in my hotel room went on the blink. I only mention the fact because it led to an interesting conversation with the old electrician sent up to fix it.

His trade union was involved in its triennial negotiations with employers, and part of the package under discussion was a reduction of working hours to thirty-six a week. The proposition was causing him some alarm. I thought that it had to do with the possible effect on his future earnings but it was not the case. It was to do with, as he put it, 'All that *leesure* time I would have to put in.' The thought of how to fruitfully occupy a further twelve hours of spare time, for which he was ill prepared, mortified him.

This conversation took place long before the microchip reared its head to throw all preconceived ideas out of the window. Now, with the shorter working week a fact of life, tens of thousands of people who are tired of watching the box in the corner of their living room are faced with the same dilemma.

It underlined something that I had been cogitating on for some time: that there was a need to provide facilities to train or educate people to be able to use the free time that modern technology would force on us. Like it or not, it would be a problem. Fifteen years on I was using this argument whilst battling with government ministers to preserve the canals, but they just couldn't see it.

Chapter XIII
TRYING TO WIN

On our return from the United States we published our report, which was made available to the citizens, and showed the film that we had made. We then tried to put into practice some of the traffic management techniques we had learned. Had we received assistance from those who had the power, we could have put an end to traffic chaos in and around our city. Central control, coupled with vested interest and public apathy, killed our chances.

We convinced the city council of the need to build multi-storey car parks along the inner ring road. They agreed that if we were to cover the cost and keep the parking fees at a level which would encourage owners to use the facilities, we should follow the Chicago example and sell fuel and services.

The private sector had no interest in providing such facilities on the scale that was necessary, so it was up to the City to do so. Controlled as local government is in Britain, we had to promote yet another Local Government Parliamentary Bill. Drafting these Bills to meet the conditions laid down by Whitehall has to be carried out by lawyers well versed in this type of work. It cost time and money but we had no other choice.

The decision having been made by the council, the bill, by law, had to be put before a Town's Meeting, and if it failed there, to a Town's poll. Again, a time-consuming and expensive exercise. It was in any case an outdated process and a nonsense. Birmingham had over a million citizens. The Town's Meeting was held in the town hall, which could hold much fewer than a thousand, but we were stuck with it.

The Motor Trades' Association turned up in force. They were led by Francis Griffin and Frank Guest, who in addition to being directors of companies in the motor trade were Conservative members of the city council. They put their commercial interests before that of the city and the wish of the council.

Along with their associates in the industry, they had no objection to the ratepayers bearing the costs of providing the car parks which would be unprofitable, but objected to the City helping to offset the burden by selling fuel and services.

The Town's Meeting was chaired by the then Lord Mayor, Alderman Grogan. It opened at 7 p.m. and lasted until a half-hour past midnight. He had a very hard time trying to keep order; the Motor Traders' Association had worked hard in drumming up support and they created bedlam. At one stage the police were called to restore order.

It got so bad that a Birmingham University professor, who lectured on economic history, made a dramatic intervention which was reported in the *Birmingham Post*. Making a verbal attack on the interrupters he told the hushed audience, 'Future citizens of Birmingham will remember this as a night of shame. These proposals have been carefully thought out by responsible and adult people anxious about the future welfare of this city; they have been treated with contempt and hooliganism. This meeting should exercise some sense of responsibility. The average age of this audience seems fantastically high. As a young man I wish to record my protest against this attitude.'

His words silenced the meeting and we thought that the proceedings would be less boisterous, but it didn't last.

Delegated to speak on behalf of the council, I made it clear that if the private sector was prepared to provide the car parks we would welcome them with open arms. We had approached the petrol combines but support was not forthcoming either. I added, 'Those who are here representing the motor trade saw the car parks as milch cows, they want the ratepayers to have the end you feed while they have the end you milk.' I went on to say, 'If we are to deal with the growing traffic problem, we needed sufficient car parking spaces, and must face the fact that ratepayers must either subsidise these car parks or have the power to run services to help pay for them.'

I reminded those Conservatives who were present that one of the most famous members their Party had produced was a great believer in municipal enterprise; I meant of course the Rt Hon Joseph Chamberlain. It was of no avail, and the clause was voted down. It proved the point made to me by Robert Moses. The public had not yet developed sufficient interest in the growing problems caused by vehicular traffic.

One of the questions that I had put to Robert Moses during our meeting in New York was on the reaction of the car-owning public in America to the use of kerb side parking meters. He told me that if kerb side parking was to be allowed, the fairest way of both controlling and making the best use of it, was by the use of parking meters. 'Of course,' he said, 'car owners object, but it is the only way to ensure that drivers don't hog limited space too long.'

He went on to tell me the story of the Mayor of North Dakota who, when up for re-election, was worried about the protests against the parking meters he had installed in their downtown area. With his re-election prospects fading, he announced that he would bow to the demands of the motorists and have hoods placed over the meters, suspending their use.

That weekend, the tempers of drivers motoring around the shopping area looking for a car space boiled over. Seeing those who had got there before them hogging the space, hour after hour, led to fist fights. On the following Monday the hoods were off, the meters working and the Mayor's policy justified. He was re-elected with an overwhelming majority.

I remembered Moses' story and in 1957 began to sow seeds in the minds of my colleagues in the hope that I could get their support for the American idea of having parking meters in our main streets. Again I was surprised to be told that we, the City of Birmingham, the largest all-purpose authority in Britain, would not be allowed to put in meters without the permission of Whitehall. I put the idea on the back burner.

By the end of the year the parking problem in the central environs had grown so bad that without my having to raise the matter again, the members of my committee proposed that meters should be installed in the main shopping streets. We would have been the first in Britain to install them, but we hadn't counted on opposition from our own Chief Constable, Sir Edward Dodd.

He was a well groomed, handsome fellow who had an ability to charm his committee, on which were a number of lady members. We all knew that he had the Watch (Police) Committee in the palm of his hand and that his wish became the law of the Medes and Persians. He convinced them to oppose the proposition that parking meters be introduced. I decided to make an effort to avoid a confrontation between the two committees by arranging to meet with him and his chairman, Alderman Lummis Gibson.

About 9.30 a.m. on the day of the meeting I had a call from a Sir Alex Samuels to tell me that he was down from London to attend the 11.30 a.m. meeting, and could he see me an hour before? I had absolutely no idea who he was and how he came to be invited to a meeting that I had arranged; nevertheless I agreed.

He was a small, dapper character with a tanned, much lined face and tiny twinkling eyes. He suggested that we walk the streets where I hoped to place the meters. Samuels explained that he was the London traffic adviser to the Minister of Transport and that he and Colonel Young – who was, I believe, the chief of the metropolitan police force at that time – were here at the invitation of Edward Dodd. This piece of arrogance, ignoring protocol and totally lacking in courtesy, demonstrated Dodd's low opinion of council members. I was astounded but didn't raise this with Samuels.

During our walk, Samuels, a voluble character, stopped every now and again to stress a point. At one stage he said to me, brushing his hand on my coat sleeve in a downward direction, 'You must learn to rub people the right way.' Then, running his hand in the opposite direction, he added, 'And not the wrong way.' I was furious. We walked on a few steps and it was my turn to stop. Endeavouring to stay calm, I asked, 'Where did you stay last night?' Before he could answer I went on, 'Never mind, I'll tell you. You stayed with Ted Dodd. You would appreciate him, he is an expert in the art of rubbing people up the right way – but not this time!'

I turned around and headed for my office in the department, leaving Samuels to consider who the hell he thought he had been talking to.

At the meeting I sat at the head of the table, Dodd, his chairman and Colonel Young on my right. Sir Herbert Manzoni, and surprisingly, Sir Alex Samuels, were on my left. Dodd hadn't bothered to introduce the 'out of towners' or to explain or apologise for inviting them without reference to me.

I opened by outlining my committee's reasons for wanting to introduce parking meters to the city. The chairman of the Watch Committee, who was the general secretary of what was then the Clerical and Administrative Workers' Union, and a respected member of the council, had been fully briefed by Dodd. He led off with a blistering attack on parking meters and me for even daring to suggest that they should be introduced into Britain.

I glanced across at Samuels, whose face was contorted with anger. He called across the table, 'I am amazed at your ignorance! You haven't a clue what you are talking about. I doubt whether you have ever seen a parking meter or visited a place where they are in operation, and obviously have no idea how the system works. I think your comments are outrageous.'

After his outburst silence prevailed.

'Sir Alex,' I said quietly, 'you may not be aware that it was I who arranged this meeting. I was unaware until we met that you and Colonel Young had been invited.' The Chief Constable sat quietly so I continued. 'However, since you are both here I would like to welcome you and may I ask, in the nicest possible way, if you will endeavour to try *not* to rub those with whom you differ, up the wrong way.'

Only he saw the funny side. Unabashed, he went on to stress the need to control the very limited space available in city centre streets and, looking at Gibson, he pointed out that it ought not to be the job of policemen to be spending their valuable time dealing with parking; they should be fighting crime.

'I would have thought you, as chairman of the Watch Committee, would be the first to recognise that,' he ended with a flourish.

Sir Edward Dodd agreed that we had a problem but suggested that the blue disc system, as applied in Paris and Bordeaux, would be the best way of handling the problem. In order to get through the meeting I suggested that perhaps someone should visit these cities to ascertain just how effective the scheme was. This agreed, I closed the meeting. I was to meet Samuels many times in the future.

Because of what I had seen in the cities I visited in the United States I now found myself in France. Our first stop was Paris. Getting through the security system to visit the Head of the Paris Police Force in his office was interesting, to say the least.

Sitting there with Sir Edward and Sir Herbert, a lot of time was taken up with the two Police Chiefs exchanging views on general policing matters. When we got around to discussing parking, I made it clear that I was proposing meters in my city whilst the Chief preferred his disc system. I added, 'We are here to get your opinion on how your system works.'

The Police Chief raised his eyebrows and his hands. 'Monsieur, let me make it clear, it is not *my* system. But surely this cannot be!' he exclaimed in a voice which registered disbelief. 'You are the politician, are you not, and Sir Edward is the policeman.'

I thought, *He won't like that description, mate.* Then the Frenchman went on, 'I am the policeman and I am in favour of the parking meter. It is the frightened little politicians who insist on this *stupid blue disc.*'

I kept my eyes firmly fixed on him and my mouth tightly closed, trying to image what was going in Dodd's head.

When we got outside Dodd turned to me, flushed and almost out of control. 'You cheeky little bugger!' he blurted out, 'You insulted me in front of a fellow officer – and a bloody foreigner at that!'

Off he stomped in a huff. Manzoni looked at me and as soon as Dodd was out of earshot we both began to laugh.

'What the hell was that all about?' I asked.

Manzoni said nothing but looked totally bemused.

While we were staying overnight in Paris, Manzoni tapped on my door. He knew that once Dodd had cooled down he would reflect on his comments and realise that he had overstepped the mark. I gathered that Manzoni was there to suss out what my reaction would be once we were back in Birmingham. They were, after all, brother officers, and he knew by this time that I was no fool and carried weight with the council. He was aware that I could have created a great deal of fuss out of the incident, placing Dodd in some difficulty. What he didn't know was that I had no intention of doing anything of the kind but decided to let Dodd stew for a while.

After Manzoni left, I slipped down to ask the concierge to recommend a nightclub where three English gentlemen might enjoy the evening.

'Le Naturiste,' he answered, with a wicked glint in his eye, and proceeded to book a table.

I called Manzoni and asked him to ensure that Dodd would be joining us for dinner; what he made of that I never knew.

We had a quiet meal during which I spoke hardly a word. Leaving the restaurant, I hailed a cab and without being overheard gave instructions to be taken to the Le Naturiste. I jumped out first and marched through the entrance; Manzoni and Dodd followed. I had arranged for a table near the stage and was sure that they enjoyed the champagne and the show. As we were leaving, Dodd, who had fully recovered from the morning's meeting and now more light-hearted, thanks I suspect, to the dinner, the show and the wine, turned to me.

I realised what he was about to say and held up my hand. 'Not a bloody word, my friend, not a single bloody word.' He looked down at me and for the first and only time said, 'Frank.' That was all, just 'Frank'.

After returning to Birmingham, we had no further objections from the Watch Committee. The end to this story is that we applied to the government for permission to install parking meters, only to find that Sir Alex Samuels had in the meantime travelled to Paris and returned to recommend to the Minister of Transport that the government try out a pilot scheme in Westminster. He wanted him and his minister to have the credit, not some councillor from the sticks.

I think that the decision to put traffic wardens under the police force was a mistake. I had been advocating for sometime that there was a need, as I saw in America and other countries, for a special highly trained traffic force separate from the normal police service. Today traffic wardens can be seen in most police stations carrying out duties that should be the job of civilians. The force increased its in-house establishment without questions from the Establishment Committees, and had control of the money collected from the meters which should be devoted to providing off-street parking facilities.

Chapter XIV

CHANGING THE IMAGE

Birmingham had regular spasms of creativity. Joseph Chamberlain – who was then a Liberal – began the trend in the 1800s when he convinced the city to take giant strides in municipal enterprise. He believed that public spending on the right projects was beneficial – unfortunately clearing the slums was not part of his plans – subsequently the city owned its own water, gas, electric and transport undertakings, and later its own bank.

During the 1880s he had the council purchase the freehold of the land in the centre of what was then a town, and rented it off on ninety-nine year leases so that it would benefit the citizens of the future. His intention was twofold; one that the ratepayers would enjoy the increase in values, and the ownership would allow the council to control its renewal programme without having to purchase the land and property.

Unfortunately, in the 1970s the Conservatives chose Francis Griffin to lead them and the council. He was an extreme right wing Tory who decided to sell the freeholds to the leaseholders. He suggested that we would be selling the assets to our citizens. They were in fact the multiple retailers, banks, insurance companies or pension funds. Like Mrs Thatcher, he believed that ownership and profit should be the preserve of the private sector.

As sitting tenants, he sold the freeholds for far less than their true value. He tossed away, at a knock-down price, the city's investment, which had been built up by Chamberlain and with it, the ability to renew its central core without the burden of buying the land. As I said at the time, 'Joe Chamberlain would be revolving in his grave.'

However, those of us who were members of the city council during the 1950s and 60s were fortunate to be serving during another period of creativity, one of its greatest up to then. We launched into a dramatic programme of change which was to improve the quality of life for tens of thousands of our citizens.

With the Austin and Morris car manufacturers and hundreds of companies making their components, we were Britain's car city, playing a part in their growing ownership which was to bring with it problems that the national administrators consistently failed to comprehend. The desire, as Robert Moses had described it to me, 'of people wanting a combustion engine under them', was making itself felt in the early fifties.

The sad thing was that we had the will and the ideas to deal with the impact, but were kept in a Central Government straight-jacket. Provincial cities such as Manchester, Leeds, Liverpool, Newcastle and Plymouth, like Birmingham had progressive Chief Engineers and Town Planners who were trying to plan for the future, only to be frustrated time and again by Whitehall.

In Birmingham, we were fast clearing the slums and improving the environment as we progressed. We recognised the need to keep the centre of the city vibrant and prosperous. Catering for the car and improving the standards of our public transport was a priority.

Our city, like others, had grown by absorbing surrounding villages, and as more people moved into these areas so their shopping facilities expanded. Over the years the main street in these 'villages' were extended and improved to resemble small town shopping centres. Its effect on Birmingham's city centre was not severe because they didn't attract large department stores, and we had a public transport system which was clean, regular and reasonably priced. We pioneered free rides for old people, and although we owned the transport we had obtained parliament's permission to achieve it. Once we'd won that battle, the rest of the country followed our example.

We were well aware that the growing car ownership would create problems, and if we failed to provide adequate and reasonably priced car parking facilities the owners would go elsewhere to shop. It didn't need a genius to realise that without them, the threat of American-style out-of-town shopping malls would present itself. And so it did.

The failure to provide adequate off-street car parking on the edge of the town centre, and the difficulties in controlling traffic movement within the core, were just a few of the reasons given to town planners by property developers to enable them to cash in by buying greenfield sites on the edge of populated areas to construct large shopping malls.

With massive free car parking and land that was far cheaper than it was in the centre of town, they were also able to offer lower rents to traders. The effect on many towns has been devastating. Their main street shopping centres were denuded of quality traders and the vacated properties declined into third-rate facilities, with many remaining empty.

Those British planners who became enamoured of these well-designed covered centres with copious parking space that took cars away from the congested inner city areas failed in their enthusiasm, to take note of the harmful consequence to the appearance and rateable value of recognised commercial centres.

Those who recommended planning permission be refused were in many cases overruled by the Government Ministry Inspectors on appeal. By allowing these developments they eased the traffic in the town centres temporarily but depressed them both financially and visually.

Had the government encouraged and assisted local authorities to construct adequate off-street car parking facilities on the outer rim of the commercial centres, and actively fostered the development of the park and ride schemes, I feel sure that we could have saved the spectacle of seeing so many town centres deteriorate.

What I have never understood is why the effect that these centres had on towns in the United States, which was there to see, failed to have any effect on the decision making process. In the lovely town of Wilmington, North Carolina, on what should have been a busy midday period, I found its downtown district deserted. Needing to change money, I made my way to the premises of a leading bank which I had visited some years before. It was established on the ground floor of a high-rise commercial block. The notice on the window informed me that it was closed, permanently. Looking up at the rest of the building I could see that it too was mostly empty.

Many of the stores and shops in the surrounding area were also closed. It had become a commercial slum, a victim of the out-of-town shopping phenomenon which changed the image of what had been an attractive district.

In order to save the commercial centre of Birmingham from deteriorating, I wanted to see the land within the confines of the inner ring road developed in a manner which would enlarge its central retail and entertainment facilities. My aim was to obtain the interest of the large departmental stores, by providing adequate low-cost car parking facilities around the inner ring road, and jump-on jump-off buses to carry shoppers into the centre.

I was convinced then, and am even more so today, that had Britain followed the trend towards regional autonomy, a goodly number of our problems would have been speedily dealt with. My views on this was strengthened in 1962 when I had the good fortune to be asked by the Macmillan Government to join a small delegation to study local government in West Germany, as it was then.

Macmillan, being concerned about the desire of local authorities to loosen the control of Central Government, which raised its head from time to time, set up a series of study groups. It disturbed the Whitehall mandarins. This was patently obvious for when I met the other members of the delegation I found there were only two local government representatives, the other being the Mayor of Norwich who, for reasons I never discovered, was not a member of their council. This in itself demonstrated Whitehall's attitude.

The Secretary, who came to take notes and keep us in order, was a civil servant. We toured the Province of Schleswig-Holstein and met the President. I had an opportunity to have a chat with him in private. It turned out that he had been a political prisoner held by the Nazis for many years, and on his release by the British army he'd been sent to England to study how our local government operated.

As their district was in the British sector, they wanted him to install our system which they thought was the best; they would, wouldn't they? Having studied our way of doing things I asked if he felt it superior to the present German system. He asked me in turn if those elected members in local government were happy being so closely monitored by Whitehall. I got the point.

He outlined the cultural, financial, economic and social benefits that were the result of what he called local state government. The day we visited Trävemunde, the President hosted a dinner party in the restaurant of a large hotel which had its own casino. After the meal I enquired if he had any objection to me looking in to the casino and maybe playing for fifteen minutes. He asked, 'Why should I object when, as we are partners in this enterprise, you will be contributing to our exchequer?'

In Kiel, he took us to a performance in the opera house, also owned and managed by the Province. Twenty per cent of the seats were sold to students at a discounted price.

'We encourage the arts; by providing entrance to performances in theatres and other cultural places we are educating our future local tax payers to support the arts. We think it makes sense,' he told us, with a hint of pride.

When our delegation returned to Britain we were told by the Acting Secretary that he would be circulating his report. I had to call him to enquire why so many favourable points of the German system were not mentioned. There was no reaction, so I wrote to say that I couldn't agree with his summation and enclosed what I suppose was a minority report. Neither I, nor for all I know any other of the members of the group, heard anything more. I suspect that Harold Macmillan didn't hear a word either.

This took place thirty-seven years ago. The trip convinced me of the benefits of devolving much of the power of Central Government to a new regional government set-up, moving power closer to the people. Today it seems that all political parties are expressing favour for such a move. A partial devolution for Scotland, Wales and Northern Ireland has recently taken place and yet I still have doubts that the British Parliament will hand over much of its powers to the regions. The mandarins wouldn't allow it.

After I returned from my trip to Schleswig-Holstein I realised that until such time that we had a government that was prepared to take this up seriously, we needed to create in the minds of people outside its boundaries that Birmingham was not just a centre for 'metal bashing'; it was a 'capital' city. We needed to impress other countries to see us as something other than just another British provincial town.

To assist in achieving this, I urged the building of a large central Sports Hall capable of staging world events and international exhibitions. In 1963, I had a series of meetings with the trustees of the Alexandra Stadium, the home of Birchfield Harriers. It was in a rundown state, and as I was then the chairman of the Parks Committee I suggested that we take it over, offering them the same facilities they enjoyed. They turned the offer down. Today it is owned by the city, has been extended and is world renowned.

I pressed that we should improve the attraction of the city centre by developing a theatre and entertainment district on the scale of London's West End. When the chairman of Moss Empires, who was known as 'Prince' Littler, made an approach to the Planning Department to redevelop their Theatre Royal in New Street, I thought that it might present an opportunity towards achieving our aims.

Questioning his reason, he pussyfooted around, finally admitting that Jack Cotton, a local man who had by then become one of the biggest property developers in the UK, had made him an offer his company couldn't refuse. It didn't take much imagination to realise that Cotton wasn't about to go into the theatre business.

I explained to Littler that its demolition would constitute a change of use under the planning code and would require the permission of my committee and the city council. Once Jack Cotton heard this from Littler he sailed in to see us. He admitted that his client, F W Woolworth, wished to build another store in the city. He had made a very good offer to Moss Empires and he intended to erect a building to meet his client's requirements: three floors, basement, ground and first for the store, and offices above.

Privately, I had to admit that a theatre on a site in one of the busiest shopping streets in the city centre with no parking provision, a heavy traffic flow passing its doors and a pavement that was none too wide, was not ideal. Even so, I wasn't of a mind to see another one of our theatres disappear. I asked Sir Herbert to arrange a meeting with members of the Moss Empires Board.

No one appeared except Littler. I outlined our plans to zone an area for entertainment facilities and that his Hippodrome Theatre lay at its centre. I undertook to seek the council's permission to demolish the Theatre Royal and to offer his company a site in the entertainment zone for a new Theatre Royal. It would be ideally situated, adjacent to underground car parking, on a bus route and would be offered to them freehold or leasehold; in either case, on very favourable terms.

If his company accepted this offer, planning permission would be given for the change of use of their present site. They would be making a handsome profit on its sale to Mr Cotton, and would have a brand new theatre. He was left to consider the proposition.

Littler contacted Sir Herbert agreeing to the deal. We offered Moss Empires a prime site on a corner of the inner ring road opposite the new Albany Hotel. He gave us to understand that they accepted and were in the process of designing the new theatre. This was reported to the Public Works Committee, who approved the recommendation which in turn was reported to the city council. They welcomed the proposal, and on the basis of Prince Littler's word, planning permission was given to demolish the Theatre Royal.

Assured that everything was going according to plan, we waited. A little more than a year went by without any move from Moss Empires, so I sought a further meeting with their Board, insisting this time that the Board of Directors be present.

The meeting fixed, I asked the new leader of the city council, Alderman Harry Watton, and Mr Reginald Ross, the Chief Estates Officer, to accompany Manzoni and me. We met in Moss Empires' offices at three in the afternoon. Littler was in the Chair. His demeanour suggested that he had enjoyed a good lunch. With heavy eyes and a partly smoked cigar in his mouth, he opened the meeting. The West End Impresario, Val Parnell and Littler's brother, Emile, were among the Board members present.

Littler mumbled on about the last time we had met and how

much he admired Birmingham and its people. We were as embarrassed as his brother and the other members of his Board. I waited for him to complete what I gathered was his address of welcome before introducing my colleagues and laying before them a plan of the proposed theatre area. Marked on it, was the existing Hippodrome, the Alexandra Theatre and the site of their proposed new Theatre Royal.

The look on the faces of his Board members was enough for me. I said to Harry Watton, 'They are going to renege,' but he didn't see it that way. The meeting rambled on and on, with one after another of the Board members apologising as they left the room and the meeting ended without a definitive answer to our queries. Val Parnell took Harry aside; I didn't hear what was said but it turned out that he and I had been invited to meet him at the Palladium that night.

When we arrived, the house manager was waiting to escort us to what we thought would be Parnell's office; instead he took us to two seats in the stalls. During the interval we were taken to the VIP suite to be greeted by Parnell. He asked, 'Would you like to meet the star of the show, Liberace?' He appeared disappointed when I said that we would settle for a drink.

In a moment of brutal frankness, Parnell told us that his chairman was out of his mind. The Board were never told of Littler's commitment to us and that they never intended to build another theatre in Birmingham.

I hit the roof. 'He gave us his word!' I almost shouted.

Parnell looked at me and came out with a comment I will never forget.

'My dear young man, when someone gives you his word, always insist on having his bond.'

Times had changed. Not bothering to stay to see the rest of the show, I made my excuses and left alone to make my way to Ronnie Scott's jazz club, hoping that the music would lift my blues. It didn't. Sitting there I thought, *Another lesson learned…*

At that time Birmingham was described, by those who didn't know it, as being a 'cultural desert'. Although unjustified, the comment was repeated so often that it became generally accepted. Few outside the city of a thousand and one trades were aware that most of the legendary actors and actresses of stage and screen had learned their craft in Birmingham at Sir Barry Jackson's Repertory or Salberg's Alexandra theatres.

Both were subsidised by the city council, as was the Birmingham Symphony Orchestra, one of the finest in Europe, even though it performed in a town hall not famous for the quality of its acoustics. It must be said that every year we had to battle with some of the Tory backwoodsmen who fought against subsidising anything remotely connected with the arts. Thankfully, the majority were not of that mind.

In the council chamber I sat on the opposite side of a gangway to a cheerful, bouncy Conservative named Collett. He had a thing about, as he put it, 'ratepayers' money being wasted on the arts. Charlie, as he was known to one and all, had a cherubic face and a head as bald as a new-laid egg. He was one of the council's characters.

On the day our annual budget was discussed we could count on him making an impassioned speech, and it was always against what he termed 'propping up the City Orchestra'. On this particular day he decided to include in the image the theatres, the Museum and Art Gallery and City Library. I caught the eye of the Lord Mayor to indicate that I wanted to follow Charlie.

Once the Chamber had settled down after his lively contribution, I rose to speak. Moving into the gangway standing next to the seated Charlie, I looked around the Chamber and then down at him. During this pregnant pause with the members expecting me to make a hard-hitting attack on what he had propounded, I patted his baldpate, simply saying, 'I really am at a loss to understand just what goes on in here.' Then I resumed my seat.

The council sat in complete silence until they realised that that was all. They laughed, none louder than Charlie.

His compatriots once again didn't bother to support him, and the City Orchestra and the other institutions he had attacked survived for another year. Opposition to assisting the arts there was, but we could always count on a majority from all sides when the vote was taken.

Birmingham has one of the finest museum and art galleries,

the greatest number of free public libraries, and its Central Library houses the largest and most important Shakespeare and Shaw collections. We built a new Sir Barry Jackson Repertory Theatre, and the city allocated fourteen acres of a City Park to enable me, along with John English and a group of enthusiastic citizens to develop the first, and I think the only Arts Centre for Young People in Great Britain, if not the whole of Europe.

Much later, the city constructed the finest concert hall in the country for its world renowned Symphony Orchestra, and it is just a part of a complex which includes the country's largest Convention Centre and close by a superb International Indoor Sports Hall. The council even forgave Moss Empires, helping them out by buying their Hippodrome Theatre as a home for the National Ballet Company. Last year the Royal Command Performance was staged there, the first time it had taken place out of London. Ronnie Scott, who realised that the city welcomed all cultures, opened a jazz cub. Some desert!

One of the important contribution I made during my period as chairman of Public Works was the massive central area redevelopment. The destruction of the slums and the construction of what I called 'The Five New Towns in Birmingham'. But few people know that the catalyst was Winston Churchill.

Haunted by the broken promise made to the fighting forces returning from the hell of Flanders in the 1914–18 war, that the government would 'build homes fit for heroes to live in', as prime minister during the Second World War Churchill aimed to put that to rights. Looking back it is truly amazing that with the country on the edge of defeat, Churchill took time off early in 1942 to set up a committee with the remit to prepare plans for dealing with Britain's bombed and blighted towns as soon as the war was over.

By this time our City Engineer and Surveyor, Herbert Manzoni, had built an enviable reputation, and he was chosen to sit on the committee. It gave him the opportunity to bring about what he had spoken of at the meeting to the boys' club my brother Eric had attended long before the war. With his input, the committee produced what became known as the 1944 Blitz and Blight Act.

They adopted his ideas on slum clearance as a model, and by the time the committee's plans and recommendations were ensconced in an Act of Parliament, he had already prepared a scheme for Birmingham. In 1946, he placed this revolutionary plan before the newly elected Labour Council, not expecting them to grab it as they did. They immediately ordered that an application be made to parliament, now under a Labour Government, to proceed under the Act. The rest is history.

No other authority in Britain had the foresight, or the courage, to jump at the opportunities provided by Winston Churchill's Act, and no other authority was to achieve what we did over the next fifteen years.

Having heard of what was being done, an American Senator came to visit the City in 1954. I took him on a tour of the five designated areas and was able to show him the appalling conditions to which the Act applied and the work being undertaken. I explained that parliament had given us powers to acquire the land and property in these quite large areas. Asking how this was done, I set out the terms of the Act.

'We, the city council, publish a "Notice to Treat" delineating the boundaries of the areas to be included. By that notice we were exercising powers vested in us by Act of Parliament namely to take ownership of everything in the area, setting aside the matter of compensation to be dealt with at a later date. In short, we had powers to confiscate all the land, and the property that stood on it.'

'Good God!' exclaimed the Senator, 'That's a piece of unadulterated communism. Whose idea was it?'

I realised that he was under the mistaken impression that only a left-wing government would have dreamt up such a scheme, so I was delighted to be able to answer, 'It was Winston Churchill's and it works.'

After I filled in the background he began to realise that it was the only way we would be able to tackle the redevelopment of thousands of acres of slum properties in a reasonably short period. After he'd seen inside some of the hovels and met the families who had to live in them, I was able to convert him.

I could understand why the people still living there just didn't believe that it was really going to happen. Having lived in one of these areas and heard politicians promising year after year that 'something will be done', I wanted desperately to prove to them that this time the promise would be kept; that we were on the threshold of building a 'New Birmingham'.

In an effort to convince them, I wrote a series of articles called 'The New Birmingham' which the *Birmingham Mail* printed each day for a week. It wasn't just propaganda; we were really on the move and I wanted the people to know. The demand for the newspaper was so heavy that the *Birmingham Post* and *Mail* reprinted the editions in the form of a booklet and their readers were sending them to their friends and relatives in other parts of the world, proudly announcing what was being done to their city.

The five designated areas were called, for instance, 'The Summer Lane Slum Clearance Area', and to respect the dignity of those that lived there I wanted the names changed. I asked the editor of the newspaper to help me. I wanted to remove the stigma of living in the slums and to give the residents a feel for the new era. Once again he agreed to help.

They ran a competition to choose new names for the five areas, the response was overwhelming. The newspaper had contributed its services once again, succeeding in getting the message across that this time things were really going to change. A panel was set up and the names that were put forward were Duddeston, Highgate, Ladywood, Lee Bank and Newtown. These names were chosen and remained after the redevelopment was completed. I'm proud of that.

When we launched into the scheme it created a stir far beyond the city's boundaries. The Civic Trust asked if they could make a documentary film during the first phase of what was to be known as Lee Bank. It featured a number of high-rise flats set in a green open space where hundreds of back-to-back houses and grim factories once stood.

Whilst I was off camera waiting to be interviewed, two young boys came to see what was happening. I asked them where they lived, and they pointed to the top floor of one of the tower blocks.

'And where did you live before?' I asked.

'In a back house in Latimer Street,' came the reply. It had been demolished.

Wanting to get their reaction to their new surroundings, I asked if they liked it better than their old home. They looked surprised, which was answer enough. 'Why?' I asked. Then it was my turn to be surprised. The elder boy told me that just before he went to sleep he could look out of his bedroom window and, as he put it quite poetically, 'See the lights in the street stretching out like stars lying on the ground.'

The younger boy was more prosaic. 'When I go to the lav,' he said with a serious look on his face, 'I don't have to keep my foot up against the door.'

I knew exactly what he meant, having shared the indignity of having a neighbour push open the door to see me sitting on the lavatory.

What we were engaged in created a great spirit in the Departments who had the task of planning the repair and maintenance of the mass of outdated dilapidated property until they could be knocked down. To be involved in the planning of the new streets, providing the green open spaces, seeing the trees and flowering shrubs planted in areas once paved over, and the building of the new homes, made it an exciting and satisfying time.

Birmingham was long on families waiting for homes of their own, and short on land to rehouse them. We could have moved faster and also avoided having to construct high-rise flats had we been able to convince successive governments that the towns in the West Midlands were faced with the same problem as the London Boroughs. We too needed a new town.

The government sitting in Britain's capital appeared oblivious to the problems we had. They left us with no alternative other than to build multi-storey flats. To meet the needs we had to move, and move quickly and in our hurry to provide decent homes for our people, we made mistakes. The Ministry of Housing and those in local government responsible for building homes, acting on the advice they were given, fell for the private building companies' 'system building' proposals. Homes would cost less and could be built fast. Many proved to be awful to look at, and in too many cases disastrous to live in.

Mistakes were also made in housing and rehousing families. The elected members thought, as we are all prone to do, that the experts in their field knew best. Our Housing Management Committee employed as their chief officer a man who was reputed to be one of the finest in his profession – a man who had worked for the Greater London Council, whose advice they thought they could count on with impunity.

The fact was that the GLC made the mistake of breaking up family units in the East End of London when they were rehoused. Yet having worked there, the housing manager still failed to recognise the simple fact, that keeping family members living reasonably close by paid out all kinds of dividends.

Living in what they called the 'old area', when one of the family married, the mother would have a word with the landlord's agent to see that when a property nearby became vacant they would be given first chance to rent it. In this way, the people in the slums had their own built-in social security system.

When a member of the family unit was ill and needed to be cared for, one of their kin at best, or a close neighbour, was nearby to assist. One would have thought that the importance of this was simple enough to recognise and understand. Unfortunately, neither the housing manager, his staff nor the committee members appeared to be able to comprehend that by sending them to different parts of a big city hindered them from keeping in close touch. It was a most dreadful mistake.

Putting parents with young children in the upper storeys of high-rise apartment blocks also put a strain on families. Mothers could keep an eye on their children in a backyard or a garden. Living in an apartment several levels above ground made it impossible. Although the Departments were working under pressure, little if any thought was given to these very real problems by the architects or the housing managers and, to be fair, the elected members.

When I met the official in charge of housing in the Israeli city of Haifa, I questioned him about the difficulties he faced in accommodating Jewish immigrants from the ghettos of Europe and other parts of the world.

He told me, 'Many of them had no experience of living in a modern home and were bound to find it difficult to cope. I soon recognised the need to train my staff to patiently, and sympathetically guide and assist these families during the transition.'

He added that he quickly realised that splitting up friends and families would be counterproductive, so he worked hard to keep them together.

'Although at first it added a further strain, we learned that in the end, it made our job and the job of those working in Social Services, much easier.'

Our own problems were not too dissimilar, but with the added language and national differences, we had nothing like as difficult a task as theirs. Unfortunately, I met him too late in the day.

As we were so short of land and forced to put people into flats, I suggested that when we came to relocate small factories, to save land, there was no reason why *they* should not be placed in multilevel accommodation. In March 1954, we opened the first purpose-built municipal flatted factory in the United Kingdom. It was built to rehouse some of the small factories we were about to demolish in our slum clearance programme. We were trying hard to overcome our shortage of land, but our pleas for a new town still fell on deaf ears.

Through my service on the city council and in the government-appointed jobs I was to hold, I learned that those who sat in Whitehall simply couldn't, or wouldn't try to understand the problems facing cities far away from the south-east. I also began to realise that too many of those whom we elect to the Mother of Parliaments, once reaching ministerial office, became, albeit unwittingly, virtual prisoners of the system, and totally dependent on the advice and guidance of their senior civil servants. There were many who were superb but too many of them were Oxbridge Classics scholars who had little or no experience of the real world.

We also had our share of intellectual idiots among our elected representatives who didn't appear to have even a glimmer of basic common sense. The late George Brown, of fond memory, once described this to me in graphic terms.

We had arranged to meet for lunch at 12.30 p.m. on a Thursday, the day the Cabinet met. I arrived ten minutes early. By 1.30 p.m. I decided he wasn't coming, so I sat at the table I had reserved and ordered my meal. A few minutes later George came in and I could see that he was in a foul mood. Knowing him, I decided to speak not a word until he chose to.

When coffee arrived he turned to me apologising for being late. Holding up his hand to indicate that I should remain silent, he told me that the Cabinet meeting was still going on when he left.

'I was so angry,' he said in that booming voice we all grew to accept, 'I told them as I left, all you do is practise intellectual masturbation.'

'They do what?' I asked.

'They play with themselves intellectually. Instead of making what you and I would see as a straightforward decision, they get involved in an intellectual exercise playing with it between themselves and getting nowhere,' he explained without a smile. He obviously meant it.

Whatever advice ministers were given in respect of our problems in Birmingham, they and their successors in office certainly 'played with it' to the cost of much unhappiness and our reputation as a progressive, caring council.

The Midlands Conurbation was bursting at the seams. Year after year we made a copper-bottomed case for the development of a new town for the West Midlands. A number had been set up in the South to ease the pressure on London, but our appeals fell on deaf ears until it was too late.

The only thing Whitehall came up with by way of what they *thought* would be a solution was what they termed 'Overspill'. In truth, what they were doing was kicking our demands for a new town into the long grass, a tactic at which the Whitehall mandarins were adept.

This lamebrained idea was to induce rural towns to allow the city to build council houses in their district. It was fraught with problems. In addition to being too slow, it was too small to meet the problem we and surrounding towns faced. If their plan was meant to keep us quiet, it failed miserably.

The Shropshire Urban District Council of Dawley, the site of the first Industrial Revolution – and it showed – was more than thirty miles from the city and difficult to get to. It was one that the Ministry recommended. Desperate, we arranged to meet a delegation from this small town. They had with them the clerk to the Shropshire County Council, Mr Geoffrey Godber, a bright and charming man who had one brother who was or had been the Minister of Agriculture and Fisheries and another who was a chief medical adviser to the Minister of Health. Years later I was to become closely involved with Geoffrey and Dawley.

During the discussion that went on for some time, the question was raised by the chairman of the Urban District Council as to the type and quality of tenants we would be sending. We knew perfectly well what he was getting at but I asked if he would be a little more helpful by telling us the type and quality he had in mind. He raised a laugh when he replied, 'Well people like you, for instance.'

'Not from the slums?' I countered.

'No, we would prefer others.'

Alderman Sir Albert Bradbeer, who was chairing the meeting, told his opposite number, 'Councillor Price, who is as you suggest the type you would like as a resident, was born and reared in the slums and we don't want to lose him.' I pleaded with the Dawley chairman not to be embarrassed.

We did build a few houses in his district, but as an answer to our problems it was a minuscule drop in a very large bucket. As it turned out, Dawley was soon to be declared as the area where a New Town Corporation was to be set up... too late to avoid the building of residential tower blocks in Birmingham and the overcrowded towns within the region, for which we, not the government, had to take a great deal of stick. This criticism usually came from wiseacres who didn't have the responsibility of having to deal with our enormous problem.

In Birmingham alone, we were faced with rehousing more than 30,000 families from the slums, and providing for another 60,000 families who had no home of their own. With no land and no help, from whichever government was in power, we had no other choice but to build up.

Ministers and their civil servant advisers have always laboured under the impression that they know what is best for local authorities. Nothing seems to have changed. A prime example was the Rt Hon Richard Crossman – an intellectual bully who didn't care to listen to anyone he felt to be his inferior, be they political friend or foe. Too many times he was simply wrong, but he rarely if ever admitted that it was possible.

The Ministry of Defence decided that Castle Bromwich Aerodrome was surplus to requirements and offered it to the city. It was on our northern boundary, it was very large and very flat, and we jumped at the offer. Crossman was the Minister of Housing and Local Government, and his Ministry got involved with our Architect's Department in the planning of the site. As it was flat they decided to cover it with system-built tower blocks and a few bungalows for elderly people.

When the minister came to Birmingham we were given to believe that he wished to discuss the plan with the members of the council, but not long into the meeting it became pretty obvious that this was to be less of a consultation and more of a lecture.

Crossman sat at the head of the long committee table, and although I was the Lord Mayor at the time, I chose to sit further down the room next to Alderman Francis Griffin, the then leader of the Conservative Group. There came a point when I decided to express my concern about the density of the development and the total lack of social facilities in what was to be, in effect, a small township.

Having ascertained that the government was not going to fund any such facilities within Castle Vale, as it was to be called, I suggested that we leave one of the large hangars, improve its outward appearance and allow the city, in cooperation with social and sporting organisations, to turn the inside into a multi-purpose centre for the community.

Annoyed at being interrupted, Crossman looked across at me and shouted, 'What kind of bloody foolish idea is that?'

I stood up and retorted, 'Minister, if you had to live with your family in one of these tower blocks, on the outer edge of the city miles from any shops or social facilities, I would respectfully suggest that you would then have more sense than to dismiss my idea as bloody foolish.'

He was furious, but I wouldn't give way. I concluded, 'You obviously have no idea what it will be like for these families, and I'm sorry to have to say, I believe you never will.'

All that Alderman Griffin had to say was directed at me. 'How can you speak to him like that?' he said. 'He's one of yours.'

'You seem to forget, Francis,' I replied angrily, 'that I'm here to represent the people of Birmingham, whether he is one of mine or not.'

Dick Crossman never forgave me and took his revenge on two separate occasion, which I will come to.

By the time that Whitehall recognised the desperately urgent housing need in the West Midlands, Sir Keith Joseph had been appointed as the minister.

Without taking the trouble to consult with any of the local authorities directly affected, he made the wrong decision in respect of the siting of the first Midlands New Town. It was par for the course (see the chapter entitled 'New Town Blues').

During my public life, I have always believed that those who have the responsibility of making decisions that could effect people's lives have with it a responsibility of explaining directly to them what is being proposed, and to listen to their response. Too few do; they duck out of face-to-face meetings for fear of what they think will be strong opposition. They rarely understand that much of the opposition usually arises because the people concerned feel that they have been ignored.

On the various redevelopment and road schemes my committee planned to carry out whilst I was chairman, I always arranged for a public meeting to explain it in detail and to take note of the views put forward. My officers and my committee benefited enormously from this policy of two-way communication.

I carried on with this in the New Town of Dawley – now Telford – and during my long tenure as chairman of the British Waterways Board. On many occasions, I acted against the expressed advice of my officials. To be fair there were some who not only understood but welcomed my approach, which eased the burdens we were all carrying.

Public Works covered a wide variety of activities, but even so I sometimes went outside my remit. An example was the lack of imagination shown by the owners of shops and stores, and almost without exception the multiple companies, in the main streets in the city centre. I called a meeting via their Chamber of Trade, suggesting that they should follow the example of the London's Regent Street Traders' Association in respect of Christmas lights; this was in 1958.

I promised that I would obtain the support of the council if they agreed to pitch in. The negative reaction of some of the more prosperous businesses was hard to believe. Because some of the multiples owned more than one shop in the centre – trading under different names – they declined to participate.

Try as we may, they wouldn't budge. With the agreement of those anxious to see it happen I had the Architect's Department draw some designs and a visual impression of what it could look like, and then held a press conference. The designs were published along with a report naming those traders who had agreed to participate. It also listed those upon whom we were, as I put it, awaiting a decision. I stated that it depended on them whether their customers, within and outside the city, would enjoy the spectacle of Christmas lights or not. Those who had hesitated came into the scheme and the lights have been erected every year since.

One of the multifarious functions falling to the Public Works Committee was street cleaning and caring for the city's public buildings. As autumn drew close, just before dusk, the sky above the city centre was almost blacked out by swarms of starlings coming in to spend the night. They perched in the trees or on the ledges of the offices having no respect for the buildings, the people inside, or those in the streets below.

Their nightly presence became a matter of public debate. Having eaten outside the city during the daytime they left the refuse of their bodily function on the window sills and the pavements, and sometimes on the heads of those passing beneath them in the early evening.

The public reaction was divided. Those who were not affected by the nuisance far outweighed those that were, and so the majority were somewhat ambivalent to the outcry against these feathered creatures. This meant that we were on the horns of a dilemma.

We lived in a big city and the majority of its people live and worked away from the zone the birds occupied. Regular visitors *to*, and those working *in* the city centre, ran the risk of being 'hit' on their way home in the evening. Those working in offices during the daytime, after the birds had left, ran the risk of being overcome by stench of rotting excrement if they opened a window.

Office workers were in a mutinous state of mind in respect of this invasion and, being chairman of the committee responsible for street cleaning and public buildings, I somehow became the target for the 'get rid of the starlings brigade'.

When I tried to effect an answer, those who believed that the invaders should be left alone, criticised me for even trying to shoo them away. For many reasons, but most of all because of the mess they made, I sided with those who wanted to be rid of the troublesome invaders.

I held a council of war, sifting through the ideas that came by every post. We first decided to send trucks out after midnight when most people, and the birds, were asleep. The vehicles were those used for dealing with the tall streetlights and high wires, etc., so we provided them with tubes connected to a gas tank and they proceeded to put the birds to sleep, permanently.

As luck would have it, they were spotted by a late-night bird enthusiast who collected a few of the expired creatures and got a picture of himself and his haul in the local paper. It put an end to this particular method. Someone came up with what he suggested was a painless repellent. He presented us with tapes of the cries of female starlings in distress. Once they hear this they will hightail it out of town, he told us with great confidence. I thought it worth a try.

As the birds began to swarm, circling over the city to choose their landing spot, out went the trucks, this time with loudspeakers strapped to the ladders broadcasting the cries of the female starlings whilst driving around the central streets. I am not too sure about the effect on the birds but it scared the life out of many of our citizens, so we discontinued the practice.

The news of our efforts was, surprisingly, reported in newspapers around the world. A Canadian industrialist who heard of our dilemma sent me a few samples of lifelike rubber snakes which he assured me would do the trick. He predicted that when the starlings spotted the snakes they would fly off. We placed these on the window sills and awaited the result.

After a number of circuits and bumps the birds were observed landing on the sills, walking up to the snakes and contemptuously nudging them off their perch. We let the Canadian know what had happened. He said that the birds must be Russian. Make of that what you will.

Rentokil, an internationally famous company who had made a reputation on their ability to rid the world of pests, came forward with the idea of painting the window sills with a gelatinous material. The idea being that it was clear so would not affect the appearance of the buildings and the birds wouldn't see it until they tried to land. Finding themselves on an unsure footing they would buzz off. By this time we were prepared to try anything, so Rentokil got busy.

This went well until a Kamikaze starling decided to take a chance, regardless. It skidded and rolled in the material and fell with its feathers glued to its side. Again, as luck would have it, the unfortunate bird fell on to the head of a passer-by, who just happened to be an officer of the local RSPCA. He came storming into the office and that put an end to that experiment. We tried putting bright lights in trees in the parks on the outskirts of the city. This didn't fool the birds for long. In the end we placed electric wires on the ledges. It was expensive, but it did the trick. Where the starlings decided to go we didn't know and didn't care. A few days ago I read that the citizens of Rome are being bombarded; they will need a lot of wire.

The press had fun with it at my expense but I had learned enough to know that the reporters had their job to do, and in public life you were there to be shot at. There were times when the local newspapers, who could not be described as being favourably disposed to the Labour Party, could have purposely decided to show a lack of understanding even though they were in possession of the facts. It is not uncommon with some papers, but I must say that during my period on the city council, as far as I was concerned, it was never the case.

I was – with one exception – able to trust the municipal reporters. Roy Smith of the *Mail* and John Lewis of the *Post* always treated the confidence I placed in them with respect. This didn't stop them publishing the opposition's criticisms of my actions, or belting me when in their view I was out of line.

To do justice to their job they required background knowledge of what we, the council, were trying to achieve. I explained in some detail proposals that were being considered by my committee. They appreciated that these were non-reportable briefings and never 'jumped the gun'. Nothing was ever published before decisions were taken and without exception they always acted honourably.

A prime example of their cooperation was in the case of the green pastures of Edgbaston, a district less than a quarter of a mile from the heart of the city. Warwickshire County Cricket Club, the Birmingham University, the Queen Elizabeth Hospital, Priory Lawn Tennis Club, Edgbaston Golf Club and the Edgbaston Reservoir are within its boundaries. It is a green and pleasant place close to the city's centre.

The houses on what was known as the Calthorpe Estate were what you might call 'grand'; they stood in large gardens in quiet tree-lined roads. They were leasehold and the leases were running out.

Being short of land to build low-cost houses, my colleagues were naturally casting their eyes on this low-density estate. Brigadier Sir Richard Anstruther-Gough Calthorpe, the head of the family who owned this vast acreage, had commissioned John Madin, a bright young architect planner, to prepare a scheme ready for redevelopment. Although the plan introduced some apartment blocks in addition to houses, they were not designed for the lower income group.

When John Madin asked to meet my committee in order to discuss the plan, I warned him to take care. He was aware of the desire to take over the estate but I didn't tell him, or my colleagues for that matter, that I had already made up my mind that covering it with council houses was not a good idea. Sutton Coldfield and Solihull – towns on the borders of Birmingham – had already siphoned off too many members of the professional class from the city; I wanted to stem the flow and the Calthorpe development plan could help.

Convincing the rest of the Labour Party faced with a massive housing problem wasn't going to be easy. I asked Madin to hold off and suggested that we have a quiet chat about the future of his client's land. Over a pot of tea in my office in Baskerville House I gave him a rundown on the difficulties of trying to convince the council to approve his plan. He was an earthy, intelligent and likeable fellow who grasped the point. I asked if Calthorpe owned any land outside, but near to, the area which we understood as being 'the Estate'.

'Yes, they have land on the other side of the Bristol Road,' he replied quizzically. Before he left he mentioned that the press knew about the plan.

I didn't want anything published before I had a chance to try to convince my colleagues of the wisdom of allowing the development to proceed. I wanted to retain a mixture of income groups close to the centre of the city. I explained this to the reporters and they held back from releasing what was an important piece of news.

I knew that Madin would report my comments to his client so I suggested that Sir Richard come up from his other estate in Hampshire to talk. His being a leading member of the Hampshire County Council proved to be more of help than a hindrance. Having explained to him that I was not in favour of a further watering down of the city's social mix, but faced with an over-whelming shortage of land for low-cost housing, I would have difficulty in convincing the rest of my Party to see my point.

I asked, in view of our problems, 'How can I possibly convince the council to agree to your architects' plans?'

He quickly picked up my drift. 'You were enquiring about the land we own on the other side of Bristol Road. Just what have you in mind?' he said, not taking his eyes off me.

Before he left he agreed to sell us his land, which stretched between Pershore Road, and Bristol Road at a price fixed by the District Valuer as a quid pro quo for the council looking kindly on their scheme. This was the sugar on the pill which enabled us to preserve a reasonable balance and maintained the almost rural ambience that is Edgbaston. Both Anstruther-Gough Calthorpe and I knew that he could have applied for planning permission and fought the case had we rejected it, but his local government experience allowed him to see both sides. I can't say that I met with the same receptive approach from the local brewers.

Grandfather Frederick George Price. Taken in the summer
of 1931. He played for Aston Villa in 1896.

Top: Boxing for Aston ABC at Bantam Weight.
Bottom: With Sir Herbert Manzoni and Neville Borg. We cleared Birmingham's massive slum problem and was frustrated by central government from curing it's traffic problems.

Top: Standing in the Bull Ring with the Rotunda as a backdrop.
It was much criticised but became a symbol.
Bottom: With Marcus Sieff, Chairman of M&S, in happier days.

Top: Shirley Maclaine in Las Vegas. She remembered me from way back.
Bottom: Caught in a war with the Starlings.

Top: With Prime Minister, Harold Wilson.
Bottom: My son Noel (8 years old) with me in Cornwall.

Top: With Willie Brandt, Mayor of Berlin, 1965.
Bottom: Tulip Festival with tulip girls sent from Holland.

Lord Mayor of Birmingham 1964.

Before taking the Queen Mother for a sail on the Regents Canal.

Top: Opening of the Bull Ring Centre, Birmingham, 1964 – my first brush with Prince Philip.
Bottom: Princess Margaret and Lord Snowden looking at the model. John English on the right.
Midlands Art Centre for Young People, 1965.

Top: Greeting Prince Charles on the Sunday after his engagement to Princess Diana. Inaugurating a boat for handicapped in Lancashire.
Middle: Opening a lock on the SSYN.
Bottom: Prince Philip joking with canal enthusiasts on the K&A.

Top: With Admiral Sir William O'Brien and General Sir Hugh Stockwell, on the Sunday after I had retired from BWB. Opening the Dundeas Aqueduct on the K&A, 1984.
Bottom: Gas Street Basin in the centre of Birmingham. I was criticised when I started its regeneration. It's now a thriving tourist attraction.

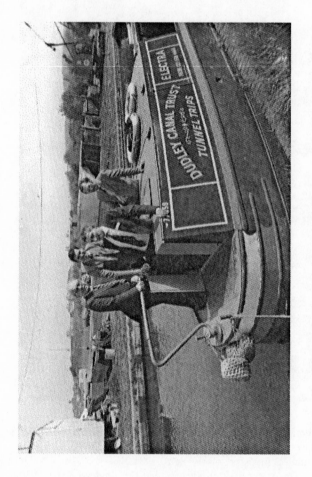

On board Dudley Canal Trust electric boat Electra. Used for trips inside Dudley Tunnel, but on this day to go inside Netherton.

PALACE OF HOLYROODHOUSE

4th July, 1984

Dear Sir Frank,

Thank you for sending me a copy of your booklet.

I am sorry to hear that you are leaving the Board.
I doubt whether anyone has done as much for the waterways
of this country during this century as you have. You
will always have the satisfaction of knowing that apart
from commercial regeneration your efforts have brought
pleasure and relaxation to millions of people.

yours sincerely

Philip

Letter from Prince Philip on my retirement from BWB.

On the day I retired from BWB. My three secretaries, from the left: June Pell, Gwen Hill and Mu Cope.

My brothers and I in Whittington – four old men reliving the past.

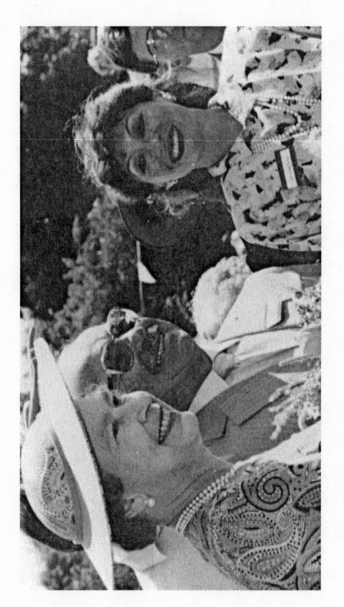

The Queen and my wife, Daphne. Opening of the K&A Canal.

Chapter XV

DEALING WITH OTHER VESTED INTERESTS

Over many years, Mitchells and Butlers and Ansells had acquired sites in areas were they knew the city would expand. When enough potential clients had taken up residence they applied for permission to build their pubs. Consequently they owned most of the pubs in Birmingham.

As chairman of the Public Works Committee responsible for town planning, I sat on what was called the Licensing Planning Committee. Licences for pubs was issued by the Licensing Justices, but applicants had first to prove need and obtain permission from Licensing Planning. The committee was made up of an equal number of Justices and members of the city's planning committee. The chairman was always a member of the Justices, and at this time it was Sir Charles Burman.

As the City was disturbing a large number of their pubs in the redevelopment areas, the brewers saw what they thought was an opportunity of obtaining compensation for what they claimed was loss of trade. They sought the support of the Licensing Justices, who always appeared to be well disposed towards them. As the two brewers had a virtual monopoly and their customers were simply being redistributed, I challenged their claim for loss of trade.

I asked the Licensing Planning committee to call in a Licensing Valuer from outside the city to evaluate the claim. I had done my homework and knew that in the North of England they judged compensation for loss of trade on what they called 'Loss of barrelage'. As the redevelopment was reducing the numbers of pubs but not the numbers of 'drinkers', the brewers' claim was a nonsense.

As I expected, the Justices sided with the brewers and my plea to Sir Charles got nowhere. Seeing the ratepayers stumping up hundreds of thousands of pounds to the brewers was unacceptable, so I asked Sir Herbert Manzoni to find a reputable Licensing Valuer from the North of England, in order that we could put forward a professional case against the claim. I wanted the best in the country, one who was not in the pocket of the brewers. He found Mr Pothelthwaite, whose qualifications were unquestionable.

Having taken a month to study the distribution and ownership of the pubs throughout the city, and in particular those to be disturbed in the central areas, he gave the Public Works Committee his professional advice about our situation. It was that loss of barrelage was the only way to fairly assess compensation. I was happy when he added, 'As drinkers are being redistributed, coupled with the monopoly situation in this city, I cannot see any claim for loss of trade being justified.' The committee appointed him to represent us if we were forced to take the matter to the courts.

As Sir Charles Burman was an Alderman, and former Lord Mayor of the City, I thought it proper to advise him. I was amazed when he dismissed my suggestion that he call on Mr Pothelthwaite to address the Licensing Planning Committee, so I decided to go to the top. I asked for an appointment with the then Home Secretary Sir David Maxwell Fyfe, who had as part of his remit to appoint the Licensing Justices.

Fully briefed, I travelled to London. Maxwell-Fyfe was a leading Silk with a tremendous amount of charm. He introduced Mr Allen, his Permanent Secretary – later to become Lord Allen of Abbeydale – a tall, slim austere fellow who was highly respected by both political Parliamentary Parties.

I explained in some detail the problem we faced with the brewers, and handed him our Licensing Valuer's report. I added that the chairman of the Licensing Justices had dismissed my suggestion that his committee should hear Mr Pothelthwaite's opinion, and ended by saying to the Home Secretary that we needed his help. He had listened intently to what I had to say and after hesitating for awhile said, 'Although I have some sympathy with your case I am reluctant to interfere in local matters of this kind.'

Depressed by his answer, I said, 'Home Secretary, I hope you understand why I can't allow the brewers to take what could be a considerable amount of money in compensation from the ratepayers when it is not justified.'

He didn't respond, and, realising that his support was not forthcoming, I added, 'Since you feel you cannot intervene, and as there is no one else to whom I can appeal, I have no alternative other than to say, sir, that the chairman of the Justices like me, is a member of the city council, but unlike me he is a member of the Conservative Party, as are a number of the Justices. I hope you will understand why I make the point and why I can't allow this matter to go by default. I will not hesitate to raise this if we are forced to fight the case through the courts.'

Maxwell Fyfe thanked me for arranging to see him and wished me well. As I left his room Mr Allen followed, motioning me to follow him to his office. He began to upbraid me for what he said was a veiled threat to the Home Secretary.

'Mr Allen,' I responded, 'I repeat: I am here to protect the interests of the ratepayers of my city and I will not allow them to be cheated. If I have offended the Home Secretary in the course of what I see as my duty, I will go back and apologise.'

'There is no need for that, Councillor,' he replied, and I left.

At the following Licensing Planning Committee, the chairman told us that he had consulted the Home Secretary. 'It seems that he has interested himself in the case of the public houses that are to be demolished in the redevelopment scheme,' he announced. 'He has recommended that we invite the Licensing Valuer instructed by the Public Works Committee to give us the benefit of his advice, and I have asked him to be present.'

He didn't mention my visit to Maxwell Fyfe, or the fact that he had been summoned to meet him. Having listened to Mr Pothelthwaite, and after asking him a few questions, the Justices accepted his advice. We heard nothing more.

On the industrial front, we were concerned at the cost of replacing the sewers being destroyed by the untreated trade effluent being poured into them by some of our larger industrial concerns and the fact that we were having to treat it. The country had not as yet woken up to the environmental damaged being caused by indiscriminate polluters.

The city's Chief Analyst had suggested to me that, if a company like ICI treated their effluent and extracted and recycled the suspended solids, instead of pouring it into our sewers, they could cover the cost of treating it and have money left over. He had put this to them but they couldn't agree. They were not alone.

Here was another case where we had to raise another Parliamentary Bill in order to obtain powers to force them to either treat their own trade effluent or compensate the city for doing it. We prepared our case and knowing that we would be faced with a barrage of eminent Queen's Counsel acting for the industrialist and the CBI, we employed the services of leading Counsel to represent us when we went before the House of Lords Committee.

Sir Herbert Manzoni, the City Analyst, the Chief Medical Officer and I were called to give evidence. The companies' QCs made little progress when cross-examining our professional team, so they called on me as the policy witness, in the hope of scoring points. I was what they called the soft target, and they were right.

I had been warned that the simpler the question the more careful should be my answer. 'One simple question,' I was told, 'will lead to another, which could in the end have you in difficulties.' And so it turned out. The time came when I was asked a question which was so naive that remembering the warning, I hesitated.

I asked the barrister if he would mind rephrasing the question. He pushed his wig aside slightly, looked around the room then back at me, and said, 'Would *I mind*, Councillor?' He again looked round the room. His tone and his gestures indicated to all present his exasperation. I recognised the histrionics. 'Councillor,' he said, 'Birmingham is a big city, is it not?'

'Yes, sir,' I replied. 'It is considered to be Britain's second city.'

'And you are the chairman of its Public Works Committee, are you not?'

'Yes, sir.'

'Would I be right in saying that it is one of the main committees of the city council?'

'One of them, sir.'

'Not to put too fine a point on it,' he continued, 'as its chairman, it would be reasonable for my Lords to suppose, that in choosing a chairman of one of its prestigious committees, the council would take care to choose a person who would be considered to be reasonably bright, would they not?'

Before I could reply, he said in a much louder voice, 'And this being the case it would be reasonable for their Lordships to expect that you would be able to understand the simple question that I have just put to you.' He almost shouted his last few words.

I was on the spot trying to figure out where the hell he was leading me when Lord Latham, who had been a member of the Greater London Council, interjected. In a quiet voice, meant I felt sure to emphasise the barrister's last effort, he said, 'I consider myself to be, as you put it, reasonably bright, but I'm bound to say that I too didn't quite understand your question.'

'Quite so, my Lord,' said the barrister, resuming his seat.

I looked across at Lord Latham, who smiled and lowered his head. We both knew that he had just got me off the hook.

The end of this story was that the city won its case, and some years later when I was sitting next to a director of ICI at some function or other, he reminded me of it.

'You know that we put in a treatment plant, as your chappie suggested. It saved us a great deal of money.'

Chapter XVI
NEW HORIZONS

With the overwhelming support of my colleagues, I had been in the Chair of the Public Works Committee for almost six years without a hint of opposition to my continuing there. When it eventually came, it arrived from a most unexpected quarter.

The desire for power can drive some people to do things that you believe to be not in their nature, but in the event, one can never be sure. Councillor Dennis Thomas was a strange mixture, a devoted member of the Labour Party, intelligent, a fervent anti-communist with a dour disposition, and at times self-destructive. He was a close friend.

Together with men like Stanley Evans, a Midlands MP, Denis Howell (before he entered parliament), and three or four Party members, including Thomas, we met on some Saturday mornings. Because of our opposition to the 'extreme' left and that we worked hard to expose those who infiltrated into the Party and the unions to serve the Trotskyite and communist movements, we were considered to be on the extreme right of the Labour Party; it was an exaggeration.

At this point I should tell you about Stanley Evans. He was at the time a junior minister in the Ministry of Agriculture and Fisheries in the Atlee Government. An intelligent kindly man, he, like most Midlanders had a tendency to speak his mind. He became wealthy mining and selling industrial sand and still retained his broad Black Country accent.

On the Saturday morning after he had resigned his ministerial post, I asked him why.

'Resign?' he said. 'I dain't bloody resign, I wus sacked!'

He explained that in addressing a meeting of the farmers' union he told them that they were the most featherbedded community in the country, a view most Parliamentary Members hold, but few have the courage to express. In addition to getting under the collective skins of the farmers, his remarks received a considerable amount of publicity, not much of it complimentary.

He told me, 'Clem – the prime minister – sent for me. I went into his room and he sat there doodling at his desk. Without looking up he asked, "Evans, did yo tell them farmers that they wus featherbedded?" and I told him, "Ar, I did," and still with his head down he said, "Then, Evans, yo'm fired."'

Stanley laughed at my look of disbelief. 'Frank,' he said, 'if yo have any doubts about it, yo will see an indentation in the pavement outside Number Ten Downing Street where my arse hit it.'

It was typical. He was known from then on as 'Featherbed' Evans.

I digress. Dennis Thomas, unlike the rest of this small group, was far too bitter and he allowed it to overcome him at times. Normally quiet and reserved, he would sometimes tackle a situation which required calm and careful judgement like a bull in a china shop. It antagonised his friends as well as his adversaries and it exposed him to counteraction which led to trouble.

There were one or two members of the council who had been or were still undercover members of the Trotskyite movement. We knew, and waited for the right moment to deal with the situation. A few days before a local government election, Dennis, whilst being interviewed by the press chose to mention the fact. The result was banner headlines in the morning and evening papers: RED HAND OVER THE COUNCIL HOUSE. It could only harm our chances at the election.

At times like this, when he realised that he was in deep trouble, he would approach me to support him publicly. Although my views were well known, those on the left of the Party trusted and respected me and so I was able to protect him, but on too many occasions he would alienate those who would normally have supported him.

His and my friends couldn't understand why I put my political future at risk to continually bail him out. Some began to suspect that I lacked judgement when I recommended that he be placed on the Public Works Committee and convinced the members to elect him to the Chair of the powerful Town Planning Committee. It was a position that gave him considerable credibility and allowed him to use his undoubted talents.

We both belonged to an organisation known as IRIS. It was this group that supplied Woodrow Wyatt, then a Labour MP, who wrote a weekly column for a national Sunday newspaper, with some of the evidence of the flagrant misuse of power by the President and Secretary of the Electrical Trades Union. It was these articles that led to an inquiry which convinced leading communist members of the union to leave the party, and give evidence which led to their expulsion and brought an end to the communist domination of the union.

To sum up, I had every reason to believe that Dennis was a true and trusted friend. In May 1958, a few hours before the annual general meeting of the Labour Group, he asked me if I wanted to stay on in the chair of the Public Works Committee. I enquired why, and he replied that if I did I could count on his support. I expected nothing less and although I thought his question odd at the time, I dismissed it.

Having settled in my seat at the group meeting, the time came for the leader to read out the names that the officers were recommending to take the Chair of the various committees. When it came to the Public Works Committee, Alderman Tegfryn Bowen rose to his feet. He began by saying how in 1952 the group had placed a young, relatively inexperienced councillor in the chair of the committee at a most difficult time; how he had risen to the task to become nationally recognised as a leader in his field. Bowen finished his glowing oration by suggesting to the group that it was now time for a change.

When he was followed by two further members using the same line I realised why Dennis Thomas had approached me. He was covering up the fact that despite our long friendship, his ambition to become the chairman had led him to lobby to have me dumped and to take my place. It was too much.

I rose to my feet and the leader called on me. I said that the members knew me well enough to know that I wasn't in the business of special pleading; if they felt it was time for me to step down I wouldn't argue with that. Thanking Bowen and the others for their fulsome praise I said, 'I now know how, in his dying moments, Caesar felt about his erstwhile friends.'

As I resumed my seat the Group began to applaud. Unabashed, Bowen moved that Thomas be appointed to the Chair. Just four members voted for his motion, Dennis Thomas being one. I thought, *Yet another lesson learned.*

Later that year I was invited by the Town and Country Planning Association to speak at their Conference on Urban Renewal at the Middlesex County Hall. I had intended to decline, but having had the honour of being elected to sit on their council, had second thoughts. It was to lead me into a phase of my life which was to open up new horizons.

As I was sitting on the platform a card was handed up to me, asking if I would be kind enough to have a word after the meeting. I turned the card over to see that it was from Field Marshal Sir Claude Auchinleck. Looking around the hall and spotting his famous craggy features, I nodded.

I expected the Field Marshal to have the same manner as some of the other military officers I had met but he turned out to be the gentlest of men. Sitting alongside him it was difficult to imagine that he was the man who, short of supplies, equipment and men, had stopped Field Marshal Rommel from taking Cairo.

This encounter led me to meet Walter Flack who, in addition to being one of the most well read men I had ever met, was both humorous and warm-hearted. He was a 'character' with a touch of genius and, like most so endowed, suffered his highs and his lows.

Walter Flack had formed a property development company and had a reputation for being able to spot a good property prospect more clearly than most. He prided himself on the quality of the developments he had been involved with and of his hand-picked team. He had the confidence of those he had around him, even when he took enormous gambles.

When I got to know him he told me that he had dreamed of having his own property company when he was serving under Auchinleck in the desert. Some fourteen years after the war, he achieved two of his ambitions, one to own a respected property company and the other to have the Field Marshal as its chairman.

Walter Flack was a Jew, and when war broke out he joined the London Rifles. Although considerably more intelligent than many in his unit, he only made the rank of Sergeant. During his period in Egypt he became deeply disturbed by the plight of the poorer Arabs, as he put it, 'Of having to scratch a living out of a few square metres of sand.' He was convinced that they had no real hate for the Jews and he fumed about the British Government's action over Suez. He demonstrated his anger by standing outside Number 10 Downing Street waiting for the prime minister, Anthony Eden, to leave. It must have been quite a sight, a Jewish millionaire shouting, 'Resign, resign!' on behalf of the Arabs.

As a London estate agent, he purchased, on behalf of a company owned by a Cecil Lewis, a property owned by Kunzles. They were chocolate and cake manufacturers who owned a number of restaurants in Birmingham. Flack linked up adjoining properties, and with Seymour Harris as the architect, created for Lewis a very profitable development. Subsequently both he and Harris had to fight for their fees. It was then that he decided to strike out on his own.

He bought a small publicly quoted house-building company near to the Murrayfield rugby ground in Edinburgh. In the process of building a team around him, Harris recommended that he should talk to me. He did so initially via Sir Claude Auchinleck.

Unaware of any of this, I accepted an invitation from Harris to join in the stone-laying ceremony of a project he had designed in Basildon New Town. I had visited a number of new towns, but not Basildon. It was during this visit that I first met Walter Flack. During the journey back to London he asked if I would be interested in joining the company; I thanked him but declined. We had a late lunch in London at which I was introduced to his wife and his Board members. This over, he insisted on driving me to the station to catch my train back to Birmingham.

Still excited by the day's events, he told me that his father had been a tailor in Poland and had escaped from one of the many pogroms against the Jews, bringing his family to England settling in the East End of London. He had worked hard to ensure that Walter had a good education. Leaving the Merchant Taylors'

School, Walter studied at the College of Estate Management and then joined a well-established London estate agency. When war was declared he enlisted.

Standing on the platform he repeated his offer. I thanked him but again declined. 'I know nothing about the property business, Mr Flack; I would have nothing to offer and wouldn't enjoy being a passenger.'

As we shook hands through the lowered window of my departing train he called out, 'If you ever change your mind, give Sir Claude or me a call.'

In 1954, my wife and I bought our first house on a new Bourneville Village Trust Estate and during the following heavy winter I caught what I thought was the flu. I carried on working until I realised it was more serious. My home was on the south side of the city; my GP, who I had never had reason to consult, had a surgery in Aston not too far from the city centre. It was 8.30 a.m., and knowing that it would be closed, I drove to his home on the far north side. When Doctor Massey saw me he realised that I was in trouble.

After an examination he asked how I had got there. He asked for my car keys telling me that an ambulance would be taking me to Selly Oak Hospital, which was nearest to my home. On my arrival I was greeted by Dr Nussey, an Austrian who had escaped when the Nazis moved in.

He was a small man, very Jewish, with a great sense of humour. I didn't laugh when he told me that had I been a smoker he wouldn't have been able to save me. I had been suffering from a severe dose of pneumonia for more than two weeks. He gave me an injection, placed me in an oxygen tent and left me to sleep. Thanks to Massey and Nussey, I was discharged a month later, but even now, forty-seven years after the event, if I catch a cold I have to be careful not to let it develop.

At seven o'clock in the evening on the 20 December 1957 in the same hospital, Maisie gave birth to our first – and only – child, my son Noel. It filled me with a feeling of joy that I had never experienced before and it continued during his early years. As he was growing up I tried hard to maintain for him that feeling of magic that we all enjoy as children but lose all too quickly. I'm happy to say that he got to university and now works hard to help the less privileged in our society to do the same.

Early in 1958 when I was still employed by the Birmingham Co-operative Society, the incoming President of the Association of Municipal Engineers invited me to present a paper to their Conference which was to take place in Blackpool. It was the first time that an elected member in local government had been accorded such an honour. It was to bring me to another crossroads in my life.

During the previous eight years I had attracted a considerable amount of publicity for my work on the city council. Photographs or stories in the newspapers, coupled with radio and television interviews, kept me in the public eye. It was bound to give rise to a certain amount of jealousy but I didn't expect it to lead to a further threat to my earning a living.

The management of the Society gave me a considerable amount of support but a week before the Municipal Engineers' Conference was to take place, chatting with my immediate superior, I mentioned in passing the honour the incoming President of the Municipal Engineers had done me by asking me to speak at his inauguration. The manager ushered me into his office.

Sitting behind his desk, with a gravity in his voice I hadn't heard before, he counselled me on the attitude of some members of the Board. He warned me that there were those who wanted to curb my local government activities and one or two who had even questioned the wisdom of retaining my services. He suggested that it would be in my best interests to forgo the Conference. I was shaken by his advice, which I was sure was given with the best of intentions.

As I returned to my office, it took some time for his message to sink in. My immediate reaction was to walk out but I decided to curb my pride, not to take precipitous action but to calmly consider my position. I now had a son, as well as a mortgage. It was too late to cancel my agreement to address the Conference, and the more I thought about the situation the more angry I became. The fact that my means of earning a living was once again being placed in jeopardy filled me with despair. I knew that, come what may, my happy days with the Co-operative Society were over. I began to look for another position.

The management was unaware that I was disenchanted although I suspect my immediate boss had an idea that this was so. It was ironic; a few months before, the Board secretary had called me to a meeting of the top management, at which there were directors of the Co-operative Wholesale Society. They were gathered to discuss the wisdom – or otherwise – of taking a large amount of space in a new development on the opposite side of the road to the main store.

As chairman of the Public Works Committee, I was publicly involved in the details of all major developments, including the scheme in which they were interested. They looked to me to advise them whether the position within the scheme was the right one and if so, how they should approach the promoter, Jack Cotton, in order to obtain a satisfactory deal; in other words, how much a square foot should they offer.

This was because of the position I held on the city council and my knowledge of both the site, its promoter, and values. I gave them advice which they followed and yet a few months later I was warned that some members of the Board wanted to see the back of me because of the prominent position I held on the council.

Sir Claude Auchinleck, who was making one of his regular visits to the city to see the Medical Officer, who had served under him in the desert and in India, called to invite me to join him for lunch. Having failed to find a suitable position elsewhere, and though some time had elapsed, I was tempted to ask whether Flack's offer was still open. In the event I didn't need to. In passing on Walter Flack's good wishes, he enquired whether I had given any further thought to accepting the offer to join the company. I didn't tell him of the bind I was in but replied that I would like to meet Flack again.

His secretary rang to ask if I could arrange to meet in the offices of Walter Flack, Kemp and Partners in London's Albemarle Street. On arrival I was greeted by Alan Wright, a young partner, who kindly entertained me until Walter Flack arrived. During our discussion I repeated that I had no experience on the commercial side of property development and that I could not and would not help the company in planning matters in the city of Birmingham. Flack replied rather sharply that his interest in me had nothing to do with my position there.

He then repeated how he had entered into the development business himself, and going over his unfortunate experience at the hands of Cecil Lewis, added, 'Had it not been for him and the fact that Seymour Harris urged me into going it alone, we wouldn't be sitting here.'

The penny dropped. I remembered that I had met Seymour Harris when I was asked to perform the opening ceremony of a multi-storey factory he had designed for a furniture manufacturer in Bath Row, Birmingham. Over the lunch that followed he had mentioned that his partnership had ideas on town centre renewal and were interested in the speeches I'd made and the articles I had written on the subject of urban renewal. I realised that it was Seymour Harris who had suggested to Flack that I would be an asset to his company. It was he who had invited me to Basildon with the express purpose of giving Flack an opportunity to look me over.

During my discourse with Flack, he agreed on my insistence that if I decided to join the company and after a twelve-month period either of us was unhappy with the arrangement, we would part without acrimony. His reaction was to say, 'I will bet that within twelve months you will be questioning, not why I need you but why you need me!'

I still hesitated, and it was not until 1959 that I decided to take the plunge and to give my notice to the Co-operative Society.

I made an appointment to see the leader of the Labour Group to give him the whole background as to why I was joining a property company and to tell him that I would be resigning my position as chairman of the Public Works Committee.

Having listened carefully, Alderman Watton said that he couldn't see any reason why I should vacate the Chair and pleaded with me not to do so. I countered by saying that being in charge of the Planning Committee and being associated with a property company could, and would, be misinterpreted.

'The Conservatives have directors of building companies and their suppliers on the committee; you could do what they do, declare an interest when necessary,' he replied, still urging me to stay on.

I had no intention of placing myself in a position where my integrity could be questioned, and had made up my mind to go.

In March 1959, the Public Works Committee passed the following resolution:

> This committee resolved that it was with their profound regret that Alderman Price had found it necessary to relinquish the chairmanship which he has filled so competently since 1953. And do hereby place on record their sincere appreciation of the able and efficient manner in which he has at all times discharged the arduous duties attaching to the office, and of the time and energy which he has so unsparingly devoted to the furtherance of the work of the committee in all its aspects. In this connection they would make special reference to the drive and enthusiasm with which Alderman Price as constantly fostered and pursued the policies of the committee which have contributed in such a large measure to the commencement of many great projects, including the inner ring road, and the unerring vision which has enabled him to recognise so clearly the advantages accruing to Birmingham from making known, both nationally and internationally, the potentialities of the City and increased business and commercial opportunities resulting from the Redevelopment Programme.

This glowing testimony was unanimously endorsed by both the committee and the council. Sir Theodore Pritchett, leader of the Conservative Group, with whom I had crossed swords many times, called me to say that he deeply regretted my departure from the chairmanship of Public Works.

The day I stepped down, the local newspaper carried the headline: MR BIRMINGHAM RESIGNS. It was a compliment, embarrassing but nevertheless appreciated.

I had expected a reaction from the left wing of the Party but they continued to support my re-election as deputy leader of the Labour Group and later to the leadership. It was a genuine and much appreciated vote of confidence.

I joined Walter Flack's Murrayfield Real Estate Company and

it proved to be an exciting roller-coaster ride which started in 1959 and ended nine years later (see the chapter entitled 'A Man "in" Property').

Now that I'd retired from the chairmanship of a major committee, the leader of the Labour Group took me to one side. He wanted me to be in the chair of a council committee and suggested that I took over the Parks Committee after the May elections. This I did and enjoyed every minute of the four years I spent in the job, during which time I introduced a number of events that built up the department's international reputation.

Four months after I became chairman I had an idea to brighten up the city, after what proved to be a long, cold, dull winter. I had heard that the Dutch were organising what they called a 'Floriade' to celebrate the 400th anniversary of the introduction of the tulip bulb into Western Europe from Turkey; so during the council recess, which lasted from the end of July until October, I made a decision to hold what I called 'The Tulip Festival' in the spring.

Colonel Ross, the Parks Department's general manager, was not enthused when I informed him of my intention. He asked how was I proposing to achieve it.

'Well, I said, 'to start, unless we already have sufficient tulip bulbs, we should order enough to flood a park and the public flower beds around the city, now.'

He protested that we hadn't the money in the estimates, and reminded me that neither did I have the committee's approval. In return I reminded him that during the recess I had been given powers to act and that was what I was doing. To calm him down I told him, 'The festival will make a profit, so don't worry.'

As I had built up a reputation in my previous council position for getting things done, he went ahead and ordered £9,000 worth of tulip bulbs: not an inconsiderable sum at the time. I then arranged to fly to Holland to see if I could obtain the help of the Dutch Government in promoting the Festival.

I had arranged to meet representatives of the Dutch Tourist and Trade Departments. My line with them was that both their agricultural and tourist industry would benefit from making a contribution to our Festival. I made them aware that I understood that it would coincide with their Floriade, upon which they were fully pressed, but that our Festival would be complementary, bringing publicity to their efforts in a city which was the centre of a population of more than five million people.

After a long discussion and an even longer lunch, they agreed to help. Among other things, they promised to set up a mock Dutch village with a windmill in the park. They would also send over a clog maker, a lace maker and two-dozen pretty girls in typical Dutch costumes who would hand out fresh tulips which would be flown over every day on the scheduled flight to Birmingham Airport. They even arranged to have a smoked eel stand and also made a present of a thousand tulip bulbs. Along with Colonel Ross, I was overwhelmed by such munificence.

During the trip they introduced me to the Boesmans, who were famous among the international ballooning fraternity. The Boesmans agreed that for a fee of £400 they would bring their balloon to the festival. I asked whether they would permit us to place an advertisement around the balloon and they agreed. Colonel Ross, hearing me confirming the deal to spend more money, was having a fit.

He whispered, 'How do you propose to get this through the committee? They haven't even heard of the festival yet.'

'Profit, Mr Ross, we are going to make a profit,' I repeated.

Booking the Boesmans turned out to be a blessing. I had suggested that as Cannon Hill Park was close to the city centre opposite the Warwickshire County Cricket Ground, and had a good public transport connection, it should be the place to hold the festival. The problem was that it was held in a deed of trust.

As soon as I got back to Birmingham I made arrangements to meet the chairman of the trustees, Mr Charles Smith-Ryland, a descendant of the donor. He was not at all happy with the idea. I explained that I had gained the cooperation of the Dutch Government and, more as an aside that anything else, mentioned that the Boesmans had agreed to join in.

'Good God, do you know the Boesmans?' he exclaimed. 'Are you aware that when Cannon Hill was the estate where my ancestors lived one of them was a balloonist who used to fly from there with Royce of Rolls-Royce fame?'

He was quite excited with the fact that I had actually met the Boesmans and convinced them to come to city and to bring their balloon with them. He rose to leave.

'Excuse me, sir,' I said. 'Does this mean that I have your permission?'

'I should say so,' he replied, 'and many congratulations!'

With that agreed, I gave a press conference, not expecting the furore that was to break over my head at the first meeting of the Parks Committee after the recess. When I entered the committee room I was surprised to see the town clerk, who rarely attended meetings other than the general purposes and the full council. He sat on my right with a smile on his face. He had been made aware of the storm that was about to break and was no doubt looking forward to being present to witness it.

Two of my political colleagues had laid down a censure motion and the opposition were of course only too happy to support it.

'Before I put this to the vote,' I said quite coldly, 'let me tell you that I have gone through the costing and projected income and have estimated that the Festival will make a profit. I am committed to it. If you wish the city to pull out then I will resign from the Chair and with the council's permission will cover the costs and run the thing myself.' It was yet another gamble.

Alderman Mrs Annie Wood was the leader of the Conservative members on the committee. Addressing me, she said, 'I am disgusted that your colleagues should put down such a motion,' and, turning to the committee continued, 'if other members haven't faith in the chairman and what he has achieved so far, I have. I move that we go ahead with the Festival.'

Along with the other members I sat silent, stunned by her outburst. The committee clerk brought me back by whispering, 'Chairman, the question – you must put the Notice of Motion, it was withdrawn and Alderman Mrs Wood's motion was carried.'

I breathed a sigh of relief. The town clerk made his excuses and departed, no doubt disappointed.

The next day I arranged to meet Sir Eric Clayson, the managing director of the *Birmingham Post* and *Mail* group. He agreed to support the event with editorial and a photographic competition, guaranteeing plenty of free publicity. Realising that the Boesmans would be flying their balloon across the areas where his newspapers were sold, he offered £600 for the advert which was to be wrapped around it. Ross and I left the meeting showing 33 per cent profit and an overwhelming amount of free advertising. Colonel Ross began to warm to the idea of the Tulip Festival.

Weeks before the event was to open we suffered a severe cold spell and the parks gardeners were fearful that the quarter of a million tulip bulbs would fail to flower on time. I had the workshop make semi-triangular shades under which we placed electric strip lights. It not only helped the bulbs to flower on time but it added to the attraction as dusk fell over the park, illuminating the flower beds.

On the Thursday before the opening we enjoyed the hottest spring weather for years. Knowing that I had been flying by the seat of my pants, Ross called it 'Chairman's weather'. He began to believe that I had a Midas touch and supported every other scheme I dreamed up without question.

There were two other pieces of luck connected with the Tulip Festival. Having made the decision in October, we planned to erect an open-air theatre and to book professional artistes to entertain the crowds we expected, during the day and until 10 p.m., when the firework display would take over. Among those we booked to entertain was a little-known song and dance man by the name of Roy Castle.

The following January he had appeared on a television programme in the United States and earned rave reviews in the press. He became a star overnight and his fees skyrocketed along with his new reputation. We didn't expect him to show up for the paltry fee that we were paying him. Needless to say he did.

During our conversation before he went on stage I mentioned that we were worried that he wouldn't show. He replied in typical fashion, 'Eh, when you booked me I was in need of the job. Who knows, I may need it again.'

The other piece of luck was that I heard that Max Bygraves, who made 'Tulips from Amsterdam' a hit song, was topping the bill at the Coventry Hippodrome. I rang to ask if he would open our Festival and he agreed to do it gratis.

We announced this through the press and on local radio and before the gates opened at twelve o'clock on the Saturday, thousands of people were queuing to get in. At two o'clock I introduced Max Bygraves from the stage, inviting him to declare the Festival open.

He stood before the microphone looking out at the vast crowd and said, pointing at me, 'Calls himself a chairman, he must know that you would like to join me in a sing-song, and he hasn't even provided a piano!' The crowd went wild. 'Can we sing without one?' he called out.

'Yes!' they yelled back, and so he and they did just that for a solid hour.

Bygraves then stepped down from the stage and spent time before he had to return to Coventry for his evening show, walking with the people around the showground. I apologised for not providing the piano as I hadn't expected him to sing. He replied, 'Had you done so, son, you would have been taking me for granted and I wouldn't have uttered a note.' A real trouper. Before he left he shook my hand, 'Frank, old son, you have a success on your hands.'

He was right; well over half a million people paid to come to the show.

The Boesmans arrived on the evening before the last day of the Festival. They were up early the next day to place their balloon in the centre of the display arena, and once it was inflated they gave people a chance to go up in it on tethered flights. Late in the afternoon, as the Boesmans boarded the wicker basket ready to leave the ground, thousands of visitors gathered around the ring to wave them off. As the balloon began to ascend the band struck up, 'Now is the hour, when we must say goodbye.'

It's difficult to describe the wave of emotion that swept through the crowd as the balloon gradually rose above our heads. They began to sing and weep as if they were saying goodbye to dear friends. The Boesmans let drop a trailer which could be seen as they disappeared above the tree line and out of sight.

The Festival had made its mark. A huge success, it had brought colour and a lot of fun into our lives after the winter. As people began to walk to the exits on that last evening, many stopped to shake my hand and say thank you. Colonel Ross, not one to show emotion, was standing by my side, overwhelmed.

The staff of the Parks Department had worked hard to make the Festival the success it turned out to be. Max Bygraves, in making his contribution, set an example to stage stars appearing at the Coventry Hippodrome who followed his lead. Jimmy Edwards, who brought along his trombone, and his horse and took part in the gymkhana, Dickie Henderson, Russ Conway, Harry Worth and many others were kind enough to follow Bygraves' early example, contributing their time freely, helping to make future Festivals successful.

Our first effort proved to be financially beneficial and a few weeks later I convinced the council to allow me to use the profit to provide much needed hot shower facilities near the football and rugby pitches in the city parks – something for which Denis Howell had been campaigning for years. Had I not had the support of a political opponent, Alderman Annie Wood, I doubt if any of it would have happened.

On the Monday after the end of the Festival, as I was about to leave the Councillors' Library, Annie Wood – who was then quite old – asked if my car was parked below. I thought that she wanted a lift home. We went down to the parking area and I pointed to my car. As it turned out, she wasn't seeking a lift. She directed me to her car and opened the boot. She told me to take the four leather-bound volumes that were lying there. They were the biography of The Rt Hon Sir Joseph Chamberlain.

'I met him when I was a child,' she said. 'He was my hero, and you have the same kind of love for our city that he had. I want you to have them.'

I protested that they really ought to go to the Conservative Party Headquarters library, or at least the city. She wouldn't hear of it. I have the books on my shelves now.

I stayed on to organise three more Tulip Festivals. Before I left the Parks Committee I also ran Water Festivals, Military Tattoos and used our open-air theatre to bring such bands has Ted Heath and Humphrey Lyttelton to the park. I started the first Guy Fawkes Bonfire Night Festivals for those kids who lived in flats or on housing estates and who would miss the thrill of watching a bonfire and organised firework displays.

It was the idea that Councillor Mrs Johnson had put to my predecessors over the years but had been dismissed as a nonsense. They were so wrong; I was pleased for her that they turned out to be so successful and have become a date in the annual calendar of outdoor events in the city.

I also obtained the support of local sports personalities such as Ann Jones, who became a Wimbledon champion, to give training sessions for the children in the parks. I had the railings around many of the parks removed. Again, this idea had been promoted by a Councillor Watts but dismissed out of hand. I was not one of his favourite people, but when I took up his idea he appeared to view me in a different light. We also set up a tree nursery, and a Children's Tree Lovers League.

By the time I had to approach Charles Smith-Ryland again, the Queen had appointed him Lord Lieutenant of Warwickshire. On this occasion it was for something far more important than all of what had gone before.

Chapter XVII
CULTURAL ORPHANS

I had been aware that the lack of money helped to contribute to making most arts a preserve of the wealthy. Many of the middle class thought subsidising the arts an unacceptable burden, which meant that the poor had no chance to share in the pleasure the arts brought.

Birmingham City's Parks Department did sterling work during the war years, helping to keep up the spirits of those working long hours on sparse rations and not much to smile about, by creating what was called 'Holidays at Home'. They laid on events, among which was 'Plays in the Park'. John English, an amateur actor and playwright, along with his wife, Molly, worked tirelessly to bring some fun and a little culture into the lives of people who, at the time, had a little of either. A large marquee was erected and they ran what they called 'A theatre in the round'.

The stage was circular and the audience sat around it so that the actors (most of whom were professionals) and the audience were as one. John wrote a number of plays in which the children actually participated. The shows were subsidised by the city council and were so successful that they continued long after the war was over.

I believe it was in 1958 when I was invited to the Birmingham Theatre Guild's Twentieth Birthday celebrations. Hermione Baddeley gave poetry readings, and as part of the evening's entertainment there was a Forum. The Panel was made up of representatives of the world of the arts: the Keeper of the Museum and Art Gallery, theatre directors, the leader of the City Orchestra, an author... myself being the odd man out. I was only there, I guessed, because the council rented the Guild the building at a peppercorn rent. I was placed at the end of the table.

Questions were put from the floor, and the chairman, Derek Salberg, the owner of the Alexandra Theatre, called upon members of the panel to reply.

At some stage one of the audience asked, 'What is the future of the Theatre?' and to my astonishment Derek called on me to reply.

I said, 'It hasn't got a future.'

It stunned the assembly. Derek looked down the table at me aghast.

'Come on, Frank,' he whispered.

I decided to stand up. Looking at the audience I said, 'The question was, what is the future of the Theatre; I answered that it hasn't got a future. The chairman wishes me to expand.' I hesitated for a moment before adding, 'It hasn't got a future because of you people.'

The room exploded. The audience stamped their feet, muttering loudly their anger or disbelief. Derek looked at me exasperated, so I continued to stand. I held up my hand and when the noise had abated I went on.

'I am not a gambling man, but I am prepared to bet anyone here that if we go out into the street to ask the first hundred people we meet, "When did you last go to the theatre?" or more important, "When did your children – pantomimes excepted – go to the theatre?" we would be lucky to find more than *one per cent* who would give us the answer we would like to hear.'

The audience was quiet, so I continued, 'You stamp your feet. Let me tell you that my colleagues and I fight every year to win subsidies for the arts which would perish if we lost the vote. If you think that by going to the theatre or the concert hall you are doing your bit, you are sadly mistaken.' I made to resume my seat but decided to add, 'Unless we follow the example of the Jesuits, who know that if they can affect the first seven years of a child's life they will have won them for the future, then, as I say, the Theatre has no future.'

I stood looking at the people sitting in front of me and decided to go the whole hog. 'Don't you understand that we must take care of the cultural orphans? To welcome them in, to open up to them what the arts have to offer, to fulfil their lives so that they and then their children will nurture the future of the theatre, the concert hall, the libraries and the art galleries.'

There was no response. I sat down to a stony silence.

At the coffee break, as if I were a leper, they left a large space around me.

John English, who I knew slightly, came over to say, 'My God, Councillor, you really told them!'

I replied, 'I doubt very much that it made the slightest impression other than for them to wonder who the hell invited me.'

John asked if we could meet to discuss what I had in mind. Neither he nor I realised just what that meeting would lead to.

As I was leaving a meeting in the council house one day, I found John English sitting on a bench outside the committee room. He told me that he had heard that I was attending a meeting so thought he would waylay me. John had charm and an enthusiasm which tended to carry his listeners along any path he wished them to take. I knew that he had a burning ambition to build a children's theatre and listened to what he had to say. I had to tell him that this was not what I had meant when I spoke to the Theatre Guild's meeting. I wanted to reach a higher plain.

Outlining my idea set him back on his heels. A children's theatre was a small but important part. I wanted to build a centre devoted to all the arts; a place where young people from humble backgrounds whose parents and grandparents had, through no fault of theirs, lived without having enjoyed any of the things those who sat in the audience that night took for granted. I wanted to see a centre that allowed, taught and nurtured the cultural orphans so that they could and would participate in and contribute to the arts.

We arranged to meet again. This time John brought with him an architect who had sat in the audience that night. His name was Herbert Jackson. He had designed theatres, and although he hadn't spoken, apparently agreed with the sentiments I had expressed. I made it clear to him, and again to John, that I wouldn't be interested in becoming involved in a scheme with such limited horizons as building a children's theatre.

Setting out once again my vision of a centre which would

provide the widest possible opportunities for, as I kept repeating, those thousands of young children who had been starved of the pleasure that live music and the visual arts provided, I said again, 'I'm concerned about the cultural orphans.'

I wanted to see young people from the age of five to twenty-five, not merely watching or listening but actually participating in the arts in all their forms. I kept hammering home that if we were to start out on this venture it would be to develop a whole site with a live theatre, a small film theatre, a marionette theatre, a pavilion for live music and dance, studios for sculpture, painting and practising on musical instruments they couldn't afford. They sat listening to me as if hypnotised; I wasn't about to stop once started.

'It must be a place where the children feel comfortable, where at weekends they could invite their parents or grandparents to join them in whatever they were doing. There should be studios where young people could learn the art of film making, a library, art gallery and restaurant with a snack bar on the ground floor and a dining room above where every week the menu would change – Italian one week, French the next, Spanish, Mexican, Indian and so on... learning the art of knowing and enjoying international cuisine. This is what I want this centre to offer to those who will be lucky enough to be able to use it,' I finished with a flourish.

All through this oration, they both sat quiet, with eyes glowing. It occurred to me that I was doing 'a John English', but they thought I was preaching about the unachievable.

'The members of the Theatre Guild didn't understand that the future of the arts is with the children,' I ended.

They both asked just how much land would such a centre require and where. I shook them by saying, 'We need to build it in a place which is synonymous with enjoyment and fun – it's got to be in a park.'

They left enthused and, I imagined, thinking that I was a touch crazy.

My first hurdle was to convince the city council to travel with us. We kept the plan under wraps until we had worked out the basics, the individual units that we needed to build, and the philosophy behind the scheme. We were as one, that we needed to set up an independent trust.

I called upon Mr Bushill-Matthews, a solicitor, who I suspected loved the arts more than his profession. Having heard us, he jumped at the chance of joining in and he set about drawing up the trust deeds. Herbert Jackson prepared a plan, a schematic drawing and a three-dimensional model. We tested it out on a number of people whom we could trust to keep it quiet and who were also capable of assisting both with time and money.

The first on Board was the head of the old established company, Boxfoldia, Miss Beryl Foyle. Having listened to our aims and objectives, she became a tower of strength. She too had been at the Birmingham Theatre Guild's celebrations but never mentioned it to me. Beryl became a vice chairman along with Mr J J Gracie, who had just retired from the chairmanship of GEC.

With the support of a range of highly regarded citizens and a goodly sum of money already promised, I arranged a meeting with leading members of the city council. We put on a display of the drawings, plans and a model, along with a detailed report on our objectives, saying how with their support we hoped to proceed.

We spent over an hour answering questions, one of which was, inevitably, 'Where would the centre be built?'

My colleagues turned to me, and without blinking an eye I suggested that the only place was in one of the city parks. We were surprised by their favourable response, and even more so when the leader of the council said that he thought that it had to be Cannon Hill Park and everyone agreed.

It meant that we first had to obtain the agreement of the Ryland trustees, and then according to the town clerk, promote a Parliamentary Bill to obtain the powers. I had to say, 'What – again?'

Once we had the support of leading council members we opened up to the press. They gave me support by publishing photographs of the model and giving the plan editorial coverage. The resolution to back the project was put before the council. It was agreed without a division, subject to the agreement of the Ryland trustees. The council did us the honour of funding the legal procedures.

We had another meeting with Charles Smith-Ryland, the chairman of the trustees. Once again he demonstrated his goodwill. We were allocated a substantial area alongside the boating pool. I travelled to the House of Lords to give evidence before a committee which I was relieved to see was being chaired by Lord Cobham, the Lord Lieutenant of Worcestershire. After an hour of cross-examination he leaned forward to say, 'I can't understand for the life of me why you have had to go through this rigmarole. The trustees have agreed, the city council is supporting it, so why do we have to pass judgement on it?' To which the rest of the Lords Committee said, 'Hear, hear.'

We were not asked to wait outside the room for a decision, as is the usual practice. The committee gave us there and then the blessing of parliament. I returned to Birmingham, held a press conference and set about raising the money to achieve our aims. We instructed Bushill-Matthews to set up the Cannon Hill Trust. Its aims – to construct and manage The Midlands Art Centre for Young People.

Jenny Lee, wife of Aneurin Bevan and Minister for the Arts, came to meet the directors. After outlining the scheme and explaining that we meant to raise money from both sides of industry, she agreed to help. Sir Bertram Waring, whom I had met when trying to get a start on our inner ring road was, I was told, a hard man.

'He swims every morning in his open-air unheated pool, winter and summer. It's no good asking him to assist the arts.'

Even so, I asked if he would see me. I mentioned that my mother had worked for the firm.

'In the office?' he asked.

'No, on the shop floor,' I answered. I also told him that I had boxed against his team, and he began to warm to me. I then launched into the reasons I was seeking his support. I explained the reasons why we should help the 'Cultural Orphans'.

I mentioned the story of the old electrician I had met in New York. I told Sir Bertram of his complaining about all the leisure time he would have to put in if his union won a thirty-five hour working week. 'Like a lot of your employees, Sir Bertram, they work all their lives in jobs for which they have been trained. What they haven't learned is the art of using their leisure hours.'

This wasn't lost on him. He was aware that the working week in Britain, which had moved from sixty to fifty hours, was on its way down, and readily understood that his workers would be more content at work if during their longer leisure hours they had learned to enjoy and participate in a meaningful pastime. He saw that for some it was already too late but a start needed to be made. He saw that the Midlands Art Centre for Young People could provide one of the answers. By the time I got up to leave, he had promised to donate £100,000 from the Lucas Trust, which in the early 1960s was a lot of money… millions in today's terms.

My company's London office was in St James' Street immediately opposite the headquarters of the Dunlop Company. They had their main plant in Erdington, Birmingham. Looking across the street, I suddenly had the urge to phone the chairman.

I explained to his secretary that I was in my office opposite theirs and that her chairman knew me. It would have been more accurate to have said, knows *of* me. I asked if I could pop across to see him for five minutes. She called me back to tell me to come straight away.

I thanked Mr Beharrel for seeing me at such short notice and asked whether he had yet heard of the proposed Art Centre; he nodded. I was aware that he and Waring, both suppliers to the motor trade, were good friends. I said how pleased we were that Sir Bertram had donate such a princely sum to our cause.

He laughed. 'Bert Waring donating money to the arts – I don't believe it!'

He looked at me, still laughing, so I suggested he might call him. He did then and there. His part of the conversation went something like this.

'Morning, Bert. I have Frank Price sitting opposite me.' Pause.

'Yes, Bert, *he is* after me for money.' Pause.

'Yes he told me, I thought he was kidding.' Pause.

'How much? You're joking… really, that much!' Pause.

'Yes, I suppose he has something… okay, yes.'

He hung up the phone and called for his secretary telling her to bring in the charity file. Mr Beharrel made out a cheque for

£50,000. If I had any doubts that we would succeed they were fast disappearing as I danced across St James' Street back to my office.

My other great coup came much later. It was with Jack Cotton, who had contributed millions to a variety of charities. During the time he was trying to merge his City Centre Property company with Murrayfield, I visited him in his suite in the Dorchester Hotel, Park Lane. It was both his office and his home for five days of the week.

Around the walls hung original paintings by Monet, Goya and Renoir. His suite occupied a considerable area of the hotel's mezzanine floor. Jack was larger than life, immaculately dressed and always sporting a bow tie and a huge cigar. He had a ruddy complexion and a full head of jet-black hair, and was a gregarious fellow who allowed all kinds of people to just drop in.

Anna Neagle and her director husband, Herbert Wilcox were regulars and so was Michael Parker, the Equerry to the Duke of Edinburgh. He would pop in, help himself to a pink gin and disappear. It was like Piccadilly Circus without the plebs. It was Jack's way of keeping in with the Establishment.

During this period he was wooing Flack, and, knowing that I wasn't too happy, he invited me to lunch. He was a Brummie and knew my background. We sat in his suite with the table set for two. He said, 'Frank, we are going to have a simple meal which I'm sure you will enjoy: shepherd's pie.'

When the waiter wheeled in the trolley I looked at it and, seeing my expression, Jack smiled, saying, 'Well, it's Shepherd's Pie à la Dorch.' So I forgave him.

But that's an aside. Some time before, I had a private meeting with him about the arts centre, pointing out that he had donated millions to Israel and charities in London but not much to his native city. The arts centre was an opportunity to put that to right. I suggested that he donate the money for the art pavilion which would be named 'The Cotton Gallery'. I said, more as a joke, 'You can hang your Renoirs there.'

He called in his man Friday, who went through the large ledger listing the names of recipients and dates when money was due to be transferred from the Cotton Trust to these many and varied charities, concluding that a donation would be made but delayed for five years.

Returning to Birmingham, I thought that I had missed out. I gave some thought as to how I could speed things up. I called the *Birmingham Post* municipal reporter, informing him that a wealthy son of Birmingham had agreed to donate money to the Midlands Art Centre to build an art gallery which would be named after him. He pressed me for the name but I explained that I was not at liberty to expose it without the donor's permission, and that he must not quote me.

The next morning my secretary, Muriel, had placed the *Birmingham Post* on my desk opened at the page which reported the donation. At nine thirty, Jack was on the phone shouting that I had no right to announce that he had agreed to sponsor the gallery. I asked him where he had got this from.

'The bloody *Birmingham Post*, haven't you read it?'

'Hold on, Jack, I'll see if we have it in the office.'

I put the phone down, and after waiting for a minute, I said, 'Are you there, Jack?'

He grunted.

'Jack, no one knows that I have spoken to you; I can only surmise that this must be someone else. Another member of the Trust must have been approached. I'll try and find out and get back to you.'

'It's *mine!*' he yelled. 'You can have the money by the end of the year – but that gallery is *mine!*' then he hung up.

I slept badly that night. I knew that he wanted to contribute to a charitable cause in the city of his birth. In the morning I convinced myself that all I had done was to provide him with the opportunity, and then to speed it up.

Beryl Foyle chaired a trust set up by her late father. She convinced the other trustees to give a grant to the Arts Centre which enabled us to build Foyle House, the reception and administrative offices, which was designed like a large comfortable home. Sir Edward Boyle was a Birmingham MP, and Minister of Education when he performed the opening ceremony on 7 March 1964. By then we were well ahead with the Cygnet Theatre, the studios and the outdoor Greek-style amphitheatre, which was being constructed by volunteers from the International Youth Workforce.

It brought to Cannon Hill students from all parts of the world who camped and worked on site. Each group spent between two to four weeks with us, constructing a project that they, in all probability, would never see again. By the time this phase was completed we were receiving visits from officials in Italy, America, Greece, German, France and Russia, and they all wanted to see what they called, 'our innovative approach'.

Harry Parkinson, who was by then the town clerk of Birmingham, phoned to warn me that I would be receiving a call from the British Council. They were looking after the visiting Russian National Ballet Company. Harry explained that some of its members had asked to visit the Midlands Art Centre for Young People, but the British Council had no knowledge of our existence so had called him for help.

I was appalled that, having received so many overseas visitors, it took a visit from a Russian Ballet Company to acquaint the British Council of the fact that we existed. When the call came I agreed to make arrangements to meet them and suggested that he ask some of the dancers to bring their ballet shoes. On the day they arrived, I had organised with the manager of the Birmingham City Orchestra to arrange for some of his musicians to be at the Centre prepared to play a few excerpts from the ballet.

I then contacted a number of the schools in the central areas to bring some of their pupils to the Centre, none of whom, I was told, had ever seen a ballet performed. The Russian visitors were taken on a tour of the city and given lunch by the Lord Mayor. They were then brought to Cannon Hill. Having looked over the park, our buildings and the model of those which were yet to be constructed, we then took them out into the amphitheatre to be introduced to the children who were already sitting eagerly awaiting to see the Russian Ballet performance.

The leader of their group spoke impeccable English, and he explained to the children the excerpts that they were about to see. He asked them to close their eyes whilst he painted a word picture of what the dancers would have been wearing had they been performing on stage in a normal theatre. He did this before each excerpt eloquently and with a deep understanding of his audience. He asked them to use their imagination whilst watching the dancers.

The members of the orchestra began to play excerpts from *Swan Lake*, and the dancers, having donned their shoes, came on stage. What followed is too difficult for me to adequately describe. Standing in the wings watching the reaction on the faces of those children moved me to tears. John English, who was standing behind me squeezed my shoulder. Turning round, I could see that he too had tears in his eyes. He pointed to the children.

'That's what this is all about... you were absolutely right.'

Some time later we had a visit from the directors of the Moscow Central Puppet Theatre. We were aware that we were breaking new ground but didn't expect Valerian Nesterov, the Cultural Affairs Secretary to the Russian Embassy, to say, 'Of course, there is nothing just like this anywhere.'

To be fair, they start with their children in kindergarten, but it is all government controlled, while we were an independent trust.

They had with them was an internationally famous puppeteer who had been performing in Britain. He was so moved when he saw the children making puppets for a show they had written that he left with us a large trunk full of his own puppets.

In October 1965, we were honoured by a visit from Princess Margaret and Lord Snowdon. He was so deeply engrossed in what he was seeing, that when I passed on the message that a fog was closing in and the police were concerned about getting them to Elmdon Airport for their flight back to London, he said, 'Shush, not a word!'

He obviously wanted to spend more time in the Centre. I was duty bound to pass the message on to the Princess. Snowdon disappointed, asked if he could come again, 'Any time you want,' he was told. Unfortunately, I never met him again, but the Princess Margaret and I were to meet on a number of occasions.

The Centre was well established and accepted as part of the Midlands scene when John English and I had our first disagreement. A local businessman offered the trust a large sum of money on condition that it be used to build indoor squash courts. I said that we should politely turn it down. John disagreed. He obtained the support of the majority of the trustees, and the money was accepted. I felt then, and still do, that it was completely contrary to our aims and objectives.

Had I made a fuss, it would have created a considerable amount of press comment which would have been harmful to the future of the Centre. With great sadness I left a project that I had put forward, nurtured and helped to get up and running. I disappeared from the scene quietly.

The then Councillor George Jonas, a very able lawyer, became deeply involved in the Centre, and on meeting him in 1998, I explained the reasons for my leaving the Cannon Hill Trust. He agreed that inserting a squash club into what was an Art Centre for Young People was an unfortunate error of judgement.

However, it has now been converted, with the donor's consent, and the Centre has gone on from strength to strength. I'm proud to have been its instigator and to have worked with John and his wife, Molly, who were unstinting in the time and energy they devoted to the physical creation and success of 'our dream'.

Chapter XVIII

FIRST CITIZEN

In 1958, I had been approached to allow my name to go forward for the selection of Lord Mayor of Birmingham. I was only thirty-six years old and felt that there was still a great deal more to do before taking a break from the mainstream, so I declined. I was pressed again in 1964. I was still young to be Lord Mayor of the second city in Britain, but having left the Public Works Committee and achieved the things I wanted to achieve on the Parks Committee, I accepted.

Having been born in poor circumstances it was inevitable that the local press likened me to Dick Whittington, although unlike him, I had stayed in the place where I was born. I took on the task with some trepidation. In naming me Frank, my parents had demonstrated unusual foresight. I was and am Frank by name and frank by nature, and at times it tends to offend people. As first citizen I wouldn't be expected to be frank, and that was to prove difficult for me.

Two days after taking up the office, the Duke of Edinburgh came to the city to open the new Bull Ring Centre. He was also to visit a number of factories, one of which was owned by Oscar Hahn, who had been at Gordonstoun with him. Oscar was the son of the founder, Kurt Hahn.

The Duke's schedule was heavy, and organising the timing at the various venues was important. In order to ensure that we all knew the drill, the town clerk and his staff drew up an itinerary, tested it out and had us rehearse it to make sure that we arrived and left on time. He then cleared it with the Palace.

Prince Philip arrived at New Street Station on the Royal Train. The station and the surrounding properties were part of a large redevelopment which was, at this time, under way. Lord Willoughby de Broke, the Lord Lieutenant, the stationmaster, the town clerk and I were on the platform as the train pulled in. The carriage door opened, the Duke stepped out and the Lord Lieutenant introduced me.

The Duke looked around him and said to me, 'You building an overhead sewer here?' then, without waiting to be introduced to the others, he set off for the exit.

A large crowd had gathered outside the station. By the time we got into the Lords Mayor's Rolls we were already ten minutes ahead of schedule. Once seated, I handed him the itinerary, a copy which he had already seen. Conscious of the timing and the long day ahead, I said, 'We will need to keep to the timetable, sir.'

He replied, 'They will just have to keep up, won't they,' and turned to wave to the crowd.

I had heard that he could be difficult. He had already put my nose out of joint by his 'overhead sewer' comment so I decided to make my point.

'If that's the way you wish to proceed, I suggest that we open the windows and toss out the itineraries – then everybody will know where we stand.'

Still waving to the crowds, he slapped my thigh, saying, 'All right matey, don't let me upset you.'

Once we were in the Lord Mayor's Parlour, where he was to sign the visitors' book and have coffee with a number of VIPs, I moved away to the far end of the room. The Duke called out, 'Town clerk, I think that I have upset your Lord Mayor.'

Harry Parkinson looked at him and then across at me and said, 'Oh, I very much doubt that, sir.'

'Oh yes he has!' I called out, and the Duke roared with laughter. From then on the day went smoothly according to plan and he enjoyed himself.

When the time came for me to hand him over at the city boundary to the Mayor of Smethwick, where he was to open a new bowling rink, he commented, 'You are not leaving me, are you?'

I nodded my head.

'Why don't you come in and give me a game?' he added.

'You are out of my manor, I'm sure that they will look after you...'

At that, he shook my hand and was gone.

The press were kind to me, so I was surprised when a free paper called the *Planet* printed an article questioning my political sincerity. It was headed MR SUCCESS, and suggested that, like Joseph Chamberlain, I had represented St Paul's Ward, that we were both leaders of great Birmingham improvement schemes, both civic heads and successful businessmen, and that like him I would split my Party and become a Tory cabinet minister.

The owner of the paper wrote a letter to its editor to say that he knew me well, that I was a sincere Labour Party supporter and not a 'woolly' socialist. The owner, by the way, was Woodrow Wyatt.

At the first opportunity I had I expressed my concern about the false view that many people had of the city, that it was time that we made an effort to alter our image of being simply a large industrial conglomerate, lacking in beauty, style and culture. A few weeks later the BBC screened a documentary by a local lad named Kenneth Hill called *The Second City*.

The film suggested that people in the South saw Birmingham as a drab, dirty, dull and dreary place somewhere in the North, and that events passed it by. The programme caused such a stir that Sir Hugh Greene, the BBC's director-general, dismissed it as sardonic and humorous and not a factual documentary. The BBC refused to consider allowing someone to produce a counterbalance to the film but agreed not to show Hill's effort nationally. It just intensified my desire to see us alter the image.

It did give rise to an amusing incident. I received a letter signed by thirty-five teenage girls urging me to further *my* own reputation of being a progressive Lord Mayor by administering a 'terrific' jolt to the Baths Committee by supporting their plea to allow them to bathe in topless bikinis, which they claimed were 'definitely in'. 'Oh to be rid of those confounded shoulder straps!' they pleaded, adding that my support would be most gratefully received by an overwhelming majority of females.

The letter suggested that, 'as you are a comparatively young man compared with our council representatives, we guess you will not be afraid to have a go.' They apologised for not including their names and addresses as their parents were rather straight-laced.

The Baths Department's general manager, Mr Moss – who obviously had had an antipathy towards rolling stones – said that bye-law 24 read:

> A person while bathing in a swimming bath shall wear a costume proper and sufficient as regards thickness and otherwise to prevent indecent exposure.

He added, 'It precludes topless bathing costumes.'

I asked that he might follow the lead that the borough of West Ham had given, namely that women be allowed to wear topless costumes but only at women-only sessions, and sent him a copy of a letter from a citizen signed 34B. It asked me to keep 'abreast' of the times. The Baths Committee were not amused.

Prior to taking up the office, the Lord Mayor's secretary called me in order to go through the many invitations his office had received. He required me to decide whether to accept or decline, and proffered his advice as we went through the pile. There was one from County Galway, Eire.

'We never accept,' he advised. Apparently one came in every year but was always declined. I asked why.

'Southern Ireland, sir,' and he continued to read out other invites.

'Hold on, let's get back to Galway – you mean that because it's Eire it's turned down out of hand?' I asked.

'Yes, of course,' he replied, as if I was an idiot not to understand.

'Do we accept invites from Italy, Germany or Russia?' I asked.

Before he could answer I added, 'I would hazard a guess that we have more Irish living in this city than in the whole of Galway, and yet you are telling me that we turn their invites down out of hand. Not this time, mate.'

My private office was a few minutes walk from the council house and as I entered there was a call from the foreign office.

The official on the other end of the line suggested that it would be helpful if I changed my mind about visiting Galway. The Lord Mayor's secretary had obviously made contact. After I'd emphasised that I thought his request was a bloody nonsense he hung up, to call again later. He asked, if I insisted on visiting

Galway, whether I would agree to stop off first in Belfast to meet their Lord Mayor.

When the time came it proved to be a memorable visit. As I was to travel south, the Belfast Lord Mayor must have taken it as read that I was a Catholic; indeed he asked the question. I told him that my mother was a Catholic, my father loosely Protestant, my paternal grandmother Jewish and that I was an agnostic seriously considering atheism. He changed the subject.

Landing at Shannon Airport I was greeted by a fellow no bigger than 5'2" who asked if I was prepared to do an interview for television. He explained that there was, as he put it, 'a minor difficulty'. Due to scheduling – I believed he really meant the cost – the television crew wouldn't be able to travel to Galway.

'So would you do the interview as if you had just returned from your visit?' he asked.

'Are you asking me to be interviewed about a place I've never been to, as if I had?'

He said, 'You've got it in one, sir.'

I couldn't believe it. There stood the camera and sound crew, along with the guy who was standing by to do the interviewing, all smiling broadly. 'You're kidding me?' I said.

They shook their heads in unison.

The little fella pleaded that they would be in trouble if they went back empty-handed so after some thought I reluctantly agreed. The interviewer came forward, did a few words into the microphone to test it for sound, and pushed it under my nose, with the camera rolling.

'You are the first Lord Mayor of Birmingham to have accepted the invitation to visit us, are you not?'

'Yes, I believe I am, and I'm glad to be here.'

'Have you met many Irish people before you came here?'

I repeated what I had said to the secretary. 'I am the Lord Mayor to more Irish than live in Galway, I believe, so yes, I have met a lot who speak like you.'

'Did you enjoy your visit to Galway?'

'It is as beautiful as all the songs written about it.'

'And what did you feel about the people?'

I looked across at the little fella and beckoned him to join me.

With my arm around his shoulder I replied, 'This chap was the first to greet me when I landed here; like all those I have met he's been full of charm and goodwill.'

The interview was to be broadcast the day I was due to leave.

The 'little fella', full of excitement, said, 'Tank yer, tank yer – it will be worth a tousand votes, a tousand votes.'

A local election was due ten days later. I asked him if his politics were left or right and was mortified to find that I might have assisted a right-winger to get elected.

My visit took place during the Oyster Festival, so the cavalcade of cars taking us to Galway pulled up at a pub in Clarinbridge called Pat Burke's Oyster Bar. There I was introduced to the chairman of the Oyster Festival, taken to a seat at the bar and served a half-dozen oysters and a pint of Guinness. Although the pub was crowded there was no sound as the customers' eyes were fixed on me.

Oysters and I have a mutual dislike but on Birmingham's behalf I sunk them along with the Guinness. Before I could move, another plate was put in front of me. Again under the watchful eyes of the pub's clientele, I repeated the exercise and suddenly he onlookers erupted, cheering wildly. My stomach was less than appreciative. Back in the car driving through the now dark countryside I asked the driver to pull over. I ducked behind a hedge out of view, and threw up.

The town clerk of Galway had requested that I bring with me the mayoral robes, chain and tricorne hat. The following day, dressed appropriately and standing alongside Councillor O'Flaherty, the Mayor, behind the bearer of the heavy mace and another official carrying a rather weather-beaten sword, with the council members in their robes, we marched ceremoniously out on to the stage to meet the people.

I enquired about the sword, which was in a sorry state. Apparently a former town clerk had left in a hurry, taking with him the sword and much else. It had been found in the United States and returned some weeks before my visit.

Once seated, facing a large audience, I took out the few notes I had prepared waiting for the Mayor's address of welcome. He stood before the microphone and opened up.

'I would like to welcome to Galway, His Worship the Lord Mayor of Birmingham.'

The audience, led by Dr Browne, the Bishop of Galway, rose to their feet and applauded. I can only assume that the Mayor hadn't expected such a rapturous welcome, for he followed it with 'Let's not get too excited. I'm sure that you remember that one of his predecessors was Joseph Chamberlain, who was no friend of Ireland's.'

This wasn't quite correct; Chamberlain wanted Britain to keep both parts of it.

He went on, 'And one of the leading industries is the Birmingham Small Arms Company – and you know what their guns did to us in the troubled times!'

I was staggered. As he continued, all eyes were turned on me, so I held up the notes I had in my hand and carefully tore them up, their eyes followed the pieces as they fluttered to the floor. When the Mayor resumed his seat in total silence, the town clerk called on me to respond. I stood before the microphone for about fifteen seconds before speaking.

'*That* was an address of welcome?' I asked, raising my hands and turning to look at the Mayor.

The Bishop, followed by the rest, applauded. I thanked the good people of Galway for inviting me, saying that I looked forward to meeting them when I got out of my uniform. Turning to look at the Mayor, I said, 'I feel I must inform you, Mr Mayor, that Joseph Chamberlain's politics were more akin to yours than to mine. His son Neville, by the way, married a girl of the Burke-Cole family from Graughivel, which you all will know. Furthermore, the chairman of the small arms company you referred to was also one of yours, not mine; and by the way he was an Irishman named Patrick Hannon, who was born not too far from here!'

I was not quite sure on the latter point but I had been so taken aback that I threw it in anyway. After a pause, I continued, 'I think I should warn you, Mr Mayor, to be a little more respectful, because I happen to be Lord Mayor to more Irishmen than you.'

The audience, led by the Bishop, stood up again, cheering and clapping.

I went on to tell the audience that during times of persecution Birmingham decided to provide a haven for those who wished to worship in peace, and that the Irish who had settled in my city had always been given a square deal in housing, jobs and everything else – and that Gaelic football had a stronger following there than anywhere else in the Midlands.

When I was 'out of uniform' and mingling among the guests, Mr Bartley, the Minister of Defence, came over to shake my hand. 'Spoken like a good Celt,' he muttered as he slapped me on the back.

The Bishop had arranged a dinner for a number of citizens he thought I ought to meet; I noted that the Mayor was not included. When we were alone, the Bishop asked what he said was a couple of 'embarrassing' questions. 'How did the British view the Irish problem, and what religion did I belong to?'

I replied that to me neither question was embarrassing. I thought that most of the British people didn't know or understand what was called the Irish problem. Their knowledge of what was going on in the North, in their name, was minimal; that to some extent they could be excused because, before the war and during it, they had too many problems of their own.

As to my religion I told him that I belonged to none and with what I saw of the world would most likely remain an agnostic at best. That I didn't mean that I didn't believe that Jesus Christ had existed; rather that I wished that those who claimed to practise what he preached actually followed more closely his actions. I ended by saying, 'Now, I feel that I've embarrassed *you*, I don't mean to.'

He smiled and clasped my hand.

Galway and the surrounding countryside was, as I had told the television interviewer, like everything the songs written about it, and more. Everywhere we went we were treated with kindness and warmth that was very moving to me. I was able to forgive myself for the charade put on for the TV cameras on our arrival.

On the last night of our stay the banquet that was laid on for us developed an interesting twist. I sat next to the President of the Society that had organised the function. Halfway through the meal, the double doors at the end of this large room burst open and a man entered, almost running towards the top table. As he came closer I could see that he was emotionally disturbed and wondered just what he was going to do.

He passed me and bent down to whisper to the President. By this time all heads were turned towards us and the room fell silent. The President stood up, his face quite pale, and turned to me putting his hand on my shoulder. I thought, *Good God, something terrible has happened at home.*

He turned to face the room and in a quavering voice announced, 'Tonight, my dear friends, the last night of the visit of our most welcome and honoured guest, the Lord Mayor of the City of Birmingham…' He paused, wiping away a tear.

'I am pleased to tell you—' another pause '—that the mortal remains of Roger Casement are at last home, here in Ireland.'

With that he turned to me and began to clap, saying, 'Thank you, thank you.'

The scene that followed is hard to describe. The guests began to hug each other, laughing and crying and cheering at the same time. It took me a few minutes to remember who Roger Casement was. Ireland had been trying for forty-five years to have his remains returned. It took me a few minutes more before it dawned on me that they thought that I had arranged it with Prime Minister Wilson to coincide with my visit. I was too embarrassed to disabuse them.

Before I left the banquet, a call had come through from Dublin inviting me to stand on the podium as the gun carriage bearing the remains of Roger Casement was paraded through the streets. I declined, with the excuse that I had previously arranged important duties in Birmingham and under no circumstance could I break them. I left them to celebrate without me.

Birmingham is twinned with the French city of Lyon, and when they decided to put on a show in opening the massive Rose Gardens surrounding their exhibition pavilion, I thought it strange that they should choose to invite an Englishman from a provincial city to be, as I had been told, their guest of honour.

I was met at the airport by a high-ranking Army officer who invited me to dinner that evening. The following morning he collected me from my hotel and with police outriders took me to the pavilion to meet the Mayor of Lyon and invited dignitaries. Having been introduced to the Begum Aga Khan and Princess Grace of Monaco, I didn't need anyone to tell me that I was not the guest of honour.

After an aperitif we were asked to follow the Mayor to the place where the ceremony was to take place. As we walked through the grounds, embarrassed by what I thought had been a mix-up, I slowed my pace falling back among the huge crowd. Suddenly a distressed call came over the tannoy system.

'Lord Mayor de Birmingham.' Pause. 'Lord Mayor de Birmingham.'

As I was the only one on this hot June day wearing a morning suit and a chain of office – another piece of mistaken advice – I was pretty conspicuous.

The crowd around me parted like the Red Sea and an official hurried me to one of the three seats on the dais where I was placed between two of the world's most beautiful women to observe the long initiation ceremony... This concluded, they laid on a gargantuan lunch that lasted for five hours. On the evening, having thankfully changed into a lightweight suit, I was taken back to the Rose Gardens which sloped down to the river, to enjoy the son et lumière display. It was magnificent.

Later that evening, being the only 'Brit' at the cocktail party hosted by the Mayor, I stood by the door leading on to the terrace and away from the crowd who were milling around the more important guests of honour. An official approached to say that Princess Grace would like to have a word with me. I guessed that being the only other foreigner present, she sympathised with my situation.

She asked me to sit next to her. As she turned her chair towards me and let it be known that she wished not to be disturbed, I discovered that Princess Grace was not just a beautiful woman, she had a warmth that made it easy to converse with her. I mentioned that I had met one of her father's friends, an architect who told me about her family; that her father had been a great oarsman whose ambition had been to compete for the Golden Sculls at the Henley Regatta but hadn't been allowed because 'he had worked with his hands'. I wasn't sure how true the story was but she didn't correct me.

I also understood that her brother had contested and won the contest two years running. The Princess asked how I had come to meet the architect and I then told her that I had been in Philadelphia on the day she left to get married and had met him during my brief stay.

Watching her reaction I had the overwhelming feeling that I had somehow saddened her and said, 'Please forgive me, but I sense that you are missing your home and family right now.'

She stared at me for a moment and then touched my hand. I realised then that my senses hadn't mislead me. A few weeks on, I read that she was pregnant with her third child.

We met again six years later. I was entering the lift at the Connaught Hotel when the lift attendant held up his hand to stop me. The Princess had entered the foyer and the doorman had signalled his colleague. I stepped aside and she got into the lift. Looking at me she held up her hand and beckoned me. On our way up she turned and said, 'Hello again, it's been a long time since we last met.'

Before we could start a meaningful conversation the lift doors opened, she shook my hand and got out.

On the day when I left Lyon to fly home, the Begum Aga Khan arrived at the airport. One of her security men came across to me to ask if I was flying home via Paris, and I told him that this was so. A few moments later he returned to tell me that the Begum would be happy if I would join her. A tall, handsome women, she explained how she had been invited to the ceremony. 'I was born in Lyon,' she said. In return I explained that the only reason I was there was that Lyon was twinned with Birmingham and I happened to be that year's Lord Mayor.

During my year of office, the Lord Mayor of London called the Lord Mayors of the major cities to discuss ways of assisting the National Council for Handicapped Children. The meeting was addressed by Eunice Shriver, the late President Kennedy's sister, who spoke eloquently of her brother's help for severely retarded children in America. One of her sisters suffered from this disability, which was, the reason she was so fervent. After the meeting she sought me out to tell me that the last Bill her brother signed was for research into the cause and effect of a problem which affected thousands of families. Going on to say that they had sought the help of a famous professor in the field, who worked at Birmingham University, she added, 'Of course, you would know him.'

I didn't, so to save my embarrassment ducked the question. Once back home I looked him up.

During a long conversation, Eunice Shriver asked what I was prepared to do to help, expressing her concern that the care of mentally handicapped children in Britain was in the hands of the Ministry of Health.

'With care and dedication they can be educated,' she insisted, 'and that there is a need to educate teachers to specialise in teaching severely mentally retarded children.'

I got the message. On my return I met members of the Birmingham Society, all of whom had afflicted children. I was to discover that so many parents felt that it was somehow their fault that there was something wrong with their child. Some hid their children away, never taking them out because they felt ashamed. I put this to the professor who introduced me to a man and wife, both professors at his university, who had a family of four, one of whom was severely retarded.

'It must be a case of where the lightning strikes,' I said.

He convinced me that many of these children could be educated if we had specially trained teachers. He was right. Recently – in 1999 – a girl with Down's syndrome won a place at university. He convinced me that I should get involved and I decided to raise enough money to build and equip a college to teach teachers to teach these children, and to do what I could to assuage the feeling of inferiority which some parents suffered.

I opened an appeal with the help of Councillor Mrs Jean Cole, and addressed meetings all over the city to raise money and to help those suffering families. At one such meeting, before an audience of five hundred and the television cameras, I introduced the two professors. Before doing so I spent time giving reasons why parents should feel no shame, uttering my phrase, 'It's where the lightning strikes' – which was used time and time again during the campaign. Pointing my finger at the TV camera I said, 'It could happen to you.' I then introduced the professors who told their story.

The following Sunday morning, walking my dog across a park near my home I was stopped by a man of about fifty.

'I saw you on television,' he said. 'I have a son who is a TWA pilot and a daughter who is severely mentally handicapped. We haven't taken her outside, other than into our back garden, for years.' He became quite distressed, adding, 'You made me feel ashamed.'

It was a very moving moment. I pulled him to me and hugged him.

'Come on,' I whispered, 'you are not alone; it's because people do not understand, but they are beginning to. You have nothing to blame yourself for. Go back home and introduce your daughter to the neighbours in your road... and be proud.'

It took time to raise the money for the building but we were encouraged when Fircroft College, a Cadbury enterprise, gave us the land on which our college could be built. My friends, the architects, Seymour Harris and Partners, offered their services at cost which relieved the Society of a considerable financial burden.

During the early part of my year in office, a General Election was called. It was a most frustrating time for me. As Lord Mayor and presiding officer over the election in Birmingham, I had to stand on the sidelines, unable to be involved in helping my Party. I invited all the candidates and their agents to have coffee with me before the battle started, and they all turned up. Labour won the election with a wafer-thin majority.

A few weeks later, the chairman of the Bank of England, in toasting the city on the occasion of a bankers' banquet held in Birmingham, spent most of his time slagging off the new government. His only reference to the city was when he asked the guests to join him in raising his glass, 'To the City of Birmingham.' The Toastmaster then called on me to reply.

I had to say that I was in some difficulty in replying to a speech toasting the city when it had hardly been mentioned.

'Sitting here holding a position which is by tradition apolitical,

I wondered how I would reply if I wasn't the Lord Mayor. I thought that it would go something like this…'

I then suggested that I would have told the chairman of the Bank of England to forget *his* politics, to begin to understand that we were all in the same boat, that if we were to win we should all try and row together in the same direction. I ended by saying, 'But as I am the Lord Mayor, and have to abide by the rules, I can't say that. All I can say is, that his toast to the City of Birmingham fell short of what I had expected but nevertheless I *have* to thank him.' There I was, being Frank again.

I got a call from the Queens Own Hussars just before Christmas. They were manning the number one action station in Berlin at a time when many thought that the Russians might begin to move west. They had been on Red Alert for months and their nerves were wearing thin. The majority of the serving men and their families were from the Midlands and I was asked if I would go over to visit to meet the families and to speak over the Army radio.

I was met by Major Harry Deal-Payne, who turned out to be quite a character and highly regarded by his men. When he met me off the plane he told me that he had been expecting a much older man. Two nights later he and two of his officers took me 'downtown'.

Although the General had invited me to stay with him, I thanked him but felt that he had enough on his plate. I stayed at the Bristol Kepimski. He had made an appointment for me to meet the Mayor of Berlin, Herr Willi Brandt, and joined me on the visit. Entering the Mayor's office we were greeted by his secretary, an English lady of uncertain age. She surprised me by advising me that when the Mayor went quiet it was time to leave. To the General's embarrassment I said that if Herr Brandt ever decides to visit me in Birmingham I would accord him as much time as *he* wished, and that if he was really that busy perhaps we should give it a miss. She hurried into an office, returning to usher us into Brandt's presence.

He was, as I had been led to believe by those who had met him, a most charming man. We conversed for a while and then he became, as his secretary had warned, rather quiet.

I then said, 'I understand that you will be up for election soon, how are you getting on with the Catholic vote?'

The General rather flushed, excused himself. Willi Brandt asked how I knew that he was having difficulty in that area.

I replied, 'You have many admirers outside Germany who are anxious that you should succeed. As a Democratic Socialist I am one.'

We rattled on for more than an hour. Before I left, he presented me with what he said was a favourite vase. The General was waiting for me. He told me that of all those he had accompanied to Brandt's office none had stayed so long. I told him that I had been invited to stay over to join the Mayor when he opened the new shopping area in the centre of West Berlin on the Saturday. I would have like that but was due to return to Birmingham on the Thursday.

Harry Deal-Payne rose to become a General. It was sad to see that his batman had been picked up by British customs driving an army vehicle towing a horsebox which was full of crates of whisky. He was charged and was prepared to accept his punishment, but Harry couldn't allow that. He told the court that the batman was carrying out his orders. It cost him his career. As I said earlier, he was a 'character' – but of the highest order. I am proud to have known him, if only for a short time.

A few days after my return, in fact just two days before Christmas day, along with the then Chief Constable, Derek Capper, I was invited to the annual Christmas Lunch at the Press Club. I was unaware that they had kindly invited the chauffeurs to join us. They left the cars at the entrance in Bull Street which had a 'no parking' restriction.

Sidney Hawkins, a traffic warden on duty in the area, spotted the cars and slapped tickets on them. For Albert Colley, who had driven the city's Lord Mayor's car for the past twenty years, it was his first traffic offence. When asked for my opinion of the warden's action, I replied that he was doing his job and the fact that he booked me and his boss, the Chief Constable, goes to show that we are living in a democracy. The Chief and I both paid the £2 fine. The news spread across the world. Leonard Gollober, a friend in New York, sent me a cutting from the *New York*

Journal, reporting my comment, no doubt for the attention of their Mayor.

Looking through the galaxy of scrapbooks my secretary, Muriel, had so faithfully kept, made we realise just how full and varied my year in office had been. There were so many people, happenings and joyous moments that it would take far too much space to record, and those I have chosen to mention are no more important than so many others I could have mentioned.

In May 1965, my mother was sitting in the city council chamber during the Lord Mayor making ceremony. I had just handed over the chain of office to my successor, Alderman George Corbyn Barrow, a great-grandson of the founder of Barrow's Store. As he was making his first speech as Lord Mayor, I spotted my mother dabbing her eyes. When I stepped down from the rostrum I took hold of her.

'Mom, I can't be the Lord Mayor for ever,' I said in an effort to console her.

'It's not that, son,' she whispered. 'As Alderman Barrow was praising you, I suddenly had the picture of you standing by me at the bacon counter in his father's store.'

Not long after I stepped down, Harry Watton, the leader of the council and the Labour Group in the City, went down with what I was informed was a life-threatening illness. The Group had reappointed me as junior deputy leader, and as Alderman Horton, the senior deputy had suffered a stroke, I took over the leadership. As I was to be heavily involved politically, I felt it necessary to ask to be relieved of the non-political post of Deputy to the new Lord Mayor. So ended a most enjoyable period.

Denis Howell, who had been appointed the first minister for sport, invited me (dragooned would be more the word) to become an unpaid chairman of the newly appointed West Midlands Regional Sports Council; it was the last to be set up. The officials had already been appointed by the minister and we were fortunate that John Coghlan was the Secretary. Despite the many tasks set by the National Sports Council, he was always brimming with confidence and enthusiasm. He was like a breath of fresh air.

Our first job was to assess what our region lacked in the way of facilities and to list our priorities. We were, as I mentioned, the last regional sports council to be appointed, but thanks to my colleagues and John Coghlan and his team, the first to produce its report to the sports council. One of our priorities was to redress the loss of open-air playing space.

Some years before, the government amended the Town and Country Planning Act, inserting a clause which gave rise to a massive loss of open space. In a country that already had well below the average of open space per head of its population, the amendment proved disastrous. Today, politicians from both sides are crying out for more open space, blaming the situation, as they always do, on what they say is the ineptitude of local government. They conveniently forget that they are, for the most part, responsible. Their amendment, in a nutshell, gave landowners 'a right for alternative beneficial use'. In essence it meant that if a company had a sports field for the use of their employees, which many had, they were given the right to challenge the local plan by applying for alternative beneficial use.

Zoned as a playing field, the land was of little value. Its alternative beneficial use would normally be housing, commercial or industrial. The amendment created a land value far in excess of its present use, so under this clause the owners were given the right to apply for an 'alternative beneficial use' – 'beneficial' meaning 'valuable'. The planners, aware of the shortage of open space, would refuse; the owner would then appeal and if the local authority insisted in holding to the original use, the owner sued for compensation, which placed the council in an impossible position.

For example, under the amended act two football pitches owned by, and next to the Birmingham Battery Company in Birmingham, about two miles from the city centre, would have cost the ratepayer £1,000,000 – had the city insisted on retaining its official use. When the act was first mooted, I wrote to the city's thirteen members of parliament warning them where it would lead. I cannot recall receiving support from that quarter.

The West Midlands Regional Sports Council, in setting the priorities of need in the various towns, discovered that the priority most of them had was to build an Olympic-size swimming pool. With limited grants we were able to convince them that such an expensive facility would have to be limited within the region and shared. Money could then be spent on other facilities in short supply.

We formed a Sports Forum, upon which local government representatives and delegates from each sport would sit. We hit a snag with the cyclists. They had track, road, mountain and touring clubs, all independent of each other. Luckily we were able to convince them to choose one person to represent them all.

I served as the council's chairman for four years before pressure of other duties forced me to retire. The council passed the following resolution which was recorded on an illuminated address:

> The West Midlands Sports Council formally places on record its grateful thanks to its first chairman Alderman Sir Frank Price on his retirement from the chair, for his inspired manner in which he has promoted the best interests of sport and physical recreation throughout the West Midlands. And that by his enthusiasm, drive and enterprise the aims and objects of the Regional Sports Council have been greatly furthered to the benefit of the Region whom the Council was established to serve.

I mention it only to underline that at times one's efforts are recognised. It is not always the case.

The National Exhibition Centre

During this period the leader of Birmingham City Council, Sir Francis Griffin, asked to see me on what he said was an urgent matter. It turned out that he was considering the idea that Neville Borg, the then City Engineer and Surveyor, had put to him – namely, the development of a National Exhibition Centre. Borg had spoken to me about this when he was Manzoni's Deputy; it seemed that he had convinced Griffin to go for it.

This was municipal enterprise and Griffin, knowing that he would have opposition from his own side, needed the support of the Labour Group. I was very much in favour, and after a series of meetings with him, Borg and the town clerk, was convinced that we could pull it off. I didn't expect any opposition but some of the left wing were not happy to support what they saw as a Tory idea. At the meeting of the group, of which I was leader, I asked them to allow me to bring in the town clerk. It was a first and I doubt that it has ever been repeated.

I outlined the proposal. The town clerk was able to tell my colleagues that the idea was that of the City Engineer and that it needed cross party support. With a few voting against, it was carried. This was repeated at the Conservative Group meeting, so when it came to the city council it was approved.

We obtained support from the Conservative Government and they provided us with a grant of £11 million, about a third of the estimated cost. When the GLC heard they began to lobby the ministers to have the centre built in London. They started on a plan which they confidently thought would scupper us. The leader of the GLC invited his political colleague, Francis Griffin, to join him at his celebration party on being knighted. Griffin didn't really know him and didn't suspect that he was involved in a 'dirty tricks' campaign. By the time Griffin returned to Birmingham they had convinced him that he was wasting his time and our money. They told him that they were to build the Exhibition Centre in London. His Deputy, Neville Bosworth, warned me about what had happened. Soon after this, Noble, who was Minister of State at the Board of Trade, informed the city that the £11 million grant would be set against what was known as 'locally determined schemes'. This meant that plans to build old people's homes, schools or other projects would have to be shelved.

I spoke to Neville. 'We have a battle on our hands, we must make an appointment to meet the minister,' I said, and he agreed.

A date was fixed, and I took it upon myself to telephone Lord Thorneycroft, whom I had met only once but who had connections with Birmingham going back a long way. I explained what was going on, that I believed that the 'London lobby' was at work trying to undermine our efforts, and the reason we were meeting Noble. He promised to help. I then phoned Peter Walker with the same message and obtained his promise to help.

We travelled to London to meet the minister. Waiting outside his room we saw Peter Thorneycroft entering the minister's room. When he came out he acknowledged me, saying, 'It will be all right.'

Francis Griffin was surprised and asked me what he meant; I didn't reply. Soon after, Peter Walker came out of the minister's room, nodding to me with a smile. Griffin turned to me again but we were interrupted by being called.

Noble was sitting at the end of a long table. He signalled us to sit down. Francis Griffin asked me to open for the city. Before I had time to develop our case, the minister interrupted.

'Sir Frank, I have decided that the grant will not affect your locally determined schemes grants.' With that he stood up and left the room – somewhat unsteady on his feet, I thought.

On the train back to Birmingham I was able to tell Griffin of my appeals for help from his Party colleagues. 'You should drop them a line and thank them,' I added. He did, but it didn't occur to him to thank me. I wasn't expecting him to; he was never friendly to anyone on the other side of his political fence.

I remained on the Board of the National Exhibition Centre to see it built, to help convince British Rail to build the Birmingham International Station, to help to convince the owners of the Metropole Hotel in London and Brighton to invest in the first hotel in the area, and to welcome the Queen when she opened the complex. I was approached to become its chairman when the first chairman fell out of favour, but declined. I stayed on the Board until we landed the Motor Show, which signalled to the rest of the world that we had a success on our hands. I then resigned.

Chapter XIX
A MAN 'IN' PROPERTY

My life 'in' property had begun in 1959. Exciting and hectic as it was, it didn't quell my enthusiasm for my work on the city council. By 1961, I was playing a major role in Murrayfield's involvement in a number of negotiations to redevelop large town centre shopping areas, and was still deeply involved in the affairs of my Party and the City.

By this time a number of the major players in the world of property were becoming interested in the company. Town and City, Sunleys and Trafalgar House all made an approach to merge their interests with ours; but, for one reason or another, no agreement was reached. On reflection it was a pity. I thought that if we were to merge with anyone, Trafalgar House would have been our best bet. Unfortunately, we were to get sucked into a merger with City Centre Properties, one of the biggest real estate groups in Europe.

It was controlled by two multimillionaires, Jack Cotton and Charles Clore. Cotton started his career in Birmingham, so I knew of him, and I had heard enough about Clore to know that Walter Flack would never survive swimming in their pool. The merger, which was in truth a takeover, arose out of Flack's obsession with a famous Victorian edifice overlooking the River Thames in the very heart of Whitehall. The building consisted of luxury apartments, famous historic clubs and a restaurant. It was aptly named Whitehall Court.

Walter had heard that the owning company was in trouble and wished to unload it. He made an offer, and its chairman made a mistake in the manner in which he brushed it aside. It caused Walter to delve more deeply into why and how it was being put on the market. He discovered that the chairman had kept his Board in ignorance of the fact that he was involved with others who were bidding for the building.

Had the chairman acted differently, Walter would most probably have let it be. In the event, late one night after dinner, Walter called a cab directing the driver to take us to Whitehall Court. He asked him to continue to slowly circumnavigate 'The Court', whilst he described this old building to me in the most eloquent terms. 'It occupies the finest site in the Empire,' Walter assured me. He was so enamoured that I didn't bother to interject that the Empire was in terminal decline.

He told me of its history, the famous people who had lived there, among them Bernard Shaw, and rattled off the names of those who still did, as we circled round the building a few times. I was grateful to the cabby when he cried out, more in hope than anger, 'How many more times, guv? I'm getting giddy.'

That night as I listened to Walter Flack, it was obvious that he would not be deterred from going into battle with its owners' chairman, and he convinced the Board that we should back him. I knew that it would cost us around a million pounds, a considerable amount of money at the time; what I didn't know, was that we couldn't afford it.

Walter peppered the company with phone calls and telegrams and in the end its chairman caved in and a deal was struck. Over the next few days Walter approached the banks and the institutions to provide the funds, without success. I was never sure whether Walter ever had it in mind, but for historic and architectural reasons it was not a site which could be redeveloped.

During a meeting he was having with Jack Cotton, he mentioned the project and – surprise, surprise – Jack offered to fund it. He went on to suggest that if we sold him twenty per cent of our shares he would 'turn on the tap' to fund other schemes we had in the pipeline. When Walter broke the news to the Board he was in a buoyant mood. 'We have brought our ship in,' he enthused.

Knowing Cotton, it made me distinctly nervous.

Among my many failings is one of being unable to suppress my feelings, and my face reflects it. Walter noticed and took me aside to ask what was wrong. I told him that he would never be able to live with Jack Cotton. I didn't realise just how prophetic this observation was to be. But with Cotton's assurance the Board agreed to go ahead with the purchase of Whitehall Court and to sell Murrayfield shares to City Centre.

A few of weeks later I was called to a special Board meeting in London to be told that Cotton had reneged; his excuse being that when he agreed to merge city centre with Charles Clore's property company, a condition was that Clore had to be a party to such deals. Clore was a cold, hard-nosed property man and refused to agree to fund Murrayfield unless City Centre Properties owned a majority of its shares. I had my doubts about this but never did discover whether it was true or not.

Clore did tell me that it was at his insistence that Walter, Alan Wright and I had to sign five-year contracts. Although a compliment which proved something which had not occurred to me, namely that I had become an essential asset to the company, I was not at all happy at the prospect of working with or for them.

Walter, having imparted this piece of bad news, said that we had no alternative but to accede. Looking across the boardroom table, Sir Claude Auchinleck noticed my unease and called on me.

'I'm sorry, chairman, but I can't go along with this. I made my position clear to Walter that I wouldn't be happy working with Jack Cotton.'

Sir Claude, who I soon gathered was not too happy either, said, 'Frank, it seems that we have no alternative,' and he put it to a vote. I was a lone dissenter.

Walter asked me to stay behind after the meeting. He calmly told me that after all he had done for me, I was letting him and the side down. I felt his comment was unfair and retorted, equally unfairly, 'It's all right for you, having made enough not to be too bothered; but for me, I've got to bind myself to these people who will have my future in their hands, not by *my* choice, but yours.'

I looked at him and could tell that beneath a buoyant appearance, he was less than sanguine.

I left to return to Birmingham unaware of the true position. During the two-hour journey back home I made up my mind to go away, alone, to consider my future. I explained the situation to my secretary, Muriel Benton, and asked her to book me a flight to Majorca on the understanding that no one should be told.

Explaining this to my wife, Maisie, and giving her the same instruction, I left England the following morning. That night I called home, making the mistake of telling her the name and telephone number of my hotel.

Two mornings later the phone in my room woke me. It was Walter. I asked how he knew where I was and he said, 'I explained the position we are in to Maisie and she gave me your number.'

'What position?' I asked.

He then set out the fact, of which I was until then unaware, that based on Cotton's original undertaking he had on behalf of the company entered into a binding agreement to buy Whitehall Court. We hadn't the money, and unless we signed down with City Centre we would be sued for specific performance; in short, the company would go under. I packed my bags and returned home.

Up until that moment I had enjoyed every minute I had been with Murrayfield. I had succeeded in proving my ability and Walter, Alan Wright and another young director, David Bacon, and I had become firm friends. Before City Centre came on the scene, in addition to the schemes in Scotland, I had set up what I called the 'Urban Renewal Section' in our Birmingham office, and with two senior and one junior qualified chartered surveyors, we had landed a number of profitable developments.

Among them there were three major town centre redevelopment projects which we carried out in cooperation with the local authorities. The reputation of Murrayfield as a competent and fair dealing company was spreading.

Our first large scheme was in the city of Dundee. Walter had heard that Land Securities, the most prestigious property company in the UK, had been asked by the Dundee City Council to design a scheme around its ancient city church in an area known as the Overgate. What they put forward was not what the council wanted, and it was turned down.

Fortunately for us their Managing Director, Luis Friedman, had refused to negotiate on the design so they lost out. The Scottish representative of Healy and Baker, an old established British estate agency who had put the City and the company together, was angry at the loss of his commission and contacted us. We appointed Ian Burke, Martin and Partners, a local firm of architects, to advise us. Meanwhile, Walter asked me to fly up to see them and report my views on the potential of the Overgate.

I was met in Glasgow by Healy and Baker's Scottish representative, who I found to be a young, highly strung fellow with a ruddy complexion. He was wearing a dark blue three-piece suit and a bowler hat. On his arm was a rolled umbrella and in his hand a briefcase. He was small and painfully thin and when he handed me his card I noticed that his hand was shaking. It was my first encounter with Roderick McFarlane McLean. I was to spend four very eventful and sometimes hilarious years with him.

We got into a car to be driven, I thought, to Dundee. Instead, he pulled up at a restaurant in the centre of Glasgow, and over dinner he filled in the details of the situation. It was getting late and I assumed that we would soon be setting off to our destination, but on leaving the restaurant, when we reached the car he handed me the keys, giving me instruction on how to get out of Glasgow and on to the road to Dundee. He gave me the name of the hotel where he had reserved a room and with that wished me goodnight.

The fact that he wasn't taking time out to accompany me was not reassuring. Having driven in the dark through a countryside of which I knew nothing, in a hired car in not too good a condition, I entered Dundee and found the hotel a little before 2 a.m. The large doors were firmly shut and I could see no lights. I rang the bell and banged on the doors until a startled old retainer with a flashlight in hand opened up.

It took me fifteen minutes to convince him that a room had been booked for me. He had his doubts, and by that time so had I. In the end he decided to hand me the keys to a room. Both tired and angry, I was looking forward to my next meeting with Roderick McFarlane McLean.

The following day I walked to the offices of Burke, Martin and Partners to find the senior partner, Ian Burke, to be a 'laid-back' character, at times infuriatingly so. But he was an imaginative architect with flair and a pleasant disposition. He took me to the Overgate site and then back to his office to go through the outline scheme he and his team had drawn up. On my asking why he felt that his design would meet the wishes of the local authority, he pointed out that he was a Dundee man, that he lectured on Architecture at the local university, and he knew what the city wanted.

Impressed, my spirits rose even further when he said that he had arranged for me to meet the Lord Provost for lunch that day. Unaware that I had spent twelve years and was still serving in local government, the Lord Provost treated me with disdain. He rubbished Burke's ideas, although he hadn't seen his plans, and added, 'The fact that you have an old Field Marshal as your chairman doesn't impress me one bit.'

I simply couldn't let that one go by. It was obvious that we were getting nowhere so I countered by thanking him for taking time off to see me but that I was surprised by his reaction to a scheme that he hadn't even seen. Before he could say a word I then added, 'My Lord Provost, I feel I must tell you that in my time I have met many Lord Mayors and a few Lord Provosts who, without exception, treated me in a manner which one expects from those holding high office. They were all as courteous as they were impressive.'

Without losing eye contact, I added, 'I am sorry to have to say that you fall very far short of the standards they set.' And without waiting to witness his reaction I left the table.

He had been the leader of his political party, was in the mould of a city boss, and acted as such, which annoyed me intensely. Of course I realised that by being 'Frank' again I had shot my bolt, so I motored back to Glasgow Airport to catch the evening flight to Birmingham. Having parked the car, leaving the key where instructed, I entered the airport building. Before checking in I called Walter Flack to apprise him of my 'foul-up'.

Typically, his response was, 'Come on, Frank, you can't catch every bird that flies. Have a drink, go home and relax.'

Taking his advice, I sat in the bar with a brandy. I was still smouldering when it was announced that the Birmingham flight was subject to a two-hour delay. The drive back to Glasgow gave me enough time to consider the demeanour of the Lord Provost and to wonder how I would react to a man like him if I had been a member or an officer of the Dundee local authority. I phoned

Walter again to tell him that I was going back to Dundee. I then phoned Ian Burke.

'I am really pissed off by the treatment at the hands of your Lord Provost and I'm on my way back to Dundee. Will you please book me a room and be there when I arrive. Call that McLean guy and tell him to be in Dundee tomorrow and try to fix a meeting with the town clerk or his deputy.' Replacing the phone I began to feel much brighter.

When I arrived I found Ian Burke and his partner, Hugh Martin, keeping the old retainer happy in the bar. Both were surprised and delighted that I hadn't just given up. They had made arrangements for me to meet the deputy town clerk on the following morning. When I entered his room he came from around his desk saying that he hadn't connected my name.

'Connected?' I asked.

'Yes, I heard you speak on Urban Renewal in London some years ago, I am so pleased to meet you,' he replied, warmly shaking my hand.

The architects, unaware of my background, beamed with pleasure and obviously began to view me in a different light.

I asked the deputy town clerk if the proposed development of the Dundee Overgate was open to tender, and if so had the list been closed. His look of embarrassment spoke volumes. I decided to chance my arm.

'I must be honest, *I had* heard that your council has not yet been asked to rule on the procedure to be adopted, but having met your Lord Provost he gave me the distinct impression that the method of open tenders would not be invoked.'

Both the deputy town clerk and the architects became distinctly uncomfortable.

'I'm sorry,' I said, 'it's not my wish to embarrass you.'

He smiled, and whilst saying that the council had not discussed it as yet, wrote something on a piece of paper, folded it and handed it to me. Back in the hotel I asked Burke to call the men whose names were on the paper and to ask them if they would meet me. I was to discover that they were leading members of the council and that they had been told that there was no development company interested in putting in a scheme along the lines that would meet the council's wishes. I suggested that I could supply the names of half a dozen leading companies off the top of my head who, given the chance, would tender – adding that Murrayfield would be one.

I made it abundantly clear that I wasn't asking for any favours or preferential treatment, just an opportunity to put forward a scheme. They didn't bother to ask how I had got their names but it was obvious that they were unhappy with the way things were being run.

The Agent, Mr Roderick McFarlane McLean, had failed to show but I was to get to know him well during the next few years. He had a rare feel for property deals and a liking for his national beverage. Having said that, he was a likeable character and fun to be with, most of the time. It was he who put us on to the possibilities in Dundee and he worked hard to put other schemes to us. Walter was to appoint him as a Scottish director and he set up offices in Glasgow and Edinburgh.

The fact that my flight to Birmingham had been delayed, or maybe it was the brandy, gave rise to my return to Dundee and it had paid off. Ian Burke sent me copies of the Dundee newspaper containing reports of the rumpus which forced the issue of competitive tenders. Months later we saw the press advertisement inviting tenders which enabled us to join those who were to compete for the scheme. The rest is history.

Soon after we began work on the Overgate and before we merged into City Centre Properties, our Glasgow office was up and running with Roddy in charge. Then unmarried and working hard and long hours, he helped to advance the company's reputation. We were invited to put forward schemes in Edinburgh, Glasgow, Greenock, Ayr and Inverness. Some were dramatic; others quite nondescript.

I was always involved when we were dealing with local authorities and became quite friendly with those with whom we worked. It meant my spending a lot of time north of the border. The staff working under Roddy were very loyal to him, so much so that they failed to let me know that he was drinking heavily.

Murrayfield's advance was rapid. Within a few years we were working on a number of large development schemes on both sides of the border. We were lucky in having a lively and imaginative team of people who worked well together. Alan Wright, who led the property management and rental side under what was then the Walter Flack, Wright and Partners banner, joined in on some of the negotiations with the local authorities.

Goddard and Smith, a firm of London Surveyors, invited Walter to attend a closed meeting at which, with a few other companies, we were asked to tender for what was called 'The Old Town Hall site' in a main street in Preston, Lancashire. Again, Walter asked me to take a look and report on its potential.

I fixed an appointment with Mr Staziger, the town's Engineer and Surveyor and travelled to Preston with Goddard and Smith's brochure in hand to locate the site. Having walked around the town centre I was impressed – but not with the site I was there to see. Nevertheless I kept my appointment with Mr Staziger.

After the preliminaries I asked why they were developing a site which would make an admirable garden open space that would expose to view the Harris Library, which was one of the finest buildings in the immediate area. He agreed, but said, 'The council have been told that the site will fetch a considerable sum of money.'

I told him that we wouldn't be putting in a tender. I left his office and with a few hours to kill before my train was due, strolled around the town once more. Walking down Fishergate, one of the main shopping streets, I noticed a stream of women disappearing down a narrow passageway all carrying shopping bags. Intrigued, I followed them although I could have found myself in an embarrassing situation had they been queuing up for a public loo. As it was, they walked through a maze of dilapidated empty warehouses, workshops and rubbish dumps which lay behind the facade of main street shops.

Halfway through this conglomeration of disused property they entered what was an 'oasis' called Bamber's Yard. In it was a café which, I was informed by a lady I sat next to, 'served the best pastries in Preston'. She also told me that the passage we came along was a short cut linking the bus station to the markets. 'It's a rabbit run,' she said. 'Saves a lot of time, besides we can stop off here for a snack.'

I followed the route out through to an exit between shops on the far side of the site. There I saw the magnet which drew the shoppers through an area that looked as if it had been blitzed. It was a thriving partly covered market.

Retracing my steps I scrambled over the rubble which lay behind Market Street, Fishergate and Friargate main shopping streets and entered Lune Street, which formed the southern boundary. It was a street of what in their day had been rather fine houses, most of which had been turned into solicitors' offices and the like. There was no off-street parking, and no loading and unloading facilities to service the shops and stores in this heavily trafficked town centre. It didn't need a genius to realise what could be achieved. I simply couldn't understand why no one else had recognised it.

I entered a solicitor's office asking if I could see the senior partner. During our conversation he mentioned that he had served in the Navy. He really didn't need to tell me; I had already spotted his picture, in uniform, on the wall in the reception. He was the spitting image of the First World War hero, Admiral Beatty, of which I'm sure he was aware.

I asked if he represented any of the land or properties I have described. He didn't, so I asked, 'If my company decides to negotiate for some or all of what's there, would you act for us exclusively?'

He glanced at my card and looked at me saying, 'I have a few shares in your company, so may I ask, why would you be interested in that pile of rubbish?'

Without answering him, I extracted a company letterhead from my case and asked whether I could dictate a letter to his secretary.

She typed out a simple agreement appointing his partnership to act solely in our interests. In turn he gave me a letter accepting the commission. I then advised him not to sell his shares just yet.

A few weeks on, at my request, he organised an evening meeting with the property owners at the Victoria Hotel, close to the site. I travelled to Preston with Bob Allen, one of our chartered surveyors, who would carry out most of the negotiations if the meeting proved to be successful. We left the train and groped our way to the hotel, convinced that the thick fog which lay over the town would have kept the owners away. We entered the room that our solicitor had booked to find it full. He obviously possessed a persuasive manner.

I soon realised that addressing people I had never met before, who were naturally suspicious of London developers, wasn't going to be easy; so I introduced myself as one who had travelled far and wide gaining experience in town planning and traffic control.

'The ownership of motor cars is growing faster than the facilities to handle them. Without sufficient off-street car parking, and the provision of off-street loading facilities in the main streets, town councils such as Preston will be forced to act.'

I went on to describe what was happening in America where they had constructed large out-of-town shopping centres with sufficient free parking space that had attracted the major stores. They had moved from the town centre and taken the shoppers with them. Property values in these towns had plummeted.

'If towns like Preston are to avoid this, it is patently obvious that sooner rather than later they would have to provide off-street parking and loading facilities. To do so they will be forced to acquire back land such as yours and they will do it by compulsory purchase if needs be,' I told them. With that I sat down.

During a long question and answer session, I felt that I had convinced them of what lay ahead. When asked what my interest was, I told them that I wasn't there to try to take an unfair advantage. If the council were forced to act, they would negotiate with the owners and failing this would compulsorily acquire their land. In the event the council would be advised on values by the District Valuer.

I suggested that if they were all prepared to sell to my company – at this time the company had no idea – we would be prepared to pay them ten per cent above the value placed on their ownership by the District Valuer.

I added that any development we carried out would provide the services I'd mentioned, and furthermore, if and when we developed the land, we would agree to rehouse any business we disturbed which conformed with planning requirements.

I then placed two pieces of paper on the table in front of me, one marked AGREED and the other NOT AGREED. I asked our solicitor to take over whilst Bob and I went downstairs to the bar for a drink. When we were called back to the room we found that all but the owner of the snack bar in Bamber's Yard had agreed to negotiate. He was the only one present who was actually running a business, small though it was, and to him it was important. I promised that we would see that he continued in business at a rent far lower than anyone near him.

Bob questioned me on this but I pointed out that this small café already attracted a considerable number of shoppers to the area; it was small but it was a magnet. Walter Flack, not for the first time, agreed with my line without question.

When our local lawyer had all the option agreements in, I went to see Mr Staziger again. This time I had an outline plan of what we wished to build. It included off-street services and an adjoining multi-storey car park. I then added, without consulting my colleagues, that if we had the cooperation of the council I would convince my company to present the freehold of the land to the town, taking back a 120-years lease at a peppercorn.

Unfortunately, the town clerk proved to be unhelpful. My offer of the freehold must have made him suspicious. I received a call from his secretary asking me to phone back at a given time. It was an indication of what was to follow.

I called as requested, and the town clerk said that he understood that my company had purchased one or two properties behind the main shopping streets and asked what were our intentions. I asked whether Mr Staziger had informed him of our meeting. He brushed this aside and repeated his question.

I replied, 'You must be aware that we are a publicly quoted property company. You are mistaken by suggesting that we have purchased one or two properties; we own them all. May I ask you again, has Mr Staziger apprised you of our discussion?'

He stayed silent for a few seconds and then, ignoring my question, continued, 'I find that hard to believe; I think that we should meet.'

I contacted the company's lawyers, and John Franks, the partner who dealt with our affairs, joined me for the meeting. He brought with him copies of all the agreements. Sitting opposite was the town clerk, who without thanking us for travelling more than 150 miles to see him, asked us to show him proof of our ownership.

John was a very smart lawyer, but had, when dealing with pompous people, a short fuse. John enquired as to what right he had to make such a demand. Knowing that we would have to live with him I asked John to hand him the list. Scanning it, he called out a number. John whisked the agreement out of the pile he had on his lap and the town clerk proceeded to call out other numbers from the list. Came one which John had misplaced as he was apparently struggling to find it, the town clerk said, 'I thought so.'

Retrieving the agreement, John stood up and slapped it and the rest of deeds on the desk scattering them in the process. He was furious.

'You thought so?' he shouted. 'Let me inform you, sir, that I hold office in the Law Society and I take the greatest exception to your attitude. *You thought so.* Who the hell do you think you are dealing with?'

With that he gathered up the deeds, stuffed them into his case and stormed out of the office.

I looked at the town clerk, raising my eyebrows, my shoulders and my hands in unison, and left the room.

On our way back to London, John said, 'From what you told me, I knew how he was going to react, that's why I misfiled one of the deeds, hoping he would call for it.'

We carried out successful negotiations with the owners of property fronting the main streets, which allowed us to break through to land we had purchased at the rear. Seymour Harris and partners put in a plan which we had agreed and applied for planning permission on behalf of the company. As I expected it was turned down. I didn't bother to ask to meet the council; I simply advised the company to slap in an appeal. We secured the services of a leading Queen's Counsel named Sir Geoffrey Lawrence, who among other things specialised in matters to do with Town Planning.

As luck would have it, before our appeal was to be heard, Sir Geoffrey had taken on the defence of a Brighton doctor who had been charged with the murder of a number of his elderly patients. The case attracted considerable publicity. I think it fair to say that few people thought that Sir Geoffrey would win this multiple murder case, but win it he did. Subsequently his reputation as an advocate went up by leaps and bounds.

When we received notice of the date of the appeal, I enquired about its possible timescale and reserved all the rooms in the Bull and Royal, a relatively small four-star hotel in Preston's main street. Two weeks before the hearing the town clerk surprised me by calling to ask who was to lead for us; usually they acquaint themselves of the strength of the opposition. I asked who was leading for the Preston Corporation; I was happy to hear him say, 'Me, of course,' and even happier to impart the news that we had been fortunate enough to secured the services of Sir Geoffrey Lawrence.

'You may have heard of him,' I said as I hung up.

Six days before the appeal was to be heard, he rang again. This time he was to tell me that he had advised the council to drop the case and grant us planning permission. He went on to ask whether the offer to give the freehold of the land to the corporation was still on. It proved that Staziger *had* spoken to him of our meeting and there was no doubt in my mind that the town clerk had advised his council to turn down our application. When he realised that we were not prepared to play games he revised his view on who was likely to be successful.

Although happy that we could now get on with building our scheme, I retorted that my Board was so annoyed by the arrogant manner in which we had been treated so far, saying nothing of the unnecessary expense we had been put to they decided to turn down my request to offer the town the freehold. I went on to say, 'I trust that you will inform your council of the reason.' I doubt very much that he did.

On completion of the scheme, which was the first of its kind in Preston, we passed over to them, free of cost, the ownership of the multi-storey car park. The St George's Centre proved to be both attractive and, for the company, profitable. The Coal Board Pension Fund purchased it from us some years later.

My Birmingham office went on to win the central redevelopment of Hagley, Huddersfield and Keighley. Working with the Scottish offices, I was involved in the schemes in Edinburgh on the St James' Square and Port of Leith schemes, and in the plans to resuscitate the heavily bombed centre of the town of Greenock. Further south, I was also engaged in discussions with Wigan Corporation.

We always included in our budget what I called 'fun money'. With it we were able to add something special by way of mosaic murals, fountains or statues. In the case of Preston we created a mural based on the spectrum around the elevated central balcony. In Huddersfield we bowed to the wishes of the council by erecting a mural representing various aspects of the wool trade. In Keighley it was a replica of a mythological giant called Rombole.

The story goes that Rombole came down into the valley having had a row with his equally large wife. Angered, she rolled great boulders down on him, he picked them up and hurled them back and they broke up and scattered over the hills. And they are there today for all to see.

I had a miniature clay model made of the giant, holding a boulder above his head in the act of pitching it back at his wife. We placed the model, arms and legs spread, depicting him naked, before a council committee. A lady Alderman looking at it closely asked, 'How big will the statue be?'

Our architect answered, 'About twelve to fifteen feet, madam.'

She inspected the clay model again before saying, 'Will it be in proportion?'

Trying to keep a straight face, I said, 'Yes, madam, and mindful of the fact that you wish to encourage more visitors to Keighley, we felt that you might wish us to place him in a fountain and have him copy the actions of that statue of the little boy in Belgium which as proved to be such a tourist attraction.'

Although it was meant as a joke, had I pressed it I think the committee might have gone along with the idea of Rombole peeing in the fountain on the hour, every hour. The councillor in charge of tourism was very much in favour.

By the time the development was completed, City Centre Properties were in control of Murrayfield, and Walter Flack was

279

no longer with us. Charles Clore decided to represent the company when the town's Mayor opened the Centre. We stood in a line behind him as he was addressing the audience that had gathered to watch the ceremony which included the unveiling of the Rombole statue. Clore whispered, 'Who paid for this monument?'

I answered, 'I haven't a clue,' hoping that the Mayor wouldn't thank us. He didn't.

My involvement in the town on the other side of the Pennines was to give Richard Crossman his first opportunity to score off me, and he did so with a vengeance.

I had passed through Wigan as a boy a few years before the war, but all I could recall was the sound made by the mill girls' clogs on the cobbled street as they were making their way home from the mills. It was just past twelve o'clock on a Saturday, it was raining hard and I was sitting on the back of my father's old motorbike and sidecar, making our way to see the Blackpool illuminations.

It was an old machine which kept breaking down, and every time we had to get off whilst he 'fiddled' with it to get it started again, the seats got soaked. We got to Blackpool late and the only view we had of the lights was driving in a line of traffic along the promenade making our way to the cheap bed and breakfast boarding house. By the time we reached our goal we were soaked to the skin. The landlady, in typical north country fashion, took good care of us and after a hot bath and supper we went straight to bed.

On my next visit to Wigan, some twenty-five years later, most of the mills had closed, the cobbled streets had been paved over and the girls of Wigan wore more fashionable footwear. I was there to view a property the company owned.

Walking around the town I came across the fine-looking church on the hill which was unfortunately obscured from general view by the rundown properties surrounding it. Below stood the Market Hall, situated in crowded narrow alleyways behind the main shopping street. I decided on instinct to call on the town clerk.

The girl in reception took my card and a few minutes later the town clerk came out to both greet and surprise me.

'You are the experts in urban renewal,' he said with a smile, inviting me into his office. Over a cup of tea he asked what had brought me to Wigan. I said that I was passing through and decided to take a look round. I mentioned the church and how sad that it was hidden away.

He enquired about Murrayfield and I gave him a rundown of the places and the developments we had completed or were working on, and encouraged him to call his opposite number in those towns to check on our performance. He asked if I was staying in the area, and when I told him that I was returning south, he expressed his disappointment. He said he was sure that Alderman Ball, the leader of the council, who was in London and returning late that day, would have liked to meet me. He urged me to stay over.

It was too important to miss so I thanked him and agreed. He booked a room in the Brocket Arms hotel, but I declined his offer to cover my costs. Picking up a toothbrush, paste and a shaving kit I made my way to the hotel. It was fairly new, not too far from the centre and had a fine restaurant, which cheered me up no end. My visit to Wigan was turning out much better than the last time I past through.

The following morning the town clerk phoned to ask if I would call into the town hall at 10.30 a.m. to meet the Alderman. He was a tall thin man with a heavily lined face which made him look quite ancient. It belied his alertness and his youthful attitude to life. He was a typical Lancastrian, blunt and to the point. He asked if I knew Wigan, if I had looked around and if so what did I think my company could do to improve it. Three weeks after this conversation I was invited to meet what he called, his 'caucus'.

I travelled back to Wigan, booked into the same hotel, and since I was to report to the town hall at eight o'clock that night, got into a relaxing hot bath with a view to having an early dinner. Before I could get down to the restaurant, the hotel receptionist called my room to tell me that the Alderman was waiting for me in the lounge.

Being unaware of my background, he thought that I wasn't

accustomed to addressing a gaggle of politicians and wanted to prepare me for what he thought would be something of an ordeal. It was just one of his many acts of kindness. I listened quietly whilst he warned me not to be too erudite. 'Keep it simple, lad,' was his advice.

I sat alongside him on the platform looking out across a crowded room. The Alderman introduced me by telling the members that I had not requested to meet them, rather that he had invited me. With that said he asked me to outline what my company did in respect of the renewal of town centres. I apologised for not having with me slides or photographs to illustrate our work but outlined to them the efforts we were making in the field of urban renewal.

Whilst I was on my feet one of the councillors came up to whisper to Alderman Ball. He looked hard at me, and when I resumed my seat leaned across, whispering, 'Is he right, are you the Alderman Price of Birmingham?'

'Yes,' I replied.

He didn't ask my political persuasion but said, 'Why the hell didn't you tell me?'

'Because it has nothing to do with my company. I don't and won't try to use my connections to influence local authorities. If this embarrasses you I will leave, now.'

He stared at me and said, 'I will have to tell them.' And he did just that.

However he went on to say that neither he nor the town clerk was aware of my local government connection, a fact which proved to him that, as he put it, 'He is straight.' He then asked whether the members wished to proceed. The vote was unanimous so I stayed for an hour answering questions.

When we left he invited me to join him for a drink at his club. 'It's the Labour Club, I hope it won't *embarrass you*,' he commented with a laugh.

My God, I thought, *he thinks I'm a Tory*! As I hadn't eaten that day I asked if I could phone the hotel to see when the last meal was served. The manager told me that I was already too late. 'Would you please put sandwiches in my room,' I pleaded. 'Sorry,' was all I got.

Returning to my seat, Ball asked if everything was all right, 'No, I was too late, they wouldn't even leave sandwiches for me,' I moaned.

He stood up and indicated that I should follow him and went to the phone. He blasted the manager with a warning that he had better improve his service. 'I chair the Brewster Sessions and could easily alter your licence!' he shouted down the phone.

Alderman Ball insisted on taking me to his home and had his wife prepare a hot meal for me. She apologised that the stewed steak came out of a tin, with, 'I hope you don't mind.'

It was my second taste of Lancashire hospitality, and the tinned stewed steak went down a treat. Back in my room I found a plate of chicken sandwiches and a bottle of wine waiting for me, compliments of the management. It was late and I was full so I opened the window and skimmed the sandwiches across the adjoining field hoping the birds would enjoy them before the manager turned up the following morning.

Murrayfield was invited to work with the Wigan Corporation to renew and update the area around the central markets. It was a big scheme so we decided to employ two well-respected architectural practices to cooperate with the town's Architect's Department. We went further; we asked Professor Allen, the then President of the Royal Institute of Town Planning, to act as an independent arbiter. After two years, an agreed scheme was put forward and welcomed by the Wigan Council.

Naturally, the local traders objected and a public inquiry was held with a Ministry of Housing and Local Government Inspector in charge. It lasted near enough a month. Later that year the Ministry official indicated in favour of the scheme and we thought that we could make a start. It was not to be.

During the planning period I had a message from the Engineer and Surveyor of the neighbouring town of Bolton. He asked whether I had time to call in and see him; his name was McKellen. His committee was in the process of considering how to improve traffic flow and in the process modernise the town centre.

We drove and then walked around the central shopping and commercial area and then returned to his office. By the time our meeting had finished it was late so I decided to stay over and booked into the local hotel. He invited me to dinner so that we could continue our discussion.

Over coffee he asked whether I had ever belonged to a theatrical society. The reason he gave was that he felt that I must have had some training in that direction. Laughing, I said no, but that my mother had 'trod the boards'. He then mentioned that his son had ambitions to become an actor; he seemed rather disappointed at the prospect.

The outcome of all this was that, along with our architects and town planners in consultation with the Bolton officials, we prepared our basic ideas for the Bolton town centre. All our efforts went belly up when, on a visit to Wigan, staying at the Brocket Arms, the receptionist called to tell me that I had a visitor.

I went down to meet a man I had never seen before. He opened up by saying that he had called my office, and they – thinking it important – told him where I was staying. He handed me his card which described him as being in public relations; the address was in Bolton. I took him into the lounge and ordered him a drink. He said he was aware that my company was putting forward a scheme for the redevelopment of the Bolton town centre and that if we employed him he could ensure that we would be successful. I asked how.

He told me that he was a member of the council and sat on the committee that would be making the recommendation. Trying to appear calm, I asked which political party he belong to.

'Labour,' he replied.

I stood up and said, 'Finish your drink, my friend, and get the hell out of here – and quick!'

He spluttered, 'I suppose if I had told you I was a Tory that would be all right with you.'

I grabbed his arm and walked him outside. 'I'm a lifelong socialist, you worm, now bugger off before I get violent!'

I went back to my room and phoned Mr McKellen to tell him that we would be withdrawing our scheme.

He insisted on knowing why. I told him that I was calling from the Brocket Arms and in confidence, of my meeting with the councillor. I asked that he keep the information to himself, other than to inform his council's Labour Leader. An hour later the Bolton town clerk phoned to say that McKellen had been duty bound to inform him of the situation. I asked him to take no action other than to leave matters with the Labour Leader. He agreed, then suggested that before deciding to withdraw our scheme, I wait for a week and then call him.

I phoned Walter Flack. Filling him in with the situation I said that in my opinion if we proceeded, and this man's approach became public, although innocent we would be suspect. I went on, 'I know we have spent a great deal of money but...'

He stopped me. 'Frank, phone the town clerk, thank him for being so considerate and withdraw the scheme.'

Once again Walter had come up trumps.

A few years after we first met, Mr McKellen was killed in a car accident. He was a kind and considerate man. Reading the report in the obituary column I discovered that his son was Ian McKellen, now Sir Ian. It was sad that he didn't live to see his son's rise to the top of his profession.

On my return from Wigan, my secretary, Muriel, told me that the Ministry of Housing and Local Government had been on the phone to ask if I would be kind enough to call in and see them. Completely unaware that I was to meet the minister, Dick Crossman, I presented myself at the Ministry and was shown into his room.

I had taken no more than three steps when Crossman walked across to me. Two of his officials were sitting at the far end of the room with their backs to me, looking out of a window. I also noticed that the minister's trouser buttons were undone.

Without bothering with preliminaries, Crossman said, 'I've asked you to come in to see me so that I can tell you personally that your Wigan proposals are not good enough.'

Being brought in to be told this was in itself highly unusual and could only be interpreted as a desire to humiliate me in some way. Not waiting for a response he went on, 'It is a thoroughly bad scheme and I am calling it in.'

Still standing close to the door, I couldn't believe what I was hearing.

'Minister,' I replied, 'are you aware that two respected architectural practices, plus Wigan's Architect and the President of the Institute of Town Planning drew up the scheme?' I added as an afterthought, 'And your own ministerial inspector, who oversaw the public inquiry, came out in favour of it.'

It made no impression. 'It's a thoroughly bad scheme and I am calling it in,' he repeated.

I looked at him, understanding only too well why he had taken this decision, so I turned to leave. With my hand on the door handle, I turned to look at him. The only thing I could think of to say was, 'Are you aware that your flies are undone?' Then I closed the door behind me. It had been a bad week.

Two months later Wigan was told that they, and we, had wasted our time and money; the minister had rejected the scheme. Crossman was to demonstrate one more time that he hadn't forgiven me and just how small-minded he could be. It happened during a time when he was the Minister of Health and I was the government's appointed chairman of a New Town Corporation (see the chapter entitled 'New Town Blues').

My suspicion about why Crossman had turned down the Wigan scheme was confirmed some years later. In 1967, I received an invitation from the Anglo-American Society, to be a member of an international symposium on 'The problems of big cities'. It was to be held at Ditchley Manor, a mansion set in open country just north of Oxford, left to the Society, with all its furniture, fittings, pictures, etc., by the Tree family.

I thanked the Secretary of the Society for inviting me but told him that I was far too busy. His reply was somewhat sharp. 'We have very busy government and city leaders in the United States who will be travelling between three and six thousand miles to attend – at some inconvenience, I might add.'

I quickly apologised. 'I'm honoured to have been asked to participate and of course I will be there.'

I motored up the long drive to the front door late on the Friday afternoon. As I pulled up, a man in livery came down the steps to take my bag. He guided me to a bedroom, asking if he should unpack for me, but I declined his offer. Before he left the room he told me that during the war Winston Churchill stayed at the manor from time to time.

'You will be sleeping in his bed,' he said with a smile, which made me wonder why he had emphasised the point. He added, 'Most of the other guests have arrived; dinner will be at eight,' and he closed the door behind him.

I got down early so that I could nose around a little. It is a most splendid house, set well back from the road and surrounded by manicured lawns, a profusion of flower beds and overlooking acres of rolling countryside. The Secretary informed me that the party would meet for drinks before dinner, at which time he would take us through the arrangements for the weekend. The American visitors were all leaders in their fields ranging from sociologists, town planners and city managers to state and federal government officials.

Walking in the grounds during a break in the proceedings, I was joined by two senior civil servants from the Ministry of Housing and Local Government. It turned out that it was they who had been standing by the window when the then minister, Richard Crossman, dropped his bombshell about Wigan. One, the Ministry's senior architectural adviser, mentioned the incident. Without actually spelling it out, he confirmed my suspicion that the decision to turn Murrayfield's Wigan scheme down was made by Crossman alone and had nothing to do with the merits of the scheme.

I had spent a great deal of time and effort on the proposal and Crossman's decision had left me completely shattered. A week or so later Walter Flack told me that he had booked me into a Town Planning Conference taking place in Puerto Rico. I knew that it was his way of getting me to take a break. When Jack Cotton heard he called me in to see him.

'As you will be passing through New York, would you take a couple of days out to find what is holding up the permission on the office deal we are involved in?'

He was referring to what turned out to be the PANAM Building. He left one of his minions to fill in the details.

City Centre Properties had entered into an agreement with a New York property tycoon to erect a huge office block over part of Grand Central Station and their plans were held up by the

287

planning authorities. I agreed to make a few enquiries. Once there I revisited my cousin, Polly, and her family in Westchester, north of New York City. Her daughter, Joan Leslie, worked for CBS and commuted into Grand Central daily. She described to me what it was like during the morning and evening rush hours, and having stood outside the station watching the massive movement in the restricted area known as the Loop, I could understand why the planners were concerned.

I called the Port of New York Planning Authority and made an appointment with Mr Jackson, the officer to whom the Loop area was delegated. He also commuted into Grand Central every weekday from his home in Poughkeepsie, a very long journey in British terms. Jackson said it was the only time he could get to read the newspapers.

We walked around the area adjacent to Grand Central. He didn't need to point out to me that the construction work on the planned office tower would bring this busy area to a standstill for long periods. I understood why it was considered unacceptable. I spent the next two days walking in, out and around this magnificent railway station. It was more like a gigantic coliseum than a place one visited to catch a train.

It was obvious that the only way that planning permission would be forthcoming was if an answer could be found to avoid the chaos the construction traffic would create. It was also obvious to me that the rail company, whose air space above the station had no value unless the development proceeded, would have a real interest in finding a solution. I talked it over with Mr Jackson and we concluded that if one of the railway lines could be allocated during the night to allow the construction material and equipment to be brought in, so avoiding the use of the streets, the planners might agree to stomach a little chaos whilst the foundations were laid and a platform constructed overhead to receive the materials. It was simple enough, but no one had given it a thought.

Mr Jackson said, 'Fine, but I doubt that the rail company will agree.'

I sent a telex to Jack Cotton and caught my flight to Puerto Rico. That was the sum total of my involvement.

Murrayfield had at this time been absorbed by Cotton and Clore's company. Along with my colleagues, Walter and Alan Wright, I was invited to a lunch on the occasion of the City Centre Properties Annual General Meeting. It was held at the Dorchester Hotel. In the centre of the enormous banqueting room, a sheet held by an overhead cord like a huge mosquito net was hiding from view whatever was on the table beneath it. Among the hundreds of guests was a large international press corps and at every place setting there was a 4" record in a sleeve on which was written: SPECIALLY RECORDED BY THE CBS CHOIR.

The meal and the normal toasts concluded, the chairman of City Centre Properties, Jack Cotton, rose to address us. As he finished his speech the lights were dimmed and a spotlight focused on the covered table. At that precise moment the sound of the CBS Choir came over the intercom singing a song with words specially written for the occasion starting with, 'It's the biggest, it's the greatest, it's the finest office building in the world!' I kid you not.

As this was going on, before a startled audience the cover was gradually lifted to expose a model of the building over Grand Central, alongside a model of the proposed Monaco development in Piccadilly. This stage-managed event was as corny as it turned out to be disastrous. The press panned it unmercifully.

Leaving the room I noticed that, like me, the other guests had left behind their free record disc. The outcome of this bizarre episode was that the GLC, having given outline planning permission for the development of the Monaco scheme, refused full planning permission when this was applied for. Cotton had jumped the gun, and the GLC planners took umbrage. It was not a good reason for turning it down, but turn it down they did.

To add to his misery, when the PANAM Building was finally finished, they had trouble, finding tenants. The lack of rental income from this massive building almost ruined Cotton's company. The only reason it was named PANAM was because that company had taken a number of the top floors and, knowing that they were the first and only tenants at the time, insisted on the building being the named, as it still is to this day. It gives them an amazing amount of publicity which would have cost millions of dollars in normal circumstances.

As I had predicted, Walter's normally cheerful personality changed during the following months and as I had feared, on 15 January 1963 he resigned from the City Centre Board. It meant that he had lost Murrayfield, a company which he had built up from scratch, to become respected and admired by those in the business. For me, a light went out.

The fun in working for the company, without him at the helm, had gone. He had remained unaffected by his wealth and as one of his directors I had been happy and content. From the first day we met we shared a mutual respect which grew into deep affection. As I had forecast, he couldn't get along with Cotton and Clore; he was out of a different mould. When he left, Murrayfield was never the same. He died sixty-six days later, an unhappy, dispirited man. It left a big gap in my life. Strange to say, Jack Cotton died in Nassau twelve months later, to the day.

My Murrayfield colleague, David Bacon, had been Walter's accountant and he convinced his widow to pass over the controlling shares in the estate Agency left to her, to Alan Wright. It had not been easy, as during Walter's last year she had grown to dislike Alan. She agreed to David's suggestion on the understanding that the partnership would retain Walter's name, and that Alan would divide the shares with those who had helped to build up the partnership and Murrayfield. The shares Alan offered to the other partners was so derisory that I resigned from the partnership. After Louise Flack died, Walter's name was removed.

Not long after I left the partnership I was called to London to be told by Edward Footring, the then CEO of City Centre, that Alan and the City Centre Board had had a bitter disagreement, and that Alan had resigned both from the Board of City Centre and Murrayfield. He asked me to take over as Managing Director. Although not happy at the prospect, I was under contract and, I accepted. It was at a time when I was deeply involved in a number of major developments in Scotland.

Shortly after taking over, Edward Footring broke the news that the Board would like to pull out of Greenock, and asked how much that was likely to cost the company. We had been working on it for more than two years and the architects' plans had been completed. I wasn't sure how I was going to set about extricating the company and just what in meant in compensation terms. We were committed to the town and the professional advisers involved.

As luck would have it, Greenock's town clerk called to tell me that the Liberal Party had captured control of the council and the new leader had asked to see me. Two days before I was due to meet him the town clerk rang to warn me that I would be appearing before the full council, so I arranged for members of the professional team to join me.

The Liberal Leader informed me that the council had decided that they would carry out the development scheme themselves. I asked how he proposed to compensate those who had already spent a considerable amount of time and money on plans which had been completed and accepted by his predecessors. He consulted the town clerk and recommended a break in the proceedings whilst he conferred with me.

In the privacy of the town clerk's office I told him that I admired the fact that they wanted to proceed to redevelop the town centre themselves and suggested that rather than start from scratch, they take over our scheme, along with our architects, surveyors and estate agents. He literally beamed. I said that of course my company would need to be compensated and suggested a figure of £10,000. He ask me if I would leave him and the town clerk to think about it.

Waiting outside, the professional team were naturally downcast. Called back into the town clerk's office, I was told that the leader had accepted my terms. I was able to report to the team that their position and their fees were secure.

Returning to London, I told the City Centre Board that I had successfully extracted them from their Greenock commitment and had secured the position of the professional advisers so that we didn't have to compensate them. I slipped across the table the cheque made out to the company for £10,000. I ought not to have been surprised when Footring commented, 'Couldn't you have got more?'

I pushed back my chair and left the boardroom in disgust. And I didn't get a thank you from Alan Wright for securing his partnership's considerable fees; but the architect, Ian Burke, rang to say he appreciated my efforts on their behalf.

I was very unhappy in my job and concerned about the future. If the policy of the company was to back out of the schemes I had worked on for so long, there would be not too much joy in continuing with them. However, my days were cheered up early in 1966 by a letter delivered to my home enquiring whether, if Her Majesty the Queen considered offering me a Knighthood, I would accept. I was then forty-three years old and couldn't quite believe what I was reading. Someone must have put my name forward, someone whose reputation was respected, but who...? I never did find out.

The following November I was asked to attend the investiture. The invitation specified that I could be accompanied by my wife and one member of my family, which in my case meant my son, Noel. I had never been in any doubt, that without my mother's dedication I would never have survived let alone reach this stage, so I decided that she and my father should somehow be involved in this important day.

We spent the previous night at Whitehall Court, and my secretary Muriel knowing my mother's liking for the music hall, booked a box at the Victoria Palace which was staging a season of the *Black and White Minstrel Show*. At the end of the performance as the cast were receiving a standing ovation they turned towards the box, calling out, 'Congratulations!' and giving us a royal bow. My mother was overcome with emotion. I could only suspect who it was that had let them know what was to happen the following day.

In the morning, being driven down to Buckingham Palace, we reached the Victoria Monument and were held up by a police sergeant. He opened the door and asked to see my invitation card. He looked at my family and before he could utter a word I said, 'Officer, may I introduce my wife and son, and this is my mom and dad, if they can't go in then neither can I.'

He handed back my invitation and saluting said, 'Quite right, sir.'

Then he closed the car door and waved us through the gates.

Whilst my wife, son Noel and I were guided into the building, the driver took my parents around the grounds to see more of the Palace than we did that day.

Before the three to be knighted were due to kneel before the Queen, a Colonel of the Coldstream Guards instructed us on the procedure.

'You will be standing at an entrance to the Gold Room where the guests will already be seated. Her Majesty the Queen will enter the room from the other side, she will welcome the guests, whereupon the official will begin to read out your citation.

'The first in line – you, General, sir—' he nodded to the man next to me, '—will start slowly to walk towards him; when you reach him you will stop. When he mentions you by name he will nod, you then take twelve paces forward, stop, turn left, two paces forward, bow to Her Majesty, and then kneel with your right knee on the stool with your head bowed. You will be kneeling on the very stool used by Sir Francis Drake. Her Majesty will place the sword, which her Majesty Queen Elizabeth the first used to dub Sir Francis, on *your* shoulders.'

He waited for that to sink in and then added, 'Once Her Majesty removes the sword she will ask you to rise. You will then step forward, Her Majesty will say a few words, you will then take three steps back, bow to Her Majesty, turn right and leave through the exit facing you. And that, sir, will be your lot.'

While standing, waiting for the Queen to appear, we could hear a band playing softly in the minstrels' gallery. On the raised dais facing the families sitting patiently in the room, stood a guard of honour made up of members of the Gurkha Regiment. The Queen entered directly opposite to where we were standing. A few feet in front of us was the orderly standing by a microphone. The Queen stepped on to the dais, said a few words of greeting to the assembled guests, then nodded to the orderly and the ceremony began.

The General in front of me was called and went through the routine which had been outlined to us. The other person who was standing behind me whispered that he had already forgotten the instructions. I told him that I was watching the General. 'He should know,' I muttered. 'I'm watching him, you watch me.'

As the orderly began to read out my citation and I stepped into the Gold Room, the band started to play softly, 'You'd be far better off in a home.' I glanced up at the minstrel's gallery, thinking, *Well, thanks very much*... After rising from the kneeling stool I approached the Queen, who passed a few pleasant comments. I backed away, bowed, turned right as instructed and left the room. As the man had said, 'That was my lot.'

That day the Queen presented decorations for what must have been two or more hours. I cannot imagine anything more boring than having to stand handing out these honours and having to say a few kind words to people one has never met before, and to do this at least twice every year.

In March of the following year The Rt Hon Mrs Barbara Castle breezed into Birmingham. There is no better way to describe a visit from this effervescent lady. She had come in her capacity as Minister of Transport to discuss with the councils of the West Midlands the merging of their independent Public Transport Departments into a single Passenger Transport Authority. It meant that we would no longer be in control, either in management or fiscal terms, and there would be no compensation for their loss.

Birmingham had already lost its profitable gas and electricity undertakings. All had been efficiently managed and answerable to the locally elected representatives who, unlike Central Government, rarely interfered in their management and we received nothing for them. Some years later the same happened to our water undertaking. When all these were sold to the private sector the government forgot where they had come from and kept the money. And now we and the other local authorities in the West Midlands fell for the Transport Ministry's idea and lost control and the profit of our transport undertakings produced for the ratepayers. You will never witness slicker confidence tricks than that, all carried out in the name of democracy. Had we, like Kingston upon Hull, who owned and kept control of its telephone company, held on to our assets, ratepayers would have enjoyed, as Hull does today, the fruits of ownership.

But back to dear Barbara and her meeting held in Birmingham's Council Chamber. For anyone other than

Mrs Castle it would have been a daunting prospect. I sat in the meeting marvelling at her bloody nerve. The towns north of the city are inhabited by tough, fiercely proud people who had an historic uneasy relationship with what they called 'Big Brother Brum'. I didn't fancy her chances in obtaining their support. I still think that had it been any other minister trying to sell this bill of goods, he or she would have bitten the dust.

Not so Barbara; she took away with her all that she came for. She couldn't have realised – I hope – that she had handed Whitehall their future plan to privatising public transport, on a plate. The democratically controlled transport committees, answerable to their respective elected councils for the economic, social implications and general efficiency of their transport service, would no longer exist. In their place would be a Transport Executive managing a conglomerate over which the elected representatives would have little or no control, and from whom the general public would be even further removed.

Whilst watching her devastating performance, a Ministry official passed me a note. It read: AFTER THE MEETING WOULD YOU CALL AT THE ALBANY HOTEL, IN ORDER THAT THE MINISTER COULD HAVE A WORD. My first reaction to the missive was one of suspicion. Was I being lobbied? If so, she had obviously mistaken my position in the city council hierarchy. Although I was at this particular time, the leader of the opposition, I had little to do with the transport committee. My predecessor, Alderman Harry Watton, had been its chairman and watched over its affairs like a jealous lover. In short, if calling me in was the minister's tack, she had chosen the wrong man.

At the hotel I was ushered into the presence. This was the first time that I had been within twenty yards of her. I was struck by this diminutive woman who exuded tremendous energy and enthusiasm; it simply sparked off her. Still stunningly attractive, she had obviously been a great beauty in her time. She had well-coiffured auburn hair and penetrating bright green eyes. They must at times been quite soft to look into but on that day they had the sharpness of needle points.

There were no preliminaries. She asked, 'Frank, what do you know about canals?'

'Canals,' I could only mutter, 'I beg your pardon? What the devil was she on about?'

'Canals, Frank,' she repeated.

'Not a lot, Minister,' I stuttered, but as an afterthought added, 'my father spent time when he was unemployed fishing in the cuts around the city. He had as much success landing a fish as he had at landing a job.'

My attempt at humour bounced off her. 'I am led to understand that you are something of an irritant.'

I thought that provocative comment required a tart reply.

'No more than you, I suspect, Minister.'

Without a flicker she retorted, 'In my book, young man, that's a compliment. You have spoken about the preservation of the canals around this city in the past and I want you on the British Waterways Board. Think about it; if you would like to serve will you contact Jimmy Jones at my Ministry.' With that I was dismissed.

Jimmy Jones turned out to be the Permanent Undersecretary to the Ministry of Transport. We had met on two previous occasions. He had been a witness to my confrontations with Dick Crossman during his period as Minister of Housing. Jones must have been the source from whom Barbara had got her 'irritant' comment. The other occasion was during the Anglo-American Society seminar at Ditchley Manor.

On 20 March 1967, I received a two-page letter from the minister inviting me to join the British Waterways Board; I was formally appointed one month later. This was my introduction to our inland waterways, which turned out to herald the most turbulent period of my life. I didn't know it then, but accepting the part-time membership of the British Waterways Board offered to me by Barbara Castle was ultimately to lead me out of the upper echelons of the property world into national service. It carried with it far fewer perks, a great deal less money, tremendous problems but a great challenge coupled with genuine job satisfaction.

During the same year, 1967, David Bacon introduced me to Bruce Woodall, the managing director of the merchant bank Armore Marden, part of the London and Hong Kong finance group. After a number of discussions with this intelligent and charming fellow he asked David and me to consider joining his Board. John Marden was the chairman of Wheelock Marden, a well-established multifaceted Hong Kong company, of which the husband of Princess Alexandra, The Hon. (now Sir) Angus Ogilvy, was a Board member.

A few months later we set up Armore Marden Midlands Limited, fifty-one per cent of which was owned by Armore Marden. David Bacon, Douglas Ellis (Chairman of Aston Villa FC), Sir Neville Bosworth, a senior partner in a Birmingham local law firm and Kenneth Purnell, chairman of KBP Holdings, joined the Board, mainly due to my reputation.

Things were going well until David called to tell me that he was worried about Armore Marden's annual report which he had that day received. Pouring over the accounts with him it became obvious that at a time when the money market was volatile, the company had entered into a number of questionable contracts loaning money over the long term at low rates of interest. We decided to challenge this at the next Board meeting which Mr Marden was to chair.

Raising the matter, which in our view was placing the company in a vulnerable position, we expected the chairman at least to listen to our concern, but within minutes of David's opening remarks he interrupted and in an angry outburst told us to back off.

I interjected to say, 'If you are not concerned about the reputation of the members of the Board, I am. Will you please take the time to listen to what Mr Bacon and I have to say.'

He adjourned the meeting. I told David that I was worried about those friends I had convinced to join the Birmingham Board. If Armour Marden began to fail, then the Birmingham operation would also suffer. I wasn't prepared for that to happen and would resign from the main board.

David said, 'If we resign it will be picked up by the financial press and the spotlight will be on the company.' He told me that Angus Ogilvy was on the Wheelock Marden Board and might have some influence with John Marden.

I called him and we met the next day. I explained the situation in which the Wheelock Marden subsidiary was most likely to face in the future and that the chairman just wouldn't listen. I added, 'When David Bacon and I resign the press will want to know why. They will trace the company back to the Hong Kong group and your name will be picked up. I do not want to fire that torpedo whilst you are on Board.'

Angus said that he was due to leave the UK with the Princess on a goodwill tour to Canada and the US, and would be in Hong Kong in two weeks' time. He would then meet Marden and would get back to me. I undertook that David and I would take no action until then.

As good as his word, he called me from Canada to say that he had made arrangements to see Marden and would keep in touch. On his return he let me know that John Marden had realised that he had made a mistake in dismissing our observations and would arrange to see us when next in the UK. In the meantime he was asking his chief accountant and secretary to the Board to meet us. We made little progress, so we made it clear that we would not be continuing our membership on the London Board but would delay any announcement until after our meeting with the chairman.

David and I informed the Birmingham Board of the situation, and they suggested that Marden should meet them and us in our Birmingham office. I was surprised when Marden agreed. I guessed he thought that he could convince them that David and I were supernumerary and the Birmingham Board could continue without us. He could not have been more wrong.

He came with the chief accountant, the secretary and two main Board members. His pompous attitude didn't help his case. Then our colleagues made it clear to him that if – when – David and I resigned they would go with us, which in effect would have closed down the Birmingham subsidiary. Neville Bosworth (now Sir Neville) made it clear that he wouldn't be associated with the name Armore Marden (Midlands), and that if it was to continue it would have to trade under another name. The accountant clearly understood how the City would have viewed this and suggested that the meeting be adjourned whilst they considered the matter.

About an hour elapsed during which my colleagues became increasingly agitated. In their view they wanted to disassociate themselves from Marden's company by buying him out. When he and his party returned, before he spoke I informed him of the local Board's views. The outcome was that David and I would resign from the main Board; that if asked, the reason would be that we wanted to concentrate on the Birmingham operation, which would be set up in the name of Birmingham Midland Investments; that if Marden wished to keep his fifty-one per cent interest he would deposit with the company a £250,000 unsecured loan for ten years.

Four years later Guardian Properties made a bid for the company. Its managing director, Harvey Sonning, with my agreement, flew to Hong Kong to meet John Marden, who was very happy to agree the deal. After all, his money would be more secure in a publicly quoted company. One of the conditions of the sale was that I would join the Board of Guardian.

Harvey was a young, personable, intelligent property man, the son of an East End market trader who was the company's chairman. He had a habit of entering a room and interrupting whatever discussion was taking place and whispering into the ear of his son. Harvey obviously loved his dad dearly, for he never remonstrated with him in public or privately; so Harry kept on whispering.

Unfortunately, Harvey became overambitious. Wishing to build up the company's property portfolio without referring to the Board, thinking that he had been offered (privately) a bargain, he bought a group of properties from James Goldsmith's Cavenham Foods. The first I knew of it was from reading the announcement in the *Financial Times*.

Having heard of Goldsmith's business acumen, I called to ask if I might have a look at the schedule and travelled to London the following day. I divided the properties up into three categories: those with good tenants and reasonable leases, those that could be sold on at a profit or at least at no loss, and those that were overpriced. It didn't take much time to realise that the bargain was no bargain.

When we spoke, Harvey soon realised that he had overtraded and that the banks would soon get to know of it. He asked me to stay over. The next day he called me in to a meeting between him and his friend, Eric Miller, the then chairman of Peachey Properties. Dressed in what looked like a dark red smoking jacket, Miller sat there smoking a huge cigar and giving no words of comfort to Harvey or me.

Knowing that what I had to say could only depress him further but nevertheless needed to be said, I told him, 'Harvey, you must call an emergency Board meeting, and after explaining the position warn them that, having been made aware of the situation, they must not in any circumstances sell any of their shares.'

They did the honourable thing, and they and I lost a considerable amount of money when the company went down.

On David Bacon's invitation, I was to be called in to three substantial companies which were in trouble to act with him as company doctors. It was interesting but less than profitable to me personally, and looking back I can't for the life of me understand why I put myself to so much trouble.

The only one I will mention here is the case of Wharf Holdings Ltd, a company that in its day had been very profitable. When I was asked to join the Board its blood was running under the door. My time with them was short-lived but provided a safety net to its many shareholders.

I had been placed on the Board at the request of a number of major investors, and within a few months the chairman, Ronnie Mann, who was also a director of Grindlay's Bank, asked if I was prepared to succeed him. The Board agreed and I began to grasp some of the nettles.

We sold off the loss makers – Beagle Shipping and Union Lighterage. The general manager had entered into an agreement with Compass Securities, a development group who wished to buy the company's headquarters, Beagle House, situated on Gardeners Corner near to the borders of what is known as the City. There were two problems, one that they required a government office development certificate, and secondly, they needed to obtain planning permission. This had been held up by the Greater London Council, who had failed to find an answer to the traffic problems surrounding this busy island site.

The first problem was overcome by Overseas Containers Limited, who had agreed to rent the office block when completed;

but Compass Securities failed to find a solution to the second problem, having been unsuccessful in obtaining planning permission and also its appeal had reached a stalemate.

I was to discover that the GLC had been tinkering with the traffic problems of Gardeners Corner for twenty years without coming up with an answer and during this time had placed a 'blight' on the area.

I thought this totally unacceptable and sought the advice of Richard Seifert, an architect who had made a name for being able to overcome such difficulties. It was said that Richard knew the planning code backwards. On my recommendation the Board agreed to appoint him to act on our behalf.

I informed Compass Securities that as they had failed to produce, our agreement with them was at an end. Their chairman wrote to say that if we wanted to take over their client, Overseas Containers Limited, we could do so by compensating his company for a sum of £250,000.

As the client would only be the client if there was a building for them to rent, which Compass had failed to provide, it was obvious a 'try on'. I tried to contact the chairman of Overseas Containers Limited, but his secretary said that he was far too busy to see me. So I decided to go to their offices.

The chairman's secretary insisted that Lord Aldington was not available. I asked whether he was in the office, she said yes he was but he would not see me. As I hadn't disclosed what I wanted to see him about I couldn't understand the problem, so I just sat there. Aldington came out of his office, spotted me and said, 'Aren't you Sir Frank Price, what are you doing here?'

'Trying to make an appointment to see you for a few minutes.'

He took me into his office.

I quickly explained that I was the new chairman of Wharf Holdings and that I was aware that he had agreed to occupy offices on the Beagle House site, that he knew that Compass Securities had failed to obtain permission to build and that Wharf was going to apply and, if successful, to build. What I wanted from him was his agreement to be our tenant.

He replied that he had heard that the planning permission had been turned down, but that he still felt that the position of the site was exactly where they wanted to be. I then asked if he was tied to Compass.

'Why should we be, for heaven's sake?' he said.

So I then showed him their letter.

'Two hundred and fifty thousand pounds – the cheeky blighters! I'll write you a note,' he said. And that I thought was that.

Seifert drew up a scheme and applied for planning permission on our behalf. He weighed in heavily on the twenty years that the GLC had placed a planning blight on the area and provided them with some ideas as to how the traffic could be handled. He won the day and the company had a valuable asset.

No more than a few days passed before I received a call from Jeffrey Sterling (now Lord Sterling, the chairman of *P and O*), the young chairman of Sterling Property Guarantee Trust. He said we should meet as he had acquired a large number of our shares and was in the process of mounting a takeover of the company. It was clear that he had heard about the planning permission to develop our site and, as an intelligent and aggressive property man, had moved quickly.

We arranged to meet with our financial advisers. I had no idea at that time just who our advisers were; I was informed that they were Baring Brothers Bank. We met in their offices; Sterling was accompanied by a team from Slater Walker. It didn't take long to realise that they had a very strong hand and that I was faced with trying to get as good a deal as I could for the shareholders and the people the company employed. I decided to ask Sterling if he and I could leave the meeting. Baring, who was in the chair, became quite angry and said, 'This is quite unusual!'

I replied, 'Yes, I know,' and left the room.

Jeffrey Sterling followed me. I opened with, 'Although I have a good idea where you got your information in respect of the planning permission, what I am sure of is that you recognise its value.'

He didn't comment, and I then said, 'The value your people are putting on the shares is ludicrous and you know that, but this aside, I'm concerned for the future the company's employees and I would like to be satisfied that they and their pensions would be protected.'

He gave an undertaking that they would be.

He asked me what arrangement I had. He was surprised when I told him that I had no contract, that I only owned £1,000 worth of shares and that there was no suggestion of there being a golden handshake. We re-entered the room and I told Baring that so long as we could obtain a fair price, taking into account the value of the planning permission for the development of the Gardeners Corner site, I would recommend that the Board consider the deal.

Once this had been done, Jeffrey Sterling called to ask me to continue as chairman of Wharf Holdings and its subsidiaries. I declined. I didn't want the shareholders, even though they were to receive a considerable uplift on the value of their shares, and the employees to think that I had done other than my best for them. I cleared my desk and left.

Chapter XX

CHANGING DIRECTION

The British Waterways Board was born out of the British Transport Commission which was set up at the beginning of the war to take control of the railways, the canals and river navigation. The waterways were placed under a separate authority in 1962, and Sir John Hawton was appointed as its first chairman.

Sir John had served as the Permanent Secretary to the Ministry of Health during the post-war Labour Government; his minister was the ebullient left-wing Labour MP, Nye Bevan. Their backgrounds couldn't have been more different.

Bevan, like his father and grandfather before him, had worked in the coal pits of South Wales. He first admired, and then became disillusioned with, some of the orthodox Trade Union leaders, who he felt let the miners down. It turned him into an adversary and he remained so until a few years before he died.

I first met Bevan in the flesh in 1948 when he addressed a meeting in the Delicia Cinema close to the city centre; it had been converted into an all-purpose hall. I was acting as a steward and he appeared to me to be a big man, well built – the sort you hesitated to pick an argument with. He had bushy eyebrows and a mop of thick, dark grey hair, a lock of which had a tendency to fall across his brow when he was in full flight. He would on these occasions hold his head high with his chin jutting out, and despite his slight stutter, or maybe because of it, he could overcome any hostile audience and then hold them in awe. I know; I watched him operate.

A well-dressed man of about forty had pushed all the way forward to occupy a front seat. As Bevan was getting into his stride the man stood up and began to heckle, using a few four-letter words. I moved towards him but Bevan pointed at me and called out, 'No, boyo, let him speak. He is demonstrating better than I can just how those who feel that they are our betters act when they are faced with the truth.'

The man sat down deflated. When Bevan stepped down from the platform he went over to shake his hand.

He was to become one of the House of Commons' most passionate and feared orators but his pugnacious appearance belied his nature. He was at heart a romantic. He had seen the working class misled and misused and was always ready to do battle to defend the underdog, right or wrong.

Bevan realised at an early age that if he was to be of any help he needed to be where the 'power' lay. According to the story he told, he got himself elected to the town council because he was told, 'That's where the power lies.' He was to discover that if there was any, it was in short supply. The same was said of the county council, so he got elected to that body only to find that there too it didn't amount to much.

One of his elders advised him, 'Parliament, that's where the real power lies, boyo!'

'But when I got there,' Nye said, 'I found that backbench MPs didn't have the power either. It was the government, meaning those in the cabinet, that had the real power.'

Seeing the way some ministers fell under the spell of their civil servants, he suspected that they didn't have it either.

Bevan first tasted the power he had been looking for when he became the Minister of Health in the immediate post-war Labour Government. He and his Permanent Secretary, John Hawton, had the task of getting the Government's National Health Service Bill on to the statute book. He was soon to find that the British Medical Association – he called it the doctors' trade union – had power.

Aided and abetted by the Conservative Party, they gave him a hard time, refusing to cooperate and using all the shots in their locker to scupper the Bill. Hawton worked long hours stitching the Bill together, using all his considerable diplomatic skills negotiating with the BMA in an effort to achieve a compromise so that the Bill would have a relatively smooth passage. Once it was on the statute book, Hawton's health gave out and he was forced to take early retirement.

Speaking of this period, Sir John told me that to reach agreement he had to convince Bevan to bend to some of the outrageous demands the consultants were making. He was well aware that it wasn't in Bevan's nature to capitulate to what he saw as part of the Establishment, but he also knew that Bevan had a passionate belief in the proposed Health Service. John Hawton was able to use this to persuade him to do a deal, however distasteful.

Sir John said that Bevan wanted to take the BMA on, but I had to convince him that the delay would jeopardise the chances of the Bill becoming law. He was concerned that his comrades would think that he had 'sold out' and was left with the unenviable task of selling to them the amendments he had agreed with the BMA. He added, 'No minister other than Nye Bevan could have convinced the left-wing members of the Labour Party to succumb to the demands of the doctors, mainly the consultants.'

The job done, Hawton collapsed and was ill for some time. After a long period of convalescence, in 1962 his civil service colleagues advised the Minister of Transport to offer him the chairmanship of the newly created British Waterways Board (BWB). He and I met on the day of my first Board meeting five years later. I was still Managing Director of Murrayfield.

I was placed next to Sir Alex Samuels, whom I remembered from our 'clash' in Birmingham in the 1950s when I was trying to introduce the parking meter into Britain. He attended a meeting I had arranged, to which he hadn't been invited; by me at least.

Samuels was small with black wavy hair, an olive, wrinkled complexion, a permanent smile and small twinkling eyes. A loquacious man, he had the air of a cheeky cockney, which indeed he was. Always smartly dressed, with a flower in his lapel, he was irrepressible.

Raised in London's East End, as a youngster he went to the aid of a policeman who had been struck down during the National Strike. Some years later, having bought a clapped-out old cab, he went to the local police station to obtain a hackney carriage licence. The desk sergeant went outside, took one look at his motor and told him to 'bugger off'.

A Superintendent entering the station at the time asked Samuels what he wanted. He explained and was taken into the Senior Officer's room; it turned out to be the policeman he had assisted. He got his licence and from that single old cab, built up a prosperous taxi and garage business. His knowledge of London and its traffic, coupled with his gregarious, pushy nature and natural intelligence, led him up the ladder of success. He became the personal adviser to successive ministers of transport and was labelled by the 'press' as Mr Traffic.

Although he had been a lifelong member of the Labour Party and had served for years on one of London's Borough Councils, when Barbara Castle took over the Transport brief she dumped him. He claimed that it was because he had served such staunch Tory Ministers as Lennox-Boyd, Boyd-Carpenter, and Ernest Marples; but I doubt it.

Despite his oft-used phrase about the need to rub people up the right way, he had a manner which many people couldn't stand. It had obviously offended Barbara Castle. He left the Ministry and as a consolation was offered a seat on the Waterways Board.

I found sitting through the monthly Board meetings insufferable. The role played by members of the Board was disappointing, if indeed we actually had a role. I asked Samuels, 'Are the meetings always run this way?' and wasn't happy with his reply. Mr A W Allen, the general manager, dressed and acted like a 'resting' thespian. In his checked shirt, flowered bow tie and coloured waistcoat, with a shock of red hair over a ruddy complexion, he sat next to the chairman paying him little notice. It was he, in effect, who conducted the meetings.

I soon realised that Sir John Hawton was a sensitive, intelligent man who had a deep insight into the workings of Whitehall but was surprisingly and painfully shy. So much so, that in order to avoid bumping into members before Board meetings he had his secretary scout the corridors between his office and the executive loo, before answering the call of nature.

We received reports which were of a general nature, and I sat observing the general manager's performance, soon to take the view that, intentionally or otherwise, he was undermining Hawton's authority. The chief officers who ran the major departments were only allowed into the meeting when he called them. When present, they appeared to me to be far too subservient. Maybe because of my background, I couldn't abide being treated by them with what they may have felt to be due deference.

In these circumstances I felt unable to make a contribution to the Board and after six months had elapsed I made an appointment to see the chairman. I mentioned my concern, making the point that Board members didn't seem to have an opportunity of forming overall policy. He didn't appear to have taken my comments on board. I had a great deal of respect for him but left his office thinking that I had wasted my time.

Over the next few months it became obvious, to me at least, that his relationship with the general manager and the deputy manager, who had worked with Allen previously, was fractured. Consequently he was as he appeared, a very tired, unhappy man – and that annoyed me no end. With his long experience in the highest echelons of the civil service, it seemed odd to me that Allen and his deputy appeared to be too much for him to handle.

It occurred to me that I may have been mistaken. Perhaps he was just coasting. He was isolated and may have decided to live with it, but I couldn't quite swallow that. I began to wonder what the hell I was doing sitting on his Board.

There was another matter that offended me but not, it appeared, the other members. The Secretary to the Board, who in 1925 at the age of seventeen, started work with the Regent's Canal Company, went through an intensive course specialising in modern techniques, which over the years he introduced to the inland waterways industry. The company merged with the larger Grand Union Canal Company, and John Backhouse was appointed assistant secretary to the Board. Absorbed into the British Transport Commission, when BWB was formed he was appointed its Secretary.

Yet with all his experience, Backhouse had to sit at a small table placed in a corner of the boardroom to record the minutes, never being called upon to express even an opinion. I mention it because this intelligent and kindly man, who had more knowledge of the canal system than anyone sitting at the board table, including the general manager, was treated like the Dickens character, Bob Cratchit, and virtually ignored by all present. That got right up my nose.

During one of the few conversations I had with Sir John Hawton I began to suspect, probably mistakenly, that he welcomed my rather pugnacious approach, but his Whitehall training kept his caution uppermost. On one single occasion I thought that he was on the verge of committing himself but he quickly withdrew behind his protective screen.

After ten frustrating months trying to get to grips with the making of Board policy, I felt as if I was swimming in a bath of rice pudding. Relationship with users of the system and their organisations was one of mutual distrust and there appeared to be no way that the general manager and his sidekick was going to allow anyone, other than the Ministry officials, to interfere with the way he ran the Board. I decided to abandon ship.

My next meeting with Sir John was to tell him that I was resigning. He gently asked why. As I was quitting I decided not to hold back. It came as no surprise to me that my observations appeared to have little effect on him. He was as always, as inscrutable as a Chinese diplomat. His only reaction was to ask if I would delay my announcement for a month. Speechless, I just nodded and wished him good afternoon. This was early 1968, when unknown to me my name was being discussed in another Government Ministry.

Four years previously, the high-minded Rt Hon Sir Keith Joseph, then Conservative Minister of Housing and Local Government, concluded that the Midlands Local Authorities were right after all, the area *did* need a new town. Yet without consulting any of those for which the new town was planned – which, judging on past performance, was not unusual – he made the mistake of choosing the wrong place to build it.

The Urban District of Dawley in the County of Shropshire was in part surrounded by marvellous countryside, and in others was an industrial muck heap left behind by the ravages of the first industrial revolution. Joseph, it seemed, was moved by the idea of rejuvenating this historic area, and simply ignored the logistics.

The only decent road to it was the already treacherous A1. On the line of a Roman road, it was flat, straight and for miles only single carriageway; consequently the death toll was already too high. Dr Beeching, who had been a director of ICI, knew nothing about transport, so was thought by government to be the ideal man to run the railways. He had set about emasculating the country's rail system and in so doing had turned the proposed new town's railway connection into a sideline. The fact that the physical communications were abysmal, placing the area as they say now 'out in the sticks', hadn't even crossed the minister's mind.

Had Keith Joseph taken the trouble to consult the Midlands local authorities, they might have been able to convince even his closed mind to look elsewhere. It was another example of Whitehall believing that it knew best. The final piece of bad judgement was his choice of its first chairman. To have chosen a retired Managing Director of a car manufacturing company from the South of England was the height of stupidity. He was a pleasant, very capable fellow who had no local government experience. It was unfair to him and to the new town project; he didn't stand a chance.

These points should have been obvious, but not to some of the educated idiots in Whitehall. With their heads in the clouds, and their feet very far from the ground, they doomed the New Town Corporation of Dawley from the start.

In January 1968, the office of the Permanent Secretary to the Ministry of Housing and Local Government – then under Labour – made contact, asking, 'Would I drop in for a chat with his minister, Anthony Greenwood!'

I had visited the old Ministry building at the end of Whitehall many times, once to that unpleasant meeting with the then minister, Richard Crossman. This time I was greeted by Sir Matthew Stevenson, a dour Scot who left me in ignorance as to the purpose of the meeting, simply guiding me into the large ornate conference room.

The Rt Hon Anthony Greenwood – son of a famous father, whom I had first met during his visit to Birmingham – came across to shake my hand. He was a handsome man, tall, slim and urbane. He was always dressed immaculately, the right tie in a Windsor knot, a handkerchief draped from the top pocket, and like the products of most public schools tended to speak without appearing to move his lips.

In addition to the minister, there were two junior ministers, his parliamentary secretary, the Permanent Secretary, and a number of departmental officials. They had obviously been in conference. Had they asked, 'When did you last see your father?' I doubt that it would have surprised me. What Greenwood did ask was, 'Do you know Dawley New Town?'

I answered, 'Yes, of course.'

His next question was, 'What is your view of it?'

'My honest view, Minister?'

He leaned forward to tell me to be completely frank. I had to say that in my view, and that of almost everyone else in the West Midlands, was that Dawley New Town was a total disaster.

There was a shuffling noise behind me, caused I felt sure, by my comment. He pressed me further. I looked around the room, addressing them as well has him. 'Minister, you don't need me to tell you that it's going down the tube.'

Silence prevailed for what seemed like minutes. Greenwood sat back with the fingers of both hands clasped under his nose as if in prayer, looking at me. I couldn't determine what was going on in his mind but he gave me a tight smile and offered me a glass of sherry. I realised that the meeting was at an end.

On Thursday, 15 February I was invited to meet him again. This time he asked whether I was aware that the chairman of Dawley was leaving. I said that I had heard the rumour. He asked whether I would be prepared to take the job on. This I hadn't expected.

I mentioned that the Birmingham Alderman, Tegfryn Bowen, who had been the deputy chairman of the New Town since its inception, was expecting to be appointed.

'We are of course aware of his expectations,' the minister said rather dryly, 'but under no circumstances would we appoint him.'

A few days previous to this meeting I had been offered the Chair of the British Waterways Board (see the chapter entitled

'Water World'). So I hesitated and then asked whether he was aware that Mrs Castle had offered me an important post.

'Yes, I am, but the position I am offering you is more important to the government at this time.'

I thanked him for considering me and asked for a few days to think it over. He agreed and made me undertake not to mention his offer to anyone.

On the Monday of the following week Roy Jenkin's secretary phoned to ask me if I would call in at Number 11 Downing Street to see the Chancellor on the Wednesday. It was unusual because we had a standing arrangement for me to visit him at 6.30 p.m. for a drink and a chat. Although I enjoyed these visits I was always embarrassed when he entered the room followed by two men carrying the famous red boxes. Seeing the number made me aware of his heavy workload. Each time I mentioned this, Roy always insisted that he enjoyed my being there, if only for a short time.

On this occasion he told me that my name had come up at a Cabinet meeting. 'It seems,' he said, 'that two ministers are fighting over your body.'

He asked whether I had made up my mind which job to take. I answered that I didn't want to fall out with either minister and would be turning both jobs down. He then informed me, that in order to keep the peace, the prime minister had suggested that as the jobs were part-time, I be asked to take them both on.

Roy sat waiting for a response. I replied, 'I'm the Managing Director of a company and although I would be prepared to take them on, I am still under contract.'

He nodded and said that Harold Wilson was going to ask me to accept the jobs and added, 'Frank, if you do, I would advise you to insist on being able to keep a foot in the private sector.'

I knew full well what he meant. Serving ministers can prove to be hazardous, and as I had an independent streak, I might not stay the course. Before I left he told me to expect a call from Number 10.

I met the prime minister in his room at the House of Commons. He asked if I had decided which job I would accept.

After repeating what I had told Roy, he asked if I was prepared to take on the two jobs. I explained again that I was on a contract. The prime minister said that I should consider that I was being 'called up', and that he would clear it with my company chairman, George Bridge, who was also the deputy chairman of Legal and General.

Accepting Roy's advice, I agreed, subject to my being released and being permitted, if I wished, to continue to participate in the private sector. The prime minister kindly agreed. It occurred to me that he was glad to get shut of what was to him a minor problem. Again I was asked to keep our conversation confidential.

A few days later George Bridge rang. 'Frank, I've been asked to call at Number 10 to see the prime minister. I understand that it's something to do with you, can you tell me what it is all about,' he asked.

Trying to sound surprised, I replied, 'No, George, I can't.'

I didn't add that I had given an undertaking not to tell anyone. 'Will you let me know how you get on?'

I was being what Mrs Thatcher was to instruct Lord Armstrong to be during the infamous Spycatcher trial – 'economical with the truth'.

George phoned to inform me of what I already knew, and that the Board had agreed to release me on condition that if I gave up either of the jobs, I would return to the company. This was another show of confidence, but flattering as it was, I was glad to be leaving them.

I took the Dawley New Town job on the understanding that as soon as I had got to grips with it I would put forward recommendations on what I felt needed to be done to make it succeed. If these were accepted I would continue; otherwise I would step away from it. Although this was never recorded, the minister was left in no doubt that it was not my intention to wreck my reputation on the rocks of Dawley.

Before my appointment was announced I had an embarrassing encounter with Alderman Bowen, who was still the deputy chairman of the New Town. Waiting on the platform with John English to catch the London-bound train, Bowen got into the same carriage. He was in high spirits and told John and me, in confidence, that he had an appointment to see the Minister of Housing and was expecting to be appointed to the chairmanship of the New Town. Honour bound not to say anything about my forthcoming appointment to the job, I was mortified. Worse still, I knew that Bowen was actually going to be fired that day. It was purgatory having to sit there for over two hours listening to him telling us how he was going to handle the job.

The news broke on 22 April 1968, and Bowen didn't speak to me for the following two years. The announcement in parliament brought the Conservative Member for Wenlock, Jasper Moore, and John Biffen, the Member for Shropshire North, to their feet. They objected to my appointment. According to them I was nothing more than a Party hack.

Two years later John Biffen graciously withdrew his objection. I got to know him during my period in the New Town, and although at times he took exception to my approach he recognised the battle I had on my hands and how it was being won. He was, I believe still is, one of the brighter members on the Conservative benches. Jasper Moore, who is no longer with us, couldn't bring himself to accept that I had given up a very well-paid position to try to save the New Town. To him I was a socialist, and therefore unacceptable.

My departure from City Centre Properties did little to improve my impression of its Board members. George Bridge, as an appointee of one of its biggest shareholders, sat in the chair. He was a pleasant fellow who was guided by the tycoons who made up the rest of the Board.

Leonard Sainer, being the brains behind the success of Charles Clore, was a wily bird. His light-hearted approach was a smokescreen hiding a hard, calculating character. Tall and lithe, he always appeared on the surface to be in a jocular mood. A senior partner in one of London's brighter legal practices, he made sure to have his supporters placed in positions of power. His sister held a top post in Selfridges, owned by a Clore company, and Edward Footring, a junior partner in Titmus, Sainer and Webb, was appointed CEO of City Centre Properties.

On 21 March 1968 it was Footring who called to say that

Charles Clore had arranged a farewell lunch with the Board at his house in Park Street. I asked him to thank Charles for the thought, but I would prefer to go quietly.

Footring's reaction was, 'Charles rarely invites people to his home, in fact I have never been myself. He will feel most insulted if you refuse.'

It was obvious that if I declined he would be denied the opportunity of seeing inside the great man's home, but that was not the reason I accepted. I wanted to see the show Clore would put on.

The door was opened by a butler in livery wearing white gloves; a bit over the top, I thought. He guided me up to the first floor where the rest of the Board were already assembled. I sat down and was offered a gin and French. I declined, saying that I preferred my gin with tonic; it never came.

Lunch was announced and we traipsed down to the ground floor dining room which was over full of objects d'art. A Canaletto stretched over the large fireplace and I recognised a few Renoirs and the odd Van Gogh. Charles Clore sat at the top of the long dining table and I was placed next to him. Not famous for his ability to converse, he hardly uttered a word during the meal.

This over, he raised his glass and in a very few words thanked me for all I had done for Murrayfield. It was probably the longest speech he had ever made. I didn't expect to be presented with a farewell memento from a grateful Board, so I wasn't disappointed. When he resumed his seat, Clore leaned towards me holding my wrist, to ask if I knew that his Lewis' Department Store in Birmingham was divided by a road.

'Yes, it's called "The Priory",' I answered.

'Will you see whether you can get us permission to build over it?'

I thought, *You cheeky bugger, this is what the lunch is all about*! But I said, 'I'll write to you.'

Happy to be freed from the company but sorry to have to leave those with whom I had worked with in our Birmingham office, I did what I had promised Clore; I wrote to him:

Dear Charles,

Further to your request that I see if I could obtain planning permission to extend the Lewis' store across the road known as The Priory. As I am no longer employed by you or the City Centre Group you would naturally expect me to charge for my services. I await your instructions to proceed and will then forward you a contract. Many thanks for the lunch.

Needless to say I heard nothing more.

All those who knew me well, or otherwise, were – and some still are – under the impression that when I joined a property group I became a millionaire. Most of the people with whom I worked during the period did achieve that status, but for me it was never the case. I earned more money than I could ever have dreamed of, but gave much of it away.

Looking back I realised that had I concentrated on making a fortune it would not have been too difficult, but money has never been a driving force for me. Coming from such a humble background it sounds unbelievable, but it happens to be true. I wouldn't have taken on the government jobs had I been money orientated; my salary alone was cut by half.

Chapter XXI
NEW TOWN BLUES

It was April 1968 and I was in need of a rest before taking up my new duties so I took my family off to the South of France. Before doing so I phoned the general manager of the Dawley New Town Corporation, Mr Penryn Owen, who gave me the date and time of the next Board meeting. I asked him to let me have a draft of the papers to be presented. These, for what they were worth were delivered to me before I left for France.

During the days I spent on holiday I tried to make sense of the papers that were to be presented to the Board. Having spent almost twenty years studying committee reports I thought myself capable of combing through the fuzz, but after three attempts I had to admit that I couldn't make top nor tail out of most of what I had been given. The reports were all signed by the general manager, be they on planning, finance, engineering or estate management, etc., and there appeared to be few clear recommendations.

Arriving in England on the morning of 23 April, I travelled to London to speak with Sir Matthew Stevenson. During our discussion I let him know that I wasn't happy with the way reports to the Board were presented. He simply said, 'Sir Frank, you are in charge.'

At 8.30 a.m. the following day I walked into the Corporation's Headquarters based in Priorslee Hall. I asked the lady who was vacuuming the carpet in the entrance to show me to the chairman's room. I sat at the desk which had nothing on it other than a telephone without a dial. There was no list giving the internal phone numbers of the various officers, no filing cabinet and nothing in the desk drawers. I decided to walk around the building opening doors – on which there was no information to indicate who or what one might expect to find behind them.

On my return to the chairman's room, a flushed general manager was waiting for me.

'You should have warned me that you would be arriving early,' he protested. I was about to ask him why but decided to give it a miss. I shook his hand and asked him to let me have a mint copy of the Board report. I also asked him to arrange for me to meet the chief officers before the Board meeting. I was smiling, so *he* didn't ask 'Why?'

I introduced myself to the officers and asked their name and function, saying that I hoped that we could work happily together, that I would arrange to meet them individually, and that my door would always be open. After they had filed out, the Board members filed in. Christopher Cadbury, who knew me and Isaiah Jones, who was the chairman of the Rural District Council and had served on the Board from the beginning, appeared happy to see me. The other members, Viscount Boyne, Lieutenant Colonel Morris-Eyton and Mrs Wilson, appeared uncomfortable.

After coffee we entered the boardroom where the general manager and Mr Thomas, the Board's legal adviser and Secretary, were already seated. I waited for a while then asked where were the other chief officers.

'They are called in when they are required,' I was told, and began to get a glimmer of how affairs were being operated.

We went through the report, and at the end I asked the general manager and the Secretary if they would mind leaving whilst I had a word with the Board members. Once they had left I outlined my concern about the way the reports were set out, the fact that they were all signed by the GM, and not many had clear recommendations. I asked them to turn to the housing report. They were somewhat startled when I said that it, like most of the reports, was 'gobbledegook'. I enquired whether they would mind if we suspended any decisions made that day until the following week; they agreed.

After the members had left I apprised Mr Owen and Mr Thomas of the decision. Owen told me in no uncertain manner that he was not at all pleased with the suggestions I had made. I asked whether there was anything further, and as he didn't reply told him that he had misinterpreted the position.

'It was not suggestions, Mr Owen, it was an instruction,' I said firmly.

Before they left I asked Mr Thomas to arrange to have a phone with a dial put in my room, along with a list of the chief officers' internal phone numbers an that their names and function be put on their office doors. I also asked that the press cutting books for the previous two years to be placed on my desk, and when he thought I could meet the chairman's personal secretary. Thomas said that on the rare occasion when my predecessor required to dictate a letter, the general manager's secretary would oblige.

It confirmed just how matters had been run in the past and the difficulties that lay ahead. It was no fault of the general manager that he had been left to deal with almost everything. He had become used to the idea that he was controlling the future of *his* New Town. I was faced with the unenviable task of letting everybody employed by the Corporation know, that however distasteful it might be to them, I was a 'hands on' chairman and things were going to change.

Having spoken to the chief officers individually I sensed the lack of comradeship that one would have hoped for. I asked Mr Thomas to arrange for a large round table I had spotted to be placed in the staff canteen and to ask his fellow officers to stay over and join me for tea. It sounds corny now, but it worked. In those days I could read people pretty well; looking at my guests, I could tell those that resented my presence.

For the first ten minutes no one spoke. I broke the silence by asking them if they had any idea why I arranged that we sit at this round table. There was no response, and I guessed they thought it was a nonsense of a question, too silly to require an answer.

I opened up with, 'I may be wrong but I sense a lack of team spirit here. I have already spoken with the Board and the general manager. From now on your reports to the Board will have a cover sheet setting out in clear and simple terms the basis of the report – let's call them headlines. It will have your recommendations and your signature. You can attach as much detail as you feel is absolutely necessary – let's call that the news. You will also sit with the Board at its meetings and join in their deliberations.'

I paused again; still nothing. 'If any of you feel uncomfortable with that, please let me know.'

As they still sat there without a word of protest or agreement, I added, 'What I intend is that *we will*, not should, *will* work together. We are all equal under the flag, and if we are going to rejuvenate this place we will all cooperate, and I mean from the chairman to the girl who does the post.'

I noted a few wry smiles, so left it at that. The look of satisfaction on the face of Mr Thomas spoke volumes.

I was aware that starting up a new town was no easy matter and that the Board had introduced some innovative ideas. One that should have been followed by every municipal authority in the country was the Madeley Education and Recreation Centre, MERC for short. With the Shropshire County Council they built the first large school in which was encompassed a sports and community centre. Unlike most schools which were closed after school hours in the afternoon, weekends and the long school holidays, the playing fields, swimming pool, assembly hall and canteen were open for the use of the residents of the area out of school hours. It was brilliant in its conception and construction.

However, the New Town Corporation was not attracting enough industry or siphoning off enough people from the overcrowded Midland towns nearby which was the reason for its existence. It was failing to justify the vast government investment. I had a feeling that the chief officers appeared not to share the Ministries concern about the gravity of the situation.

I wasn't surprised by Owen's outburst after his colleagues had left my little tea party. He made it clear that he wasn't happy with the changes I proposed and that they would not be tolerated as long as he was in charge. He reserved the right to make his feelings known to the Board members.

'I have no problem with that,' I told him, 'so long as my instructions are put into practice for next week's meeting, and that your objections are put to the members of the Board collectively.'

When the Board reassembled and we sailed through the meeting they appeared to be satisfied with the new arrangement. That being so, I hoped that Mr Owen would have sensed it and reserved his judgement. Unfortunately he asked to see the Board alone. I agreed and stepped out of the boardroom and into my office.

About thirty minutes later Isiaiah Jones popped his head round the door to ask if I would go back to the boardroom. When I entered Mr Owen was not present. Once I was seated, Christopher Cadbury opened up.

'Mr Chairman, you are new here, my colleagues and I expected some changes but we thought that it would take you some time to settle in. We hadn't expected you to grasp the nettle so soon. What I am saying is that we hope that you are not under the impression that we are happy with the present situation.'

'Are you telling me that you approve of the changes I have made so far?' I asked.

The Board members said 'Yes' in unison. I knew then that we would succeed in turning the New Town around.

I didn't blame Mr Owen too much. He was a nice man but it was obvious that his previous chairman, who was an industrialist, had leaned on him giving him full charge of the New Town. After five years in the job, I could understand why he wasn't happy with the change, but I hoped that the atmosphere between us would improve. Unfortunately it remained strained. I asked the members to take time to consider what action the Board should take if the general manager persisted with his objections, and to let me know by the next Board meeting.

The press cuttings made dismal reading leaving no doubts that the New Town Corporation was extremely unpopular with the adjoining local authorities, especially the Dawley District Council. I realised that I faced an uphill struggle to redress the balance. I phoned the Dawley Council Chairman asking him if I could meet him and his members for a private session in their council chamber. The clerk to the council advised Mr Owen, who made it clear that the meeting was in his opinion unwise and that nothing would be gained.

Having read just a few of the criticisms of the actions of the New Town Corporation, I knew that fences needed to be mended and quickly, so I carried on with the planned meeting. Presenting myself at the Dawley Town Hall, the fact that I was alone impressed the members. I had seen pictures in the press of

Councillor Powis, who was the main antagonist, and looking around the Chamber I noticed that he wasn't present. I asked the chairman whether he was attending.

'He is in the building,' I was told, so I said I would wait until he was in his seat. As Councillor Powis walked into the room it was clear that I was in for a drubbing.

I opened up by saying that I really hadn't come to make a speech, I had come to listen and hoped that they wouldn't pull their punches. They accepted the invitation with alacrity. Every one of the members of the Dawley Council spoke of their concern at the autocratic manner adopted by the Corporation. They left me in no doubt as to their bitterness about the manner in which their protests over the years had been ignored. Such things as closing ancient rights of way without notice, explanation or consultation would, had I been a member of their council, been an act of war. I understood why Councillor Powis waded into me.

Like many politicians when they feel that they have the opposition on the run, he rather overcooked the goose. I sat there quietly listening whilst he enjoyed himself verbally bouncing me around the room. I had been long enough in politics to know that if I kept quiet his rhetoric would prove to be counterproductive. I simply nodded my head and some of his members began to sympathise with me.

At the end of the meeting I thanked them for giving up their time and for their frank observations, and added that if I had offended anyone by being equally frank I hoped they would accept my apologies.

'I am a new boy and know that I will tread on people's toes. But having spent almost twenty years in local government, I understand and sympathise with your position. I want that we should work in partnership and suggest that the council and the Board meet four times a year, alternately in your Chamber and at Priorslee Hall. The agenda should be agreed jointly and our discussions be free and open.'

I was startled when a member jumped to his feet and made an emotional speech concluding with an appeal to the members to withdraw the motion of no confidence in the New Town

Corporation which they had that week sent to the minister. He moved a motion and it was carried unanimously. From then on our relationship with them and the other adjoining authorities was vastly improved. It didn't mean that we never had problems, but they were dealt with through joint discussion, rather than by simply ignoring their wishes.

The meeting was reported in the press. Isaiah Jones, being both a member of the Board and a chairman of one of the local authorities, must have had a hard time of it. He was overjoyed by the press report and from that day on became one of my most ardent supporters and a close friend.

I had already decided that the Board should have among its members more of the local public representatives and that Isaiah should fill the role as my deputy chairman; the minister agreed. The Board members also agreed with my suggestion that they attend an advice bureau on a rota basis, so that the residents could have a direct contact with the Board. This new relationship that had evolved with local towns and our tenants helped enormously when the plan to increase the size of the New Town from a planned population of 50,000–250,000 was under consideration.

Although I saw it as the only hope for survival, it had become bogged down at ministerial level. I asked to meet the Minister of Housing, the president of the Board of Trade and the Minister of Transport jointly. To my surprise they agreed. We met in Whitehall; the Ministry of Transport and the Board of Trade were represented by their junior ministers, which I took as a sign that the future of the New Town was not very high on their agendas. It was nothing new to me. I outlined some of our difficulties and the fact that if something radical wasn't done then Dawley would be the first New Town in Britain to have failed.

What we urgently needed was a plan setting out the line of a new motorway from the M6 to the New Town and committing the government to build it, but I wasn't insisting on a start date. I asked the Minister of Housing to hasten government approval to the extension of the New Town to take in Oakengates and Wellington, and that once announced the name of the New Town be changed.

To the Board of Trade Minister I added that whilst respecting the government's adherence to the industrial development certificate policy, which directed industries to depressed areas, we were ourselves in a depressed state and only a few miles from one of their designated areas.

I was asking the Board of Trade, if I was able to convince a few large industrial companies to set up in Dawley, to grant the necessary industrial development certificates. The minister, Mrs Gwyneth Dunwoody dismissed my suggestion that Dawley was depressed as utter nonsense, along with my plea for IDCs. I apologised to Tony Greenwood before saying to the other ministers, that they might not be too disturbed if the New Town went down the tube, but I wasn't prepared to go down with it. Unless some real help was forthcoming then I would not stay. Again I was chancing my arm.

As I was descending the Ministry stairs leading to the front door, Gwyneth Dunwoody came alongside. I said, 'As a very young man I once met your father (Morgan Philips, who had been the powerful Secretary of the Labour Party). Coming from South Wales, *he* would have recognised a depressed area when he saw one. You should come to Dawley and see for yourself.'

A month later she did just that and as a result the policy was eased for us. Shortly after her visit we did actually land a few big 'industrial' fish.

Four months after this meeting the plan to extend the New Town was agreed, and in accordance with the rules I set myself, I spoke to Sir Matthew Stevenson to suggest that those that were effected should have an opportunity to express their feelings on the plan. He asked me what I had in mind. I said I felt that we must hold a public meeting.

'Are *you* prepared to do that?' he asked.

'Who else?' I replied.

'Who else indeed. If you need any help let me know,' he said and hung up.

The meeting was organised in the assembly hall of a major college in Wellington. It had been well publicised and maps and plans were on display for a week before and after the meeting. On the night the place was packed, with three or four rows standing at the rear of the hall. I asked the Corporation's chief officers to sit on the platform ready, if called upon, to answer questions. They were seated when I arrived and without exception their faces appeared to be paler than normal; they were expecting trouble.

Stepping up to the microphone, I thanked the audience for coming to the meeting and then introduced the Officers by name and function. I then began the task of explaining the plans. I overstepped the mark by saying, 'Together, we, you the government and the corporation are to be involved in building a city.' Then, carried away by my own oratory, I described it as a 'New Jerusalem'. The audience were very attentive, and unlike those in many public meetings I had attended, offered no heckling.

The only two questions I can remember came from a clergyman and a teacher.

'If you are building a city, does that mean we are to have a cathedral?' asked the cleric.

Before I could answer the teacher was on his feet asking, 'If we are to have a city are we to have a university?'

'Yes!' I called out. 'Why not both? If you gentlemen will see me afterwards we can start to plan how the both of you are to set about raising the money.'

My answer brought both laughter and applause.

However, I was later to be metaphorically beaten over the head with my 'Jerusalem' comment. With restrictions laid down by the Ministry on size, facilities and costs, the design of public housing was strictly limited. Some were pointed out to be what the public called 'little boxes on the hillside'.

Having been given the nod on the IDCs, a little later the Ministry of Transport agreed a line for a new motorway. It assisted us tremendously. I didn't realise that the Minster was deeply worried that Qakengates and Wellington, both proud of their heritage, wanted the town named after their Authority.

On a Sunday evening he rang my home.

'I hope I'm not disturbing you, Sir Frank,' he said, 'but I've come up with a name and I would like your view. I am suggesting that we call it "Telford" after the famous Engineer who worked in the area.'

Frankly, I was only concerned that the name be changed to

anything other than Oakengates or Wellington. Had he pitched for one or the other it would have caused a minor war in the area, so I said, 'Brilliant, Minister.'

'Do you really think so?'

I said, 'Minister, it is inspirational, you should announce it right away.'

I was happy to see an end to the competition.

Wellington had one of the best semi-professional non-league football clubs in Britain. Non-league meaning not in the Football Association professional leagues. I visited their ground at Buck's Head to watch them play and was invited to sit with the chairman. The ground was typical of small non-league clubs, but the team had potential. My thoughts went to how best the Corporation could help the club and in turn the New Town.

Back at Priorslee Hall, I spoke with Mr Thomas, who in March 1969 had succeeded to the post as general manager. 'Don't think I'm crazy, but will you have the architects draw up a design for a decent stadium on what is now Buck's Head?'

'What are you up to now, Chairman?' he asked.

'Suppose I could get Wellington Town football club to change its name to Telford United?'

I didn't get any further. 'They will never agree to do that, Chairman,' he said.

'But suppose we could, help them by providing them with a plan for a new stadium and help to build up a successful team, it could put the town on the map,' I countered.

He just smiled.

Ron Flowers had been captain of Wolverhampton Wanderers, just south of us. He had won a number of English caps. In addition to being a remarkable footballer, his brains were not just in his feet. In those days footballers' wages were not as they are today. Ron had recently retired and had a small sports shop in Wolverhampton. I suggested that he be approached to ascertain whether he would work part-time for the New Town and take on the job of player-manager of the club, if I could arrange it.

With a large, full colour schematic drawing of the proposed new stadium, I met the Wellington Town FC Board of directors. Speaking first about how the New Town would be successfully expanded to a population of a quarter of a million citizens, and how their band of supporters would grow with it I suggested that they would need a decent stadium and if their ambitions to win a place in the Fourth Division of the Football Association's League, they also needed a top-class player-manager.

I then pegged the architect's drawing on their notice Board. Above the entrance to the stadium were the words: TELFORD UNITED FOOTBALL CLUB. Lowering my head, I waited for the screams of abuse. One of the directors asked, 'Who are they?'

The chairman answered, 'Can't you see, you bloody fool, that's us! He wants us to change our name.'

'No bloody fear!' the director shouted.

I said, 'Okay, I'm sorry, I was trying to get you to lift your eyes off the floor to look at the stars. Listen, if I could induce Ron Flowers to be your player-manager, and join in helping to raise the money to build what you see there, will you think about changing the club's name? After all, Wellington is in Telford and Telford is going to be the finest new town in Britain. Think about it.'

I then departed, taking care to leave the plan on the Board.

The directors followed my advice, and in 1970, as Telford United, Ron took them to Wembley to play Macclesfield in the final of the Football Association Challenge Trophy; they lost. They had played at Wembley and thought it was the greatest achievement in the club's history. They were wrong.

Ron Flowers repeated it again in 1971, playing against Hillingdon. At half-time Telford was two–nil down but came out to score three goals to win the highest accolade that non-league football has to offer, the FA Challenge Trophy. Their run in the cup brought much needed publicity to the New Town, and that year we encouraged industry to take up over a million square feet of factory space. These were heady days; the Board, its staff and I knew that we had at last got a success on our hands.

During this period I was still the leader of my Party on the Birmingham City Council, was a member of the Midlands Economic Planning Council, chairman of the British Waterways Board, a Director of the National Exhibition Centre, on the council of the Town and Country Planning Association, chairman of the Midlands Art Centre for Young People, a Member of the Convocation of both Aston and Birmingham Universities, chairman of the West Midlands Sports Council and a partner in a Birmingham company. All of which gave rise to a great deal of travelling and little time for my family or recreation.

At the time I drove a Jensen Interceptor, a very fast car in the days when there was no speed limit on the new motorway system, which started at its northern end at Watford Gap. My days were long and full and most of the time I had to hurry to keep appointments in places between Shropshire and London.

Within a few minutes of leaving the New Town Corporation offices I was able to get on to the A1, and then had to drive hard to get to my next meeting on time. The day came when the Chief Constable of Shropshire phoned to ask to see me; it sounded ominous so I agreed to go to his office, but he insisted that he would visit me. I was sure that, for reasons unknown, he was about to 'nick' me.

Like most chief constables he was tall, and in his uniform with his medal ribbons, silver laurel leaves on each collar and carrying a stick under his arm, he was most impressive – even more to a small working class boy like me. He placed his hat and stick on my desk and sat down.

'Cup of coffee, Chief?' I asked.

'No thanks,' he replied.

He had yet to smile. 'I want a word with you about that car of yours.'

I began to speak but he held up his hand. 'I appreciate just how busy you are with important appointments here, in London and Birmingham, and that you are doing a good job for us. The last thing I want to do, Sir Frank, is to have you nicked.' He leaned over the desk. 'My chaps have reported that you go past them on the A1 like a bat out of hell!' He paused; I didn't know how he expected me to respond, so I kept mum. 'Tell you what,' he continued. 'You have your secretary call mine half an hour before you are due to leave here; it will give time for my patrols to withdraw until you are out of my manor.'

With that he stood up, shook my hand and left. I was both relieved and very grateful.

The government having agreed to the plan to expand the designated area of the New Town, we needed to decide how best to plan and develop, what would be the heart of the town. The Board decided to call in a leading firm of estates surveyors who had experience in the field of major shopping centres, along with a well-known economist. Their remit was to advise us on the first phase of what was to be Telford Town Centre. They looked at our ideas and we took them to the 'greenfield' site upon which town centre stores, shops and so on would be built.

There initial report was disappointing. It suggested that we should start off by building a supermarket and three or four standard units. It was not my idea of a first phase of the New Town central commercial area. The consultants were adamant that with Wellington and Oakengates nearby and Shrewsbury but a few miles away we would be unable to attract major national companies until the town was much further advanced.

I had read in the *Financial Times* that a French hypermarket chain had failed for the umpteenth time in its efforts to obtain planning permission to build in the UK. The name of the chain was Carrefour. With the general manager and the chief estates officer I flew over to France to see their operation and meet the directors. Their stores, with plenty of car parking spaces around them, were large and busy. They bought their merchandise in bulk, stacked it high and sold it cheap. There were no frills other than in their food sections. The operation was very professional.

I sat in front of their directors and intimated that I was aware of their efforts to open up in Britain and their failure so far. I said that we could not only offer them a site, we could also guarantee that they would receive planning permission. The site would be on a twenty-year lease with options. The fact that they may be on an open site for some time with no significant traders nearby didn't bother them. To obtain a permission to open up in the UK was an offer they couldn't refuse.

Having been in the business of town centre development I was able to use my contacts with the estate managers of the major multiple retail companies. I asked Sainsbury's if competing with the French company worried them. It didn't, and they agreed to come in, so did Boots the chemists, and because of them Timothy

White and Taylors. Before too long we were able to start a respectable first phase. So much for advice from the experts.

I had a good relationship with Sir Marcus (later to become Lord) Sieff of Marks and Spencers, and he agreed to allow us to reserve a site for them without entering into a contract. Seeing a large site boarded with their name on it encouraged others. Before the first phase was half completed, we had arranged to begin the second leg. Had we followed the advise of the experts, our central shopping area would have endured many years before it even looked anything like a town centre should.

Telford was expanding and attracting industry. Copying the ideas of George Cadbury, the founder of the world famous makers of chocolate, who built what he called his 'factory in a garden' in Bourneville, Birmingham, we began to plant trees and lay out gardens around our factory buildings. With the increase of industrial units the population of Telford was increasing, and the Regional Hospital Board realised that the local 'cottage hospital' was totally inadequate to cater for the needs of the new town.

The Ministry of Health had stated in a letter to their chairman, that if an appropriate site was found for what they called 'a best-buy hospital' they would put it in their building programme. A number of sites were put forward suitable for the District Hospital but for one specious reason after another they were rejected. Frustrated, the local hospital coordinating committee approached me for help. They handed me a letter they had received dated December 1968 signed by Richard Crossman, who was at the time the Minister of Health. It accepted a site at Nairn Farm as being suitable, but no progress had been made to build.

The committee had arranged an appointment with the minister and asked if I would lead the delegation. I wasn't too happy about the prospect of meeting Crossman again, but after being pressed further I agreed. The delegation travelled to London and were placed in one of the Ministry's meeting rooms. I had asked Mr Thomas to make a photocopy of the minister's letter and have it handy in case it was needed.

Crossman and his officials entered the room and he beckoned me to sit next to him. I thanked him on behalf of the delegation for seeing us and began making a case for a decision to start on the hospital building now that the minister had agreed on the site. I got no further.

'Agreed on the site, what are you talking about?'

I asked Mr Thomas for the copy of the minister's letter. I apologised that it was a copy and not the original. Crossman leaned back in his chair and read through it. He placed it on the table and said, 'You can read anything you like into that letter, it was written that way.'

I looked at him and then down the table at the rest of the delegation, almost speechless. Turning to Crossman, I asked, 'Do you really mean to tell me and my friends here that the letter, which is clear to me and them, doesn't mean what it says?'

The Ministry's Senior Medical Adviser sitting opposite me, started to explain but I interrupted. 'No sir, I am asking the minister.'

Crossman, completely unflustered said, 'Yes.'

I sat for a while trying to control my temper. I pushed my chair back, stood up, and turning to the delegation, who were sitting at the table quite bewildered, and said, 'I am sorry, I can't stay here and listen to this.'

I looked across at the embarrassed Medical Adviser and then down at Crossman, turned and walked out of the room. It took some years before the hospital was finally built.

Telford was expanding at apace when for reasons best known to them, *Private Eye* began to print short notes suggesting that I was corrupt. They stated that a large Birmingham construction company had never won a contract in the New Town until I was appointed, not saying but leading its readers to suppose that I was receiving a kickback. They were wrong; the company had built roads, bridges and houses long before I arrived on the scene.

As was normal practice, a contract was advertised and this company's tender to build five hundred houses was recommended to the Board by its officials. Once approved, it still had to be submitted to the Ministry for *its* approval. No one was aware, other than *Private Eye* it seemed, that the company was under investigation. This was the subject of the magazine's story and they tried to involve me.

On advice, I arranged to see Lord Goodman, who had

represented other people maligned by the paper. He listened to my complaint and asked if I wished him to sue them on my behalf.

'Before you answer,' he said, 'let tell you that I have had numerous requests to take them to court. They were all under the impression that they would obtain a vast sum of money because of the amount of damages announced in the press, most of which has never been paid.'

He looked hard at me and went on. 'You have been in public life for some time, you should have developed a thicker skin by now.' He paused. 'Do you realise that it will take more than a year before your case could come to court, and through all that time they would put you through the mincer and at the end of the day, you may get an apology.'

I stood up, thanked him for his advice and asked what I owed him. With a dismissive wave of his hand he showed me the door.

The Conservatives had been re-elected, Peter Walker had been appointed Secretary of State for the new Environment Ministry, and his minister in charge of Housing and Local Government was Paul Channon. A few days after the piece appeared in the *Private Eye*, Channon had his officials contact my officers giving instructions to send all the papers concerning the contract with the Birmingham Company to the Ministry. I blew a fuse.

I phoned the Ministry, who were obviously embarrassed, and were of no help, so I sent a missive to Channon. I wrote that ordering the papers be sent to him was suggesting to the officers of the Corporation that there was something to the piece in *Private Eye*. I pointed out that as the minister, he ought to know that contracts of this nature have to go out to tender, the Board had to approve and in turn, their recommendations had to be cleared by his department, who had done so. I suggested that his decision not to raise the matter with me, but to go through his officials who contacted mine was both ill mannered and a sign of his lack of trust. In so doing he had placed me in an impossible position. I finished up by saying that unless I received a written apology, the Secretary of State would have my resignation on his desk within forty-eight hours.

Channon phoned and without apologising tried to make light

of the matter.

'Not good enough, Minister,' I replied. 'If I fail to receive a letter from you I'm on my way out of here.'

He had his apology delivered by hand the following day.

On a lighter note, something came up which had nothing to do with the New Town, other than what was to follow. The National Folk Club of Great Britain, who were raising funds to expand the influence of traditional song and dance in the UK, hired the British Waterways *Lady Rose of Regent's*, inviting a number of Britain's wealthier citizens to dine on Board whilst cruising along the Regent's Canal. As Princess Margaret was a supporter she graciously agreed to join them, which encouraged the said wealthy citizens to join the party. I was invited to act as host for the evening.

Rory McEwen, a cousin of the Princess and a well-known folk singer, was among the party, along with Ian Campbell, the Scottish leader of a well-known folk band. The Palace had informed the organisers that the Princess would arrive promptly at 7.45 p.m. and leave at 11 p.m. She arrived 8.30 p.m.

After dinner, when the boat had returned to its mooring in Little Venice, she insisted on McEwen treating the guests to a song or two. Ian Campbell's folk group were ensconced in a local hostelry and she insisted that they be brought on board. It turned into a Royal Command Performance, with Campbell and his Group going through their repertoire.

Consequently the dinner, which was due to end before eleven to comply with Palace instructions, went on until two the following morning. By this time the staff were becoming understandably bolshie, and I mentioned this to the Princess.

She turned to me and said, 'Are you kicking me off the boat?' and stood up to leave. I escorted to her car, which had been waiting for hours. Before she got in she added, 'I will never dine with *you* again.'

Four days later, on 29 June, she was due to pay a visit to Telford New Town to have lunch with the Board and to visit the Ironbridge Museum. I don't think she realised that I was the chairman when the invitation was accepted.

The cars drew up in front Priorslee Hall where, along with the rest of the Board members, I was waiting to greet her. The Lord Lieutenant of Shropshire, Lieutenant Colonel Heywood-Lonsdale, stepped out of the lead car and led the Princess forward so that he could present me. He didn't expect what was to follow.

'I don't wish to speak to him,' she said quite loudly.

I didn't intend to be embarrassed further so I took the bit between my teeth and held out my hand, bowing and leaning forward, I whispered, 'Are you going to behave?' Then quickly added out loud, 'Welcome to Telford, ma'am. May I present my vice chairman, Isaiah Jones.'

She gave me a wicked half-smile and continued to shake hands with the rest of the Board as I presented them.

During lunch she conversed with Lord Boyne, a member of the Board whom I had placed on her left. Towards the end of the meal she finally turned to me to ask, 'What are we going to do about poor George?'

I had no idea to whom she was referring.

'Good God, I thought he was a friend of yours. We had him round to tea on Sunday, he's in quite a state.'

She was referring to George Brown, who had just lost his seat in the General Election.

She continued, 'Although he has embarrassed me so many times, we are really very fond of him.'

'I didn't realise that you were close,' I mumbled, and suggested that although George would hate it, having been a Secretary of State and a Privy Councillor, he would no doubt be elevated to the House of Lords.

'Not his scene,' she replied, and she was absolutely right. She went on to say, 'George is a character, that's what I like about him. He's not a cardboard cut-out, as are so many one meets today.' She was right again.

The lunch over, we toured Coalbrookdale and the Ironbridge Gorge and the Ironbridge Museum site. I mentioned to her that along the way a man whose family had made coracles for generations would be waiting by the roadside with a model of a coracle which he wanted to present to her. I introduced Mr Rodgers, and Princess Margaret stood conversing with him for some time. She told me afterwards that he was the most interesting man she had met that day. I couldn't help saying, 'Oh, thanks very much.'

She laughed, a sure sign that she was enjoying her day.

Although it rained, thousands of people came out to see her. The press reporting on the visit wrote:

> The bravery and charm of the Princess in very inclement weather and the obvious delight with which she received all who took part in the Royal Tour of Telford New Town was appreciated.

That about summed it up. Her last words to me before she left, 'It was a fabulous day,' were obviously sincerely meant, and indicated that she had forgiven me.

Princess Margaret is certainly not what she called 'a cardboard cut-out'. Although she has a reputation for being difficult, at the time she was not only the most beautiful member of the Royal family, she was one of the smartest. Having a capacity to charm the birds off the trees, if she was in the mood, she could also freeze you out with just a look if she thought that you had overstepped the mark. Proving that if people, having spent time in the company of members of 'the Family', think that they have been accepted, they're fooling themselves.

Late in 1971, I asked to see Peter Walker to tell him that I was tired and wanted to stand down from the Telford Board. Although there was still a lot to be done, I told him that it was now a pianola, and with the right man putting in the music it would play itself. He was very kind, saying, 'Why now, Frank? All the hard work has been done – you can rest on your oars and enjoy the fruits of your labour.'

I thanked him but insisted. He asked me to help find and approve a successor.

Attending my last New Town Chairman's Conference early the following year, I was approached by the new Minister of State, Julian Amery, whom I had never met before. I found him to be a pompous little man who appeared to mimic Winston Churchill when he spoke. He came to the lunch and appeared to have 'had enough' before he even sat down. He made an innocuous speech which meant nothing to those having to listen to it.

After lunch he came over to me and muttered, 'You're Price – Telford, I presume.'

'What can I do for you, Minister?' I asked.

'Your successor, I've chosen him…'

I interrupted, 'Peter asked me to be involved in the approval.'

'Done – it's done, old boy… Dugdale, Lord Lieutenant of Shropshire, don't you know,' he said, brushing me aside.

I protested, 'You've made a mistake. It's unfair to him, Telford may still need a "gut" fighter. Dugdale would be admirable in three years – but not now.' It fell on deaf ears.

At my last meeting with the Board, Mrs Wilson, an exceptional and intelligent lady member, who on my insistence had been joined by a further woman member, cried a little. It surprised us all because we never suspected that she had an emotional streak. There had been many occasions when she had whipped me with her tongue. She surprised me further some years later.

She had passed away and through her daughter had left her instructions that I be asked to speak at her memorial service. I travelled to Shrewsbury to comply with her request, which included a note 'to make it cheerful'. Telling stories about the headbutting sessions I had had with this remarkable woman brought gales of laughter to the crowded cathedral. I hope I did her instructions justice.

Two weeks after my departure from Telford, Mr 'Tommy' Thomas, the general manager, called to ask if I would attend with him a dinner which, he said, had been arranged some time previously and which he had accepted on my behalf but failed to tell me. I reluctantly agreed. He sent the chairman's car to collect me from my home in Birmingham.

I wasn't made aware of the venue, so as we drove slowly past the entrance of a well-known restaurant which was lit up with a crowd and TV cameras and photographers gathered outside, I asked the driver what was happening there.

'Haven't a clue, sir,' he said. He then drove round the square and back to the entrance of the restaurant we had past a few minutes before. He gave a blast on his horn as we slowed down. The door was opened and flashbulbs began to pop. The television crews asked me to pose before being led through the door. I had been conned.

Inside, I stood facing a broad flight of stairs. On both sides on each step was a member of the local authorities in the Telford area. As I climbed the stairs they clapped, and on entering the dining room I saw the large banner draped from the ceiling which read: FAREWELL SIR FRANK. A JOB WELL DONE. It was as unexpected as it was moving.

In the after-dinner speeches, those who spoke were kind enough to forget to mention the times they must have taken umbrage at my actions. They gave me a night that I will never forget.

Chapter XXII

WATER WORLD

A Voyage of Discovery

As I have mentioned the British Waterways Board was born out of the British Transport Commission set up at the beginning of the war to take control of the railways, canals and river navigations. The canals were placed under a separate authority in 1962, and Sir John Hawton was appointed as its first chairman.

Early in 1968, having spent almost twelve months sitting on Hawton's Board, I came to the conclusion that I was wasting my time and informed him of my intention to resign and returned to Birmingham. My secretary, Muriel, passed on the message that the Ministry of Transport had been on the phone to say that Mrs Castle, the minister, wished to see me. Asking whether they had given any idea as to what it was about, the answer was 'no'. Naturally.

It was during a very busy period in the House of Commons. The government was battling to get their massive controversial Transport Bill through, so my instructions were to go to her room in the House of Commons. During the preliminaries, Stephen Swingler interrupted to clear a number of matters that he was having to deal with on the floor of the House. I thought that the reason I was there might be to discuss my desire to leave BWB, but I was getting nowhere.

Stephen was a Midlands MP I had met before. I was shocked by his appearance; he looked totally knackered. The sessions were going on through the night, and as Minister of State he bore the brunt of the opposition's onslaught against the Bill. He died soon after it went on to the statute book and many members were convinced that the burden that he had carried had contributed to his premature demise.

After Stephen had left the room I waited for Mrs Castle to open up; she still hadn't told me why I had been summoned. She looked hard at me, slapped her desk and said, 'We are going to get out of this place, you are taking me to dinner.'

I asked to use the phone and reserved a table at l'Écu de France in Jermyn Street.

Barbara Castle was, and still is, an intense political animal, and during the meal all she talked about was the main points of the Transport Bill, part of which was for the first time to give a Charter for the Canals. She put her hand on my arm to tell me that great things were in store for the BWB.

I thought, *All very interesting, darling, but I'm on my way out.* I started to tell her but she parried my opening gambits like a matador does with his prey. Once the coffee was on the table she fixed those needle-sharp green eyes on me, saying, 'Now, my lad, I hear that you want to resign.'

How the hell does she know? I thought. *Only John Hawton was privy to my decision.*

'Before you say anything, let me tell you that I want you to take on the chairmanship of the Board.'

After the initial shock, I explained that I held an important job and couldn't possibly take on the appointment. 'Even more important than that,' I added, 'I wouldn't consider stabbing John Hawton in the back.'

Obviously surprised, she said, 'Stabbing him in the back? It was he who suggested that I should offer you the job, and if you accept, he would like to serve under you as your vice chairman. That's the way he wants it.'

Clever devil, I thought, *he wants to sit back and watch how I perform against the general manager.*

All this time the minister had a smile of expectation playing around her mouth as if she had just handed me a birthday package and was waiting to see my joy when I opened it. I explained to her as clearly as I could that I was not free to accept the appointment but would give it some thought, promising to let her have my answer within a week. As I have already mentioned, on the following Monday I was asked to take on the chair of Dawley New Town. It changed the course of my life.

I succeeded Sir John Hawton in June 1968. When he was congratulating me on becoming chairman he had a twinkle in his eyes I hadn't seen before. He suggested that I take over the services of his secretary, but I was too long in the tooth to agree to that. She had served him for six years and as he was to remain on the Board as the vice chairman, her loyalty to him would remain; he knew that, but so did I. Thanking him, I said that for the time being I would make do with a girl from the typing pool. The future was to reveal that my instincts hadn't let me down.

I had been honest with the minister when I answered her original question – that the sum total of my knowledge of Britain's canals was gleaned sitting on the banks of the 'cut' in the Midlands watching my dad fish when he was out of work. I didn't know then that by agreeing to become involved, I would be embarking on a long, sometimes very rough period which was to save the canal system from disintegration. It cost me the loss of a potentially lucrative future in the property world, and sixteen years of my life fighting political friend and foe to save and to improve Britain's Inland Waterways.

At 8 p.m., on the day my appointment appeared in the press, two men called at my home. The elder of the two apologised for the intrusion and introduced himself.

'I'm George Andrews, chairman of the Wolverhampton branch of the Inland Waterways Association.'

He was an industrialist who for many years had cruised the canals with his wife and their pet parrot in their converted narrowboat complete with its double bed. Before he and his colleague left that night I had been fully briefed on the antipathy their Association had towards the Board and its management.

They outlined the desperate state in which many of the canals were in, and were convinced that the policy of the Board was to allow the canals to deteriorate until they were virtually unusable. I could only say that it was not my intention to preside over a dying industry, and that they should allow me time to prove it.

A few days after my appointment a Councillor Albert Jackson – a city council colleague – phoned to add his congratulations and invited me to join him on a trip on which he was to embark that weekend. It was the beginning of a voyage of discovery.

He was to sail his narrow-beamed yacht down the Grand Union Canal to London, enter the River Thames and then go out to sea. Having never sailed on a canal I jumped at the chance. With the mast safely strapped along the deck so that he could navigate under the bridges and through the tunnels, using his auxiliary engine we set out along the Birmingham Navigation on to the Grand Union heading for Stoke Bruern. He had arranged for a car to bring me back to Birmingham.

When we reached the Blisworth Tunnel, the longest on the system, so long that it takes one-and-three-quarter of an hour to navigate, he said that the yacht was too wide to allow another craft coming in the opposite direction to pass. We moored at the mouth of the tunnel and climbed up the embankment to the road to phone the office at the other end. They told him that a boat called the *Kingfisher* was by now halfway through the tunnel and that they would hold up further traffic to allow us to proceed once it had exited.

It was a hot sunny day so we sat on deck drinking a can of beer waiting to continue our journey. As this splendid craft appeared we saw a fellow sitting astride the front and as it cleared the tunnel the man steering the craft exclaimed, 'Good God, it's the chairman!' and promptly ran aground.

Allen, the general manager was with his family and friends enjoying a trip on the boat left to the Board by its predecessor, the British Transport Commission. It had been used by Sir Reginald Kerr, a member of the Commission who, like many high-ranking officers in the armed forces, had been handed a government job to supplement his pension. Kerr was appointed to supervise the canals and spent most of his time out of the office, cruising around Britain with his wife, living on the *Kingfisher*.

He ran the operation as if he was still a serving officer, issuing general instructions, setting out standard procedures for the – as he put it – 'wearing' of flags by powered craft owned by the Commission. No flags other than those laid down by him were allowed to be worn in any circumstances other than the Red Ensign.

There was a House flag, but when he was aboard his special flag was 'worn'. When afloat, his general manager had to 'wear' a swallow-tailed flag; craft carrying a divisional manager showed a triangular pennant. As for the Red Ensign, the rules said, it could be worn by all vessels but along the lines of the edict he had set. He even took the trouble to specify the pattern, colour and size of each of the flags – his being much larger, naturally.

Travelling at no more than four miles an hour, mostly out in the countryside, I guess he had plenty of time for this nonsense. When Sir John Hawton took on the chairmanship of the newly created organisation, he let it be known that he had no intention of following Kerr's example. He cancelled the flag drill and never set foot on a canal boat. It appeared that the general manager had commandeered the *Kingfisher*, now aground.

After we helped to refloat it, Albert and I sailed through the tunnel and moored outside the Stoke Bruern Canal Museum. We took the opportunity to look around its small but interesting exhibits. Allen had obviously phoned to warn the staff that the new chairman was on his way, for as we were leaving, the gentleman sitting at a table near the exit with two of his staff standing to attention, rose to introduce himself to Albert.

'I'm the Curator, sir, I hope you enjoyed your first visit to our museum.' He handed him a pen and went on, 'Would you be kind enough to sign our visitors' book, Mr Chairman?'

Albert, being a tall, rather striking-looking fellow, laughed. 'I'm not your bloody chairman,' he said, and then pointing at me added, 'he is!'

The Curator looked at me in dismay. It was apparent that to him, Albert looked more like a chairman should.

The trip from Birmingham to Stoke Bruern was an eye-opener. The locks we had to use, and long stretches of the canal bank, were showing signs of neglect, as were the tunnels, and yet I was told that this was considered to be one of the better parts of the system. I began to understand what George Andrews had complained about and made up my mind to see as much of the system as possible.

Once I had settled in I asked the general manager to arrange for me to take a boat out at weekends so that I could inspect the system. A few days later a craft was placed at my disposal at the Board's Birmingham depot near the centre of the city, and my home. On the next free weekend I drove my wife, son and dog to the depot. I had expected to set out on my first solo trip in a boat somewhat like the *Kingfisher*; instead, I was taken to a large inspection barge named the *Swift* moored alongside one of the Board's warehouses.

A man had been instructed to show me how to handle the boat and to take me through the first lock. He, being a 'Brummie', knew of me, and once we'd been seen off by a smiling depot manager and his staff he said, 'I think they are setting you up, sir.' He explained that the inspection craft which was long, wide and, had a deep draft, was difficult to handle even for the normal crew of three experienced canal men. A novice like me would soon find himself in trouble.

My new-found friend showed me how to take the craft into a lock and to empty or fill the lock as needs be. He also decided to stay with me until he felt confident that my family would be reasonably safe. Some miles and a number of locks later on, we moored outside a pub, and after a pint I arranged for a taxi to take him home.

The weekend proved to be a test of endurance – planned, I felt sure, to put me off the idea of cruising the system. It didn't work. Not for the first time, my background led some to consider that I was not too bright and therefore easy to handle. My trip on the inspection Barge had given me my first taste of the problems I was to face, but difficult as it was I took the monster out during the rest of the summer months.

Having familiarised myself with the Board's Melbury House headquarters, and the staff that worked there, I had the general manager organise a more manageable cruising boat. We named it after the famous canal engineer, Telford. I travelled many miles on the canals and river navigations, using weekends and holidays to meet the men and women who worked along the canals and many of the users.

I was invited to attend their boat rallies which took place in various parts of the country so I was able to get close to them and hear their comments, which were usually uncomplimentary. Mooring alongside a country inn I took my family for a pub lunch. As I approached the bar to order our meal, the three fellows standing there made comments such as, 'The bottoms too near the top.'

It was of course aimed at me, but it was the first time I had heard the phrase. I didn't respond. In my defence the man behind the bar shouted, 'You can cut that out or leave the premises!'

He was also a boater and although he no doubt felt the same, didn't mention it. He, like them, had recognised me, and as he kindly put it, 'You're new at the job, it's nowt to do with you.'

The cruising fraternity got to recognise the *Telford* when it was out on the system. When we moored alongside a pub for lunch or to bed down for the night, we got to talking with them and learned a great deal about their frustration with the Board. This was in the main due to a lack of communication. Even so, they always made us feel welcome. They told me, 'Seeing you out on the canals and being able to talk about the problems face to face makes us feel that at least you are on our side.'

It was useless to try to convince them that the Board members were as interested as they were in improving the system.

As good as her word, Barbara Castle had included in her massive Transport Bill a Charter for the inland waterways. The Queen signed the Royal Assent in July 1968.

In October, Trevor Luckcuck who had answered the advert and applied for the vacancy left by the death of Mr Backhouse earlier that year, was appointed as Secretary to the Board. I knew of him when he worked in the Birmingham town clerk's department, and although I was aware of his talents, felt it unwise to join Sir John and the general manager on the interviewing panel. Trevor proved to be a tower of strength during the sixteen years that I was in the Chair.

The history of Britain's canals dates back almost 250 years. They were originally financed by local businessmen, designed by the country's leading engineers and built in the main by Irish labourers, nicknamed 'navvies' because they were digging out the navigation canals. The canals reduced the cost of transporting coal and other bulk cargoes and helped to improve the economies of industrial centres. Their history has been well documented.

The decline of the system started with the introduction of the railways. Both suffered when road transport became a priority in respect of government support. Both systems fought for survival, but later civil servants were seduced by the 'Road Lobby', and ministers found it easier to let them do their thinking for them. With Barbara Castle in the job and her Charter on the statute book, we were convinced that at last we had someone who would do battle on behalf of Britain's waterways and we saw a bright future for the inland shipping and the commercial waterways industry. It didn't last.

Within a few months of my appointment she was moved to another Ministry, and although we didn't know it, the future of the waterways was once again in jeopardy. Her Charter had divided the canals into three categories: 1,100 miles were designated as cruising waterways; 340 miles as mainly commercial – but also used for leisure; and the rest, some 600 miles, which with the inane logic of the parliamentary draftsmen, were put into a class to be known as 'remainder'. It meant that we were only allowed to spend money on them if they presented a danger to the public or to property.

The Board owned a number of docks, warehouses, freight-carrying craft, and leisure boats which were hired out. We also had land, an asset which a future government did all they knew how to force us to sell. The Act included the setting up of an Inland Waterways Advisory Council, on which the users' associations were to be represented. Before she was moved, Mrs Castle held a press conference to launch this new venture and introduced me to its first chairman, Illtyd Harrington.

She had previously informed me of her intention that in his capacity as chairman of the council he would have a seat on the Board. I warned her that being a member of the Board would place him in an impossible position. His function was to represent the interests of the leisure users and there would be times when the Board would be forced to take decisions which would create problems for him and his council. We would expect his support, to which the users – mainly the cruising and fishing fraternity – might object.

'In short,' I told the minister, 'you are asking him to wear two hats. Having divided loyalties would place him in a no-win position.'

She couldn't see my point but had obviously told Harrington. It explained his frosty greeting when we were introduced. My fears proved to be right. When the time came for him to retire from the council his successor was not given a seat on the Board.

Illtyd was an attractive bearded fellow who was always ready with a funny story, and along with his roguish manner it endeared him to those he met. He was an extrovert who taught at a school in London's East End, and was a leading member of the Greater London Council. He was to become its chairman just before Mrs Thatcher decided to close it down. As one would expect from someone brought up in Wales, the son of a Welsh mother and Irish father, he was gifted with a 'silver tongue'.

He was a friend of many famous stage and film stars, and Bing Crosby asked him to watch over one of his sons whilst he was studying in London. A few weeks after Crosby died, Illtyd introduced me to his widow, who was in London negotiating film rights. At his request I invited her to lunch and as she was so recently bereaved I tried to ensure that she was not bothered by the press. When I went out to greet her I was surprised see her posing before a galaxy of photographers. She had her press agent arrange the photo call. So much for the grieving widow.

Illtyd was an amusing raconteur with a deep respect for the environment, and he was much admired by many users of the canal system. He was at times a great asset to the Board. A left-wing socialist, he had the unfortunate habit of dipping his 'silver' tongue in vitriol when face to face with Conservative ministers. During a dinner to which the then Minister of Transport, John Peyton, was our guest, Illtyd took issue with him. Despite my protestations he was to lose his seat on the Board – and at a time when I needed all the support I could muster.

His vice chairman of the Inland Waterways Amenity Advisory Council (IWAAC) was General Sir Hugh Stockwell. As a serving soldier he had the unfortunate job of having to lead the ill-fated British Task Force in the Suez fiasco. He was a great character and every bit the commanding officer.

He and his wife had paddled a canoe along the Kennet and Avon canal at the time when it was in a desperately sad condition. When they came to places where the canal was unusable they carried the canoe along the towpath and camped on its banks. They were both active supporters of the Kennet and Avon Canal Trust, a voluntary body whose aims were to restore this beautiful inland waterway which stretched from the River Thames at Reading across to the River Avon in the city of Bath.

The K&A, as it is popularly known, runs through one of the prettiest stretches of the English countryside, and for the most part it was listed as a 'remainder waterway'. When its President, Lord Methuen, retired, Sir Hugh succeeded him and some years later became a member of my Board.

Soon after my taking over the BWB chair, the General asked if I would perform the opening ceremony of a lock that the Trust had recently restored. This done he took me to one side, saying, 'My chairman (Illtyd Harrington) and you will save the canals.'

I bristled and retorted, 'General, I need IWAAC like I need a hole in the head. If I can't reverse the present process and save the canals without its help, I'll resign.'

It was an intemperate outburst, but during the previous week I had been verbally mauled by the chairman of the Inland Waterways Association (IWA), at their annual dinner, and was still feeling sore.

The IWA was formed for the purpose of safeguarding the canals as part of Britain's heritage. It had hundreds of members from all parts of the country and had support – but not enough – from both sides of parliament. I had been in the Chair for a few months when, against the advice of the general manager, I accepted an invitation to their annual dinner and to reply to the toast to the British Waterways Board.

I arrived at London's Royal Lancaster Hotel to be greeted by Sir Alan Herbert, their President, with, 'Thank you for coming, I'm sure that you will enjoy the evening.'

He was sadly wrong. Sir Alan was the author of a best-selling novel called *The Water Gypsies*. A humorist, playwright and member of parliament, his love affair with the River Thames earned him the title of the 'Thames MP'.

The dinner was a rather grand affair with some members wearing full evening dress, most of the others dinner jackets, and the ladies dressed, as they say, appropriately. Numbered among the guests were members of both Houses of Parliament, and of course the press. My wife was placed towards the end of the long top table, next to Robert Grant-Ferris, a Conservative member of parliament. Grant-Ferris asked her about my background and when he discovered that I had represented St Paul's Ward on the Birmingham City Council he interrupted his meal to come along to speak to me.

I was able to tell him that as a child, I had with my mother been driven by him in his open Lagonda to the polling station when he was the municipal candidate for St Paul's. He won the seat so I was able to tell him that my mother voted Labour. He was more excited by the fact that I remembered his car, which had been his pride and joy.

After the meal came the main speech, which – including the toast to BWB – was made by their chairman, Captain Lionel Munk. He had arranged to see me prior to the dinner and gave me the impression that he was happy with the 'new start' provided by the Charter, as well as my appointment. This hadn't prepared me for his verbal onslaught.

I had placed the notes I had prepared to help with my reply to his toast on the table in front of me. I was sitting next to the President, who saw me tear them up as Munk proceeded with a tirade of insults and jokes at the Board's, and my, expense. His speech was greeted with much clapping and laughter, and grinning faces turned towards me to see how I was taking it.

When Sir Alan rose to introduce me, he stood for some time without saying a word and the audience fell silent. He looked around and began, 'The British Waterways Board now has a Charter. It also has a new chairman.' He paused. 'Sir Frank, who is our guest of honour, has only been in his post for a few months.' He then apologised for what he described as a lack of respect to my Board and me and then asked, 'Sir, do you wish to reply to the Toast?' – giving me the chance to duck out.

I stood up, and glanced both left and right and then at the people sitting at the long table in front of me; the room had remained quiet. I turned to Sir Alan and thanked him for his courtesy. I then addressed my remarks to the members of the Association, saying that by their reaction to their chairman's speech they had confirmed what I had been told but had dismissed: namely that they were more concerned with the past than the future and that they would not be interested in listening to anything I had to say as the chairman of BWB.

I went on, 'Well, tonight you've made that perfectly clear, so let me say that if you are under the impression that I would allow you to use me as a target for your misplaced humour or venom, you had best understand that you have chosen the wrong man. Having heard Captain Munk, and taken note of your response, whether you believe me or not is now no longer of interest to me. I will do my job to fight to improve the waterways, with or without your help.'

I stood waiting for my words to sink in before turning to Sir Alan.

'Thank you, Mr President, for showing me and my Board a measure of courtesy here this evening. I hope that I have the pleasure of meeting you again.'

Neither they nor I knew that within two years the very future of the system would be placed in jeopardy and that it would draw the Board, the Association and most users of the system closer than we had ever been. Neither did they realise that whilst I was fighting Conservative ministers in order to save the system, one of their future chairmen, in letting his ambition mislead him, sided with the government who were about to tear up the Canal Charter.

The ordinary IWA members didn't know, and I am sure that many are still unaware, that their future chairman would – almost did – sell them out. He gave written evidence supporting the dissolution of BWB to a Select Committee of the House of Commons; and yet later, after *we* had won the 'war' against those who wished to devolve the system among the Regional Water Authorities, he had the brass neck to seek the chairmanship of the Board. Fortunately, and just in time – in fact, two days before I was due to leave – a new and more assiduous Secretary of State blocked his appointment. But that was twelve years on.

It took some time before they really understood just what the incoming government planned, but in the end, with the exception of the man they were to elect as their chairman, they joined forces with us to secure the preservation of the system against a government hell-bent on divesting themselves of the responsibility of maintaining it. Everyone now agrees that had the Board failed to take issue with the government the system would not now be the recognised national asset it is.

It was to prove to be a long, hard and sometimes bitter battle, most of which went on behind the scenes. Neither the Association nor the users, past and present, realise how close we came to losing. Had it not been for the support of the majority of my Board, colleagues and our staff, there is no doubt whatsoever that the canals, as we now know them to be, would not have survived.

But this was two years away. Barbara Castle had been replaced by Richard Marsh, who joined me on a number of visits to the canals and the boat clubs on the system. He had an easy, laid-back manner coupled with a jolly personality which appealed to those he met. We got on well together and I hoped that we would be seeing some progress, but he also had British Rail under his command and it took up most of his time. He was to leave parliament to be appointed BR's chairman, and some time later was elevated to the House of Lords.

Dick was followed by Fred Mulley, another easy-going fellow who is best remembered the time when, as Minister of Defence, he fell asleep whilst sitting next to the Queen watching an RAF fly-past. He certainly didn't leave his mark by anything he achieved for the Waterways as Minister of Transport.

Four months after my appointment, Mr Allen, the general manager, informed me that he was leaving to rejoin the United Kingdom Atomic Energy Authority. I am not sure but, as a civil servant, he believed that he would succeed Sir John Hawton to the Chair; apparently Barbara Castle, advised by Hawton, didn't quite see it that way. As I had yet to appoint a private secretary I decided to ask Gwen Hill, who had been working for Allen, to fill the vacancy. It proved to be a good choice, on my part at least.

Being new to the job, I took advice on who should succeed to the general manager's post. His Deputy's name was recommended; it was a mistake, but as it turned out, it was a fortuitously short appointment. He departed before the end of the year and was replaced by the Board's Chief Accountant, Mr David McCance.

We began a process of reorganising the structure of the Board to meet the challenge that faced us, both on the freight services side as well as the growing interest in leisure activities on and alongside our waterways. Harry Grafton headed up our Freight Division and Alan Blenkarn the Amenity Services.

The Board's Solicitor retired and I was told that his deputy had been promised the post. I called Mr Rutherford into my office to tell him that I wasn't happy with the concept of Buggins' turn, and that the post would be advertised, adding that it was not a reflection on his ability. He agreed by saying that he would prefer it that way. He applied and got the job in the face of some heavy competition. The process proved to be good for him and the Board. Without his loyal support and impeccable guidance during our long fight to save the canals from being split up, I am sure that we would have sunk without trace.

A Deal With a Dash

Although my appointment was for two to two and a half days a week, I found that I was spending more and more time on the Board's affairs. During the reign of Dick Marsh we were faced with a damaging strike at the Regent's Canal Dock in Limehouse, the heart of the East End of London. It came as a surprise because the Board's relationship with our dockers had been good.

There were a number of ships in the dock waiting to be unloaded when the dockers decided to walk off the job. It meant that the Board would be faced with mounting demurrage charges the longer the strike lasted. We knew it, and so did the men. Based on our past relationship I wasn't convinced that the problem could not be solved, so I asked them if they would care to meet me.

They agreed to come to our Melbury House offices. They were led by Jack Dash who, not in our employ, was there representing the union. Dash had built up a national reputation and according to press reports was a firebrand. The Ministry heard of the meeting and insisted on having one of its officials present. I think they were worried that since I was a socialist and a trade unionist, I would side with the dockers.

I found Jack Dash – a small, perky fellow, as one would expect of a true cockney – to have a great deal of charm coupled with a matching intelligence. He held strong views and expressed them whether his listeners like it or not, but he was no firebrand. He was my kind of man, and I knew within minutes of meeting him that we would understand each other. He liked to paint in his spare time, so did I, and we found that we shared the same views on literature.

When they were seated I asked him if he minded if Mr Luckcuck took minutes of the meeting. 'No problem, guv,' was the response. I then asked if he would set out his members' complaints, having first mentioned how surprised I was that they should be taking action when I had been under the impression that we, the Board and they, had enjoyed such a good working relationship. The real basis of the problem was money, I was told.

I laid before him the docks accounts which had been showing a deficit for a number of years. He countered by saying, 'That's because you have spent too much money on the dock's facilities, and this has nothing to do with the men.'

I asked him to illustrate what he meant by too much money, and on what. 'Are you suggesting that the Board have acted frivolously, and if so how?'

Each time he mentioned what he thought was an unnecessary expense I was able to prove that it had been at his members' insistence. It was recorded in the joint committee meetings. The new lighting in the sheds, repairs, and even the annual painting of the edge of the wharves were all done at their insistence.

Dash countered by saying, 'You are a new chairman. Let me tell you, guv, the real problem is that the Board don't know how to run the dock – *we* could do it better.'

I responded by saying that as it had lost money over the past few years I thought he may have a point, to which he said, 'Are you be prepared to minute that?'

To the general manager's consternation I instructed the Secretary to do so.

Then, turning to Mr Dash, I said, 'Now then, Mr Dash, you said that you could do a better job of running the dock than us, I tell you what, you can *have* the Dock.'

The Ministry official stiffened and whispered to me, 'Are you serious?'

I nodded and sat watching the reaction from the other side of the table. The man from the Ministry appeared to be in a state of shock. The union members and Jack Dash were looking at each other down the table. I stood up.

'Mr Dash, you said that you could run the dock better than us. I suppose that you mean that you could make it profitable, so I propose that we withdraw to let you and your colleagues consider my offer.' Then we trooped out of the room.

Once outside, the man from the Ministry repeated his question. I responded with a question to him and the officers of the Board. 'For heaven's sake, what do you think they are now talking about?'

There was no response, so I said, 'Well, let me tell you. Someone is going to ask Jack Dash, "If we take over the dock, who is going to pay our wages this week and the next?"'

The man from the Ministry was not convinced; he rushed off to phone his office for advice.

After an hour we were called back into the boardroom and I was asked if Mr Dash and I could have a word in private. We adjourned to the next room and there he told me that although his members could in his opinion run the dock successfully, they didn't feel inclined to accept my offer.

'Why not?' I asked.

'They don't want to become capitalists,' he answered.

I sat there puffing on my pipe. I had watched smarter men than me use their pipe as a tool when a few histrionics were called for. After a moment I looked at him and said, 'Come on, Jack, that's all balls and you know it. We can't afford to increase their pay, the dock is losing money, the government read our accounts and are continually breathing down my neck. I'm having a job justifying keeping the bloody place open, you must know that.'

He looked me straight in the eye for a good minute before uttering a word.

'So what are we going to do to settle this dispute?' he asked finally.

'Jack, there are just three options. One, you take over the

Dock; two, you get the lads back to work; or three, I will be forced to close it down. I've no choice.'

He knew that I wasn't kidding and I knew that they had to save face.

'Okay, they will stay out for the next four weeks and then I'll get them back.'

'Four days,' I countered.

'Six,' he replied.

'Done,' I said, and we shook hands.

As good as his word, the dockers went back to unload the ships that stood in the dock and we had no more trouble.

During this time London's river traffic was falling off. Constant walkouts in the main docks, due to bad management, lack of communication and a recalcitrant workforce eventually killed them off. It was a tragedy. Sadly, we had to close our dock a few years later. It has, like so much of Docklands, been redeveloped with luxury apartments.

Chapter XXIII

THE BATTLE TO SAVE THE CANALS

In 1970, the Conservatives were returned to power and John Peyton was appointed Minister of Transport. He had a pathological dislike for Harold Wilson and when in opposition went after him on every conceivable occasion. I believe that his elevation to a post was a reward for being his Party's thorn in Wilson's flesh. As Wilson was responsible for appointing me, I didn't fancy my chances with John Peyton, but I was mistaken; he treated me with respect and appeared to take notice of what I had to say.

On 16 October of that year the restoration of the thirty-two mile stretch of the beautiful Monmouthshire and Brecon Canal was completed. The Ministry having listed it as a 'remainder waterway', its restoration was brought about by my obtaining the cooperation of the Brecon and Monmouthshire County Councils. Having paid the costs they agreed to share its future maintenance cost with the Board.

Lying in the magnificent Brecon Beacons National Park, it was opened by the new Secretary of State for Wales who, whilst saying how this would help bring tourists to a depressed area, did nothing to help. On the other side of the coin, in Scotland we were faced with the Stirling County Council's development plan, which envisaged the Union Canal being filled in and used as a highway. But when we applied a little pressure we were able to bring about a change of heart with them and other authorities north of the border.

In 1971, the Conservative Government merged the Ministries of Housing and Local Government, Transport, and Public Buildings and Works into a super-ministry which became known as the Department of the Environment, DoE for short. Peter Walker, the member for the city of Worcester, was appointed as its

Secretary of State. John Peyton was appointed Minister of State, with Transport as part of his brief.

Although nothing had been mentioned in their manifesto, the new government promoted a Bill to Regionalise the water industry, taking over those water undertakings owned by the local authorities – who received no compensation for their assets – whilst those in the private sector did. The Secretary of State appointed the chairmen of these Boards and naturally, with only one exception, they were all Tories. No cry of 'jobs for the boys' was heard on this occasion.

It came as no surprise to me that a number of high-ranking civil servants applied for well-paid jobs in the new Boards. One, who had been responsible for setting the salary structure for the senior officers of these newly created Boards, without a twinge of conscience, applied for and got one of the top posts. Not a word of protest was heard from the minister, the ministry, or parliament.

I was reminded by the now retired Secretary to BWB that at the time I told him that the move to set up these Boards was a precursor to them being 'privatised'. I'm not alone in believing that the permanent secretaries who head government departments, referred to as the 'mandarins', have their own agenda. Benjamin Disraeli made the point. 'The world is governed by quite other people than the citizens imagine.' I knew full well where the future of these Regional Water Authorities lay although I doubt that it had occurred to Her Majesty's Opposition.

The mandarins carefully read the Parties' political manifestos and mould their own ideas into the one that belongs to the Party that gets elected. Placing the water industry under regional control was not part of the Tory manifesto, but the Labour Opposition couldn't cry, 'Foul!' After all, they had regionalised local government transport, and in the case of some cities like Birmingham, they had nationalised and then regionalised their electricity and gas undertakings.

A National Water Council was appointed to supervise the water industry under the chairmanship of Lord Nugent. The membership of the council was made up of the chairman of the new Regional Water Boards plus a few who were termed 'independents'. In practice the Regional Boards were supervising themselves.

Part of the Government's White Paper, 92/71, proposed to scrap the Canal Charter so recently passed by parliament, and envisaged the abolition of the British Waterways Board. Its canals, reservoirs and assets were to be split up and transferred to the various Regional Water Authorities. I knew nothing of these proposals until John Peyton phoned just before lunch to tell me that Peter Walker was to announce in the House of Commons that afternoon plans for changes which would affect the Board.

I asked, 'What changes?'

'Oh,' he replied, 'a few alterations to your commercial side, nothing of great consequence,' and hung up.

Just after 4.30 p.m., Denis Howell, one of the Opposition's spokesmen, rang to ask if it was true that I had agreed to the changes Walker had announced. He then read out some of the proposals. Contrary to the information Peyton had passed on to me, the plan was to kill off the Board. Howell told me that on being questioned, Walker had replied that I had been consulted and was in agreement with the proposed changes. Howell asked me if this was true.

I contacted the Permanent Secretary, Sir David Serpell, to tell him of the call and to complain that not only had Peyton misled me, but according to Howell, Walker had misled the House of Commons. I was unaware that Serpell was at the time sitting with John Peyton. He asked what I had said to Howell. I told him that I had said that the idea that my Board be abolished was news to me. Peyton took the phone, yelling into it, 'This is war!' and slammed it down.

David Serpell rang me later that evening recommending that I take care. The subject of my call had been passed on to Peter Walker who had obviously been given the wrong information. He apologised to the House for his error.

Howell called to say that he had made it clear to the House that the minister's policies would be carried out 'over his dead body'. However when *he* became the Minister of State, he had either forgotten or had his mind changed for him. It was hard for me to accept that when his time came, he would allow his 'mandarins' to convince him to follow a line not too dissimilar from that of his predecessor's; but convince him they did. He and I were to butt heads over this in front of meetings with a House of Commons Select Committee (see Select Committee Reports).

I doubt that it had occurred to the ministers, or even members and officers of the Board, that I would take up the cudgels to preserve the system. After all, those with whom I was to cross swords could fire me.

Eldon Griffiths, who at this time was the member of parliament for Bury St Edmunds and a journalist by profession, had been appointed Peyton's junior minister. He was in a different class to his boss and stood much further to the right.

He lacked Peyton's style. Griffiths who was tall and thin, with a clipped manner of speech, an arrogance that grated, and no sense of humour. Soon after his appointment he invited me to call in at the Ministry to meet him.

At this point I should put you in the picture as to how meetings with ministers at their offices take place. During my sixteen years as chairman of BWB, I was called to meet an ever-changing collection of personalities who occupied ministerial chairs, so I got quite accustomed to the form.

Driven to the appallingly ugly high-rise monstrosity which housed the Department of the Environment and its ministers in Marsham Street, Whitehall, I would take the lift to the top but one floor to be greeted by Harry, the one-armed porter, who was a kind of general factotum.

As I was a regular visitor over the years, Harry and I got to know each other well. He would escort me to the little room where he worked, look at his watch and say something like, 'You know the form, Sir Frank, we've time for a cup of tea.'

The 'form' was that ministers always kept visitors waiting for at least ten minutes. It was a way of suggesting that they were frightfully busy. Another ploy used was when they wanted to end an interview. Sometimes they looked at their watch and sighed, 'The House of Commons is a strict taskmistress; I'm sorry, but I have to leave to get there to vote.' Alternatively a 'primed' junior would interrupt to say, 'You are needed at Number 10, Minister.'

I got so used to it that I was almost out of the door before they had finished the line.

During my meeting with Griffiths he made it clear that in his view I was no more than a minor appointee of the Labour Party who wouldn't present any problem with which he couldn't deal and who would soon be replaced. He was to discover his mistake too late to save himself or the intentions set out in his Government's White Paper.

Before he closed our discussion that day he asked, or rather told me, that he wanted to meet the members of the British Waterways Board, saying, 'I intend to explain to them personally my government's proposals.'

'I'm sure that they will be overjoyed,' I cracked.

It went straight over his head. He just beamed. He had been chosen to get that part of the White Paper dealing with BWB accepted by the Board, and the users of the system, in order to ensure the proposed Bill's smooth passage through the Commons. He proved to be a bad choice.

In trying to win over canal enthusiasts and their organisations he employed all the tricks in the trade. His first move was to appoint the new chairman of the Inland Waterways Association to a post which he simply created, that of canal adviser to the minister. It was obvious that he had spotted his appointee's ambitions and believed that the move would gain the support of IWA members. By his bumbling, Griffiths did more to antagonise the users than to obtain their support. Fortunately, because of his underestimation of them and me, his arrogance led him to fail to realise that he was losing the battle. He kept falling down holes of his own making.

His meeting with my Board fixed, Trevor Luckcuck met him and his officials at the entrance to the building. He escorted them to the boardroom on the third floor and I introduced the members individually. I sat alongside him whilst he glossed over those clauses in the White Paper which affected the Board.

He had already informed me that he wasn't prepared to answer questions, so, when he had finished, I thanked him for taking time out of his busy schedule to meet us. He began to rise from his chair but I placed my hand on his arm and he resumed his seat.

Addressing the members, I said, 'You have heard the minister's interpretation of the White Paper 92/71 which involves the future of this Board and the inland waterway system. Now let me underline what the Paper actually means.'

I explained just how the Canal Charter, so recently placed on the statute book, would no longer be honoured, and that if the White Paper was accepted, the future of the canals would be in jeopardy. The members were staggered, and so was the minister. White with anger, he pushed back his chair and without a word to the members stalked out of the room. The Board Secretary and I hurried to join him.

Walking down the corridor to the lift, no words were exchanged. I pressed the button, the lift doors opened, Griffiths stepped inside and glared at me, stabbing a finger in the air.

'I want to tell you...' he began, but before he finished the sentence the doors closed, we could hear a muffled voice shouting in the lift as it proceeded to the ground floor.

The members sat stunned by the minister's performance. Going round the table I asked each of them what they thought we should do. They all agreed that we could not stand by and let the proposals go through without a fight. I was pleasantly surprised that both The Hon Alexander Hood, a direct descendant of the famous admiral, and General Sir Hugh Stockwell, who had recently been appointed to the Board, agreed; all the more so because I knew of their links with the Tory Party. It wasn't long before I was disillusioned.

At the next meeting of the Board, Hood referred to our press release, which recorded the Board's opposition to the White Paper. He claimed that the Board minutes which recorded the decision to fight the proposals were not true. The minutes had been read, passed and signed as being a correct record of the previous meeting; even so Hood suggested that they were completely untrue. When asked in what particular way, instead of justifying his comments he merely replied, 'I have nothing more to add,' whereupon Sir Hugh Stockwell, who had mentioned that the previous weekend he had spent time with the minister, John Peyton, at his cottage, proposed 'that we burn all the minutes and records'.

I realised that we had two members upon whom I could not depend. With the battle that lay ahead this was not easy to bear.

We waited for the next move. Trevor Luckcuck had developed a link with a sympathiser in the Ministry who tipped us off that Eldon Griffiths was to call a meeting of the user organisations to be held in Church House, close to the House of Commons. We decided to start our own offensive by preparing a document setting out all the reasons why the White Paper could not be supported.

Without any previous official notice, we received invitations to the minister's meeting just two days before it was to take place. On the day, I had a copy of our document setting out the Board's opposition placed on every seat in the hall and ensured that our chief officers were sitting in prominent positions before the meeting was due to start. I took a seat at the end of a row so that if I decided to get into the act I could move into the gangway to perform.

The chairman of the IWA approached me to say that what the minister was proposing would provide all the money needed to put the canals into good condition.

I looked at him and said, 'That's bullshit, and you of all people should recognise it as such. At least I now know where you stand.'

He shrugged his shoulders and moved to a seat on the platform in order to smile at his unwitting members.

When the Minster led his team, which included the Reverend Lord Sandford, into the room, it was packed to capacity. A Ministry official came to tell me that the minister wished me to sit on the platform. I was placed at the end of the table next to His Lordship. Griffiths rose to thank everyone for attending and then launched into a defence of the White Paper, telling those present to ignore the Weary Willies and Tired Tims who were against change. This would bring in a new era for the canals, he told them.

As he went on at some length along these lines I felt that as a seasoned politician with the ability to sway an audience, his experience should have let him know just when to switch off. It didn't, and he overcooked the goose. Before he sat down, he had that look that politicians have when they are convinced that they have their audience in the palm of their hand.

Under the impression that he had won them over he looked along the platform and with a broad smile called out, 'Perhaps the chairman of the Board might wish to say a few words.'

Although I hadn't been forewarned I was not surprised by this piece of chicanery. It proved to be a mistake on his part.

I first explained to the audience that unlike theirs, my invitation from the minister to attend had only been delivered two days before the meeting; that unlike the rest of the platform party I was only invited to sit on the platform just before the minister opened the proceedings, and that I had only just heard that he wished me to speak.

'However, I can tell the minister that I am not a Tired Tim, but I will admit to being a Weary Willie.' I turned towards Griffiths. 'Minister, you are obviously unaware that you have been addressing a room full of Weary Willies. They, like me, are weary of those who profess to support the canals but fail miserably to do so. They, like me, are wearied by the fact, that just two short years after the canals were given a future through a Charter, such as it was, we now hear from you that you intend to toss it into the dustbin.' I was held up, and encouraged, by a loud and continuous round of applause.

I continued, 'The White Paper that you so eloquently presented doesn't guarantee a tangible future for the system or to those that use it. Your White Paper doesn't guarantee any more money, neither does it guarantee that those to whom you intend to transfer the canals would face up to dealing with the huge backlog of maintenance. It does not guarantee that those to whom you would entrust our national heritage, would find the money your government and previous governments have failed to provide.' I was again interrupted again by a burst of applause.

Pointing to his invited audience I added, 'Minister, these Weary Willies know that you are just moving pieces on the chessboard without a guarantee that they will be able to stay in the game, let alone win it. You are aware that I and my Board are totally opposed to your White Paper – not because we want to keep our jobs; we are more likely to lose them by standing against it. We are opposed because we know that the problem my Board and the canals have is simply a lack of resources. What you propose has not, and does not, provide the answer to the problems facing Britain's Inland Waterways. You are asking these people to agree to your proposal to turn the clock back. Minister, I don't think for one single moment that they will agree to that.'

As I sat down and the whole body in the room stood up to applaud, Lord Sandford shook my hand and said, 'I didn't realise that you were such a powerful speaker, Sir Frank.'

I replied, 'I know, My Lord; your minister didn't either. More to the point, he is labouring under the impression that I'm a bloody idiot, but he's going to find out just how wrong he is. You would be doing him a favour if you told him.'

The minister, having seen and heard the reaction from the floor, made yet another mistake. He invited questions from the floor, thinking that they would be put to him. Most of those who spoke denounced the contents of the White Paper, and asked me to elaborate on various sections. Griffiths was furious.

The meeting over, I got down from the platform and as I was leaving the room an official came after me to say, 'The minister wishes you to join his party for lunch.'

It confirmed my view that he thought me to be none too bright. 'Please thank him,' I said, 'but tell him that it's a bit late, I've made other arrangements.'

From there on, Griffiths set out to bury me.

He decided to have the Board take him on a tour of the canals, and to arrange lunch meetings with the local canal societies and boat clubs. It was an effort to gain their support, so I stayed with him all the way. His plans, as I suspected they would, backfired.

On one of these occasions we met the Wolverhampton Society and its chairman, George Andrews, who I mentioned earlier had visited my home just after I had been appointed. Without me having to say a word, George gave the minister such a roasting that I doubt he has forgotten it. It was a repeat of the scene he had met in other areas, but the Wolverhampton meeting brought to an end the Eldon Griffiths roadshow.

Invitations to address canal societies came in from all over the country. It was tiring, but worth the effort. A groundswell of support was building up, newspapers began to take notice and local MPs were being badgered by those in their constituencies who used, or had a feeling for, this environmentally friendly leisure facility, which if lost would never be replaced. Things got so hot that the Secretary of State, Peter Walker, sent for me.

We met in his room at the House of Commons. I had been led to believe that it was to be private, with no officials and unrecorded; it turned out not to be the case. When I arrived I was taken up to Walker's room to find that he had with him his Ministers of State, Junior Ministers, his parliamentary private secretary and one or two I didn't recognise.

The room was divided in the middle by a partition that stretched almost to the window, which overlooked an inner courtyard. We were sitting on one side of it, and Peter Walker began to question my opposition to the White Paper. Before he got into his stride the division bell rang, calling the members to vote, and the room emptied. I got to my feet and walked to the window. Turning round, I saw a fellow sitting at a table against the wall on the side of room which was hidden from where I had been placed.

I greeted him with, 'I see you are taking notes,' and he nodded; what else could he have done? I said, 'Please tell Mr Walker that we have met, and that's why I decided not to wait.'

I hurried out of the parliament buildings expecting an angry call from the Ministry. It didn't come.

I admired Peter Walker; he was one of Mrs Thatcher's 'wets', leaning more to the left than most of his colleagues. Normally he would have been above such tactics, but he was under pressure from the civil servants and his junior ministers. However, before he was moved to another post there was a further occasion when I 'upset the apple cart'. This time it was in his office in the Ministry building.

I was asked to call in to have a drink with him at the usual time, 6.30 p.m. Entering his room he offered me a seat in a comfortable but low armchair next to his desk. In the room were his ministerial team and three or four civil servants. Peter offered me a drink; I asked for a gin and tonic, which was placed on the desk alongside me. I looked around the room to notice that no one else was drinking; neither were they talking.

Peter walked in front of me and began lambasting me for what he called my senseless intransigence. I had the gin and tonic in my hand but had yet to even sip it. He continued to harangue me so I placed the untouched drink back on the desk and stood up.

'Peter, you invited me for a drink. You have your colleagues and your officers, and I am here alone. Don't you feel that your invitation, to say the least, was both misleading and palpably unfair?'

He looked at me, but before he could reply I added, 'I'm not prepared to stay here, Peter.' Then, with all the injured dignity I could conjure up, I walked out of the room.

Peter Walker was big enough to see that the meeting, arranged no doubt under pressure from Eldon Griffiths, was a mistake. By this time he was beginning to realise that they were losing the battle, but he bore me no grudge.

The year 1973 brought in a number of Cabinet changes. Listening to the news on a Sunday night I heard that Peter had been replaced by Geoffrey Rippon QC. We had yet another new Secretary of State.

It was a little over ten years since the Board was formed and we had already decided to hold an exhibition to show that despite the lack of funds, advances had been made during the decade. I wrote to our new minister inviting him to open it in the tentative hope that he would accept. He surprised us by accepting.

We called the exhibition 'The last ten years'. In view of our continued opposition to his government's bill, and not being sure where the new minister stood, he surprised us again when seeing the banner displaying the words: THE LAST TEN YEARS, he said, 'Don't you mean the *first* ten years?'

We were so suspicious that we didn't know how to interpret this remark. Did it indicate his support, and if so would he be strong enough to have the civil servants back off?

Whilst the battle to save the system was going on we continued our efforts to improve and increase the transport of cargoes by ships and barges on our commercial waterways, which would have taken many juggernauts off the roads. Further studies had shown the prospect of a substantial increase in tonnage on the Sheffield and South Yorkshire Navigation (SSYN). We resubmitted the scheme for the improvement to this waterway in the North-East requesting the DoE to approve our application to place our bill before parliament.

The improvements would allow the navigation to be used by 700-tonne craft from Goole on the Humber Estuary to Rotherham in South Yorkshire. At an estimated cost of £7.82 million, almost everybody was in favour apart from the Ministry. We requested the government to give approval and make an immediate application to the EEC for a grant.

Our submission had been held up by the department's officials, because, we thought, the future of the Board was uncertain. But on 25 January the government had announced that they had shelved the idea of dismembering our organisation. We had won the battle.

Now that we were no longer under threat I asked for a meeting with the new Secretary of State to discuss the reasons for the delay. I met him in his room in the Ministry. He sat on a chair away from his desk with his deputy secretary, John Jukes, on his left. He indicated that I should sit on his right directly opposite Mr Jukes. I enquired why our submission to promote our Bill was again being held up, adding that in order to proceed, the application had to be cleared by the Ministry before November.

Rippon turned to Jukes, who said, 'Minister, it ought to go before the Treasury.'

I protested, 'The department has had it long enough to have been placed before God almighty.'

Rippon looked at Jukes and asked, 'Ought, or must, Mr Jukes?'

He replied, 'Ought, Minister.'

In dismissing me, Rippon said that I would hear from him within twenty-four hours. Before that day had past, a phone call told us that permission had been given to go ahead. The minister had proved that he was his own man. Mr Jukes called the general manager to warn him that this didn't mean that the money for the construction had been given. They were aware that we knew this, but no doubt thought that they should let us know that they were still in charge.

The news that dismembering the Board had been dropped, however, proved to be a false dawn. We should have known that the Whitehall officials never give up. They should have realised that neither did we. The battle we fought to save the system was to be rekindled in the future, this time by a political colleague, someone I had considered to be a close friend.

However, BWB was gradually gathering support from members of all parties in both Houses of Parliament, and from the leader writers of the quality press. Articles in the major newspapers along with documentaries produced and screened by the BBC and independent television companies was awakening the public to this great forgotten resource.

Increased support was also coming from local authorities and work was under way on canals in the 'remainder' category, on which we were restricted in spending money. In many cases they had been so neglected that they were turning into desolate eyesores. With the joint effort of local councils, the Board and enthusiastic volunteers, these sow's ears were being turned into silk purses. The overgrown towpaths became pleasant walkways; in what had been polluted water, fish were breeding, and the depth of weed free water allowed boats to cruise on them once again.

Canals in the north such as the Ashton, Lower Peak Forest and the Caldon were well on the way to being fully restored with the help of volunteers. Press and television coverage on what became known as 'Operation Ashton' showed men and women from all walks of life covered from head to toe in sludge, happily helping in their leisure hours to restore a piece of our heritage.

They were demonstrating in a positive way their belief in the need to preserve the canals for the future, but the government at best didn't understand, or at worst, didn't care. They continued to starve the Board of money sufficient to do the job that the 1968 parliamentary bill had delegated to us.

On the 1 June 1973 my first term of office was due to end. In normal circumstances I would have been approached six months before to be offered a further contract or be informed that I was no longer required. In the event I heard nothing until 30 May when it was announced that I had been offered a two-year contract.

On the following day a banner headline, PRICE OF FIGHTING WHITEHALL, appeared in *The Times* 'Business Diary'. It question the reasons why my contract as chairman of British Waterways Board had been delayed until the last moment and why it was for two years, and not the customary five. It suggested that the reason might be because I had scotched the Department of the Environment's plan to scrap the board, and that my dismissal would have created an uproar, but after two years it might have been forgotten.

In the event I was to continue running the Board for a further eleven years, serving two Labour and two Conservative Governments; but both appeared to go along with the civil service line, that the commercial use of inland waterways was of little interest and the sooner they got rid of the responsibility the better.

In July 1973, a Select Committee of the House of Lords published their report on Sports and Leisure. Making many references to BWB's role in waterways recreation. The Lords Committee took the view that:

> ...every inland waterway capable of being restored should be treated as eligible for restoration and that the Board should be allowed to contribute more towards the cost of restoration.

The members of the Select Committee were obviously unaware that we were not being provided with funds enough even to keep those waterways which were outside the 'remainder' category in good order, but their support was welcome. However it didn't really help us. As is the practice, the recommendations of Select Committees are normally ignored by governments. Why members of both Houses allow this is beyond me. It was unusual for me to get too depressed but I was beginning to feel as if no one in government would ever understand what I was fighting for. However, something which had nothing to do with canals helped to keep me smiling.

With the help of the generous citizens of the Midlands I had raised sufficient funds to complete the first college in Britain devoted to train teachers who wished to specialise in teaching mentally handicapped children. It helped to convinced Prime Minister Wilson to change the long established anomaly in these children's education and care. He transferred responsibility from the Ministry of Health to the Ministry of Education.

On 28 February 1973, Queen Elizabeth the Queen Mother, in her role as President of The National Association for the Mentally Handicapped, travelled to Birmingham to receive from me the deeds and the keys of the new College.

As she was greeting the large crowd who had gathered to see her, I was distracted by spotting my dad standing at the back of the crowd. The Queen Mother, who misses nothing, enquired who it was. When I answered she suggested that I call him over to be introduced. I did but he was too shy to respond. When I met him later I told him that the Queen Mother had asked to meet him. He never forgave himself.

My depression returned when the news that Geoffrey Rippon's period as Secretary of State was to end. Before he left he appointed The Rt Hon Lord Feather and The Rt Hon Sir Frederick Corfield, QC to the Board. They were to be of enormous help to the cause in which we were involved.

In February 1974, the Labour Party was re-elected with a majority of four, and Tony Crosland was appointed Secretary of State at the DoE. Bill (now Lord) Rodgers took over the Transport brief. We first met at the annual Fabian Society Summer School when he was its Secretary, held at Beatrice Webb House. I recall playing in the Society's cricket team against the village. As most of our side had been to university I was under the mistaken impression that some were cricket blues. They didn't do too well with bat or ball, but some did better politically, achieving positions in future British Governments. Neither Bill nor Tony bothered to pay BWB or me any attention. So much for me being the best bowler in the side.

With such a small majority they and the rest of the ministers kept their heads down and BWB was left, as it were, floating on still water. After eight months, Prime Minister Wilson, knowing the government wasn't making any progress, called another election and the Labour Party was returned with a working majority of forty-two.

The Board's commercial side was making profits, the number of pleasure boats on the system had risen, and despite the shortage of funds we were improving the standard of some of the amenities, and from the environmental aspect, the standard and appearance of our buildings. This led to the Board winning the European Architectural Award; but the general condition of the canals, tunnels, bridges, reservoirs and locks were deteriorating.

The appointment of Sir Frederick Corfield QC strengthened the Board. Having held a number of important posts in the Conservative Government – Minister of State in Housing and Local Government, Minister of State at the Board of Trade, Minister of Aviation and Minister of Aerospace – his knowledge of the system and his contacts proved to be of immense help.

Lord Feather, who as plain Vic Feather had been the popular general secretary of the Trade Union Congress, added colour to our proceedings as well as gaining us more attention from the media. Fred Mulley, who had returned as our minister appointed The Rt Hon Lady White, who had held ministerial posts in the Foreign and the Welsh Offices. He also reappointed Illtyd Harrington. General Sir Hugh Stockwell left us in April, as did Lieutenant Colonel Richard Seifert who, as one of Britain's foremost architects, had provided the Board with free advice on planning and architecture, which had been of enormous help.

I was sorry when in the following June Sir John Hawton decided to retire from his position as vice chairman. I doubt if any of those canal enthusiasts who criticised the board during his Chairmanship ever realised the contribution he made towards the formulation of the 1968 Transport Act.

I was asked by the Secretary of State if I had any objections to his appointing Lord Feather to be my vice chairman. Of course I had none, but when this was announced Sir Alex Samuels amazed the members by taking me to task at the Board meeting because I had failed to recommend him for the post. I was pleased for his sake that Vic Feather wasn't present during this tirade.

I was told that Samuels had contacted the minister, which could have been the reason for him not being considered. Six months later at the end of his term, he was not reappointed to the Board. Unfortunately Vic Feather's association with the Board was brought to an abrupt end after only two years. He passed away after a short illness in July 1976.

The Board continued to press the new government to take notice of our complaints about the years of insufficient funding. Knowing that it meant that we were unable to meet the conditions that *they* had laid upon us in their 1968 Act, they continued with their policy of providing us with the shadow, not the substance.

By this time the arrears of maintenance had reached a stage where the system was at risk of collapsing. For years we had supplied the department with reams of evidence as to deterioration, but nothing was been done to alleviate a situation which was getting worse year by year. We discovered that in order to delay making a decision, the civil servants convinced the ministers that they could not rely on the reports of the Board's engineers in respect of the worsening conditions, and urged that they be checked by outside consultants.

I rang Mulley, who had been reinstated as Minister of State, to tell him that it was 'a bloody insult to our engineers, and the Board'; but by this time I had grown accustomed to the weakness of ministers who hadn't the courage to seek out the truth for themselves. It was far easier to side with the mandarins and ignore those professional engineers who were closer to the problem and employed to protect the canal system.

At great cost to the taxpayer and further delay, which was to cost even more when the consultants' report came out, the minister buried his head in the sand. It was par for the course. Meanwhile, the Board was left to carry on patching up a fast collapsing system, undermanned, underfunded and lacking in the elementary support that we had every right to expect. I should have walked off the job then.

Peter Fraenkel and Partners were commissioned to:

> Study the maintenance needs and to examine in detail the condition of the waterways, its structures and its reservoirs and to advise on the necessary works and costs of operating and maintaining the system, having regard to the Board's statutory duties and other obligations.

The wording was unbelievable: 'having regard to the Board's statutory duties'. How did the civil service have the nerve to write this when they had assisted in denying us the money to carry out the statutory duties and other obligations since 1968? By this time I didn't bother to ask. The minister, by not having the sense to recognise the irony of the situation, confirmed that he, and more so his officials, were colluding in yet another delaying tactic. It was an outrageous insult to the Board, its staff and the general public.

It made me realise that the Ministry officials, who had been supplied with all the relevant information year in and year out, were sitting on it awaiting a government who would follow their advice to get rid of the responsibility of maintaining the canals. It was what was known in the corridors of power as 'Kicking it into the long grass'. To those less naive, it was another demonstration that the mandarins in Whitehall had their own agenda and were determined to apply it.

The consultants undertook to complete their studies by the summer of 1975. It was handed to the ministry in November 1977 'to await their observations and ministers' decisions.' In any other sphere it would have caused considerable embarrassment to find that the expensive consultants' report that they had advised simply confirmed the advice that our engineers had presented to them seven years earlier; but not in the case of Ministry officials. No one apologised and no one was fired; nor did they provide us with the wherewithal to allow us to carry out 'our statutory duties and other obligations' as referred to in the minister's instruction to Fraenkel and Partners. They continued to ignore the warning, even though it was underlined in their consultants' report, of the dangerous condition that many of the waterways were in.

Whilst we waited, there were more canal breaches. Reservoirs and bridges became dangerous, and to add to our problems, we were advised that more of our building and structures were to be listed as ancient monuments, or of special architectural or historical interest. These, under government statute 'had to be maintained in good order'. It was almost beyond belief that this listing was done by the same Ministry who was starving us of funds.

Again, the same Ministry gave approval to increase the size and weight of lorries using Britain's roads and called for the canal bridges to be strengthened, which placed on the Board an extra financial burden.

This was followed by the passing the Reservoirs Bill, which was so badly written that many of our canals were defined as 'large raised reservoirs'. The Board, through our legal department, had to get their Bill amended when it went before the House of Lords. The Bill, written by officials who in effect controlled our money supply, were imposing on us a duty to appoint a 'supervising engineer for each of our 96 reservoirs', when they knew that we hadn't got the money to even fill our existing establishment. These anomalies would have been known to a minister who was even half awake, yet none of them or members of parliament bothered to raise the matter. It became more obvious by the day that the inmates were running the asylum.

The Llanfoist embankment on the Monmouthshire and Brecon Canal collapsed. The torrents of water, boulders and other debris caused extensive damage to properties, horticultural and farming land for miles around. When the canal near the centre of Coventry collapsed, the lower floors of the nearby hospital were flooded and patients had to be evacuated. I called the officials in the Ministry to ask, 'What needs to happen before you realise that we have a problem?'

The Secretary of State, Tony Crosland, had been moved from Environment to become the President of the Board of Trade, taking Bill Rodgers with him. A few days after the changeover, Bill hailed me as I was crossing the central lobby in the House of Commons. He told me that they were to set up the English Tourist Board, and asked if I would become its chairman. I was sorely tempted to opt out of the problems of BWB to take on a new enterprise which was being heavily supported by an enthusiastic department and government funds, but couldn't bring myself to do it.

I suggested he approach Sir Mark Henig, who was highly respected for his work in the city of Leicester. Bill understood my reluctance and later appointed me as a part-time member of the ETB. Mark Henig did a wonderful job as its chairman.

Peter Shore, very much the academic, took over at the DoE, and Denis Howell joined his team as Minister of State. He was, or had been, the President of APEX – the trade union that sponsored Fred Mulley, who still held the Transport brief. Without any consultation, Mulley agreed to pass British Waterways over to Howell, removing us from the Transport division. I protested, but to no avail. It was clear that transport on water was of no interest to Howell. All his attention was concentrated on recreation, yet Mulley, who knew or should have known of the Board's interest in the transport industry, in which it had a considerable financial involvement, handed it over without a peep. I'm convinced that Mulley, being a sponsored member of APEX, was the reason why he acquiesced so easily to his President's request.

What followed was both distasteful and counterproductive. It was an eye-opener to those who were still under the impression that ministers who on the surface appear to be strong and decisive can prove to be anything but...

Chapter XXIV

INLAND SHIPPING AND THE BACAT FIASCO

During the early 1970s we held discussions with inland shipping interests on the Continent, meeting in Rotterdam, Paris and Munich. It didn't need a genius to realise that the benefits that the improvements to our outdated commercial inland waterways, which we had recommended, would help to take hundreds of juggernaut lorries off our roads.

Our commercial waterways already carried over six million tonnes. The schemes we put forward would have accommodated barges of a size that would move a vast number of bulk loads by water, be five times more economical in fuel consumption than road transport, be far cheaper to maintain, and would reduce accidents and air pollution. Unfortunately, our message to the minister was ignored and our efforts frustrated by the actions of his officials.

Our coal and steel industries exported to the Continent and we already carried their products to the coastal ports. British Steel also imported iron ore. We held talks with both to see whether we could jointly build a barge-carrying ship to transport their products door to door. As I expected, the mandarins would have none of it. A consortium of Norwegians who had heard of our ideas decided to invest in the design and construction of a barge-carrying ship called *Bacat*, short for 'barge on catamaran', capable of carrying barges that would fit our system.

Unlike the UK, Germany had embarked on improving their canal system by constructing a connection between the Rhine and the Danube to link the North Sea to the Black Sea. It opened up the possibility of transporting cargoes deep into the heart of Europe, to and from the British Midlands via the Sheffield and

South Yorkshire Navigation, the River Trent and the North Sea. The Germans were investing hundreds of millions in the project, whilst our commercial waterways were being allowed to deteriorate.

The *Bacat* ship was introduced in March 1974. The vessel carried ten barges of 140 tonnes capacity and three lash barges of 370 tonnes capacity. Both types could be lashed together end to end or side to side to form a push-tow train. With foreign private enterprise demonstrating confidence in our inland waterways transport, it would have been reasonable to expect the Ministry of Transport to show even a modicum of interest. Not a chance. Neither the investors, BWB or the inland shipping industry received any encouragement or support.

Whilst I was working hard to keep the interest of the industry alive the Ministry were busy confirming the view that it had no future. They were firmly committed to the road lobby. This became so obvious that the BBC took an interest by producing a series of damning programmes called *Brass Tacks*.

They exposed the way large juggernaut lorries, some with as many as twelve wheels, pounded their way through country towns and villages destroying property and the environment. The BBC team travelled to Holland to demonstrate how continental inland waterways had assisted in transforming Rotterdam, which at a time when the Humber ports were the busiest in Europe, had been just a small fishing port. Rotterdam is now one of the world's premier ports, in contrast to the Humber ports which are in terminal decline.

Brass Tacks became essential viewing. In their penultimate programme, the BBC invited the then Minister of State, Denis Howell, to appear. During the interview he gave his support to the road lobby, discounting all the evidence the programmes had produced in support of transport on water. They invited him to debate the subject with me on television but he declined.

Our lack of involvement in the investment in the *Bacat* system was to create problems for the company. Had we been involved we would have taken part in the negotiations with the dockers' union, which in our view would have helped to avoid some of the difficulties that later arose. As we were not, when the *Bacat* shipping company entered into discussions with the British Transport Docks Board regarding the passage of the barges through the Humber ports, which included the Hull docks, the dockers dictated the terms.

The dock workers, although members of the Transport and General Workers' Union, were in a section known as the Blue Union. They were a law unto themselves. When it suited them they acted independently of the TGWU, who failed lamentably to control them. Their employer, the British Transport Docks Board, was equally weak, but much more so than we could have even guessed.

The manner in which the local leaders of the dockers controlled matters in Hull was reminiscent of the Hollywood movie *On the Waterfront*, a film which exposed how the Mafia-led union controlled the docks in New York. I doubt if there were many outside Hull, the local union and the passive directors of the Docks Board, who knew just how much of a stranglehold the Hull dockers had over their employers. The battle over *Bacat* was to expose just how far the Docks Board and the TGWU had lost control.

The situation began to unfold when the dockers decided to 'black' the *Bacat* operation along with BWB's freight services. Although we had a lot riding on the success of the *Bacat* system we were unable to intervene. The Hull dockers were calling the shots.

Their employer, The British Transport Docks Board, took no action, and before long trouble erupted. I wrote to Jack Jones, who was then the general secretary of the union, pleading for help and asking for a meeting. There was no reply. There was no need for the barges, once they'd been dropped off the mother ship bound for inland river or canal side wharfs, to be held up in Hull. However, the dockers insisted that one out of every three of the barges would have to be unloaded and then reloaded by them before proceeding to their destination. The *Bacat* Company were being forced to pay fees to the Docks Board for a service that was not required.

There came a time when even the dockers thought that unstuffing a barge and then restuffing it was a waste of time, so they left it and played football on the dockside until they felt it time for the barge to go on its way. An intrepid local newspaper reporter snapped them, and the illustrated story that followed exposed that they were being paid more than the professional footballers playing for Hull Football Club at that time.

Following an appeal to the Secretary of State for Employment, Michael Foot, a meeting was arranged. As my General Manager David McCance, Trevor Luckcuck and our Freight Services Manager Harry Grafton, and I were climbing the steps to the entrance to the Ministry, Michael Foot was making his way down.

I greeted him with, 'Hello Michael, I thought we were to meet.'

Without stopping, he muttered, 'Albert Booth, the Minister of State, will see you,' and went on his way.

For those who have little or no knowledge of the man I should explain. Michael was as decent as he was intelligent; by that I mean that he was not in any way like the picture the Opposition and the media painted of him. Because he was considered to be on the extreme left of the Labour Party, right-wing Tories who didn't measure up to him, ethically or otherwise, tried hard to ridicule him in the press.

A prime example was when he became the leader of the House of Commons and Lord President of the Privy Council. It was assumed that at the State opening of parliament he would wear the traditional uniform allotted to the post: a dark blue single-breasted coatee with gilt buttons and stand-up collar, white breeches, white silk stockings and a sword. This was never Michael's style. On the occasion he wore a dark lounge suit.

Nicholas Fairbairn, a barrister, farmer, Scottish Tory backbench member of parliament and an 'oddball', had never held ministerial office. He attended the same ceremony dressed in a grey frock coat, a wing collar with a cravat and diamond pin, and carried an ivory-topped cane. He was, as you will gather, a dandy.

After the ceremony he spoke to the media accusing Michael of turning up dressed like a demobbed soldier. Some of his colleagues leapt on this and tried to make a meal out of a morsel. This unfair criticism rolled off Michael like water off a duck's back; I doubt if he gave it a moment's thought.

Michael Foot never forgot the way the dockers were treated in the Twenties and Thirties, so I wasn't too surprised that any battle with the unions, in which he might have to take sides against them, was not welcome. He ducked out. Needless to say, we got little joy from meeting his junior minister, Albert Booth.

The following Easter I took my family for a holiday to La Rochelle, a resort north of Bordeaux. During the first week I received a telexed message which informed me that one of BWB's Hull barge captains had been attacked by the dockers and tossed into a lock, sustaining a suspected broken jaw. I asked for details and having read them knew that we had reached the breaking point. I telexed a statement to be issued to the press, knowing that it would cause an uproar.

The following day the leader of the Transport and General Workers Union, Jack Jones, who I knew and liked, sent a message to say that it was urgent that we meet. My press statement had had the desired effect but it was too late. I telexed him to ask whether his reply was an answer to my request of December last. He was not amused. We never did get to meet, but I knew that had the meeting taken place I would be wasting my time.

However, for those who don't know him and assume that he is a weak man, they would be mistaken. The only people who could handle the leaders of the Blue Union were the members. Jack is a true democrat, not one of the armchair variety. When the fascist insurgents began their war to overthrow the democratically elected Spanish government, he joined the International Brigade and fought in Spain. Since retiring he has continued tirelessly to campaign on behalf of old-age pensioners.

It was bad judgement on his part not to have taken on the cabal that led the Hull dockers. Defending their jobs could have been forgiven, but he should have made himself aware of the operation in which some of his members were engaged. It was to bring the union into disrepute.

He wasn't alone. A well-known left-wing Birmingham MP, Jeff Rooker, who incidentally is now a bright minister in the 'New Labour' government and now a member of the House of

Lords, spoke harshly in parliament about my battle with the dockers. When the truth came out he hadn't the good manners to apologise.

I decided to abandon my holiday and phoned Trevor Luckcuck, the board's secretary, asking him to set up a meeting with the Minister of Transport. Then I motored from La Rochelle to Bordeaux and flew back to London.

We entered the Ministry room to find the chairman of the Docks Board, Sir Humphrey Browne, and his CEO already seated. They had obviously been called in by the Ministry officials. After a few moments, Dr John Gilbert (now in the House of Lords), who had replaced Fred Mulley, entered the room. He was smoking the remains of a cigar and carrying a vessel that looked like a shaving mug. It contained his after-lunch coffee.

I had seen it all before. I'd met Wedgwood Benn who, sitting in an unusually – for a minister – sparsely furnished office with a huge trade union banner leaning against the wall behind him, had offered me tea in a fine china cup. He drank *his* out of a similar mug to that which Gilbert was holding. I put it down to some odd inferiority complex they shared. Drinking out of mugs made them feel closer to the working class they thought they represented but didn't quite understand.

Gilbert, who had no doubt been fully briefed, nevertheless welcomed me with, 'What's the problem?'

I let it pass and proceeded to outline the difficulties we faced, due in the main to the actions of the Blue Union in Hull. Before I got into the detail he said, 'Sir Frank, you do not seem to understand how trade unions work.'

I didn't let him get any further. 'Minister, please don't insult me,' I cut in. Taking my trade union membership card from my breast pocket I slid it across the table to him. 'I've been a member of a trade union since I was sixteen years old, and although I have held top managerial positions and directorships in the private sector I'm still a member. I doubt very much that you or anyone here can say the same. I also doubt if you know as much as I on how, as you put it, trade unions work.'

Gilbert had blown the gaff he had been briefed and wasn't

about to cross the line. The meeting droned on without any progress being made. We left as expected, empty-handed.

Convinced that we were on our own, left to take on the dockers, I asked Trevor to arrange for me to travel to Hull to meet them. I was advised against such action but I wanted to at least try to break the deadlock. I first contacted the leader of the Kingston upon Hull Council, a long-serving Labour supporter. He knew of my work in Birmingham and we talked of the future prosperity of his town. He was well aware of the problems we faced with the dockers and suggested that we should examine more closely just what was going on in the docks. The importance of this piece of advice didn't register with me until Woodrow Wyatt and his team of researchers exposed it.

I met the dockers in a large hall placed at our disposal. I noticed Kevin McNamara, a local MP, sitting at the back of the hall. He seemed to be enjoying the tirade emanating from the floor but as he depended on their votes at election time, I guess he had no other option. Sad, really.

It was little use appealing to their sense of justice, but over the noise I stated our case. The police suggested that for my personal safety I should leave the hall by the rear door. I thanked them but thought that it was not a good idea. I stepped down from the platform and made my way through the bustle, being shoved, pushed and threatened right to the front door.

All through this sorry saga the Docks Board remained silent for, I believe, two reasons. If they upset the Blue Union their other docks could be threatened, and as inland waterway transport was competition – however small – they preferred goods to be transferred from their docks by road.

Three days after my experience in Hull, I took Woodrow Wyatt to lunch. He wrote for a leading Sunday newspaper and I was aware that he had a team of investigating journalist helping him with his copy. I mentioned the advice that I should examine more closely what was happening in the docks, which was the reason for our lunch date.

Looking at the wine list, Woodrow asked who was paying.

'You are a guest of the Board,' I told him.

'In that case,' he said, 'there is a bottle of claret on this list that is frightfully cheap – I mean it's a bargain at the price.'

So to keep him happy I ordered it. I began to outline our problems, when he interrupted me to yell out across the restaurant which was full to capacity, 'For God's sake, man, hold that bottle with more care!'

The approaching wine waiter almost dropped it. Woodrow insisted on decanting the wine personally whilst I glanced at the wine list. It wasn't what I would have called cheap, but I was just a pleb. Intrigued to see him empty the remains of the bottle, sediment and all into a glass, he told me that genuine connoisseurs drank it. I made sure that the glass wasn't passed to me.

He seemed to be paying more attention to the meal and the drink than to what I was telling him, so much so that when we parted I thought that I had wasted my time and the Board's money. I was mistaken.

Two weeks later in the Sunday paper appeared a centre page spread headed: AND WHAT ARE YOU GOING TO DO ABOUT THIS, MR JONES?

It went on to expose the Mafia-type operation being carried out in the Hull docks. He should have put the question to the chairman of the Docks Board. Among other things, Wyatt reported that members of the union were running their own business operation in competition with the Board's private sector clients. They were using the British Transport Docks Board's storage sheds, moving equipment and other facilities. Whilst the Docks Board's sheds were overmanned, the sheds the dockers used were not. The article brought a stop to the blacking of *Bacat* in Hull but it was too late to save it. The company withdrew.

In evidence to the Parliamentary Select Committee 12 November 1977, Mr R Shaw, a lay member of the union, on being questioned on the *Bacat* blacking said, 'The situation in the port at that time was a "Mafia"-type situation. There was a liaison committee which consisted of some dockers, some dock leaders, and, I do not like to say this; there were also some barge owners who took off as soon as the British Waterways Board was blacked. There were haulage firms, one-man lorry drivers, all on the union liaison committee who were blacking *Bacat* and the British Waterways Board. One of the ringleaders had his freight aboard *Bacat*, shipping it to British Waterways Board depots at the same time as we were blacking British Waterways Board.' He went on, 'Please don't fall into the trap of saying that it was the Transport and General Workers Union. There was, I will say it again, a "Mafia"-type situation in the port at that time.'

This more than justified my campaign by confirming the accusation levelled in Wyatt's article, of the strong-arm tactics and the corruption. It also proved to me that the expensive bottle of claret had paid off. The British Transport Docks Board were aware of what was going on in their port but hadn't the courage to deal with it, neither had the leaders of the Transport and General Workers' Union, nor had the government ministers.

John Prescott who, at the time of writing, is the Deputy Prime Minister and Transport Primo, was, during this episode, a Hull constituency MP. Today he says he believes in inland waterway transport. We must see just how fervent a supporter he turns out to be. When with the help of the *Bacat* ship we were in a position to achieve a genuine breakthrough for inland waterway transport, I can't recall him ever uttering a word of support.

However, after thirty-two years, he has reinstated Barbara Castle's Charter, and there is a Minister for the Canals. Even so, in the latest government publication, *Waterways for Tomorrow*, there is an ominous statement which confirms my early comment that the mandarins never give up. It reads, 'The committee will ask whether the structure and ownership of their (BWB) waterways is correct.'

The *Bacat* fiasco was bad news for the inland shipping industry and the companies who had invested vast amounts of money in the hope that Whitehall would back them. The episode, in part, set back our efforts to improve and enlarge the inland shipping industry in Britain. The biggest impediment was the lack of support from ministers who simply ignored the evidence and backed their officials, who in turn overstepped the mark on numerous occasions in their support for the road lobby.

Had we had a minister with an independent streak, prepared

to consider the case that we and others were putting forward, we would today have had a thriving inland shipping industry, fewer juggernaut lorries on our roads, less pollution, less damage to the environment and a reduction in the cost of road maintenance.

Chapter XXV

ACTIONS OF AN OLD FRIEND

Denis Howell I had known for over a quarter of a century, and through the years I had spoken for him at his election meetings and canvassed for him in the streets of his constituency. When he was Minister for Sport he appealed to me in 1965 to add to my burden by taking on the chairmanship of the newly constituted West Midlands Sports Council.

We had been close colleagues for a long time but during the 1974 Labour Government, in his new position as Minister of State our friendship proved to be of little help to me or British Waterways when he became the minister covering our affairs. Whether it was a case of familiarity breeding contempt, it's hard to say, but I was soon faced with having to do battle with him as I had with his political predecessors in office.

Given a government of which he was a member, which six years before had put on the statute book an Act which gave the canals a Charter, coupled with the fact he had publicly stated that the Tories' proposals to emasculate the British Waterways Board would happen 'over his dead body', it was reasonable to expect that he would be strong enough to stand up to his officials and pay a little more attention to what we had been, and were, saying. I hadn't allowed for the ability of the mandarins to continue to have things their way.

Howell set up a panel of what he called the 'agencies', made up of the chairman of government-appointed bodies, and various people who had anything to do with recreation, however remote. At the first meeting I was surprised to see Lord Taylor of Gryfe, the chairman of the Forestry Commission, Lord Porchester, the Queen's racehorse trainer, and an official from the Ministry of Agriculture and Fisheries. The latter gentleman was to give us a long lecture on the dangers of rabies. The reason? I still have no idea.

There must have been forty or more sitting at the huge conference table. Half of them were civil servants who appeared to show little interest in the proceedings. When we broke for a buffet lunch set up in an adjoining room, three of them and myself remained in our seats. I overheard their conversation, which had nothing to do with the morning's discussion; they were concentrating their thoughts on their future pension arrangements.

The minister set up a number of working parties to study and report back.

Lord Taylor was selected to chair that which was to research water-related recreation. His responsibility being timber, I thought the choice about par for the course. Lord Taylor asked if we could meet later that week. He suggested that as he had little experience in the subject, I prepare a paper on recreation on water with recommendations, which he would then place before the working party. The paper I produced homed in on the problem faced by the users of Britain's rivers and canals. Because there were many waterways controlled by different bodies, the users had to apply for numerous licences and to obey different sets of rules and conditions, all of which added up to unnecessary confusion and frustration. I recommended that the rivers and canals should be administered by a single authority.

On my presenting this to him he thanked me but gave me no indication of his opinions regarding it. It was never fully discussed by his working party and I was therefore surprised when it appeared on his submission to the meeting of the agencies. It was the only one that Taylor had submitted, and when called upon to comment on it, he denounced my recommendations.

I was staggered, but before I could respond Lord Porchester expressed his surprise. 'How can the chairman put forward his group's paper when he disagrees with it, and why should he object to its recommendations, which I find admirable?'

It was obvious to all those sitting at the table that Howell wasn't happy with Porchester's comment, and the manner in which he led the subsequent discussion exposed the fact that he and Taylor had put their heads together to scotch it. Being the editor of the paper under discussion I expected him to call on me; when he didn't, I tried to catch his attention but failed. I declined to attend any further meetings and sent along a substitute.

Some months later a Parliamentary Select Committee concluded that there was a need for a National Navigation Authority, with which the minister agreed, and that the British Waterways Board was best suited to run it, with which he did not. The select committee's findings were therefore ignored. Twenty-six years later it is now back on the agenda. Amazing!

It wasn't long before I was summoned to the Ministry to discuss the board's affairs. Denis Howell sat behind his desk, and an official I hadn't met before sat in an armchair against the wall to his left; he was Sir Robert Marshall. He had been the Permanent Secretary at the Department of Trade and Industry but for some reason he had been moved to the DoE as 'second' Permanent Secretary, which in itself was interesting.

The minister opened up with, 'I have good news for you, your money problems are over.'

'That's nice,' I muttered.

He then went on to explain what he said was his plan. Oh oh... The Board's engineering and maintenance departments, the largest part of our workforce, was to be split between the Regional Water Authorities. I couldn't believe my ears. Before he went any further I blurted out, 'You are kidding me, of course?'

'No,' replied the minister and turned to his civil servant, asking him to tell me how it would all work.

Marshall described the plan, part of which was that minister would appoint me to succeed Lord Nugent when he retired from the chair of the National Water Council. I rose from my seat and looked at my colleague the minister.

'I really can't believe this. Have you forgotten the Tories' White Paper and your publicly announced objections to it? Can't you see that this idea, which surely can't be yours, is doing what they tried to do but through the back door?'

Marshall started to object, but I stopped him. 'I am addressing the minister, so would you please not interrupt.'

Still looking at Howell, I went on, 'Do you really think that by offering me the chairmanship of the National Water Council I would renege on my Board and everything that they and I have been fighting for over the past three years? I'm disappointed, Minister!'

At this Denis began to bluster but I interrupted. 'Minister, it took three years before your predecessors were forced to publicly drop their plans. If you are now intent on starting this up again, then let me tell you that I will fight you as I fought Eldon Griffiths and his advisers. He lost – and so will you.'

I was addressing someone I considered to be a close friend; I was devastated. I turned and left the room.

It was late and the building was virtually empty as I walked down the corridor to the lift. Marshall came after me and, placing his hand on my shoulder, said, 'Frank, you mustn't accuse the minister of trying to bribe you by offering you the National Water Council. Can't you see this could lead to other things? He is doing you a favour.'

I was angry enough at what the minister had proposed, but Marshall's comments caused me to boil over. I stopped, removed his hand, and, trying to contain myself, said as politely as I could, 'Why don't you fuck off?'

The plan to subjugate the Board was never again referred to in my presence, by the minister or his officials. I was not appointed to succeed to the Chair of the National Water Council when Lord Nugent retired, but the civil servant, Robert Marshall, was.

On 18 March 1976, the government published a White Paper, a document which once again threw the future of the British Waterways Board and the survival of the canal system back into the melting pot. Just how we kept our workforce together in the light of all this was a managerial miracle. We did lose and could not replace a number of senior officers.

This 'new' White Paper envisaged that the Board should be merged into a proposed National Water Authority, which in effect was an advisory body. I spoke privately to the Minister of State, asking how he expected us to go on; he replied, 'I don't.'

Like one of his predecessors, he had underestimated me and the canal enthusiasts. Whether he thought that as we were members of the same political party I would succumb, I know not, but he had made a big mistake.

For the second time in under five years a proposal had come from the Secretary of State, via his Minister of State, to transfer the Boards, undertaking to other authorities. I asked many members of parliament I knew, 'How could any industry, private or public, be expected to run their organisation successfully on such an unsatisfactory and indeterminate basis?' A few such as Nigel Spearing understood and tried to have it debated on the floor of the House, but with little success.

We were starved of resources to carry out the tasks placed upon us by parliament, constantly investigated, and our professional staff's reports were questioned and brushed aside by civil servants who had little or no experience of the world outside their domain. Our complaints at last began to sink in and evidence of the fact was soon to surface.

It was coincidental to the announcement of the White Paper that the report of the government's appointed consultants into the operation and the cost of maintenance of the Board's waterways had been completed. Peter Fraenkel and Partners had carried out a thorough investigation in accordance with the mandate given to them by the Ministry. To their surprise, but not ours, it confirmed the Board's own reports to them, made more than five years before.

The Fraenkel report, which was eagerly awaited by the canal enthusiasts, underlined the concern, which we had constantly put to the Ministry, about the 'dangers of neglect where impounded water is concerned'. We thought that the department would be deeply embarrassed, if that was possible, and waited for their response. Their chosen independent consulting engineers confirmed that there was a considerable amount of work to be done – most of it desperately urgent.

While we waited for the minister's reaction, the arrears of maintenance continued to mount. Now that they had the report there should have been no further excuses but they continued to hold back. Their delaying tactics became blatantly obvious to anyone who had been or was still involved. They were counting on the White Paper being approved and that they would be saved at the end of the day, but they were wrong again.

In March 1977, Howell's office called to inquire whether I had any objections to Mr C W Plant being appointed to fill the vacancy left by the death of Lord Feather. Plant, a friend of Jim Callaghan, had been general secretary to the Inland Revenue Staff Federation; he was given a Peerage later that year. He was a tall, heavily built man with an air of self-confidence.

At the end of his first Board meeting, occupying the seat on my left, he commented, 'You got through that rather quickly.' Then, looking down the table at the Board members, he added, 'You seem to have them well trained.'

He was referring to The Rt Hon Sir Frederick Corfield QC, Bernard Gillinson JP MA, Geoffrey Godber, DL CBE, Illtyd Harrington JP, Edward Standen, Frank Welsh MA and The Rt Hon Lady White MA. Had he said it as a joke I would have let it pass, but he meant it.

I asked the Members to remain seated and quietly asked what he meant. He said that I hadn't allowed them much time for discussion. I turned to the members.

'Mr Plant feels that I have not allowed you adequate time to discuss the items on the agenda. If you feel that I have in any way made it difficult or stopped you from questioning the general manager, the officers or me, or that I have rushed you through the agenda I would be happy for us to go through the reports again.'

They were stunned. Eddy Standen wondered why I had put such a question. I glanced at the new vice chairman but he sat there poker-faced. Before he left the building he knocked on my door to apologise. We left it at that.

Just after I was appointed to the Chair, I suggested to the Board that we consider holding at least three of our monthly meetings in other parts of the country. My idea was that they would have an opportunity to inspect the system and to meet our people working on the canal bank, and they us.

Four months after Plant joined us, our 'out of town' inspection trip was held in Birmingham allowing us to look at the canals in the Midlands. The Board stayed overnight at the Albany Hotel on the city's inner ring road; naturally I slept at home that night.

Turning up the next morning to join them on the coach we had hired I was met by Sir Frederick who said, 'I'd like a word with you, Frank.' He told me that Cyril Plant had told him and Geoffrey Godber how embarrassed he was about questioning my chairmanship now that he had got to know me, and what the Board was up against.

I said, 'Let's forget it, Fred,' but he went on to tell me that over a nightcap after dinner, Plant told him that he was Denis Howell's nominee and that he had been put on the Board as Howell wanted me out, presumably to put him in the Chair.

Having been on the political scene for so long, nothing surprised me.

'It's outrageous!' Fred exclaimed. I shrugged it off and got on the coach. Geoffrey Godber signalled me to sit by him. During the drive he repeated Sir Fred's story, but it's strange how malevolent actions can rebound. When Cyril Plant took his seat in the House of Lords he spoke eloquently about my efforts with the Board to save the country's canal heritage, which to Denis Howell must have gone down like a lead balloon.

Chapter XXVI

THE SELECT COMMITTEE TAKES A HAND

Our first real break came when a House of Commons Select Committee decided to investigate the Board's operation in 1977–79. The committee was set up by standing order of the House of Commons and was answerable not to the government but to parliament. Their findings cannot be tampered with by government, and are published.

The problem is that the government of the day 'takes note' but rarely takes action or allows parliamentary time to debate the findings of the Select Committees on the floor of the House. If the recommendations of a Select Committee are unacceptable to the government, nothing happens. It is only when the matter being investigated becomes an embarrassment and the media decides to expose it that the 'fur begins to fly', which was the case in respect of the affairs of my Board.

The membership of these committees is around ten to fifteen and made up of backbench members of parliament from all sides of the House. They have the power to call upon anyone, and I mean anyone, to appear before them. Those that refuse to attend, including ministers of the crown, could find themselves standing before the bar in the House of Commons to answer to their peers.

Meetings are held in large, dark-panelled rooms on an upper floor of the Palace of Westminster. The members of the committee sit on one side of a horseshoe-shaped table at the far end of the room; the witnesses at an oblong table facing them. In between them sits a stenographer concentrating on tapping every spoken word into a small mechanical device placed on the lap.

The chairman of the committee sits at the centre of the table and behind sit House of Commons' lawyers and clerks. The members of the media and others, whoever they might be, sit at the rear of the room behind the witnesses.

As I took my seat on the morning of Tuesday 15 November 1977 facing the chairman, I recalled watching the American Senator Joe McCarthy's 'Star Chamber' cross-examinations, but this was very different. No loud interruptions from the chair, no shouting, banging of gavels or bullying tactics to extract answers the committee wanted to hear; it was all very civilised. It occurred to me that the American CBS programme, which finally helped to debunk McCarthy would have done well to have televised our system at the time, if only to show their countrymen the difference. The sad thing is, our admirable system is not all that it seems.

The committee's members normally do a good job of extracting information, which allows them to report on what actions they feel parliament should take, but their efforts are usually pigeonholed. Someday, the people's elected representatives will rise up against the executive and insist that these committees be given 'teeth'.

Although I felt a little nervous, the chairman soon put me at ease by smiling when he thanked me for agreeing to attend. I thought, *I wonder what you would have said had I not*? But that's the British way. I knew that the Minister of State had either already been interviewed or, if not, would be soon. It was not until I read the Select Committee's deliberations that I fully understood the lengths to which Howell had gone to help his department's desire to see us wiped out.

I soon realised from the questions being put to me that the members of the committee were well informed on the work of the British Waterways Board and the problems we were facing. I sensed that they understood the simple fact that the House of Commons, in passing the 1968 Act, had placed on the Board onerous responsibilities and since then, had continued to fail to provide the finance to allow them to carry them out.

Towards the end of my first session with the committee, the chairman asked, 'Sir Frank, how would you describe your relationship with the minister?'

It was not a question I wished to answer. After a few moments

I said, 'Sir, if you will forgive me, I would rather not say.'

An official standing behind him called out in a loud voice, 'Order, order!'

'What the good clerk is telling you, Sir Frank,' said the chairman, 'is that if you refuse to answer me now, you can do so before the Bar of the House in the morning.'

Suitably admonished, I asked if he would kindly rephrase the question. 'No,' came the reply. I looked hard at the chairman and then at the rest of his committee.

'Well, sir, the only way I can answer you is to say that if I don't ring him, he ain't likely to ring me.'

There was a burst of laughter from his colleagues. The chairman sat silent for a moment then replied, 'Very well, Sir Frank, on that note we will call it a day, but I hope that we will be seeing you again.'

I thanked him and the committee for their kind interest in my Board's affairs and bid them good day. Five days later they called the Minister of State, Mr Denis Howell.

He soon came under fire when he protested that my Board and I were misinterpreting his White Paper. He wasn't going to split up the canal system; all he wanted to do was simply to transfer it to the National Water Council, who would divide it up between the Regional Water Authorities to manage. Asked why, he made the mistake of underestimating the serious manner in which the committee had gone about its inquiry.

Giving his reasons, he cast doubts on the competence of the Board. By asserting that we had not assessed our priorities, that we had not surveyed the system, and had insufficient qualified staff to carry out these tasks properly. It was both pompous and stupid, in the light of the Fraenkel report, which had borne out all that our engineers had reported to the Ministry over a period of years. The committee were also aware that the government's pay restraint and the threat Howell and his predecessors had hung over the Board for years was the recent for our depleted staff.

Underestimating the committee, Howell boasted that he had made a grant of an extra £750,000 for urgent maintenance work. On being questioned on that point, he admitted that he had given the Board specific instructions as to which maintenance work the money was to be applied – namely, that which members of parliament had brought to his notice. In effect, he admitted that he had actually taken over the Board's responsibilities to decide its priorities.

Astounded, the committee began to challenge his assertions. They stated, quite categorically, that they found Howell's comments about the professional competence of the Board quite astonishing, and in total contradiction to the impression they themselves had gained during their meetings both at headquarters and in the regions.

They went on to say that in their view, 'The minister's slur on the Board's competence was unwarranted and that the Board's case for a continued injection of funds to meet the maintenance backlog had been made out.'

The committee were very critical of the minister's performance. When he left the House of Commons that evening he was greeted by the notice on the newsvendors' boards: HOWELL IN HOT WATER. It was only then that Peter Shore, the Secretary of State, and other members of the Cabinet began to take an interest on what we had to say.

When Lord Nugent gave evidence for the National Water Council he completely undermined the Minister's White Paper. In answer to the committee chairman's question, 'What you are really saying is that, apart from having the word "Water" in their titles, the roles of the water industry and the BWB are quite different, and the contributions made by each to the other are quite minimal?' Lord Nugent replied, 'Yes, that would be a fair summary.'

The chairman went on, 'You say that there are no insuperable practical difficulties in the British Waterways Board being a subsidiary of the National Water Authority, yet you go on to point out that would involve assuming executive responsibilities totally different from the relationship with the rest of the water industry; is this not illogical?'

Nugent's response was illuminating. 'I think it more semantic than substantial. In our judgement not much would be gained by it.'

There was one more action of my old friend that shook me.

The report publishing the committee's findings stated that the minister had held meetings with union representatives of NALGO, GMWU, NUPE and the TGWU, whose members worked for the Board. In an endeavour to obtain support for his idea to emasculate British Waterways, he offered the bait that if they were transferred to the National Water Authority their pay would be increased. He was well aware that it was the government, of which he was a member, that had restrained the Board from increasing its employees' pay, and the unions knew this too.

The minister had given the Select Committee to understand that the unions were in favour of his plans to change the status of the British Waterways Board. It must have come as a quite a shock when he read that one of the unions had sent a letter complaining that he had misrepresented the facts.

'We read with dismay,' they wrote, 'that the Minister of State, The Rt Hon Denis Howell, in answers to specific questions, inferred that the TGWU had changed its views on his White Paper.'

The Select Committee decided, embarrassing as it was to the minister, to include this letter in their final report to parliament.

Having been under the threat of being disbanded for seven years or more, the Board found it difficult to recruit staff. We had lost our Solicitor, Chief Finance Officer and Chief Estates Manager. We could not recruit suitable replacements because of uncertainty and the government's restriction on what we could pay. Howell was well aware of this; so were the unions and the committee.

It was a great disappointment to find that my friend of many years had descended to such a level in his anxiety to see the department's plans fructify. In doing so he had overstepped the mark, losing face with his parliamentary colleagues. I was also less than amused.

After Denis Howell's dismal performance, the Select Committee decided to call Peter Shore, the Secretary of State for the Environment, to appear before them. A few days before the meeting he ordered Howell to 'no longer delay the publishing of the Fraenkel report', which was headed: THE WATERWAYS OF THE

BRITISH WATERWAYS BOARD. A STUDY OF OPERATING AND
MAINTENANCE COSTS.

It had been three years from the date that it was commissioned,
seventeen months after the Ministry received it and seven years
after the Board's engineers had reported to the government the
dire situation that existed.

The cost of overtaking the arrears of maintenance at
March 1974 as reported to the Ministry by the Board, after four
years' delay, had increased to £34.6 million.

The Fraenkel report drew attention to arrears that required
immediate attention in the interests of public safety. It
recommended that a programme of action and expenditure to
restore the waterways to a sound condition be undertaken.
Shaken by the event, Peter Shore took it in hand and announced
that he was to make a sum of £5 million available for the fiscal
year 1978–79, in the interests of public safety.

In true parliamentary fashion, he didn't say, 'in order not to
embarrass my officials'; he formally accepted the Fraenkel report.
None of those responsible were publicly criticised for the manner
and quality of their advice, which had cost the taxpayer millions of
pounds. Had this been in the private sector they would have been
fired.

I received a message from the prime minister's office asking
me to call to see him in the House of Commons. I presented
myself at the desk in the central lobby where Lord Murray was
waiting to take me to Wilson's office. On the way he asked why
the PM wanted me. I didn't know, but thought, why should I tell
him, so I answered, 'Private matter, Albert,' and left him to
ponder. As we passed along the corridor I noticed a number of
backbench members I recognised – standing there hoping to catch
the PM's attention, I suspect.

I sat waiting in his room. Harold burst in.

'What a day... hello, Frank, don't get up, would you care for a
drink?'

'If you are having one, prime minister.'

'Brandy suit you?'

He then asked if I would like a cigar and I went through the
same procedure. So there I sat drinking his brandy and smoking

one of his Havanas, waiting to hear what I was there for.

We talked for more than half an hour before I left and I still don't know what it was all about. I certainly wasn't about to complain about culpability of one of his ministers, if that was what he was expecting. I knew, as he did, that Denis was no supporter of his and that he had worked hard in trying to have someone other than him as leader of the Party. Had I decided to be as disloyal to Denis as he had been to me, the pattern of my life might have changed dramatically; but it was not in my nature.

Harold Wilson had from time to time approached me through a third party, once to help sort out the problems of Labour Party properties which led me to project manage their new headquarters in Walworth Road, and I was also recruited to the Labour Party's 1972 Industrial Group. To my surprise it was made up of leading industrialist and men from the City who were supporters of the Party.

The Group was set up to advice the prime minister's office. We covered many areas, from industrial democracy, a cause that Peter Walker addressed later in his articles in *The Daily Telegraph*, to reducing interference from Whitehall in the management of the nationalised industries.

Chapter XXVII
MISSED OPPORTUNITIES

The waterways were growing more popular by the week. Applications for cruising and fishing licences were increasing. Hire craft licences were on the increase, demonstrating that more families were taking holidays cruising the canals. The number of boating club rallies grew and towns were vying with each other to hold the Inland Waterways Association's annual National Rally on their stretch of inland waterway.

Trying to emulate our success in leisure we intensified our efforts to bring about a resurgence in water-borne transport. With the help of the Yorkshire Local Authority we planned to improve the SSYN so that it could accommodate larger commercial craft.

Its freight carrying potential was frustrated by opposition from Whitehall officials, lack of support from members of parliament and shortage of funds. The plans for this improvement scheme had been rejected on one pretext or other for years. In 1972, thanks to Geoffrey Rippon during his all too brief period as Secretary of State, the mandarins were overruled and we received parliament's permission to put forward the scheme.

This done, and Rippon gone, the officers in the Ministry began their campaign to scotch the scheme. They asked us to prove our traffic forecast; it sounded a reasonable request. Having done this they asked us to produce the names of the companies who would provide the traffic. Having satisfied this request we discovered that, without informing us, they had actually sent officials around the country to check on whether the companies we had listed actually existed.

Having found that this was so they then asked the companies to sign a guarantee as to the tonnage they would ship, over a period of years. No such rules applied when it came to the construction of highways and they knew that no company could or would give such guarantees. Their actions made it clear that we were in for another long, hard struggle.

They impeded our efforts to enter into joint schemes with the private sector. Their aim was unambiguous; it was to stop the scheme at all cost. The simple facts were, and still are, that the annual cost of maintaining waterways is many millions of pounds less than roads. The cost of casualties on water is infinitesimal compared with the carnage on roads. The damage to the environment from the increased weight of lorries compared with barge transport was self-evident yet not even considered. To them, transport on water didn't count; they were and still are, totally road orientated.

There were European Community grants to be had for such schemes as the SSYN, the snag being that the government had to sponsor them and put up matching funds. Any approach to the EEC had to be via the DoE. In the light of the considerable opposition we encountered from the department it was patently clear that they would not make a move to apply. With no action from the Ministry to approach Brussels for a regional grant, I arranged to travel there to see one of the British EC Commissioners. He told me that whilst he met many people seeking grants from other EC member countries, I was the first he had met from the United Kingdom.

He put me in touch with the Commissioner dealing with transport, who was an Italian. We took him through the scheme, the improvement plan, its commercial viability and the tonnage we expected to take off the roads. I led him to understand that we were aware that the application had to be sponsored by our government, but what I wanted to know was whether there was any prospect of an application being successful before starting down that track.

He was enamoured of the scheme and the manner in which it had been presented. He said that in his opinion there would be no doubt as to it being grant-aided. With tongue in cheek, I asked if he would write to me to this effect. He did, and when the minister discovered that I had such a letter he let me know in no uncertain terms that I had transgressed.

'How so?' I asked when I knew full well, as did he, that the letter if published would embarrass the Ministry into funding the scheme. There was no reply.

The Yorkshire County Council gave us a lot of support and even offered the government one million pounds towards the scheme. Everything went back into the melting pot after the Labour Party was elected and Denis Howell had taken up the policy of burying the British Waterways Board.

His dismal failure in front of the Select Committee opened the new Secretary of State's eyes to what we were about. Peter Shore took more interest in our problems and aspirations than most of his predecessors and produced a £5 million contribution to the backlog of maintenance, with a promise that further money would follow year on year. In 1978, he authorised a start on the long delayed development of the SSYN and he accepted the Select Committee's recommendation that the BWB's autonomy should be preserved. In short, he publicly dumped Howell's plans.

The SSYN improvement scheme subsequently cost £16 million, double that which it would have cost had it been accepted when we first put it forward. Peter Shore inaugurated the scheme in April 1979 by starting the pile driving.

There was growing evidence of an awareness of the recreational, commercial and environmental advantages to be gained from encouraging the use of the Board's waterways. People began to realise that the canals aged two hundred years plus which had been left to us were an important part of our national heritage, and that their prudent use and improvement could make a valuable contribution to the country's prosperity and well-being.

Despite the need to struggle for every little gain, we felt that our efforts were being rewarded due to the intervention of the Select Committee and the resultant publicity. Harold Wilson had stepped down and James Callaghan was selected to take his place as prime minister. His period in office was short; it was not a happy time. He failed to understand the gravity of the situation in which the country and the government found itself, having for years kept a lid on the earnings of those working in the public sector. Although it was evident to almost everyone else he failed to recognise the undercurrent of discontent that was about to boil over.

His seeming lack of concern for the lowly paid and his refusal to even negotiate an increase brought about the 'winter of discontent'. On returning from an overseas trip, his comment in answer to the question about the crisis was not too bright: 'Crisis, what crisis?'

It was to rebound on him and his government. He called an Election in May 1979 and with a majority of forty-two he was the only one who felt confident. The Tories won with a seventy-one majority and were to remain in power during the rest of my chairmanship of the British Waterways Board – and well beyond.

Michael Heseltine had been appointed as the Secretary of State for the Environment; his Parliamentary Undersecretary of State, who was to oversee our affairs, was the ebullient Marcus Fox MP. A canny Yorkshireman, he was small – about my size – with a jolly, open manner which disguised a tough disposition. Marcus Fox was a political street fighter; he spent most of his time trying to force me to sell the Board's land assets with me snookering his every move. We had successfully negotiated a joint development scheme on our East End Docks land. Had we sold it and the rest of our land bank as the government wished, the improvements now being carried out, could not have happened.

Having a new set of masters meant once again being called to Marsham Street to be looked over. At my first meeting with Michael Heseltine he caught me staring at the life-size painting of Lloyd George hanging on the wall behind him. He turned to look at it, and then with a quizzical look back at me, asked, 'So?'

It caught me on the hop, and I replied, 'Sorry, Minister, I was just surprised, wasn't he a left-wing Liberal?'

'He was a Welshman and a great leader,' Heseltine said rather sharply, and that was the end of that conversation.

We went through the usual questions and answer session but it was, as all these first meetings were, a case of the minister wanting to run his eye over those whom he intends to control. As I would most probably not see too much of him after this, I took the opportunity of mentioning the recommendations contained in the Fraenkel report, which set out elements requiring immediate action in the interests of public safety.

I inquired whether he was aware of Clause 229 setting out the

Select Committee's proposal's and recommendations in respect of the Board, which underlined the initiative we took in developing the push-tow barge system. While I was at it I mentioned that the Board had had the sword of Damocles hanging over its head for too many years and hoped that we had seen an end to it.

The minister listened to me politely but I had no idea what was going on in his head. I thought that he must have been aware that the Select Committee had publicly justified my fight against his and the Labour Government's Ministers, but I wasn't about to let the committee's efforts be forgotten. Before I left I said that I hoped that we would now be left to get on with the job that parliament had given the Board to do.

Some years later, I was at a dinner at which Heseltine was the guest of honour. Having a drink after the function I sat alongside him. He surprised me by saying, 'I admire you, Frank, you are a pro. My predecessors underestimated you and allowed you to drag them on to *your* battleground and then knock them for six.' He went on, 'I think you were wrong, but you outmanoeuvred them.'

I wasn't sure whether it was a compliment or a warning not to try it on with him.

He also went on to tell me that in the early Seventies I had caused his government some concern with my opposition to their 1974 Reorganisation of Local Government Act whilst I was leader of the Labour Party on the Birmingham City Council. I had urged the city council to oppose it, saying, 'We should link up with Manchester, Leeds, Liverpool and the other major cities to oppose the plan, which simply wouldn't work.'

My comments were supported by the leader article in the *Birmingham Post*; unfortunately we were not in control so my appeal fell on deaf ears and the Bill went through. According to Heseltine my intervention had them worried.

I asked him why they felt it necessary to start 'mucking about' with local government. He replied that had Labour won the election they would have implemented the Redcliffe-Maud report which would have set up nine all-purpose unitary authorities and in effect introduced regional government into Britain. It wasn't that that bothered him; he had worked out that most of them would be Labour controlled and in case Labour won the following General Election he urged Peter Walker, who was then the Secretary of State at the DoE, to go in for their own reorganisation.

I was appalled and said, 'You mean to tell me that you balls up local government in cities like mine on pure political grounds?' He just smiled.

Within four years, their reorganisation proved be a dismal failure. The cost was the loss of hundreds of talented local government officers, all of whom received considerable sums in compensation, and experienced Aldermen. It also introduced payment and expenses for Councillors. Local government has never been the same. Some are now getting over £50,000 pa.

On the BBC *Hard Talk* programme in October 2000, Michael Heseltine admitted to being at odds with the policy of centralisation and that he believed in the idea of unitary authorities. The failure to support the Redcliffe-Maud report was a costly missed opportunity.

I believe that it will not be long before regional government is implemented. If dealt with in the right way, by that I mean a 'real' devolution of power from Whitehall to regional authorities, giving them control over their own destiny would revitalise many of the areas in the UK.

In addition to removing Whitehall red tape, which has held back improvements to traffic management, housing and so much else, it would improve the democratic process. Competition between the regions to attract industry, commerce and tourism would be encouraged, and it would be of great help to those areas that have been so woefully neglected by Central Government. Whether the present Blair Government will find the time and the will to bring it about is questionable.

As I expected, with the Conservatives back in power, the contracts of those members of my Board whom they considered to be 'not one of us' were not renewed. Bernard Gillinson MA lived in Leeds and was a friend of one of its MPs, Denis Healey. Bernard had been a loyal member for thirteen years; it ended on New Year's Eve. The Rt Hon Lord Plant and The Rt Hon Lady White, both Labour members of the House of Lords, went a few months later.

The Rt Hon Sir Frederick Corfield QC was appointed vice chairman of the Board, I was happy to say. He was a Tory of the old school, guided by his conscience rather than any deep-seated political philosophy. An example of Fred's independent spirit arose out of the actions of Lord Burton, the owner of a large estate which bordered on to Loch Lomond, of which BWB was the navigation authority. We owned a certain amount of land alongside his and he was for ever trying to buy it.

He commanded our area estate manager to present himself to explain the reasons for denying him ownership and would not accept that we needed it for operational purposes. Angered by not being able to get his way, he wrote to me. I replied confirming that the estate manager's reasons for not being able to comply with his request. Being a high Tory, he decided to write to Sir Frederick Corfield in the belief that he would receive a more sympathetic reply. He made the mistake in his letter of accusing me of being a communist.

Fred was outraged. He showed me the letter with the advice, 'Now that you have seen his outrageous accusation you are in a position to sue him. My advice is that you should do so.'

Fred was aware of my views on communism as practiced by the Party of that name, but I wasn't about to get angry about Burton's letter. I suggested that on behalf of the Board, he arrange to meet to tell him personally why the Board couldn't part with the land he coveted.

A few weeks later Fred told me of the meeting, which had turned out to be more of a confrontation. Made even angrier than he was by the letter, he stated that he now had evidence enough for my taking action against Burton in the courts.

Paraphrasing Groucho Marx, I said, 'Fred, I've been insulted by better people than him. But thanks for being so loyal.'

He proved to be so to the Board, its members and its officers until he retired.

A call came through from the new Minister of State, Marcus Fox, to ask for a meeting at the department in Marsham Street. I arrived as requested at six o'clock and after the customary wait was ushered into his office. There were four men sitting at the table, none of whom was known to me.

Fox said, 'Frank, let me introduce you to your new members.'

I was staggered and asked if we could have a word in private.

'Not necessary, Frank,' he said.

'I think it's very necessary, Minister,' I countered; but being Marcus Fox, he insisted, 'Anything you have to say can be said in front of your new members.'

'Since you give me no choice I must tell you, Minister, that you can't appoint members without my being consulted.' Fox was foxed.

He asked me to join him in the next room. He was, probably for the first time in his life, lost for words.

'Marcus, none of the ministers I have served have taken it upon themselves to appoint members to my Board without first consulting me.'

Fox replied, 'They have letters of appointment, I'm sure that they will serve the Board well.'

I told him that it wasn't the point; doing it this way was not only improper it was an insult to my position as chairman. 'You're the bloody minister, and you should know that!' I finished angrily.

Although I was annoyed I couldn't press it any harder, and to save him being further embarrassment reluctantly accepted the situation. We re-entered the room and he introduced me to Mr A D J Carratu, Mr H L Farrimond C B E, Mr D W Gravell and Mr R J Weston.

I asked if they wished to question me on any point. Jeremy Weston, who was a partner in a large estate agency in Manchester, asked about the Board's land assets, adding, 'I'm here for the sale of the century.'

There was no doubt that Fox had indicated to him that that is what he wanted to achieve, namely, as Harold Macmillan put it, to 'sell the family silver'.

I looked at him. 'I'm sorry to disappoint you, Mr Weston, but perhaps you haven't been told that the Board will not be selling anything until we are assured that any income so raised will be for the Board and will not disappear into the maw of the Treasury. We are however entering into joint venture schemes with the private sector, which have to be approved, naturally.'

I looked at Marcus Fox but he said nothing. A few days later he asked if I had any objection to the appointment of Rear Admiral Dunbar-Nasmith.

Both Weston and Gravell proved to be excellent members of the Board. Carratu and Farrimond's membership was not renewed after they had served one term.

With the experience I had in the property field, had the Board had the funds to develop its land and had we been able to enter the market without interference from Whitehall we could have substantially reduced the call on public funds. I'm sure that the chairmen of all the nationalised industries would have succeeded had they been left free to run their concerns.

Sir Geoffrey Wardale K C B was appointed Second Permanent Secretary in the DoE. I mention this because he was unusual in the fact that he actually came out of Marsham Street to visit the waterways in order that he could adjudicate fairly. Having done so he proved to be actively sympathetic to the Board and its problems. I had a great deal of respect for him and felt that he understood that I wasn't 'just being difficult', as no doubt many of his colleagues thought me to be.

During this period I was invited by the West German Government to see the programme of improvements they had embarked upon to improve their inland waterways. I was taken to one of the deep locks that was almost completed. Walking along its base I could see that – in true German fashion – the finish on the concrete lock chamber (which, when filled with water, would rarely be seen) would have befitted a cathedral. Their Rhine/Main/Danube waterway, upon which they were spending millions of marks, was to link the Black Sea with the North Sea.

We took the opportunity to meet the Nuremberg Harbour Authority to discuss freight handling facilities provided by them alongside the waterways, and formed a link which we hoped would generate business for Britain's inland shipping industry.

All our efforts in this direction was ignored by the succession of ministers who passed through the Ministry of Transport and the Environment. None of them took issue against the departmental officials' apparent war of attrition.

It would have been reasonable to expect that, having witnessed their appointed consultant engineers' confirmation of the Board's assessment of the arrears of maintenance, they would hesitate before landing us with further outside consultants at a cost to the taxpayer; but it was not the case. The results continued to prove our efficiency even under the most trying conditions. Their consultants did no other than to confirm what the Parliamentary Select Committee had found before them.

During the remainder of my term of office we were able to upgrade many miles of the 'remainder' waterways into the 'cruising' category, thanks to the help of thousands of enthusiast who gave money and physical assistance, and to those local authorities who entered into agreements with the Board by putting their ratepayers' money into improvements where the national government had failed.

None of this would have happened without the members, officers and workforce of the Board who stood by me through many traumatic years because they too believe that saving the canals for Great Britain was worthwhile.

My finale was as unusual as my entrance onto the waterway stage. June Pell, who had succeeded Gwen Hill as my Secretary, placed an invitation on my desk. It was to join Giles Shaw, a Parliamentary Undersecretary of State at the DoE for lunch at Locket's Restaurant, a haunt of ministers and top civil servants.

It was a few days before Christmas 1982. Arriving five minutes ahead of time I was surprised to see that the minister was already there. This was unusual; normally it was I who was kept waiting. We went straight to the table he had reserved and once seated he said, 'Your a claret man, I understand?'

When the wine waiter arrived I was in for another surprise. Without looking at the wine list, Shaw said, 'We will have a bottle of claret.'

The wine waiter raised his eyebrows and so did I. Shaw was highly educated and always well groomed; he was usually more sophisticated than this. He was obviously agitated.

The waiter returned with a bottle of the house claret and, after the traditional tasting ceremony, filled our glasses. Shaw raised his and blurted out, 'Frank, we will not be renewing your contract in

June.'

I raised my glass and replied, 'Happy Christmas, Giles.'

He stuttered, 'You don't mind?'

'Giles, I will have completed fifteen years in the Chair. I have survived longer than any other nationalised industry chairman has, and I have won the battle – if not the war – to keep the inland waterways where they should be, under BWB. Do I mind? Not bloody likely!'

Before the meal was over he told me who had been chosen to succeed me. It was the overambitious chairman of the IWA I have already mentioned. I suggested that he look into the records when Graham Page was the minister dealing with our affairs; that he seek out the correspondence between him and Sir Frederick Corfield QC, and the minutes of a meeting that took place with Page, two of his officials, Fred and me.

'You will then find out, Giles,' I said, 'that you have made yet another mistake.' He pressed me, but I just repeated my advice.

On the first Wednesday in June 1983, three days before I was to leave the Board, the newly appointed Secretary of State, The Rt Hon Patrick Jenkin, invited me to call at Marsham Street. I thought that it was for a farewell drink and couldn't refuse such a nice gesture. We were sitting comfortably in our chairs sipping gin and tonic when the minister said, 'Frank, I understand that you are not too happy about the person who my predecessors have chosen to succeed you?'

'Minister, you've made up your mind; what I think doesn't matter any more.'

'Oh, but it does,' he said. 'The appointment was made before I came into office and I have taken the opportunity of reading the letters exchanged between Corfield and Page and the minutes of the meeting that was held on the subject, a meeting at which you were present.'

Although it was never mentioned, I'm sure that Sir Frederick Corfield had been in contact. Patrick Jenkin then explained that he had called the person in to tell him that he was not to be the next chairman of BWB. Shaw had already informed the man of his decision to appoint him months before. He had joyously spread the news around that the position he had assiduously worked so hard to obtain was to be his; but Patrick Jenkin had other ideas.

By putting a stop on the appointment Jenkin had proved that he was his own man and a cut above most ministers I had served. He said, 'Frank, you will appreciate that it has left me in a bit of a hole. As from Friday BWB will be short of a chairman; I would like you to continue in office.'

I was too amazed to reply. I gulped down my G and T and then – for a change – kept my mouth shut.

'What terms would you want?' he asked.

'You are asking me to take on another term?'

'Yes, it would help me a great deal.'

'Minister,' I gasped, 'I have cleared my desk, and have had almost six months to get used to the idea of not being there! I've moved my home to Cornwall and tonight the Board are giving me a farewell dinner – my last supper, so to speak.' I added, for dramatic effect, 'There will be speeches and a presentation, I'm told.'

The minister interrupted, 'If you agree you will have to go through with that. You cannot tell anyone before I make an announcement to parliament that you are to continue, and I can't do that until Monday. You can then send telegrams to your members.'

He pleaded that, as he'd agreed with my views in respect of my successor, surely I could 'see my way clear to help him by staying on'. The idea of going through a charade of bidding my farewells and then staying on mortified me. Since the Christmas lunch with Giles Shaw I had begun to realign my thoughts to other matters... like fishing, painting and mowing the lawn. I had begun the process of unwinding. In a year I'd be sixty-one.

We chatted for half an hour or more. No one came to tell him that he was required in the Commons or Number 10; he was giving me time. I could have asked for, and would have been given, a further five-year term, but in the end we agreed that I would stay on for a short period whilst he found a replacement.

On reflection, with Patrick Jenkin as Secretary of State I wished that I had taken on another term. It was another missed opportunity. The only condition I insisted upon was that whoever he chose would join the Board as a member so that he could learn the ropes before taking my place. Leslie Young, who had been the chairman of Bibby's, joined the Board in the December 1983 and took over from me on 1 July 1984. He left about three years later.

On the Sunday after I had ceased being the chairman of British Waterways, at the invitation of the Kennet and Avon Canal Trust I performed the opening ceremony of the Dundas Aqueduct.

Under the 1968 Transport Act it had been listed as part of the 'remainder' waterway, which meant that money could only be spent on it if it proved to be dangerous to the public or property. Because of its inability to hold water, the aqueduct, which connected two sections of the canal, had been sealed off for many years.

Admiral Sir 'Bill' O'Brien had pointed out how stupid it was that on the east side a long stretch of the canal had been reinstated under a Government Youth Employment Scheme and it was cut off because we couldn't repair the Dundas Aqueduct. He was right, but under the Act laid upon us by parliament the Board hadn't the power to repair it.

After revisiting the aqueduct I called in the Chief Engineer to tell him that I considered it to constitute a danger to the public; he disagreed. I insisted and said, 'I intend to take this matter before the Board to obtain their agreement that as it is dangerous it should be repaired and reinstated under the Act.' Before he could contradict I added, 'If you are not called upon for an opinion, the responsibility will lie with me and the Board. Do you understand what I am trying to say?'

He wasn't happy with this subterfuge but went along with my plan.

The aqueduct was repaired and the two sections of the canal were joined up a few days before my retirement. On the Sunday after I had said farewell to the Board, I travelled down to the Kennet and Avon. There were hundreds of enthusiasts gathered at what they had turned into a gala occasion. A cairn had been erected upon which was a commemorative plaque suitably inscribed. It was a memorable end to my battle to save the inland waterways.

As far as I was concerned the struggle to stop Whitehall from backing away from their responsibilities – other than water-borne transport – had been won. The canals of Britain are now so well established and popular, that no government, or its advisers, will ever be able to do what successive ministers tried so hard to do during the fourteen years out of the sixteen I served as the chairman of the British Waterways Board. I am confident that we, my Board colleagues and the staff who stood by us, won the war to save a national heritage – the canals of Great Britain.

The thought makes those trials and tribulations well worth-while.

Chapter XXVIII

BRIEF ENCOUNTERS

Coming as I did from the back streets of Birmingham, I still marvel at my good fortune in having met so many interesting people, both famous and relatively unknown, who have added to my bank of happy memories. The following passages are devoted to just a few of them.

The Other Eden

Invited to perform the main toast at a dinner held at the Birmingham University, I sat next to the Chancellor, Lord Avon. He had been one of Britain's great Foreign Secretaries, earning the respect of the free world for his stand against the dictators between the wars. He recognised the threat that Hitler and Mussolini presented when many of his compatriots, including the then Prince of Wales, were being conned into believing otherwise.

Reading his memoirs, which I'll admit was hard going, was an eye-opener. The general public have yet to comprehend just how badly the pre-war government let him and Britain down.

As we took our seats his opening gambit was, 'You must be quite unhappy having to sit next to me.'

I was lost; I asked why. His reply was illuminating.

'I thought that as a friend of Field Marshall Sir Claude Auchinleck you would hold me partly to blame for the outrageous way the government treated him.'

Under-equipped Auchinleck had succeeded in stopping Rommel's overwhelming advance on Cairo. As Eden said, Churchill's decision to replace him *was* outrageous. He explained, 'Churchill was worrying about the morale of the British people, who sorely needed some good news; the fact that the German

Afrika Korps had been *halted* wasn't good enough for him.

'He flew to Cairo to instruct Auchinleck to drive Rommel out of Egypt. The "Auk", being short of men and supplies, refused to put his army at risk until he had the means to achieve it. The old man simply dismissed him and appointed Montgomery, who then insisted on having more men and equipment.'

He went on, 'When Attlee – who was deputy prime minister – and I heard the news we were appalled, but by the time we got the wire it was too late; the old man had done it.'

He then told me that later Churchill regretted his treatment of Auchinleck and offered to make him a Viscount, but he turned it down. I had heard the full story from the Auk, but felt it wise not to continue the conversation. I was embarrassed.

Here was a man who had walked the world stage, resigned his Cabinet post to fight for principles that proved to be right, humbly apologising to me for a disservice done many years before by a colleague to an old friend of mine.

Anthony Eden was a man of quality who proved that he was no cardboard cut-out. Politicians were not under such close scrutiny by the press in those days; had they been, maybe his contribution would have been recognised and the government of the day forced to follow his advice to take the dictators on at a time when they could have been easily dealt with.

Higher Than Everest

Having done a little mountaineering myself, it was an honour to meet one of the members of the first all-Indian team to have conquered Mount Everest in May 1965. His name is Hari Ahluwalia, an Army-Air Force Major. When we met he was in a wheelchair.

Some time after he and his team had succeeded in reaching the summit of the world's highest mountain, he was recalled to his unit to participate in a skirmish on the Pakistan border which was in danger of breaking out into a full-scale war. His sergeant, returning to base, reported to the commanding officer that Hari had been killed by a sniper's bullet.

Lieutenant Commander Kohli, who had led the Everest climb,

ordered the sergeant to take him to where Hari lay. He discovered that he was not quite dead and drove him to the nearest field hospital. They were able to administer enough drugs to keep him alive. He was then transferred to a hospital which pronounced that he would never walk again. There is little doubt that Lieutenant Commander Kohli saved Hari's life.

From then on Hari went through a series of operations and was finally transferred to the specialist English hospital Stoke Mandeville. There he stayed until he had recovered sufficiently to return home. He remains paralysed from his waist down. The Vauxhall motor company converted a car which he drove around Delhi and he was also still allowed to fly. He wrote a book about his fight to overcome his disability which he called *Higher Than Everest*.

Whilst I was in Delhi he rang to say that he would be collecting me. As ordered, I stood on the steps of the hotel. On his arrival I asked where we were going; he didn't reply. We reached our destination and a uniformed officer opened my door. Hari said, 'They will arrange to deliver you back to the hotel.' Then he drove off.

I was led into the building and sat in a room full of men in formal dress. A young lady in a sari came out to say, 'The prime minister will see you now,' and led me in to meet Indira Gandhi.

In that quiet calm voice we all got to know, she greeted me with, 'Hari has spoken of you often, Sir Frank, I'm so pleased to meet you.' She moved from behind her desk. 'Let us sit,' she added, pointing to a large settee. 'Would you care for tea?'

I still hadn't recovered.

Our conversation, which ranged over many things, was interrupted numerous times by the secretary, who kept reminding the prime minister that her ministers were waiting. She waved her away. Questioning me about the New Town of Telford, she expressed her concern for the overwhelming number of people who were pouring into Delhi and the other major cities, camping out along the roads.

She arranged for me to visit the efforts they were making to construct small communal villages just outside Delhi. Her Housing Minister, who left a lot to be desired, ignored my many questions whilst directing me around these villages.

During the discussion she referred to the attitude of the West towards overpopulation in India and China. She was concerned that both countries, which were making efforts to introduce family planning to deal with the problem, were nevertheless being criticised by the West for doing so.

Finally she told me, 'Tomorrow I am leaving to attend the non-aligned nations conference and my ministers are waiting to brief me. I must apologise; maybe we can meet again before you leave India.'

With that we parted. She had arranged with Group Captain Grewal the Principal of the Himalayan Mountaineering Institute, north of Darjeeling, for me to stay at the centre, the views from which are almost too magnificent to describe. In the grounds there is a rotunda situated so that from the powerful telescope you can make a visual sweep of most of the Himalayan mountain range. My excitement was tempered when I read the plaque on the wall. It stated that the building had been presented on behalf of one Aryan race to another: a present from Adolf Hitler.

Staying overnight there was just one other guest, a young Indian Army officer. He asked whether I had ever been to Tiger Hill to watch the sun rise over the top of the world. At three the next morning, he wrapped a blanket round me and drove his jeep over rough roads to Tiger Hill.

I was surprised to find a large gathering already there. I stood listening to the hubbub of mixed languages as the sky began to lighten. My companion placed his hands on my shoulders and turned me to where the sun began to appear over the edge of the distant mountain range. Suddenly there was not a whisper coming from the watchers. The sky was changing colours in front and around us.

The ice and snow on the mountains changed from grey to blue, to green to white and then to a dazzling pink. As the sun rose majestically over the rim of the world, up and up into the now pale blue sky we gradually turned to our left with the sun to see the reflection on the individual mountains. Suddenly a cry went up – 'Everest!' – as the crowd pointed to a rugged snow-capped mountain in the near distance.

My companion turned me away from where the others were facing. 'They are looking at the wrong one,' he whispered, pointing to a small blue-white pimple positively glowing in the light from the sun now rising higher in the sky. 'That's Everest out there in the distance. I know, I have stood on its peak.'

It was a moment I will never forget.

I shivered, not from the cold but from sheer exhilaration; I could hardly breathe. Turning to look at his young face glowing with pride as bright as the sun, I must admit to a feeling of envy, not to have been where Hillary, Tenzing, Hari, and my new-found friend had stood.

Before I left Darjeeling I paid a visit to 'Khangla', Number 1 Tonga Road, the home of Sherpa Tenzing Norgay who, at the age of twenty-one, joined his first Everest climb as a high altitude porter. Tenzing had climbed many mountains and was to attempt Everest five times before he stood on its summit in 1953 and the image of his smiling features was flashed around the world.

There was a message waiting for me when I returned to my Hotel in Delhi. I was to meet Indira Ghandi again before I left India. Whenever she visited the UK I received a message from the High Commissioner that he had been instructed to arrange for me to meet her. We corresponded for years. I kept most of her letters in the briefcase she gave me. It was taken when my apartment was burgled; fortunately I had placed some in a drawer and have them still, a memory of a great Indian leader, a charming, intelligent yet humble lady who had befriended me.

Nobody's Poodle

I discovered very early on, that many people in the public eye are not always what they seem. The late Willie Whitelaw appeared to me, and no doubt others, including many of his political colleagues, as one of Mrs Thatcher's 'poodles'. I changed my opinion when I got to know him.

He was the guest of honour at a small dinner party. With everyone present except Willie, I decided that we should wait before starting our meal. After forty minutes had passed I decided that he wasn't coming so we began to eat. A few minutes later he burst in very excited and out of puff. He apologised and took his seat next to me.

Sitting directly opposite was Bill Owen, the actor, best remembered for his part as Compo in the TV series *Last of the Summer Wine*. It was at the time that the disagreement over the sovereignty of the Falkland Islands was coming to a head. You may remember that the United Nations and the United States were questioning whether the matter should be put to the World Court.

Willie began to tell me why he had been delayed. 'Frank, I have been in a meeting with the PM and a few members of the Cabinet discussing the crisis. If ever the matter goes before a World Court we will be lucky to hold on to South Georgia. We need to avoid banging the drum and pursue the matter diplomatically.'

It was completely out of character and I looked across at Bill Owen and began to worry; Bill was quite left wing. Willie was in full flood and I couldn't stop him. He went on, 'That bloody women just won't listen to us!'

A few days later the Foreign Secretary and the Minister of Defence resigned.

I succeeded in changing the course of the conversation and when Willie turned to speak to the guest on his right, I looked across at Bill and whispered, 'Bill, this is a private party, do you understand?'

He just grinned. He knew what I meant and said, 'Yes, ain't that a shame?'

He mentioned nothing of what he had heard; had he had done so, all hell would have broken loose.

Willie Whitelaw had a great sense of loyalty, duty and fun, but he was nobody's poodle. He told me that when he was the Secretary of State for Ireland he caused a stir when he asked that a Catholic be appointed as his private secretary; he didn't win.

At times he frustrated his political colleagues by being far too loyal to Mrs Thatcher, and although he might have appeared so to some, he was no fool; he was a very intelligent loveable 'character'. And so, by the way, was Bill Owen.

Dear Bill Owen

He was nothing like the little smelly, dishevelled member of the unlikely Yorkshire trio he played in the BBC television series. I can't ever remember seeing him other than, as we say, smartly turned out. Little in stature he might have been, but in personality and talent he stood tall. An actor on stage, radio, television and films, he was also a writer, composer and director.

He appeared to be a cockney sparrow – small, bright, and chirpy. Unlike many in his profession, he believed that he had been lucky and should therefore put something back. He travelled through the UK under his own steam, never asking for fees or expenses to assist young aspiring actors to achieve their ambition.

Bill Owen and I first met when I bumped into him as I was leaving a room in a hospital near Robertsbridge. I had been visiting Nina Bourner, a beautiful young lady who worked from an apartment used as an office in Whitehall Court. We met in the bar from time to time and became close friends.

She was suffering from tuberculosis and was quite ill. As I was passing through on my way back from Brighton, I decided to call in to see her. At the time Bill was acting in a BBC series called *Taxi*. Nina hadn't told me that they were even close friends. I thought that he might think I was 'cutting in' and this was confirmed when he rang to thank me for visiting her. However, we arranged to meet and from then on became good friends.

French Connection

Whilst I spent far more than the two and a half days a week I was scheduled to do with BWB, I followed the advice of Roy Jenkin, and when I took on the government assignments I kept a foot in the private sector. With a young fellow named Stephen Goldstein I opened an office in the centre of Birmingham and from small beginnings the partnership grew.

We were asked by a French bank if we would assist them in advising one of their clients, the city of Tours, an historic city in the Loire Valley that wished to extend its industrial base. We travelled to Paris to meet the Mayor, who was also the Minister for Rural Development. He was a tall, thin man dressed in black with a pale, funereal countenance; he looked every bit the undertaker. He failed to smile all the time we were in his company.

Our first interview was conducted in French and I apologised for not being able to communicate in his language. The director of the bank translated for the Mayor and for me. Towards the end of the discussion the Mayor asked if I had seen the site planned for the expansion and if so, what was my view of it. This was translated and I replied, 'Oui. Crème de la crème.'

The Mayor rose from his seat and came around his desk. I stood up, he held my shoulders and kissed me on both cheeks, saying in impeccable English, 'You do speak French after all.'

In Tours we were taken to their Agricultural Exhibition grounds where there were two small exhibition buildings. One the Germans had built and the other Tours had built as a present to Britain. We were told that the Germans exhibited at the agricultural shows but the British did not. The British exhibition building was totally bare other than for a corrugated cardboard circular stand on which stood a two-foot plastic bottle representing Johnny Walker Red Label Whisky. It was left behind after the one and only British exhibition held there when it had opened; it hadn't been used since.

Back home I called the Trade Secretary at the British Embassy in Paris asking if there was any effort being made to encourage Britain's farming industry to exhibit in Tours. I asked if he was aware of the exhibition building and wondered why there was no picture of the Queen on the wall. He left me in no doubt that they were not interested and wished that the gift of the centre had never been accepted.

The National Agricultural Show was taking place at their permanent Show Grounds near Coventry which Birmingham, Coventry and the Warwickshire County Council sponsored. I paid it a visit and talked to a number of agricultural machine and implement manufacturers who were exhibiting. I handed them a plan of the Tours exhibition grounds and asked if they would exhibit there if they could have the site close to the British exhibition building at a reduced fee. They had heard of the show and jumped at the chance.

I first spoke to the Tours town hall; they agreed to offer the sites free of charge in the hope that the exhibitors would continue to exhibit each year. As I was meeting Prince Philip the following day I mentioned the story of the hall, the response of the Embassy Trade Secretary and the fact that there was no picture of Her Majesty hanging on the wall.

Once we knew that a number of British manufacturers were to go to the Tours Show we began to organise filling the hall with other British manufacturers. Allied Carpets agreed to carpet the place and to leave it as a gift so long as this was recognised by placing their plaque on the wall. The Birmingham silversmiths, Ellisons, agreed to show their wares and to place an engraver there during the show. Other firms followed and very soon we were turning offers away.

We then contacted our Embassy in Paris. They were extremely annoyed. Prince Philip had been on to them, and had pictures of the Queen and himself sent over with instructions to have them suitably framed and sent to Tours. They were apoplectic when they heard that that British agricultural firms would be exhibiting at the forthcoming show, along with a contingent showing off their wares in the hall.

I suggested that they lay on a cocktail party on the opening day. This they did. The Trade Secretary was in attendance with his attractive German wife, who moved among the guest obviously enjoying herself. Added to this we assisted with the development of the industrial site and at least three West Midlands firms took up units in addition to the French L'Oréal cosmetic firm.

I tell this story because the Mayor of Tours, who had already proved to be a character, decided to run for the Presidency of France. His platform was family values and the raising of moral standards among young people. He launched his campaign in his home city and it was naturally televised, although that turned out to be bad news.

The local university students occupied the first five rows in the hall and when the Mayor reached that part of his speech to do with moral standards the students stood up as a body and began to strip. The TV cameras turned from the platform to concentrate on the students. By the time the gendarmes reached them they were in the altogether. It screwed up the Mayor's opening campaign performance.

He followed it with a rally in the city of Lyon. The students there, not to be outdone by their Tours colleagues, put on a similar show for the television audience. The Mayor wisely withdrew from the race, but not before the press mentioned his mistress.

He wasn't the first French civic head I had met. At the invitation of the Mayor of Nice, Monsieur Medican, Vernon Crofts (a partner in the Seymour Harris architectural firm) and I were taken to see land and property owned by the city in Avenue Medican, named after the Mayor's illustrious father, who had been the Mayor before him.

The site was ideally situated in a main shopping area adjacent to Galleries Lafayette. Having surveyed it, checked out the boundaries and the plans, we were asked to travel to Paris to meet the Mayor, who was also a Deputy in the House of Representatives. We met in his office in a government building.

A tall, charming, good-looking man who spoke English with a Scottish accent, he had been educated in Edinburgh. His first questions ranged over my view of the site's potential. Happy with my reply he asked if Mr Crofts would mind leaving us for a moment.

Once Vernon was out of the room the Mayor opened a cabinet and offered me a drink. He then began to explain how he saw the financial arrangements of my company's acquisition of the site should be arranged.

'My Party is in need of its own newspaper. You will be required to deposit a million pounds into my Swiss account which I will then use to fund the newspaper.'

Here we were, sitting in a government office, and without a flicker of embarrassment he was asking me to arrange for my company to pay him a bribe.

Some years later, attending a private lunch I sat next to the chairman of a property company called Star of Great Britain. I didn't know him, but he was aware of my background with Murrayfield. He mentioned the 'Nice' development, asking why we had turned it down. Before answering, I asked how he knew that we had been involved.

'We were invited to take it on,' he said.

I have no idea whether they took up the offer, but I and the rest of France knows that Medican absconded and the government have been seeking his extradition for some years. He was a 'character' of the worst kind.

A Touch of Class

Lew Grade, the one-time vaudeville song and dance man who ended up with his brother owning theatres in the West End, television companies and in his case a film company, invited me to meet him in his offices near Marble Arch.

After waiting in a large room, I stood as he entered holding the hand of the Hollywood film star, Shirley Maclaine. Lew had just signed her up to do a TV series. He introduced me and we exchanged a few pleasantries before she left. I mention this because more than fifteen years later I was to meet her again.

My wife and I were in Las Vegas; Shirley was appearing at the Sands Casino, and we decided to see whether we could get to see the show. Most of the staff at Sands resembled Hollywood stars. The fellow who took my booking, and on the night guided us to our table, was the image of Kirk Douglas.

A comedian cum compère, opened the show and introduced Miss Maclaine. She sang, danced and joked for thirty minutes and came down from the stage, singing, and moved among the tables. She stopped for a brief moment at the one we were sitting at and glanced hard at us. For the second half of the show the comedian came back and after a number of fairly good jokes reintroduced Miss Maclaine. It was remarkable how she had maintained her ability to dance as she had done in her early years, and to have the energy she put into her performance. She had the audience in the palm of her hand.

The Kirk Douglas double came to the table and, leaning down, said, 'When Miss Maclaine leaves the stage, follow me.'

'Follow you where?' I asked.

'Just do what I tell you,' he replied and backed away.

As the curtain came down he tapped my shoulder and we followed him. He took us backstage and knocked on a door. It was opened and we were ushered into a spacious room with a bar at one end.

After what seemed like a few seconds Shirley Maclaine appeared as fresh as if she had yet to perform.

'Hello, Sir Frank, how are you? It's nice to see you again, how is Lew?'

I was staggered; how could she have remembered me after such a short meeting and so long ago? But remember she had. We chatted for ten minutes or so when her manager mentioned that there was a crowd of friends waiting to meet her. She asked us to stay and enjoy the hospitality but we decided to duck out.

Besides having a remarkable career on stage, films and as a successful author, which would have turned most people's heads, Shirley Maclaine had a touch of class, retaining her regard for others however brief the acquaintance. She is, without doubt, one of America's remarkable characters.

A Rose by Any Other Name

Before I became a member, the British Waterways Board had commissioned a replacement for its ancient water bus that plied the Prince Regent's canal. The new craft was delivered twelve months after my appointment as chairman. It was to be named the *Lady of Maida Vale* after the area in which she was to be moored... that was until someone mentioned that at one time the area had been well known for the number of ladies who were practitioners of the oldest profession.

I thought it wiser if we asked Dorothy, the wife of Sir Alec Rose, if she would agree that we name the craft after her. She did, and with her husband came up to London to christen it.

Sir Alec Rose was anything but the simple man he portrayed to those who didn't know him. A greengrocer in Southsea, during the war he served in the merchant navy. He told me that whilst he was escorting convoys across the Atlantic he dreamed of sailing round the world in his own yacht.

After the war, he followed Slocum, Gerbault and Chichester,

in circumnavigating the globe single-handed. Unlike them, it took him many years of sacrificing other pleasures and luxuries to save enough in order to make his dream come true. He was a quiet, dignified man.

Before I had the good fortune to meet Alec Rose, had I passed him in the street I would never have realised that I was walking close to such a courageous man, whose humility had allowed others to overshadow his achievements. It hadn't affected him in the least; he was far too big for that.

A Passionate Jewish Mayor

I met Teddy Kollek briefly during one of his visits to Britain. He suggested that if I was ever in Jerusalem I should call on him. He was that sacred city's popular Mayor.

In July 1979, I had reason to visit Israel, and whilst in Tel Aviv phoned Kollek's office. Sitting at breakfast the following morning I was called to the phone.

'Are you Sir Frank Price from England?' the voice enquired.

'Yes,' I answered.

'Will you present yourself at Mr Kollek's office at 1800 hours.'

'Yes,' I replied, and the call ended.

I returned to my breakfast. Five minutes passed and I was called to the phone again. 'Am I speaking to Sir Frank Price?'

'Yes.'

'The Mayor will see you at 1800 hours.'

Before I could reply, the phone was hung up. I went back to my table and a now cold breakfast. I pushed the plate away and asked for a hot tea. Before it was delivered I was called to the phone again.

'Are you—?'

Before the man could say another word, I said, 'Yes I am, you have called me twice already, what is going on?'

He rang off without answering.

I travelled to Jerusalem and made my way to the town hall. A man wearing jeans and a shoulder holster asked, 'Are you Sir Frank Price?' I nodded. He asked for identification, and I handed him my passport. He then frisked me.

I was led up to the Mayor's office and asked to wait; the man with the gun stayed next to me. Suddenly, there was a rush of people. 'He's on his way,' they told the man with the gun. The far door was flung open and in came Teddy Kollek.

'I'm a very busy man, being Mayor of this city is not like being Mayor of Birmingham, I'm a very busy man!' he almost shouted.

'You invited me to call on you, I have, so goodnight,' I said, and turned to leave.

'Hold it!' he called out. 'I'm sorry, I have just come from quelling what could have been a riot in the Arab quarter... please sit down.'

He then told me that Ariel Sharon, a leading right-wing politician, had arranged to have someone purchase an apartment for him in the Arab quarter. That day, with a deal of publicity he had moved in. 'He knew that it would cause trouble,' Kollek commented, 'and I have had to deal with it.'

I understood why he was tensed up.

Teddy Kollek raised a great deal of money for his city from people all over the world. He was a persuasive and popular man and many famous American film stars travelled there to put on charity concerts to raise money for the thousands of Jewish immigrants who had arrived in the country, penniless. He had worked hard to built up a relationship with his religiously mixed citizens and was trusted. Having Sharon purposely upsetting the scene had made him very angry.

We chatted for over an hour; he presented me with his book, *Jerusalem, Sacred City of Mankind*. In it he wrote, 'A memento to your first visit to Jerusalem. Come back often.'

He was a rare and dedicated man.

New Orleans Experience

Few people outside America, and due to the efforts of Hollywood even its citizens, realise that it was the American Corps of Engineers who won (if that's the right word) the West. America can thank them for its National Parks.

On his retirement, Colonel Haar, a distinguished member of

the Corps, was appointed Deputy Head of the New Orleans Port Authority. He had been involved with the inland coastal waterways and was deeply interested in Britain's inland waterway system. He brought the Mayor of New Orleans with him to see what we were doing.

Impressed, the Mayor invited me to see what they had achieved and I visited the city in 1980. I was asked to address a number of their leading institutions, one being their Trade Association, in their international Trade Centre.

Being in the 'cotton belt', I had entered every man's outfitters on both sides of the city's main shopping street only to discover that not one of them stocked hundred per cent cotton socks. Called upon to reply to the President of the Trade Association's address of welcome, I remarked on this amazing discovery. When I sat down the President leaned towards me saying, 'By next week everyone of those traders will be stocked up with pure cotton socks with no one to buy them; when will you be back?'

Mayor Ernest Morial invited me to return to his city four years later. It was to give the keynote address at the symposium on the occasion of the New Orleans World Expo. It was an unexpected honour. The letter stated that the Expo organisation would cover all my expenses, plus the equivalent of a £1,000 fee. With my wife, Daphne, I travelled to New Orleans, where we had been booked into the Hilton Hotel overlooking the Mississippi. Arriving late after a long tiring flight we went straight to the suite and retired for the night.

I woke up the next morning to the sound of banjo music. I took a shower and whilst towelling myself down pressed the button to open the curtains of the floor-to-floor, wall-to-wall window. Standing there naked, I found myself facing a triple decked Mississippi Steamboat crowded with passengers being entertained whilst waiting to set off on a river trip. They gazed up at me without blinking an eyelid.

The topic of the symposium was water, ranging from its use and abuse, to the ever growing need for this natural resource. Among those sitting on the platform was the Governor of the State of Louisiana and its Congresswoman, Lindy Bloggs. She had just returned from Washington.

Walter Mondale, the Democratic nominee for the Presidential election, had interviewed her as his possible running mate. He made the mistake of choosing a lady from New York whose husband's background was to be called into question. With the Congresswoman sitting near me, I opened up with, 'The supply and control of water – an asset that few appreciate or understand until they are faced with either a shortage through drought or an abundance through flood.'

I then questioned the wisdom of superpowers who were spending unimaginable amounts of money to explore space and to build sophisticated systems of destruction, while all the time on our planet there where millions of people suffering and hundreds of thousands dying through the lack of adequate funds and expertise to reach reserves of water lying beneath their feet.

'We, in the developed and more prosperous parts of this planet, are fortunate that the problems we are to discuss are based on how best to allocate, how to maintain quality, how to recycle, how to irrigate, how to maximise its use, etc. Yet in too many parts of the world their problem is how to find it, how to extract it and how to obtain the funds to do either or both.'

I turned to look at the Congresswoman when I added, 'It would do no harm for those who govern to ponder awhile and to give voice to the concern we may sometimes feel about the twisted economic and social logic of the direction in which countries such as the United States are aiming.'

She broke the silence that followed by standing up to clap.

Returning to England, I received a letter from the organisers of Expo to thank me and to apologise for the delay in sending me a cheque for the £1,000. It was followed a few months later with a letter and a press cutting. It appeared that the company set up to run the Expo had gone into bankruptcy. I never did get my cheque but I was not at all unhappy because they and the city had given us a wonderful time. The Governor of the State, David Treen, sent me an illuminated address making me an aide-de-camp on his staff.

Royal Interest

The image of BWB was being helped by the growing interest people were showing in their canals. Our fight for their survival had caught the imagination of the media and we were receiving attention from the serious as well as the popular press. With more radio and television coverage than ever before, members of the royal family joined in.

The Duke of Edinburgh visited the Bingley Five-Rise Locks on the Leeds and Liverpool Canal, built two hundred years before. His visit coincided with a serious drought situation which restricted the movement of boats, and they were banned from using the locks.

There were a number of pleasure craft moored – marooned would be more correct – at the top of the flight, and although the owners were well aware of the problem, when the Duke went along the towpath to speak to them they complained at not being allowed to take their boats down the deep flight of locks.

Always one to step right in he remonstrated with me in front of the craft owners.

'Why are you stopping your customers from using the system?' he demanded.

They were delighted. I said nothing until we were crossing the top lock gates.

'In answer to your question, sir, may I ask you whether you have any idea how many millions of gallons of water these locks hold?' Before he could reply I added, 'If we let just one of those boats down this flight, the rest of the canal they are now floating on would be empty for God only knows how long.' He wisely decided not to reply.

I began to understand him better some years later when we were having lunch in Newbury. He was spending the day inspecting the Kennet and Avon Canal project. The chairman of the Kennet and Avon Trust was then Admiral Sir William O'Brien (retired) under whose command the Prince had sailed during his naval days. It was the Admiral who had arranged the visit.

As I had been alongside him during the morning and was to be so during the afternoon, I thought it reasonable that during lunch he should have an opportunity to sit and talk with the other guests. When he became aware of this he insisted that he wanted me to sit next to him. I was soon to discover the reason.

We sat with General Sir Hugh Stockwell, Sir William O'Brien, the chairmen of the Berkshire and Wiltshire County Councils, the Mayor of Reading, the Lord Lieutenant of Wiltshire and John Smith, who had given generous donations to the Kennet and Avon Trust.

During the meal Prince Philip started to bait me about my role as chairman of the Board. He said he couldn't understand why a government body was involved in managing the canals.

Addressing those sitting with us, he said, 'Why do you put up with him (meaning me) running things when the canal is in your area?' Turning to O'Brien, he called out, 'Come on, Bill, you could do a better job than him, surely.'

Bill and I had become well acquainted and he knew just how much help I was giving to the affairs of the Trust and how much they depended on our cooperation.

I countered with, 'Bill, before you answer remember that I will be here tomorrow when he will be somewhere else.'

Not to be outdone, Philip commented, 'Don't stand for him bullying you!' Then he turned to the others. 'Take the bloody canal off him, you could run it far better than he does.'

By this time those sitting there were becoming uncomfortable, even more so when I decided to bite back. Turning towards him I said, 'Sir, I have always been led to understand that you were quite knowledgeable on the subject of our inland waterways and the way in which they are managed, but from your comments I can only deduce that you haven't got a clue about the state of play. If my Board stepped away, the system, including the Kennet and Avon, would be in deep trouble. I'm sorry to have to say that when it comes to the canal's future, you simply don't know what you are talking about.'

Everything went very quite. Sitting next to him, I then felt him squeeze my arm. It was then that I understood what he had been up to. He had been hoping to start a heated debate which I'm sure he would have enjoyed far better than stomping round the canal, but his audience wasn't up to it.

The only other person who spoke was General Sir Hugh Stockwell. He coughed a little before saying, 'Although I wouldn't have put it quite like the chairman, sir, I must say that you have somewhat underestimated the problems.'

Later, in the car, the Prince said, 'You must have gone three rungs up the ladder with that lot.'

'On the contrary,' I replied, 'I would lay odds that by now they will be slagging me off for having the temerity to disagree with you.'

'Never, never!' he said, slapping his thigh and laughing.

It confirmed my opinion that the reason why so many who meet him think that he his somewhat testy, is that they fail to realise that outside of the palace he gets little chance to get involved in arguments which he obviously enjoys. He therefore has to prod people in the hope that they will react. Too few do.

Unlike his father, Prince Charles, who had interested himself in the restoration of the Montgomery Canal, was shy – in fact, rather too shy. He visited Welshpool where a seven-mile stretch was being restored by members of the Prince of Wales Trust; it was the first time we had met.

He asked if I had travelled down from London, and when I said yes he asked why I hadn't let the Palace know. 'You could have travelled down with me,' he said. He had been brought to Welshpool on the Royal Train. I didn't respond but imagined how members of his staff would have reacted had I had called to ask them for a lift.

A number of youngsters from Dr Banardo's Homes were helping to clear the undergrowth along the canal bank and the Prince stopped to have a word with one of the boys. The lad was so taken aback he couldn't utter a word. Embarrassed by this, Charles quickly walked on.

He was under the impression that the boy had snubbed him, so I said, 'The lad you just spoke to is an orphan. He was overwhelmed by the fact that you had bothered to speak to him, that's why he couldn't reply. He didn't mean to be rude.'

The Prince stopped. 'Oh dear, should I go back?' he asked.

'I think not,' I advised. 'I will have a word with him later.'

431

It was then I realised that at the time, his experience in meeting what are commonly termed 'ordinary people' was limited.

His Equerry, David Checketts, was to help him over that hurdle. After this visit the prince became very interested in the restoration of canals and led the appeal to raise funds to bring the Montgomery Canal back into use. Had Checketts stayed with him I truly believe that he would have protected him from falling down so many holes, but David was out of a different mould from the rest of the Palace advisers and was soon to be replaced.

I was surprised by a call from Simon Gilliate, the Queen Mother's Equerry, to tell me that Princess Margaret had told how much she had enjoyed the trip on the Regent's Canal adding, in the most diplomatic way, that he was sure that the Queen Mother would consider an invitation to join us for lunch on the *Lady Rose* should one be sent. He provided me with suitable dates and an invitation was dispatched and accepted.

As we were approaching the area of the zoo, I indicated that we would be soon passing the Snowdon Aviary.

'Would it be in order if I stood by the window to see it?' she asked. She left her chair, bidding everyone to keep their seats, and on rejoining us asked me, 'Do you know Tony?'

She was the only member of the royal family whom I have met, who referred to 'the Family' by their given names without mentioning their title. As always, the Queen Mother charmed everyone present.

Lady Edith Foxwell, a friend of the royal family having heard that the Queen Mother had done the trip, booked the craft to give a lunch party for her friends. Although I didn't know the woman, I was invited. Among her guests were Paul Getty and Viscount St Davids, well known for his love of the waterways and raising funds for boys' clubs. He built a club alongside the Regent's Canal.

My host sat him alongside Getty and I overheard his efforts to put the bite on the billionaire. Some months later I was able to ask St Davids how his efforts had fared.

'He sent me a cheque for ten pounds,' he replied.

From a man who had a payphone in the hall for his guests, it shouldn't have come as a surprise.

As I have mentioned, I left the Board in 1984. Believing that I was to go the year before, my wife and I decided to buy a home overlooking Coverack harbour in Cornwall. Patrick Jenkin having asked me to stay on meant my commuting by train at least twice a week. Catching the 'Sleeper' or the first London-bound train out of Penzance was no fun. The five-hour journey to and from Paddington was a bore.

While I was sitting having breakfast, a friend, Michael Montague – later to become Lord Montague – boarded the train in Exeter and joined me.

'What are you doing in this part of the world?' he asked.

After I explained, he said, 'You must be crazy! You should move to the South of France – the weather is much better and you could be in London in two hours, and it would be cheaper.'

He was right; the winter weather in Cornwall was abysmal and the train journeys were fraying my nerves.

I kept it up until I finally retired.

Chapter XXIX
END PIECE

Nevertheless, we loved the home we bought from a retired merchant sea captain named Money. He and his wife were residing in Singapore when the Japanese entered the war. Like the most of us he never envisaged that they would ever be able to capture Singapore. He was at sea when they did and his wife was placed with other women in a prisoner-of-war camp.

After the war he went back to find and bring her back to the England. When he retired they moved into a home in the little hamlet of Trevalsoe overlooking the English Channel and the fishing village of Coverack.

When they accepted our offer Mrs Money confided in Daphne that she had insisted on selling the house for reasons she was keeping from her husband. Mrs Money was dying of cancer and she wanted to see that he was living in a place without memories, a smaller place, one which he would be able to manage on his own. We agreed to delay taking possession until they were settled in their new adobe.

Not having been born in Cornwall we were known to the locals as 'Emits' and would always be consider foreigners. I well understood the position because when I left the Midland I was a Queen's Deputy Lieutenant. In proffering my resignation to Captain Parker, the Lord Lieutenant of Hereford and Worcestershire (I had already held a similar position in Warwickshire and the West Midlands County) he said that the Cornish would never consider anyone for such a position if he had not been born in Cornwall. A few months later he wrote to tell me that wherever I lived I would retain the title DL.

During the winter of our second year in Cornwall I went down with a bad case of flu. The doctor's efforts were failing and both he and I concluded that I was in for another bout of pneumonia. It was February so I asked Daphne to arrange for us to fly out to a dry sunny climate.

Having taken advice from the local travel agent she booked for us to go to Mojacar in southern Spain. I had never heard of the place situated on the southern coast of Spain, but he said that dry warm sunny weather was guaranteed. He added, 'It's known as the village of enchantment.' I thought, *what a corny sales pitch*.

We were booked into a hotel on the seafront. The agent was right about the climate; I sat on the balcony for four days soaking up the sun. Feeling better, I decided to take a walk. We had been told that they had not had any serious rainfall for ten years and looking at the landscape removed any doubts that it was a fact. I began to look for a Travel Agent to get out of the place.

Always interested in property, I stopped to gaze in a Real Estate Agents window. A tall good-looking young English fellow came out of the office like a flash. 'Looking for a nice villa?' he asked.

'You must be kidding, I'm looking for a travel agency to get out of the place.' He was genuinely shocked. 'Have you had a look around?' My answer led him to invite me to a drive around the area.

By the time he dropped me back at the hotel I realised that there was something special about Mojacar and its environs. During his running commentary he told me that it had been invaded by the Phoenicians, the Greeks Romans and the Moors. 'They,' he said, 'left here just five hundred years ago; they were the last to leave Spain. This is an historic village,' he added proudly. However it was something else he mentioned that interested me. The young people had abandoned the village to seek work and it had stayed practically deserted for many years until a group of painters and writers rediscovered it. So, taken up with its serenity and the light they decided to settle there. He added, 'It was they who rediscovered Mojacar.'

Interested in painting and recognising the light that was similar to that which attracted artists to Cornwall, I was converted. Two years after our meeting we decided to settle in Mojacar.

I thought that I would miss the hurly-burly of public life, that we would miss the theatre and the museums but we discovered that we were living in a magnificent country, within easy driving distance of Lorca, Cordoba, the Alhambra in Grenada, Seville, Segovia, Salamanca, Madrid and Toledo. We began to enjoy a quality of life we had not imagined. I began to paint again but this time restaurants were asking me to hang my pictures and I have been able to sell them. I also got down to writing this book.

117

Printed in the United Kingdom
by Lightning Source UK Ltd.
9654500001B/1-12